I0768550

Fate of the Broken

Fate
of the
Broken

Copyright

This is a work of fiction. All characters, organizations, and events portrayed in this story/novel are products of the author's imagination or are used fictitiously. Any similarity to real persons, living or dead, is coincidental and not intended by the author.

Fate of the Broken

Book two

Copyright © J. Grenz 2024

All rights reserved

No part of this book may be produced in any form or by any electronic or mechanical means, including information storage and retrieval systems, without written permission from the author

Cover and header artwork by J. Grenz

Trigger warnings

Note: Fate of the Broken picks up where Soul of Fractured Fate leaves off do not read this book first.

Please be advised:
This book contains mentions of and acts of sexual assault, however, there is no on-page rape.
Gaslighting
Emotional Abuse
Verbal abuse
Love bombing
Graphic violence
Anxiety
Panic attacks
PTSD
Trauma
Sexism/misogyny
Swears/cursing
Death
Explicit sexual content
Primal play
There are dark themes throughout.

Shattered Moon

Soul of Fractured Fate
Fate of the Broken

Auburnigh

Auburnigh
N
W E
S
Colire
Light
Amara
Dreanigh
Drakomore mountains
Moradi
Shadow
Lupos
Eneara →
Marapor
Dialigh
Faeglo forest
Auroras
Wilkno
Samarria
Selk
Decantous
Serbea
Illa
Gloom grove forest
Tomarapos
Aquaveno
Lumoscavar

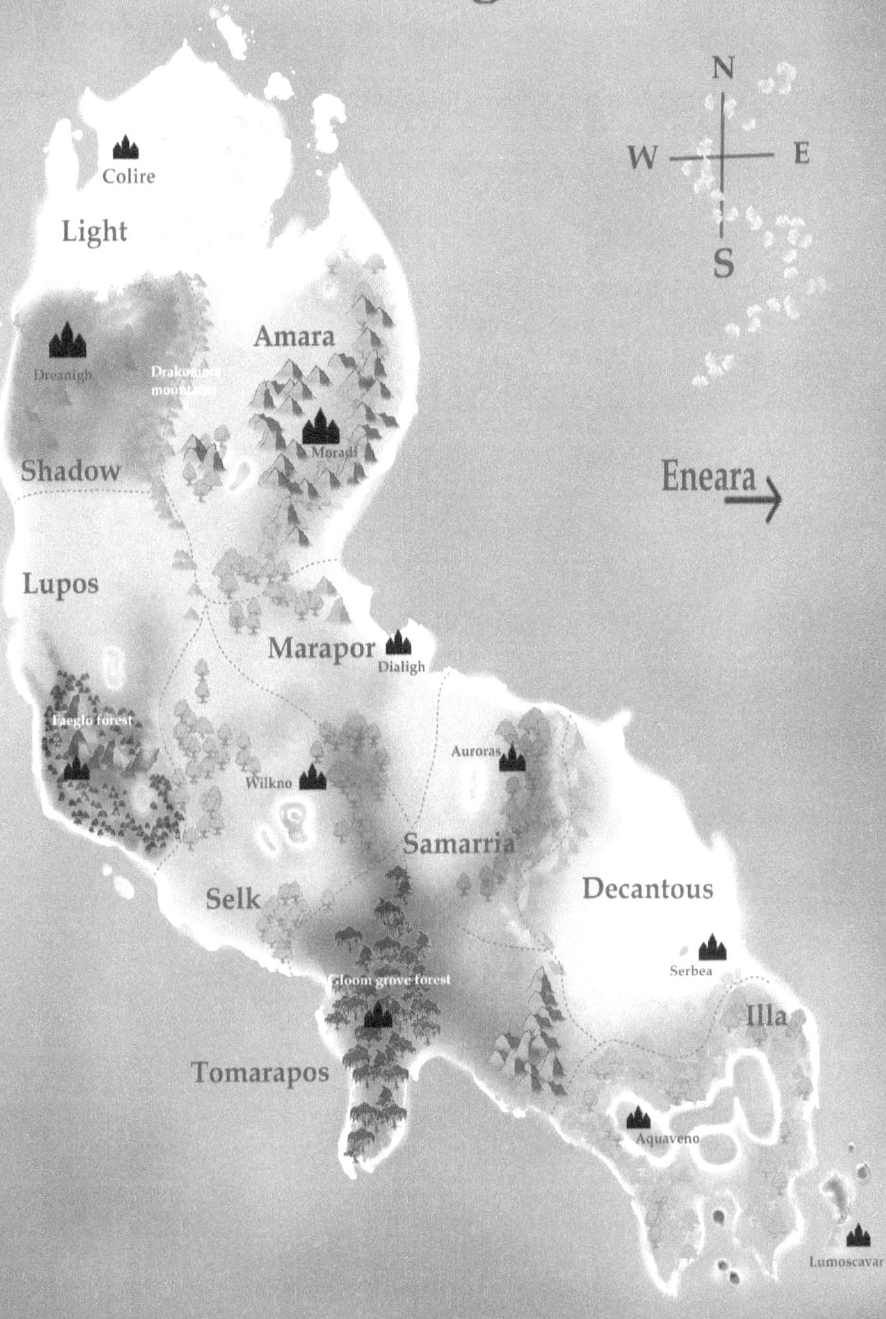

Chapter 1
Killian

I knock on the door, waiting for the goddess within to emerge so that I may embrace her. The sound echoes down the empty hallway, intensifying my nerves to a crescendo of anticipation.

Oddly, Jade didn't show up for training this morning. While she's ordinarily groggy and a bit grumpy, she always attends. "Jade?" I call through the door of her room, but there's no response. Perhaps she is sick. I knock once more, but an eerie, foreboding silence greets me. I shake off the unease that rolls through my body.

Gods, I hope I didn't offend her last night. She's my moon, and my wolf was ravenous, biting at the bars of its cage to get to her. It's okay, though; I have it thoroughly leashed again. It's been very possessive lately, and I keep feeling my hold slip; I don't want to scare her away. Damn it.

"Just try the knob; it's usually unlocked," Cat's voice carries down the hall. She must have finished training for today. She walks behind me with Ryker in tow, headed for her room. Her long strawberry-blonde hair swings listlessly, damp with the sweat that clings to her.

Ryker shoots me a grin. He is considerably less sweaty than Cat. Today, he has his long, ashy hair tied back in a low tail. He even trimmed his beard, something I never thought I'd see. His attempts to court Cat—much to her annoyance—and train her have been entertaining to watch. Ryker does nothing by halves. He pushes me toward the door as he passes.

I hate to barge into Jade's personal space, but if she's not feeling well, I'd like to help. I sigh and grab the doorknob. It doesn't budge. "Locked." I look at Cat in defeat as I shrug.

"Just use the door in my room. Come on."

I step into Cat's room, a dark plum haven mirroring Jade's with its captivating gothic theme. Unlike my bedroom, a sanctuary of soft fabrics and pastel hues, this room exudes a mysterious charm. I love that every part of the castle has various themes from different periods; only a few rooms are alike because they adjoin. Cat's rich eggplant comforter rests seamlessly over the mattress of the ornate four-poster bed, not a fold out of place. She must have sought refuge in Ryker's quarters last night. Suppressing a smile, I turn towards the adjoining suite door.

"Do you think she'll be mad if I enter her room unannounced?" I look over my shoulder at them.

"I doubt it, but leave the door open just in case," Cat replies, opening her armoire and rummaging through the dresses.

"Always have an exit plan." Ryker chuckles as he sits by the window, glancing at the pile of fae romance novels on the ground. He picks up the top book, cocking an eyebrow as he shows me the cover. *Romancing the Vampire Lord.* I grin as he shakes his head and places it back on the stack.

Resolutely, I throw on a dashing smile, smooth down my hair, and open the door.

My smile falls.

My heart stops.

Time stands still.

Dread tightens its grip on me, and I'm overwhelmed by the metallic scent of blood that permeates the room. The disarray and chaos unfold before my eyes, rooting me to where I stand. Thunderous echoes pound through my head as I battle the urge to gag. The mattress is haphazardly upended and leaning against the armoire. Blankets cascade to the floor in a morbid pool of crimson velvet. Blood streaks to a corner, staining the rug in grotesque patterns, collecting in pools that amplify the sense of visceral dread within me. At the epicenter of this dreadful scene lies a man, his blonde hair shining in the early morning light, in stark contrast to the surrounding horror.

"Call the guards! Get the King!" I shout as I look frantically for Jade in the carnage. Oh, gods, where is she? What happened? I rush to the man crumpled on the rug, his gaze drawn away from me. I check his pulse and feel nothing but his cold skin. Dead, then.

A sharp inhale sounds behind me. "Oh my god," Cat whimpers. "Where is she?" Her voice cracks.

"Fuck," Ryker breathes before I hear his footsteps retreat, thundering down the hall.

As I move around the body to get a clear view of his face, I can't help but let out a snarl. "Bravos." His expression is twisted in wide-eyed panic as he stares lifelessly ahead. His pants and belt lay open, his manhood on full display. I curl my lip in disgust. The beast inside me awakens with fury.

"What the fuck!" Cat shrieks. "Where the fuck is Jade? Why is he here? Why is his dick out? Oh, my god!" She turns frantically around. "Jay! Jay! Whose blood is that?" She runs to the bathroom, carefully avoiding the blood splattered on the floor. Returning dazed, she looks over the room before dropping onto her knees and sobbing. "Where is she?"

This can't be happening.

My wolf takes over, and I land on all fours as a snarl rips through me. The acrid tang of blood overwhelms my senses as I look for clues. My sense of smell is so much stronger as a wolf. Bravos reeks of arousal, anger, and fear. I growl, having a good idea of what he may have been doing here. I pick up the scent of sugar and vanilla near the bed. Is that a whiff of Jade's otter? The trail runs under the footboard and out the side of the bed, stopping where the blood starts. I snarl, unable to control the bloodlust coursing through my veins.

The amount of blood is staggering. I doubt Jade could have held her shifted form long after that. Back when she didn't know how to shift, she needed to relax. But I never had the chance to warn her that a life-threatening injury would also force the shift to happen.

Footsteps echo down the hallway as I catch the scent of Warrick and my parents in the air. The click of the lock alerts me that they are inside. I follow the trail of blood as I hear the roar of my father's wolf and my mother's sharp inhale.

A large blood puddle pools in the corner; my father joins my investigation as I sniff the blood trail. He growls and nudges me toward a spot on the floor I hadn't noticed. A distinct ozone and rage scent mixes with the robust aroma of iron and vanilla. I look at my father for confirmation of what he smells. The fur on my back bristles as I try to piece together what happened in this room.

"Did you hear anything last night, child?" Mom crouches down to Cat, her calming voice breaking through my thoughts.

Cat shakes her head. "I was in Ryker's room."

Mom smiles sympathetically and nods. "Corbin, Killian, did you find anything?" She stands and looks at us. The beast's rage calms with Mom's presence, and a low whine escapes me as I look at them.

Dad returns to Mom's side and shifts back, looking at me expectantly. I just want to wallow in self-pity, curl up in a corner, and pretend I'm a carefree dog. Everything I've learned is dreadful, and I don't know where Jade is. I walk toward my parents, dragging my tail behind me. My mom pets my head and motions for all of us to leave the room so Warrick and the guards can conduct their secondary assessments.

"Killian, I know you don't want to face this, but I need you to be fae right now," Mom coaxes.

With a heavy heart, I shift back and lean into my mom for a hug.

Ryker has Cat balled up in his lap, tears streaking her face. She looks at us expectantly. I stand next to my father, who has more experience in investigating than I do, and wait for him to start. My vision goes blurry as he speaks.

"From what I can tell, Bravos went into her room last night, and someone locked the door from the outside, but there is no trace of another person's scent. Based on what I scented on Bravos, his intentions were of a malicious nature." My father looks at me, and I nod, confirming that I've come to the same conclusion. "It's clear that Jade's blood is on the floor, and she was running from him."

"She was also in her otter form for a time while she ran," I say.

"While I don't know exactly what transpired, the pheromones and scent trails tell us a lot. The state of undress we found Bravos in, combined with the scraps of fabric on the floor that smell strongly of Jade, paints an interesting picture," Dad continues as Mom walks over to Cat and squeezes her shoulder in support.

Jade attempted to flee. She didn't freeze, which was her goal in training. If what I've gleaned from the room is accurate, she has made fantastic progress. Jade acted and didn't let herself shut down. At least in the end, she got away.

I run my hand down my face. "What we don't know is where she went. But we also picked up Rodan's scent in the corner."

My father nods. "I can hazard a guess that Rodan stepped in and killed Bravos, but that's where the trail runs cold."

"How could they just disappear? Could they have just walked out and locked the door behind them? Did they go out the window? What if she bleeds out? That's a lot of blood," Cat asks, looking frantic.

My parents exchange a look. My mom nods and walks over to Ryker. "I'm going to restore your memory. Unfortunately, this will be necessary." She places her hand on his temple, and his face falls slack as he looks at me. "I need you both to promise that what you learn in this room doesn't leave this room."

They nod in agreement as my mom motions for my father to continue. "I believe Rodan used his power to get her out. He can shadow walk to any location he's been before."

"But that power died with the Shadow Kingdom." Ryker glances at us, his brows pinched.

"Rodan is the last prince of Shadow," I explain. "He was smuggled out before the curse took hold of him. My parents raised us both in hopes we could restore both kingdoms together."

"Oh, shit," Cat breathes, realizing what that means. "You're the prince."

"Fuck." Ryker shakes his head. "That's a big can of worms. Any idea where he took her?"

Dad shakes his head and walks back into Jade's room, addressing the guards. "When you're done here, search the castle, find Rodan and Jade. Warrick, get the other guards on this immediately and go with them in case Rodan was unable to heal her." He closes the door behind him as he speaks, blocking our view of the devastation.

"I know this is a lot to take in, but we will find them," Mom says, walking towards me. "I assume Jade was alive when her trial ended?"

"Yes." I stiffen. The only smell of death was on Bravos. "We need to see who locked them in. We need to question Hunter." My resolve falters as I feel a lump building in my throat. I knew Bravos was a problem, but I never thought he would go this far.

"I told you we should have killed him," Ryker grumbles, somehow seeing my train of thought.

"Excuse me?" Mom cocks a questioning eyebrow. "What am I missing here?"

I cast my eyes down. I shouldn't have withheld what was going on with him. "Bravos put a collar on Jade during their first date. I had to melt it off of her," I wince.

Her eyes grow wide with horror, and rage fills her features. "How could you not tell me this? Of all the scheming, lowlife, barbaric—" She snaps her mouth shut and flushes. Taking a deep breath, she smooths down her bodice. "We will sort this out." She looks over at Cat. "I promise we will find your friend. If she's with Rodan, she's safe." Mom turns back and wraps me in her arms. "We'll find them. I'll find you later, and you will fill me in on everything you've kept secret. I will get the guards to question Hunter and everyone else in their circle. Then I have to deal with the duke to tell him his son is dead." She grimaces before walking out.

"Did Bravos...I mean, his dick was hanging out of his pants—" Cat stammers with tears in her eyes.

"No," I growl. I didn't catch the scent of sex in the room—just a lot of fear and anger. I collapse into the plush reading chair next to Ryker and watch him stroke her back as she burrows her face into his chest.

"We will find her." Ryker pulls Cat in tight, but he shoots me a weary look that mirrors my own as my heart twists.

Chapter 2
Jade

Pain lances through my head as a wave of nausea threatens to overtake me. I peel my eyes open as if it's the first time I've ever used them, straining with the effort. Light robin-egg-blue walls reach up around me to a vaulted ceiling. The attempt to push myself up fails as the bed swallows me, blankets and sheets holding me down.

Where the fuck am I?

Heavy lids shut as I take a moment to breathe and think. Sleep threatens to pull me under again. Focus. I need to focus. God, why is this sensation so familiar? Through the haze, I latch on to the last thing I remember.

I was in the hospital, and they were getting ready to discharge me. I saw a couple of police officers talking to the nurse, and then they walked into my room. They explained they had questions for me because someone had reported me missing. I agreed to go with them after they promised my mom could pick me up from the station. I was a little panicked with Ace still nearby, and I hoped that going to the precinct would help me escape him. I rode in their squad car to the station. Then, I was asked questions I had no answers for by an officer who looked less than amused.

Things get fuzzy after the questioning. I know I asked someone to call my mom and wrote her number down for them.

And then...what?

A flash of Ace talking with his father, the Chief of police. My ex-father-in-law Mark, bringing me a glass of water...

Then...

Nothing.

My heart hammers in my chest as I fight the grogginess. Groaning, I push myself up and force my eyes open. The room spins as I try to focus. I'm in a bedroom facing an ensuite. There's a double vanity and a shower through an archway. Beige carpet flows continuously from the bedroom and throughout—*gross*—the bathroom. I turn my head to look at the rest of the room. The motion feels like trying to turn a rusty screw; I wince in pain.

Two shut doors frame a large TV mounted to the wall facing the bed. An imposing wooden desk sits on the opposite side of the room. The bare room reminds me of a hotel without a decorating budget. Every wall is blank, bland, and dull in its blue simplicity.

Where the fuck am I?

Taking a deep breath, I brace myself as I pull my legs from the covers and hear the distinct rattle of metal. I pause and listen to the silence, hearing only my ragged breaths. Swinging my feet off the bed to the floor, I stare in horror as a chain rattles, puddling on the carpet next to me.

Every muscle in my body goes tense as I gawk at the cuff circling my ankle. It is tan with cream wool fluffing out the top, cushioning my skin. A large padlock connects a black band around the center. Panic threatens to consume me as I look at the long chain attached to the lock and follow it up to the wall above the bed.

Nononono!

A blast of energy runs through me as I stand and pull on the chain, then claw at the cuff. I turn my attention to the wooden mount on the wall and pull the links; nothing so much as budges.

I am shackled to the fucking wall.

Glancing out the window, my heart drops at the familiar sight. I don't even have to look out the window on the other side of the bed to know how utterly fucking screwed I am. This is the ranch, Mark's fucking ranch, outside of Morgan Hill. I am in the middle of nowhere. I collapse to the floor in defeat as I stare at the rows and rows of fruit trees lining the rolling hills. Never have I hated the sight of pears so much in my life. Not only that, but I just love the addition of bars to the windows; it really classes up the place.

If I'm at Mark's weekend house, that can only mean one thing: Ace is behind this. I am trapped at Ace's mercy and utterly screwed. Tears drip onto my legs as I pull at the lock and scream in frustration.

When I push the cuff as far down my ankle as it will move, my skin screams in protest. I claw at the band and pull on the silver lock. A high-pitched shriek of despair tumbles out of me. Cold sweat snakes down my back as my breaths come in pants between shrieks.

"Glad to see you're up."

I jump at Ace's voice as he walks through the door behind me. I scowl at the floor, balling my hands into fists as my body tenses.

"We need to talk."

"Are you kidding me?" I scream, standing to look at him. The chain rattles with the movement.

"You might fool the police, but you don't fool me. Who's the guy?"

"Let me go!"

"Answer the question, Jade," he spits.

The way he grits out my name makes my skin crawl. I seethe as I stare him down. "Let. Me. Go."

"Look, there's a lot we need to talk about, and that's impossible if you are just going to be unreasonable. Just answer the question." He uses an exasperated tone, which I've heard him direct at toddlers when they leave toys on the floor. My blood boils all the more for it.

"Unreasonable? Unreasonable! You chained me to the fucking wall, you psychopath!"

"God! I knew you were gonna be like this!" He throws up his hands. "It's a simple fucking question!"

My blood boils as I sneer at him. His face is red with anger, accentuating how pale his short blonde hair is. If he doesn't believe the truth, I'll give him a story to be mad about. "Okay, fine! You want to know? A lot of guys, an entire football team of guys! I traveled with them and let them rail me six ways to Sunday!" I shriek.

His face turns an interesting shade of burgundy at my outburst. I have to stifle the urge to grin.

His breathing grows heavy as he turns and punches the wall by the door. I jump as my heartbeat ramps up, and a soft ringing plays through my head. I continue to clench my fists to hide the tremble in my limbs.

Ace hits the wall again before his hands drop to his sides, and his shoulders slump. He pivots back to me, his head hanging, looking at the floor. I keep my sight fixed on him, refusing to yield. I won't give him an inch even as my throat begins to close on me.

He glances up and makes eye contact with me, tears rimming his eyes.

Ladies and gentlemen, prepare yourselves for manipulation. Please fasten your seat belts. It's going to be a bumpy ride. I sneer as my shoulders tense, trying desperately to keep my breathing under control.

"This isn't how it was supposed to go." He sniffles, eyes red. "I thought we could work on things. Go back to how they were in the beginning."

I stare at him, eyebrow raised. He has lost his damn mind. The beginning was the puppy-love phase of the relationship, during which he love-bombed me. That would be a hard no; it is impossible to return to that once you know someone.

"Let's start over. You'll see, things will be great. Just give me a chance." He gets on his knees in the doorway, pleading with me.

I pick up a length of the chain, holding it out in my open palm. It takes everything I have not to engage as I clench my jaw so tight I fear my teeth might crack.

"It's just a precaution. I want you to see how well I can take care of you. It's only temporary." His face morphs into a hopeful smile. I intend to break his stupid face with this fucking chain. "You're not going to say anything?"

"Let. Me. Go," I seethe.

He stands and sneers at me, pulling a remote from his back pocket and throwing it on the bed. "TV is set up so you can stream, but that's it. You can't contact anyone from it." He turns and takes a step out into the hall. "I'll bring you food, then I'm going to work." He closes the door, and I'm alone again.

I scream at the top of my lungs. Turn to the nightstand and try to pick it up, but it won't budge. Searching the sparse room, I find nothing that can be thrown. Storming into the bathroom, I knock over the shampoo bottles, which fails to calm my anger. I search the entire space for anything that might get me out of here. The chain around my ankle doesn't even enable me to get to the door. At my furthest reach, my fingertips just miss the knob.

Tears stream down my face as an ache settles deep in my chest. Despair engulfs me in the sea of darkness as my hope dissipates.

I am trapped.

Held hostage by a psychopath.

A while later, Ace reappeared with a tray of food and a cup of juice. Setting it on the floor close to the bed, he gave me a longing glance before leaving again. I sat against the headboard and glared at him, then listened to the click of the deadbolt. The rumble of the garage door sounded faintly through the silence a few moments later.

I can't believe he'd stoop this low. Of all the crazy things I thought he was capable of, this was at the bottom of the list.

I've searched every inch of this room, and there is no way out. Bars stand sentry outside the window, bolted and welded in place. The extent to which furniture is fastened to the walls and floor is reminiscent of how one would fasten things down on a ship. In short, this is hopeless unless I can convince him to let me go.

The aroma of hot food reaches me, and my stomach growls, breaking the silence. Picking up the cup of juice, I walk it over to the sink and dump it.

No more drugged liquids for me, thank you very much.

I wash the plastic cup with soap, ensuring it is as clean as possible, before filling it with water. Settling onto the floor, I look at the dried hamburger patty and a pile of lettuce smothered in blue cheese dressing.

Five years, and he still can't remember that I'm not a fan of blue cheese. Or maybe this is my punishment for not cowering to his demands. I dig into the flavorless food, and my heart sinks. The blue cheese is the best part of the whole damn plate. I drag every bite through the dressing and choke down the unseasoned, bone-dry hamburger.

It's going to be a long day.

Since he's gone, I run the shower. While searching the room, I found no clothes, so I'm stuck with this t-shirt and shorts combo. I yank off the white shirt and bra, tossing them onto the floor by the sink. Pulling down the gray shorts, I run them and my underwear down the chain. That's going to get gross exceedingly fast.

I look in the mirror in horror.

Everything has been so crazy, I haven't noticed. My tattoos are gone. Purple and blue bruises have marred my arms and ribs. A bright pink scar slices across my thigh. Not to mention my damn hair is silver, which I knew but hadn't really looked at yet.

What the hell happened to me?

Inspecting every inch of myself, I look so different; I don't understand. There are two little white scars on the inside of my thigh. My legs appear more defined than I remember them being. It's subtle, but my whole body seems slightly altered.

I spin in the mirror, taking a sharp breath as my eyes find the artwork running down my spine. It's not large, maybe the size of my hand, right between my shoulder blades. Sweeping my hair to the side, I sit on the counter to better see the mysterious tattoo on my back.

A delicate, wispy design snakes around snowflakes that twist up my spinal column. It looks like smoke and snow entwined with blank areas swirling together, creating some sort of formation. It's hard to tell what it's supposed to be with the negative spaces. Whatever it is, it's pretty, but why did I get it, and where did the others go?

What the hell was I doing for two whole months?

I take a scalding shower, filling the room with steam. The weight of the world seems to sit on my shoulders as tears slip from my eyes. My heart feels raw and split open, but who wouldn't feel this terrible being held captive? A wave of dizziness washes over me as I step out and dry off. Putting my clothes back on, I glance at the bed and TV.

With the water cup on the nightstand and the tray slid towards the door, I grab the remote. Getting comfortable, I flip to my favorite show and watch the demon enter the fairy's life. Uncontrollable tears roll down my cheeks, and my heart caves in on itself. Something about the demon makes the hurt I feel so much worse.

My head swims as I try to catch my breath. My vision tunnels...

Overwhelming grogginess pulls at my eyelids.

Oh no! The food!

The room spins.

Everything goes dark.

Chapter 3
Jade

I walk out onto the moonlit balcony, my long gown swishing. My breath catches as I look out upon the glowing garden. Towering trees surround a small blue lagoon that radiates blue light, so unnatural I wonder if it's toxic. The soft glow of the tree bark illuminates the small, smooth boulders surrounding the trickling water as it flows into the lagoon. Neon green mushrooms light paths up the tree trunks, and giant mushrooms peek out from the ground like tall lamps towering above benches.

A faint glow emanates from the grass while flowers dance in the breeze like rainbows of light. Plants with large leaves are mixed in with smaller-leaved plants, each with its veins glowing brightly in an array of highlighter colors. The garden looks like a display of neon lights.

"I thought you might like the night garden," a sensual voice says behind me.

With a beaming smile, I turn to see the man behind me. "Now, this is a magical garden."

"Bioluminescent, actually." He smiles. His wavy blonde hair catches the subtle shifts of color being cast onto the balcony. A sense of calm washes over me as I take his hand and sit. I attempt to get a better look at him before the spread of food takes my attention.

My stomach drops as I see the steak before me.

"Oh no, please tell me I didn't screw up dinner already." He sounds so sincere that a twinge of guilt runs through me at the face I must have made. "I can have something else brought up if you don't like the food."

"I'm sure it's fine. Let me try it before we make any drastic decisions." I smile as I cut a piece, noting the juice running off the thick steak.

As I place the piece in my mouth, I let out an audible and admittedly embarrassing moan of pleasure. The spices are perfect; garlic and butter round out the flavor as the piece practically falls apart in my mouth.

"Oh my god, this is the best steak I think I've ever had," I breathe, cutting into the roasted potatoes dusted with rosemary. I can't be sick of steak if it tastes like that. I could get used to the food here.

He beams as he digs into his food. "What was it like growing up in the mortal world?"

"I'd say normal, but that probably doesn't translate the same here," I say, smiling as he crinkles his eyes in amusement. "So, I went to school. My parents were pretty awesome and open about everything. I read a lot, especially books that had magic and fairytales. I used to pretend I had magic and could fly." Taking a sip of wine and giggling, I wink. "Dove off a lot of stuff and hurt myself a lot."

He laughs. "Why did you keep doing it?"

"I thought it was a mind over matter thing. I just didn't believe it enough the last time."

His entire face is lit with amusement as he laughs, shaking his head. "Determined little thing, aren't you?"

I feel my face flush. "Sometimes. What about you?"

His face goes contemplative. "As much as I'd love to tell you everything, I unfortunately can't remember much of it because of the stupid memory potion." He shrugs, tapping his fingers in thought. "I also read a lot, mostly fairy tales. I love the stories of dashing heroes saving the princesses." He winks. "Seriously, though, I was obsessed. I was already being trained in sword fighting. All I needed was a dragon to slay and a damsel to save. So, while you jumped off everything in sight trying to fly, I was probably pretending to save the fair maiden from the dragon."

"And who was this fair maiden you saved?" I grin.

His cheeks flush pink as he looks down at his plate. "She was a mop, and Rodan was the dragon," he mumbles and stuffs a sizable chunk of steak into his mouth, covering his face with his hand and looking to the side of his plate.

He looks so embarrassed; I make an effort to hold in the laugh, but the dam bursts on a fit of laughter. "That's adorable." I lift my glass towards him. "To being immensely embarrassing kids."

He lifts his glass to mine in a toast. "And probably being immensely embarrassing adults as well." He smiles.

The glasses clink.

Clink...

Clink...

The grass beneath my back is soft, and the moonlight dances with the neon glow of the garden. A steady stream of water trickles down into the lagoon, a melody that plays softly with the rustle of leaves.

My head swims with the bottle of wine I used to drown out the memories I can't seem to recall. Tears streak my cheeks, leaving cold puddles around my ears before disappearing into my hair. I glance through the strands at the man beside me, feeling defeated.

He sweeps a stray hair out of my face, tucking it behind my ear. My heart thunders as I gaze into the demon's fathomless green eyes, his long black hair gently dancing in the night breeze. My emotions feel like they will implode as I look at him.

"Why don't you go to bed?"

"Because things are just as bad in dreams as they are in the real world. I'd rather be somewhere nice," I whisper as I wrinkle my brow in confusion.

I feel like I've done this before...

"Jade."

My eyelids are heavy. Sleep is pulling me under.

"Jade, wake up. Dinner is ready."

A tear slips through my lashes. What was I dreaming about? I feel drained. My arms are heavy. I want to grasp onto the demon in my dream and stay there. It was such a pleasant dream.

"Jade." Ace's voice cracks through my thoughts.

My eyes snap open, and I take in the sight of my ex-husband standing over me, his short blond curls styled to look like ramen noodles on his head. His muddy green eyes look down at me, his brows creased in concern.

Motherfucker.

"Get away from me," I say as calmly as possible.

He puts down a tray of food and puts his hands up in surrender, backing up.

That's going to be a nope from me. I'd rather starve to death than risk being drugged again. This groggy feeling has become all too familiar.

"Take your damn food with you. I'm not eating it if it's not sealed in a package. I'd rather go hungry." Sitting up, I cross my arms. *Say goodbye to the woman who placated you. I don't care what you do to me.* I refuse to be nice anymore. My therapist said to set boundaries and stick to them; here is the perfect opportunity for me to try. Even if standing up to him makes me feel like I'm having a heart attack.

His eyes widen before his face crumples, and a lone tear streaks down his cheek. His act is revolting to watch. Nausea crawls up my throat as I hide the tremble in my hands under the blanket.

He shudders a breath. "Can we talk?"

"No." I pull my knees up to my chest, dragging the long chain; the invisible bonds that held me captive in my marriage made manifest. I hold the look of rage on my face as my heart pounds in my ears.

He sits on the edge of the bed, looking down at the floor, releasing a heavy sigh. My insides go cold as I reinforce the walls within myself. I won't succumb to his bullshit anymore. I try to suppress the lump in my throat, attempting to keep my breathing steady.

"I was so scared when I found out you were in the hospital. And when I got there, you looked so different," he says in a near whisper. He runs his hand through his stiff hair, causing it to stick in weird directions. The overhead light highlights the frizz around his face and shadows under his eyes.

Yeah, I totally believe the answer to being worried about someone is kidnapping. It seems perfectly logical when you look at it from a sociopath's perspective.

I hate you.

"Why did you get your tattoos removed? I mean, it's an improvement. I never understood why you had them to begin with, so I'm glad you finally took my advice and had them removed."

I clench my fists under the blankets and purse my lips together. I refuse to dignify that with a response. *It's not a great strategy to insult me if you want to be on my good side.* Resisting the urge to roll my eyes, I turn my head and focus on the shower stall and the pale walls of the bathroom.

Where the hell did my tattoos go? It's mind-boggling; there is absolutely no trace of them left. No scarring, no nothing. But if I could blink them back into existence, I would to spite him.

"What did you do to your hair? We'll have to get that fixed. The white looks trashy, and I'm sure that's not what you want." He leans over, raking his fingers through the long lengths.

Are you fucking kidding me? My eyes snap to his as I grit my teeth together. The sharp look makes him drop his hand in defeat. Trashy? My natural hair color may not be conventional, but I don't look trashy. If anything, it's healthier and shinier than it's ever been. While I miss the black, I won't change it because he hates it. Not that

I could change it under my current circumstances.

"I was surprised you didn't call the cops when you saw your apartment," he says, looking up at the ceiling.

What is he—?

A vision of destruction and a storm of fluff plays through my mind. The acrid smell of piss, the graveyard of books, hits me like a ton of bricks. How could I have forgotten?

When he looks at me, it's written all over his face. He's not surprised. His knowing smirk is all I need to confirm how things would have played out.

"So you and your buddies could have a good laugh at my expense? No, thank you. They all know you and probably would have locked my ass up for public disturbance if I'd even tried to report you."

He crosses his arms over his chest, smug. I hate that Ace gets away with everything because his father is the chief—corrupt assholes.

"You have an interesting way of trying to win me back. You kidnap me, chain me to the wall, and then proceed to insult me..." I grip the sheet in my fist, hoping he doesn't see my muscles tensing.

"You won't talk to me, Jade. I'm just trying to get you to talk to me," he pleads.

"Okay, you want me to talk? How about this? Fuck you, you psychopath."

He clenches his fists, balling and releasing them. His jaw ticks, and his eyes darken as he stands and walks out, slamming the door. I jolt at the sound as I try to breathe.

The door swings open again as a box of protein bars lands on the bed with a thud, followed by a bag of chips. My heart thunders as the lock snicks again. I frisbee the plate of food off the nightstand at the door before inspecting the snack bars and chip bag for tampering.

Tears stream down my face as I choke down the chalky chocolate bar. I turn the TV on at max volume, blasting the space with the fairy and demon voices.

Settling in, I watch the demon who seems to have made it into my dreams. I'll take that over the nightmares any day. I hiccup a sob, watching the demon bring the fairy the flower that will make her feel better after getting sick. The slight smirk he hides from her as she thanks him makes my heart ache.

The ache is so deep that my ribs feel like they are being pulled apart one by one.

I scream through the cacophony of noise. I hope that this keeps Ace's sorry ass up all night, because I have a bone-deep feeling that I'm never going to make it out of this room alive.

I stare at the screen, transfixed. My insides shatter into pieces as I heave a ragged sob.

Chapter 4
Killian

Mom paces the dais of the throne room, the windows casting a blue tinge over her white fur. She takes graceful and delicate steps, her feline form commanding in its presence. The warm candlelight reflects off her silver armor and in her eyes, making them shine with intent. The cobalt floor's reflection gives the impression of walking on still water.

Sitting out of the way, Cat, Ryker, Warrick, and I await our orders. The silence in the room is deafening as she addresses her guard, a small contingent of her cats.

The bulk of the queen's cats stand at the ready as she silently speaks to them, their armor gleaming in the sunlight. These are the deadly assassins who answer only to their queen's demands. They prowl silently through the halls and collect intel, protecting the castle.

I wish I could hear or understand the language Mom uses with them, but alas, I am not a feline shifter like Mom.

Cat stares in wide-eyed wonder at them, eyes bloodshot from lack of sleep. I'm sure I don't look that much better. It's been twenty-one days, and still no sign of Rodan or Jade. The wolf inside me bristles, constantly wanting out, wanting to rage at the world, wanting blood. But the hole in my chest keeps it at bay.

We tracked them to the Dracomore Mountains, to the tower Rodan has always escaped to when he needed alone time. Their scents were all over the tower, and Rodan's disappeared about a mile into the forest. Jade's scent had never so much as left the door. Fallen trees lay scattered all around the tower, and large fissures scarred the land. I'm unsure of what could have changed the landscape so drastically since the last time I'd seen it. Unfortunately, from there, the trail went cold.

It's like they vanished into thin air. The wolf paces the confines of my sanity; never have I felt my grip on it so tenuous.

My chest constricts around my lungs as I take a measured breath to calm myself. My muscles loosen as I breathe. I've been tense, and I try to take moments like these to relax.

Mom hisses some commands, signaling she's getting heated in her discussion. Typically, they communicate silently, but Mom's hissing and low murmuring indicate she is getting agitated. The guards' tails twitch almost imperceptibly, their postures rigid.

"What do you think they are saying?" Cat whispers.

I put my finger to my mouth and flick my eyes to my mom; her tail swishes as we make eye contact. Mom stares daggers at me at the interruption. Shit, I forgot to warn Cat to remain absolutely silent at these meetings. The queen's cats can hear everything, and it's very distracting.

Cat's eyes grow wide, and her cheeks pink when she looks at Mom. She sinks into her chair as Ryker picks up her hand in reassurance.

All the guards meow in unison as they break formation. Some of them form groups as they walk out of the throne room. A sandy orange tabby and a russet brown cat turn and walk towards us. They sit directly in front of Cat, who stares at them in shock.

"I'm so sorry. I wasn't trying to be rude," she says to the guards. She quickly turns to me, brows furrowed. "Am I in trouble?"

"I doubt it. Mom surely has a reason for sending her guards to you." I flash her a reassuring smile. Cat smiles weakly and waves hesitantly at the guards.

As the last of the other guards leave the room, Mom returns to her majestic fae self. With her cream gown flowing around her, the blue light tints her in shades of aqua as the gold detailing gleams. She sweeps her dark hair over one shoulder while patting the half-updo into place.

We all stand as she walks over. Warrick pulls his chair out from the wall so she can sit facing us. She nods to Warrick, who returns to my side and signals us to sit.

"How did it go?" I ask.

"They have combed every bit of the castle. I have a team searching for secret passages we may be unaware of. The team I sent into the mountains found nothing. A team surveyed the city and surrounding area, but no trail existed. They have checked and rechecked the castle grounds and gardens, but as you know—"

"Nothing," I sigh.

"We are all doing everything possible to bring your brother and Jade home. For now, the lockdown of the castle will remain in place per your father's orders. His guards are conducting interviews with everyone in the castle. My guards still go vastly undetected. I've pulled one team to be our ears within the castle, specifically."

"What can we do?" I ask as Cat and Ryker sit up straighter.

Mom's serious gaze lands on Cat. "Can you transform into a cat? Or at least something with a feline head?"

"I think so?" Cat says.

"Okay, I have two of my guards to help teach you. I believe you may have the potential to understand them, though I'm just speculating. If it's possible, they may assist you in comprehending your wild shape better. They can't change their shape as you do, but can change their size at will." Mom smiles. Cat has been at her wit's end, not knowing what to do to help. Leave it to Mom to find something to take her mind off things for a bit.

Cat's eyes grow comprehensive with understanding as she nods. "So, if I am mostly a cat, I'll possess the ability to interpret their language?"

"In theory." Mom grins.

"What about cats like Pop?"

"If you can understand my guards, you should be able to understand book dragons; the language is the same. Pop may also help you, or at least teach you about guarding books." Mom shrugs.

"Why are they called book dragons?"

I smile at Cat. "Like all dragons are known for their hordes, book dragons specifically horde books. Employing one in the royal library serves both the dragon and us. They get a horde to lord over, and we have a protector of our knowledge. Pop is rather young, but very excited to take the position. In the mortal realm, did you ever see bookstores with a cat?" I ask as Cat nods. "My guess is they are descendants of some form of book dragon."

"So, when does my training begin?" Cat looks at my mom again.

"Now, if you'd like, I think you need a break from worrying, and being productive may help. You will follow Suff and Grum on their rounds and see if you can understand their language. Learn to use your sense of smell to direct you. The three of you will start in the library with Pop. I think that should be a safe enough place to start your training. Ryker, as I know you will want to stay with them, I'd like you to be their eyes from above in your falcon form. If you all work well as a team this way, I may have use for you in the future. My guards have their instructions." Mom motions towards the door as her two guards wait for Cat and Ryker.

Ryker shifts and flies around the room, waiting for Cat. She stares at the queen's cats, scrunches her face up in concentration, and transforms into a heap of fur on the ground, her pointed ears flat against her head. She directs her blue eyes towards me in curiosity as I observe her. Okay, she didn't completely botch it this time; she is primarily a feline. However, I think their armor reminded her of an armadillo because she is sporting a shell. I stifle a smile, trying to hide my amusement.

She looks at her back and huffs a large sigh.

"Close enough. Can you understand them?" I ask, smiling reassuringly at her.

She gazes at the guards. Something appears to be communicated between them as Suff and Grum make eye contact. Cat glances up at me and nods, her eyes wide as her tail flutters excitedly behind her. Aw, she shows excitement like a wolf—that's adorable. I smile wide as she and the guards leave the room.

"How are you, Killian?" Mom leans over and places her hand on my knee.

Huffing, I choke down the lump in my throat. "I don't know what to do, Mom. I feel like my chest wants to split open. But also, like, I'm losing control of my wolf. I want to rage and destroy whoever is responsible. I've never had this much trouble keeping these instincts at bay. The more time that passes, the more worried I get, the harder it is."

"I understand. Your father, at times, has trouble as well. It's what makes you and Rodan similar—that instinct. Although he rarely cages his baser urges." She puts her finger to her temple, probably reliving some mischief Rodan put her through. "Caging your wolf as much as you do is also unnecessary. You are older now; you have more self-control. Sometimes letting out those instincts is a good thing."

"That doesn't sound like a great idea."

"At some point, you need to let those feelings in, feel possessive, rage, lust, all of it. So you can find balance and less of it feeling like 'it versus me.' While I don't always appreciate or approve of Rodan's behavior, he doesn't fight his nature. It pains me to see you fight yours."

I don't want to think about myself when they are still missing. How can I? "How could they just vanish without a trace like this?

Rodan wouldn't just run off."

"It's not like him. I'm not inclined to believe he would. Even if you and he were fighting over the same woman—" she says, lifting an eyebrow.

My heart stops. Were we?

My silence must speak volumes because Mom continues, "Love can be a strange thing. I saw the way you both looked at her and coveted her attention. I see the way you are now, a love-sick pup who lost someone precious. But that is a future problem. We will continue our search and find them."

"King Corbin is with Hunter as we speak. He maintains his innocence and won't speak of his brother's crimes. I was instructed to escort Your Majesty down to the dungeon after your meeting," Warrick says.

I stand to walk my mom out. She wraps me in a big hug as I breathe in deeply. We will find them and find out what is going on around here.

"Go lie down for a bit. I can tell by the bags under your eyes that you haven't been sleeping." Mom pets my cheek with her soft hand.

"But I—"

"Now. You can't help if you are asleep on your feet."

Dejected, I hang my head as I nod and walk towards my room.

There has to be something I missed, some clue overlooked. I turn down the hallway that leads to Jade's room instead of mine.

Someone cleaned and tidied up her chambers again, scrubbing away the blood and all traces of violence, but it still smells like her. I walk across her room to the windows, looking over the enchanted garden towards the Dracomore Mountains. The last two places that she seemed to have been. It just doesn't add up.

She was hurt. Rodan took her somewhere safe. Then what? Where did they go? I fight back the tears that want to spill as I climb into her bed, pulling her sugary vanilla scent into my lungs.

I want to tear apart the world to find her, but how can I do that if I don't even know where to start?

"Killian!"

Vanilla. I breathe in Jade's scent and pull the blankets over my head, blocking the light.

"Killian!" Cat's voice drifts through my haze.

I roll over, blinking away the groggy feeling and forcing my mind to focus.

"I think he's in here," Ryker's gruff voice says beyond the door.

Ugh.

The door flies open as Cat and Ryker pour in. "Uh, what are you—no time for that. We found something!" Cat says breathlessly.

I jump out of bed, never having felt so alert as my heart thumps wildly in my chest. It's been so long since we found anything, and I was losing hope.

"I was learning how to change my size from Grum. Did you know they can grow to the size of a house? Anyway, Pop came over and commented on my weird shell and taught me how to have wings instead, but—damn it, I'm getting sidetracked. He asked if I wanted to see something cool that he had seen. There's a secret passage in the library! He just didn't know how to open it. So I ran to get you, followed your scent here." She smiles up at Ryker, who could not look prouder.

"Show me."

We walk into a small room tucked away in the library. An oak desk stands in the center, positioned before a grand fireplace. Scattered across its surface are piles of books, with a few abandoned and forgotten on the floor. Wooden shelves tower above us and line the walls, filled with tomes of varying ages, their spines worn and faded. The scent of aged paper fills the air, mingling with a faint mustiness.

Pop sits before the fireplace, lazily twitching his tail in pride as I lean over to pet his head. Cat has shifted into the rosy golden version of Pop. She tucks her gilded wings against her back as she sniffs near the stone, occasionally sneezing from the dust.

I feel around the mantelpiece's edges, removing knick-knacks and books, searching for a button or lever.

"Meow," Cat looks up at me, dancing on her cute little paws.

Grum and Suff have a silent conversation with her. All three of them shrink to the size of mice and run against the wall alongside the fire. I lean in as they squeeze through a small, almost imperceptible hole in the far back corner behind the logs. One by one, they disappear into the crack.

Well, that's one way to do it.

I hear Cat's muffled voice beyond the wall as she squeals. Ryker moves up beside me, eyes wide with horror.

"I dislike their silent speaking. Makes her reckless," he grumbles.

"I have a feeling she's always been that way. But at least she seems to have figured out her shifting."

"Mostly. If you look closely, she had puppy feet. But the size seems to have worked out the way the queen hoped." He glowers at the wall separating him from Cat. "She better find the lever on that side before I destroy this wall."

I stifle a laugh, hiding my grin behind my hand. Breathing deeply to settle my thunderous heart, I turn to Ryker. "I thought we questioned Pop?"

"We did, but we didn't ask the right questions. Apparently, he saw this door open a while ago, when and I quote: 'the big buffoon was scaring Jade-friend in here.' It seems Jade had quite a few run-ins with Bravos that she never told anyone about, according to Pop, at least. I guess Suff told Cat that the guards all heard rumors about

Bravos constantly cornering her."

Involuntarily, I flex my hands, wanting to beat the shit out of the dead man. I wish she had told me. I knew something was wrong, but didn't want to push her. How can I help if she won't confide in me?

"Don't worry. Cat also told me Pop set his leg on fire." He gives me a knowing grin as a smile pulls at my lips. I love that little dragon.

A slight clunk and grinding sound steals our attention back to the task at hand, followed by a squeal from Cat. As the door pivots open, the fireplace grinds to a halt, leaving small openings on either side.

"I'm not sure where the lever is on that side, but I found it pretty easily on this side. Well, pretty easily for feeling around in the dark." Cat beams, pointing towards the lever on the back of the fireplace wall.

Pop walks through the opening and looks back at us. I follow the little fur ball into the darkness. Trepidation and hope blaze through me. This could be a dead end, but it could also give us clues.

The warm glow of fire sparks in my palm as I form an orb to light our way. It floats up ahead of me as I create another to follow behind, casting our shadows along the rough stonework of the tunnel. The air is musty and stale; the walls are peppered with dust. While ragged and worn, the floor is littered with gravel that scrapes under our feet. Suff and Grum take the lead, walking side by side, the size of large dogs. The firelight dances off their silver armor as they dodge cobwebs and kick crumbled rocks from the path.

Pop takes up the rear of our strange little search party, but I don't mind having a fire-breathing dragon cover us. Smoke billows from his nose as his posture stiffens to the unknown threats of the dark tunnel. His first real adventure, I'm proud of the little guy.

I glance back and see Ryker holding Cat's hand and grumbling something as she snickers. He's probably chastising her for running off without telling him. I think he is wearing her down; she has been leaning on him a lot more recently.

We reach a staircase that spirals down. I nod to the guards before they descend, with us following behind. Gripping the long dagger on my belt, I wish I'd grabbed my sword instead. This place gives me the creeps. I didn't even know the castle had passageways this old, but things were bound to slip through the cracks after a thousand years. How many hidden passages are there throughout the castle that I haven't discovered yet? This one is much more ancient than the ones I grew up playing in.

It is unsettling to consider that anyone would use this tunnel. How much has passed right under our noses?

No, I won't think like that. This may be nothing but an area that no one has visited in centuries.

"How did no one know this was here?" Cat asks.

"Castle is old. It was forgotten." I shrug.

"What do you think is down there?"

"Probably some old furniture, storage, junk, most likely," Ryker says.

"I'm all for adventures, but this place chills my bones. Granted, I probably would have loved it when I was a pup. I'm not used to feeling all doom and gloom all the time," I pout.

"Aw, Killian, it will be okay. You are the cutest love-sick puppy." She giggles. "Are you gonna wag your tail when you see Jade?"

I glare over my shoulder at her as Ryker laughs. "Are you?"

"Sorry, I'm not good at this. I make jokes when I'm upset. I know you miss her...do you love her?"

Love? My face heats, and I'm grateful the ominous darkness hides it. "I–I don't know. I just feel something with her, like a magnet...drawn, you know. I don't know how to describe it."

She quiets a bit as we continue carefully navigating the neglected steps. "Can you live without her? Like, would you want to?"

"No, I do not want to. What kinda question is that?" My heart almost stopped at the inquiry, a wave of dizziness hitting me like a ton of bricks. I don't realize I've stopped until I feel Ryker's broad hand on my shoulder. I turn and see pity flash through his features. Narrowing my eyes, I return my attention to the stairs and continue.

"That's what I thought. You can't see a future that you want without her. It's love. Don't worry, it will be fine," she coaxes. "Well, except for them being missing, Rodan also having feelings for her, the curses–" she abruptly cuts off her train of thought as she yelps and stumbles.

"Sweetheart, maybe cut the guy a break from your musing," Ryker says.

Scowling at the cracked step before me, I stomp onto it. This is the second time someone has said that Rodan was into Jade. I take a deep breath to refocus myself and concentrate on the task at hand. I can't worry about that until I find them.

"I'm sorry, Killian. I was just trying to focus on something besides my friend. I miss her. And I'm scared," Cat whimpers.

I need to believe that we will find them. Flashing a grin at Cat, I wink, letting her know we're good. I doubt Rodan would be down here, but if we find one passage, there could be more. Maybe they hid in one, and the door got stuck? I would never let Rodan live that down.

The stairs seem to go on forever as we traverse around and around; the air grows more stale with every turn, and the caustic scent of mold and rot assaults me.

Grum stops as Suff jumps over a couple of steps that have crumbled away, descending another couple of steps to make room for Grum. They gracefully clear the rubble and wait as I climb over the broken stones. Ryker holds onto Cat's arm as she falls into my arms, holding Pop firmly to her chest. As Ryker clears the steps, our guards continue. Cat sets Pop down and gives him a pat on the head.

The hairs on the back of my neck stand as we reach a long, gloomy hallway. Towering wooden doors adorned with iron line the walls. I send balls of light to the farthest end of the passage, illuminating the dingy stone corridor.

"I guess we start opening doors? Cat, stay with the guards. Pop, you back them up. Ryker, you're with me. We'll take the right; you take the left." I motion for the guards. "Don't go out of earshot," I say, walking to the first door on the right.

Ryker grumbles something about Cat as he walks to the next door. I know he wants to stay attached to Cat's hip, but she's got two guards and a book dragon.

I push open the door to a cloud of dust that assaults me. Coughing, I wave my hand around the gloom, pulling an orb of light into the room. I see a thick wooden table in the middle and torch sticks lining the walls—perfect. I grab two and walk into the hallway, lighting the fabric. Cat stands outside a door and turns when she sees the bright light. Smiling, she takes one as Ryker walks over and grabs the other.

"Room is empty except for those and a table."

Cat waits outside the door for the guards, who direct their attention towards her. "I can't understand you unless I'm a cat." She shrugs.

Pop rubs against her leg and then stretches up to tap her hand. She looks down at him as he paws at his ear. She stares questioningly at him before her face lights up. "I can't talk to them unless I'm a cat, but if I can hear them..." She scrunches her nose in concentration. Fuzzy, bright golden ears pop out of the top of her head as Ryker steps out of a room and almost falls over.

"Gods, warn a man before you do that," he pants, holding the wall for support.

Cat giggles, opening her eyes; her slitted teal irises blink at me triumphantly. "I can hear them now." She beams. "They said that room is all clear."

"So is this one," Ryker says as he looks over at Cat and shakes his head with a grin.

We continue down the hallway, checking every door. Cat translates for the guards, happily swishing her gray and black ringed tail, which I have yet to inform her she has. One day, she will get the hang of her shifting. Today is not that day.

We reach the last door on the left; after this, the only one unchecked is at the end of the hall. Cat turns the knob, but it doesn't budge. Ryker moves her aside as he slams his shoulder into the wood; it creaks and moves the smallest amount. Moving next to him, we shove as hard as we can, feeling it start to give way. One more shove, and the hinges rattle and whine as the wood scrapes across the floor.

A powerful pulse of magic and something I can't identify wafts over us, causing bile to rise up my throat. What in the gods name is that stench?

Huddled up to Ryker's back, Cat is peeking around him into the space, covering her nose and mouth with her hand. She gags and takes deep breaths, trying to right herself.

The room floods with dim light as my small fires float in. This place is much grander than the other rooms off the hallway. Next to the door is a large hearth, casting warmth over us as we descend the three steps into the space. Beside the fireplace is a table with a large glass cauldron in its center, surrounded by empty vials scattered across its surface.

To the side is a long bookcase with books, scrolls, and papers spilling out from the shelves. A reading chair situated in the corner looks out upon the entire space. A lone wooden chair sits in the middle and across from an antique carved oak desk. Mountains of books and vials lay scattered across the desk. There are cabinets filled with strange vials, bottles, and jars reminiscent of an apothecary. A rainbow of colors and textures fills each container.

What the hell?

We slowly fan out within the space. Cat drags Ryker over to the books. Grum and Suff walk over to the cabinets of strange glass jars, then disappear through a side door, likely a storage closet. Pop stands at the entrance, alert, watching for anything in the hallway.

My wolf comes to the surface, dying to investigate this strange place further. The itch to shift overwhelms me, and I give in to it.

Vanilla.

Sugar.

Jade.

I growl as I follow her sugary scent to the chair in the middle of the room. Her scent permeates the chair, but another stench in the air almost overpowers it. But I smell her—her sweet perfume. I also smell her fear—fear so intense that it sends a jolt through me.

She was here.

I work around the room, ignoring the acrid smell overpowering my senses. My eyes water as I try to piece out any other clues, but it's like Jade was in this chair and never left it. Her trail just ends again.

I snarl as I change back into myself.

"She was here!" I shout as I pick up a vial and smash it on the ground. "She was in that chair and scared to death. But her damn scent starts and ends right here." I point at the offending chair.

Cat's forehead wrinkles as Ryker turns to me. "Are you sure she didn't just sit in that chair somewhere in the castle?"

"Her scent is also lingering in front of the chair. She was here. But I can't pick out anyone else's scent." I run my hands through my hair in frustration. "It's there, but it's like...it's hidden behind something, just out of reach. I don't understand it. How can I know a scent is there but not be able to smell it?"

"Killian...you may want to look at these books," Cat says, holding one out to me, her face laced with concern.

Helplessness washes over me as my worst fears are all but confirmed. She was here. The sharp tang of her fear still laces the air.

"Killian, snap out of it," Ryker barks.

I shake my head and walk over, taking the book from Cat. The cover is old and worn in my hand. The black cover is unassuming as I open to the first page and swear.

Grimoire of the Soko family

My breath catches in my throat as I flip through pages of spells and hexes. Curses long since lost to history. I drop the book with a loud thud.

Nononono.

I grab another book off the shelf as Cat stares at me, pursing her lips. I flip to the first page.

Moria family Grimoire

Pages filled with more forbidden magic make up the compendium. My heart thunders in my ribcage as I pick up book after book, finding the same thing. Not one witch family grimoire on the shelf. None of the spell books contain anything besides dark magic; all of it is sorcery.

Shit.

This is the Obsidian library amassed by the sorcerer king. Family Grimoires of allies and enemies alike were collected with the forbidden dark magic books of old. They were believed to have been destroyed centuries ago. How did they get here?

"Those what I think they are?" Ryker asks.

"Yes," I bite out.

"You should burn them."

"What, no! You can't burn books!" Cat shrieks, looking wild-eyed at me.

"The spells contained in these books are forbidden for a reason, Cat. Sorcery is forbidden for a reason." I run my hand down my face. There has to be a good way to deal with this. "Cat, I will hand you a stack of what I believe are the most dangerous of these books. When we leave this passage, you and the guards will take them straight to the queen. Then we will have the palace guards clear out the rest of this room."

"We should all carry as many as we can. Think about it, Killian. Whoever hid them down here will come back for them as soon as we are gone," she says.

"They are too dangerous. We should burn them." Ryker punctuates his point by throwing one into the fireplace. A pulse of power slams through the room as the book hits the fire, knocking Cat off her feet and into a heap on the ground. Ryker and I steady ourselves as we observe the book in surprise.

The book shudders and lifts into the air before bolting right towards us. I duck right before it slams into the bookcase. The books on the floor shift and rise to their spots on the shelves; Ryker dives on top of Cat as books from around the room zoom past our faces, organizing themselves into the bookcase. I cover my head as the tornado of paper whips around us.

"Oh, shit," I breathe.

Cat's gut-wrenching scream cuts me off as she stares at the ceiling in panic. The color drains from her face as she tries to scramble away, pulling at Ryker's shirt.

Lowering my arm from my eyes, I glance up towards where Cat's eyes are pinned.

"You can't be fucking serious."

Chapter 5
Jade

Silvery moonlight casts the kitchen in its ethereal glow as twinkling stars dance across the night sky. Warm light radiates around the room from eternal flames mounted on the rough-hewn stone walls. The scent of spices and freshly baked bread permeates the space, enveloping me in its comforting aroma.

The cavernous room is large enough to cook for an army. A colossal hearth dominates one wall, and a smooth stone countertop runs the length of the wall. Empty pots sit ready for tomorrow's breakfast. Under the cooktop, fires smolder between stone arches. The flickering flames cast shadows across the ornate filigree carvings molded onto the facade.

I glance at the walls lined with long wooden tables and the abundance of baskets overflowing with vegetables. Trays of bread cool on racks next to enormous brick ovens.

My stomach rumbles with hunger as I search for a late-night snack. There must be something sweet in here somewhere.

"Looks like we have a pest problem in the kitchens," a low voice says, causing me to jump and spin around. The dark-haired demon leans in the doorway with a blush-inducing grin.

I let out a huff as I attempt to calm my heart down. "What the hell are you doing up?"

"Testy tonight, are we?"

I spin on my heel and flip my hair over my shoulder as I continue towards what I assume is a pantry. "Go away. I don't feel like dealing with you right now."

His footsteps echo behind me, closing the space between us. "I don't think I will. Can't have vermin in the kitchens; it's unsanitary."

I glance behind me to see the wry grin he has plastered on his face and sneer at him. "It can't be that big of an issue if they let you in here."

His eyes darken as a lazy smile sweeps his features. An arm winds around my waist in an embrace, pulling me back into the hard plains of his body. A warm hand spreads across my stomach as I gasp.

"What are you looking for, Trouble?" he purrs in my ear, sending a shiver down my spine.

Mind muddled by his proximity, I squeak, "Pie or ice cream...something sweet?"

"I'll give you something sweet," he growls, and my insides go molten. God, why does my body react this way to him? He releases me and casually strolls toward a large metal door across the room. Of course, a fridge.

I close my eyes and try to level my breathing. My face burns with the knowledge that he can smell my arousal. Stupid demon, now I understand how the fairy felt around this guy.

Bright light shines through my lids as I breathe in the fresh air. I open my eyes and blink several times as the sun brightens the horizon.

What was I—that's right, training.

The trees glow in the early morning sunlight, flickering rays reflecting off the morning dew. I turn as footsteps draw near and smile as I see the tall man striding towards me. He shines in the light, his tan skin taut with lines of muscle carved from stone. He ties his golden hair back, but little tendrils escape their confines and frame his smiling face.

"Just remember, if all else fails, no one ever sees the headbutt coming." He grins at me as I laugh. "Don't laugh. You wanted to know how to defend yourself, and that's a handy trick to know."

"Well, I hope I never have to use it because that sounds painful." I grimace.

"Oh, it sucks, but it works." He winks, handing me a sword and stepping behind me. His arm wraps around my waist, holding me tight. "This is like a dance. Follow my lead."

I nod as he runs his hand along my arm and clutches my fingers around the hilt. He raises my arm, pointing the sword at the wooden dummy, and swishes it. With his body plastered to my back, I feel every dip and weave as we methodically move around the mats. It's an unhurried, sensual dance that has my heart fluttering as I try to concentrate on the movements.

We make the same motions repeatedly, slow and steady, until it's almost muscle memory.

"You're getting better at this," he whispers.

"You're an excellent teacher." I lean into him, resting my head on his shoulder as we stop moving. I love being wrapped in his arms. He lets my hand and arm drop as he pushes a strand of hair off my cheek. Gently, he runs the back of his fingers down my temple, trailing them down my side as he holds me firmer against him.

He leans into the top of my head and takes a deep breath before nuzzling my hair and laying his head on mine. I could stay here forever like this.

Safe.

I long to question him regarding his identity. How did we end up here like this? The answers niggle at the back of my mind, but are just out of reach.

Things are getting hazy, and I can't speak...

No, no, no. Why did I have to wake up from such a pleasant dream?

I keep having these dreams with the same two guys. Aside from the fact that one looks like the demon from my k-drama, I have no idea who they are. When I open my eyes, I'm left only with this feeling of loss. Maybe it's my subconscious trying to help me in this impossible, miserable situation.

I want to escape into these dreams forever, pull a sleeping beauty, and never awaken again.

My stomach growls, reminding me I can't simply wallow in bed. The familiar rattle of chains precedes my feet hitting the floor. I lean over and dig through the breakfast bars and snacks beside the bed. What I wouldn't give for actual food that wasn't drugged. I pull out a cereal bar and groan. In the past, I enjoyed these; honey and granola used to make a nice snack. Now, they are mere cardboard that shatters with every bite, picking away at my will to survive.

A sickly-sweet scent of flowers and decay from the many bouquets fills the room. I glare at every bloom, every supposed apology they represent. Vases line every surface, plastic since I threw the first one, and it shattered into crystalline fireworks. The resulting argument landed the second vase in its stead.

Fuck these flowers. Their beauty is forever tainted.

I pause the TV, cutting off the blaring voices- the lovely point of contention with Ace, who has threatened to take away my *privilege* of entertainment. Let him. I have nothing else to lose.

I get down on the floor and throw the chain out of my way as I do push-ups. Boredom makes you do weird stuff. Even as my body thins from the lack of actual food, I've become a little stronger.

Asshole.

A creak outside my door has me scrambling up to my feet. The door cracks open.

Ace's face glances through the opening, brows furrowed in sadness. "Hey babe, I didn't realize you were up. I brought you these." He pulls red roses from behind his back.

"Cool," I grumble.

"You know I'm sorry. I just want things to go back to the way they were before."

"Well, I'm still chained to the wall, so that's kinda impossible." Not that I want that or would ever want that again.

"I should have never said anything about you cheating. I should have just moved on." His calm boo-hoo-me demeanor is laughable. He is still the victim. He ignores any mention of the chain attached to me, as if I don't bring it up. Like, I'm just talking nonsense about a fictional problem.

I roll my eyes. "Not that it does any good to say, but I'll repeat–I never cheated on you...But I should have." I mumble the last part, and my heart thunders at the admission. I've wanted to tell him that for so long.

His jaw flexes in time with his hands as he stiffens. I take a step back, heart in my throat. I watch with trepidation as he shakes his head and glares at the wall.

"I'm not trying to fight with you, Jade." He takes a deep breath. "You did what you had to do, and I did what I had to do. But things are different now. We've both been through a lot and have changed. We are ready now to give this marriage a real try." His face morphs back into pleading.

That's the subject change of the year. I have no interest in defending myself to him for the rest of my life. I'd laugh at his words if I weren't terrified by them.

The world spins while I attempt to regulate my breathing and hold my ground. "We aren't married, Ace. We got divorced. Let me go." I plead as I try to push my temper down, trying to be compliant.

His brow furrows before he adopts a neutral tone. "We vowed till death do us part. I think we should honor that. Once we have a baby together, I think your entire attitude will change. Eventually, you will see reason."

My jaw drops at this fresh horror he has placed at my feet. I have never been more grateful for an IUD than I am at this moment. I never want to be tied to this man by a child. However, this also tells me he will eventually put his hands on me again. It's only a matter of time. I feel the blood drain from my face as I struggle to breathe.

"This is for your own good. Why can't you see that? We can't work on this if you won't listen." His brows furrow, his logic lost on me.

Tears stream down my face as every last ounce of hope leaches out of me.

"Think about that. I have to go to work." He gives me a half-hearted smile and sets down the flowers and leaves.

The snick of the lock sliding into place releases the tension in my body. I sink to the floor and wipe the tears from my face.

The demon's face stares at me from the paused TV, held in a moment of utter despair that I feel down to my bones. I can't bring myself to watch anything else. When I do, the ache in my chest pulls furiously. My heart is fracturing into a million pieces; the only thing holding it together is a fictional character. If it keeps giving me pleasant dreams, I'll gladly fall into this insanity.

I want to hold on to the hope that someone will find me, but with every passing day, I feel that hope crack. Even clinging to anger is getting exhausting.

What did I do to deserve this?

This can't possibly be it. Curling into a ball on the floor, I let the unbridled tears flow as I sink into the abyss. Darkness envelops me within my mind, cast into a realm of loneliness in a place where hope never existed. The stone walls within my mind surround me, where no one can find me in the dark—an oubliette, where I can be forgotten. Never thought I'd sink back into this place of loneliness and despair, but it feels familiar in its cold embrace. I let go of that last sliver of hope and let it fall through my fingers into the bottomless depths. I welcome the pain that lances through my chest, pulsing once in its death knell—before I feel nothing at all.

So much for happily ever after.

Chapter 6
Killian

Long, spindly legs protrude from a hole in the corner of the ceiling, their inky blackness shining in the dim light. The cobwebs around the room slam into focus in their delicate weaves. More legs shove through, pulling the gargantuan body through the hole.

My heart suddenly stops in my chest as Cat screams again. Suff and Grum bolt into the room, hackles raised and hissing. I stare in horror, frozen in place, as this monster comes further into view. What the fuck is that doing in the castle?

I reach for my sword, coming up empty.

Shit!

I draw the dagger from my belt as I back towards Ryker. He pushes Cat behind the chair and congers up his war hammer.

The fire beneath my skin begs release as I try to focus. The exoskeleton on this thing may not be affected, but I pull a bolt of fire and throw it as hard as I can.

A high-pitched screech pierces the air as the spider rears back and skitters to the other side of the ceiling. Oh gods, this is the worst thing ever; I hate spiders. A shudder rolls down my spine as I attempt to hold my ground.

"Why did it have to be a spider?" I grumble.

Ryker laughs, saying, "We made it just for you."

"Dick."

Suff and Grum pace in front of us, growing larger by the second as they hiss a warning at the creature. Their giant claws tap the stone as they assess their target.

Maybe we should just run.

It's fine. It lives here now.

Just burn down the whole castle. Mom will understand.

A roar from behind shakes me out of my stupor. I whirl around, and my jaw drops as I watch another abomination of a monster slowly backing up in the corner of the room. Its legs pull it backward up the stones. Blood-red armor-like plating runs down its spine, ending in a long armored tail tipped with a stinger. Fur tufts out along its belly and chest, leading to the most confusing sight: a cat head.

Recognition hits me like a slap to the face. "Cat! Are you fucking serious right now?"

Ryker chuckles beside me, eyes glued to the spider. "Scorpion cat?"

"What the fuck?"

"Yeah, she's been working on that one for a while. I reacted the same way when I saw it." He flicks his gaze over his shoulder and flinches before returning his attention to the spider. "Gods, I'm not sure teaching her how to get big was a good idea. Fucking hell, Sweetheart."

Suff and Grum jump at the spider from opposite sides, claws bared. Grum is a blur of agile russet fur and shining metal as he grabs a leg and bites down, swinging momentarily before the leg breaks with a sickening crack, and he plummets to the floor. The spider thrashes and screeches as Suff claws down its abdomen, leaving large gouges.

Ryker hurls his hammer at the spider, which clanks against the hard shell and clatters to the ground. With a grimace, he pulls the hammer back towards him and reshapes it into a spear.

I wait for a moment when the guards are on the ground looking for another opening and cast a fireball at the beast. It turns slightly, taking the brunt of the fire to its side.

Okay, fuck this.

Closing my eyes, I pull the fire in the room towards me and feel for the lines of power. A slippery line leads to the spider, but it's loose and wiggles like a noodle. I gather all my strength, trying to will the thread to me.

Kill it with fire.

Kill it with fire.

My eyes fly open.

I can't get it. Something is preventing me from pushing my fire into its veins. No, no, no.

I stare at the nightmare and try to swallow past the lump in my throat. I can't make it combust. An icy chill runs down my spine as the spider crashes to the ground and the guards jump out of the way. Why didn't I practice on something cold-blooded?

It stands unsteady on seven legs and swipes at the guards as they circle. Standing on its rear legs, it lunges forward with its arms out towards Ryker, who throws his spear at it.

A high-pitched scream pours out of me; it's very manly, not embarrassing at all, and I fire another round of power at the monstrous thing.

Nope. I can't do this!

It rears up again, and I almost hit Suff as he leaps upon the back of the spider and digs in his claws. The spider thrashes, crushing a table and scattering glass everywhere. Legs flailing, it smashes the chair with Jade's scent, and wood splinters across the floor.

Tip, tip, tap, tap, tap. I stiffen at the clatter behind me. Movement above has me crouching and readying myself as I see the blood-red cat-thing creeping across the ceiling, its stinger poised and ready. What is she doing?

Ryker looks up at her as she positions herself above the spider, and the blood drains from his face. "No," he gasps.

Ryker furrows his brows in concentration, and the surface beneath the spider shifts, the spider sinking into its depths. Grum takes the opportunity to leap upon the beast and join Suff in trying to claw a hole in its back. Thick gouges run through the shining surface, almost cracking the shell.

The spider screeches and thrashes, the stone around its legs solid once more.

A thunderous crack sounds as the spider is shoved to the ground, held down by Cat's stinger firmly planted in its head. Icker leaks out in rivulets, puddling into the stone's crevices.

I can't take my eyes away from what I'm seeing. Cat's tail impales the spider to the floor as Suff and Grum leap from its back and bat at its legs, inspecting it for life. I blink several times before I glance at Ryker, his jaw hanging open as he drops his spear with a loud clang.

"Your girl is scary, man," I deadpan, still staring in awe at Cat.

"Yeah, I know," he says with adoration.

With a sickening yank and crack, she pulls her tail from the spider's decimated head and curls it into a spiral above her back. She skitters in the most unnerving way to the wall, down to the floor, and morphs back into herself. Her self-satisfied smirk says it all as she peruses the spider.

Her attention falls to Ryker, and she squeaks, "I thought it was gonna get you."

"Aw, you care." Ryker smirks.

"I never said that." She puts her hands on her hips, trying to hide the tremble that runs through her arms. These two are hopeless. "What the hell was that? Why is it in here? What is this place?" She is quick to change the subject.

"I have no idea, but I want to get the hell out of this room. We need to keep searching for clues. I feel it; we are so close to finding something," I say.

"You just want to get away from the spider and have someone else deal with it." Ryker nudges my shoulder with his.

"Fuck that thing."

I take one last glance around the space and leave the room. I'll have the guards come down here. The only door we haven't checked is the one at the end of the hall, and I swear to the gods–if there is another gods-damned spider, I'm out.

I have to be close to finding them. My precious Emerald is here somewhere; she has to be. I take a shuddering breath and push open the final door to yet another staircase.

How deep does this blasted place go?

"More stairs?" Cat whines, peeking around me into the claustrophobic stairwell.

I nod as I begin the descent. Fear and longing flood me; what if she's not down here? What if it's another dead end? I run my hand through my hair, trying to regain my composure as pressure builds behind my eyes. This whole situation was never supposed to happen. She would have been better off if I'd never brought her here. Or at least let her go home when she wanted to leave.

I fucked up.

A small hand slips into mine. I turn to see silver riming Cat's eyes in the dim light. "We'll find her," she whispers.

I squeeze her hand and nod once.

"We're actually pretty lucky Jade didn't see that. She would have peed herself. I mean, it was big, but a spider is a spider, and a cat always beats a spider." She snickers, changing the subject.

"Do you have any idea how dangerous that was?" Ryker chastises her.

"Yes. But I wasn't gonna let that bitch eat you. Didn't you see the web coming out of its butt? It was going to shoot it at you."

"What!" Panic causes me to stumble down a step. I grab the wall and steady myself, shooting a concerned look over my shoulder.

"Well, at least I think that's what it was gonna do, so I made my move. You like my scorpicat? I think it's pretty wicked; if I can't focus on one animal, I may as well lean into it," she says, with pride in her tone. "Don't give me that look, Grumpy. I'm tired of running scared. I saw my opportunity, and I took it."

I smile as silence descends upon us. Ryker is going to brood about this for a while. Both of them are too stubborn to deal with each other's shit.

Pop races ahead of me as the end comes into view, his hackles raised. Sconces are lit all along the room, illuminating the bars of multiple cells. A wall of reeking rot slams into me, and my eyes water at the stench.

"What the–" I breathe.

Cat gags beside me as she enters the space, with Ryker looking a little green beside her. I fight back the nausea as I step into the room. Grum and Suff guard the door, ensuring nothing sneaks up behind us.

The room looks ancient. Brittle, rough bricks line the floor and walls. Great iron rods run from floor to ceiling. A few doors rest open on rusted hinges, hanging onto their last threads of hope. Large cages line one wall, a macabre menagerie of the past. In the center of the room is a long metal table, with worn leather straps lying haphazardly across its shining surface. A smaller tray with an assortment of sharp implements sits innocently in the corner, awaiting command. A forgotten space, decaying with disrepair over hundreds of years.

"Check the cells," I say as I move towards one with its door closed.

The first cell is open, and the door lies on the floor within it. A small cot sits in one corner, threadbare fabric on its last leg. A wooden bucket in the opposite corner is the only other object in the dreary space. Three of the four walls are stone; the past occupant's only view was through the iron bars.

Gods, I know dungeons are bleak, but this is ridiculous. I'm suddenly grateful that we updated ours years ago to be brighter and more humane. I can't imagine being stuck in a place like this.

I suck in a tight breath as the next cell comes into my line of sight, and a shadowed figure lies curled on the bed. The blanket, thrown over their head in the dark corner.

I grab the bars and curse as heat boils my palms. I pull my hands away and look at the angry red lines carved into them.

"Fucking iron." I step closer, making sure not to touch the stupid metal. "Hello?" I whisper, please be alive. Please don't be a pile of bones under a blanket.

The mound shifts, and I suck in a breath. "Jade?" My voice trembles as I utter the word, conveying all my hope.

Black hair emerges, followed by a pale male face with dark eyes. His eyes grow wide with something like fear, but hope also radiates from his scent.

"R–Rodan?" I stammer out, unsure of what I'm seeing. Hope swells within my chest.

The man leans forward into the light, uttering a stream of unintelligible words in a raspy voice. He moves closer as he speaks, words growing more frantic, but I don't understand them. Grabbing onto the iron bars, he shakes them and looks at me wild-eyed.

His scent is all wrong, and his eyes are chocolate brown. He continues his tirade, rising in volume as I struggle to piece together my friend from this person who stands in front of me. I stare at him in shock, unable to move or speak.

"Oh, my god." Cat steps beside me. Her jaw moves as if she's trying to speak but can't find the words. She looks between me and this strange man. "I don't think that's Rodan...I think he's human." She pulls my attention to her and points to her ears.

Beneath the long black hair, rounded ears are just barely visible.

"English? You speak English?" The man looks at Cat excitedly.

"Yes. Who are you? How did you get down here?" Cat asks as Ryker looms behind her.

The guy scans between us and gulps before returning his gaze to Cat. "There was a girl; her skin gleamed pale like the moon. I thought she was a fan, but she kept popping up at events and whispering in my ear. Then, at a movie premiere, she sat next to me. The lights went down, and I woke up here. Please help. I just want to go home."

"Where is home?"

"Seoul," he replies.

"Oh, shit." Cat turns and grabs my arm. "I know who this is. Oh, shit." She turns back to the man. "Are you Jin Yoon?"

"Yes!" The man looks at her excitedly.

Ryker and I exchange a look and shrug. "He's an actor from the mortal realm. He stars in Jade's favorite k-drama. When we got here, we couldn't help but notice how much Rodan looked like him. Shit, someone else must have thought the same thing. This guy is supposed to be in Korea filming season two, not here." She gestures around as if we didn't guess that the guy shouldn't be here.

That explains why he smelled so off; he's human. My stomach plummets. I guess I knew this wasn't Rodan, but I'd really hoped it was. I really don't like how much he looks like Rodan. What is that? He's not Rodan. He can't have his face; it's not right.

"You guys are seriously not helping your case with the whole: 'We almost never kidnap mortals anymore' shit you try to sell me." She glares at us as if we had put the man in the cage.

"I'll look for a key. Ryker, check the other cells." I move towards the back of the room, hoping to find something to help. Gods, this is a mess. Who knows how long this poor bastard has been locked down here?

Cat continues to talk to the strange doppelgänger, hopefully calming the poor man down. If the bars weren't iron, this would be so much easier. But this was a prison designed to hold fae.

"Killian..." Ryker growls through the silence.

I turn towards the far corner to see Ryker standing before another cell and rush over. Sprawled on a cot is Calazar, his white hair caked in dirt and matted. Dried blood stains his once immaculate tunic. Gods, he's been missing for almost two months. Has he been right beneath our feet this whole time?

"Is he breathing?" I ask, my voice barely a whisper.

Ryker gives a curt nod. I continue my search for the key as Ryker runs to Pop with instructions to get more of the queen's cats. Pop runs out of the room with Suff following, and Grum maintains his position at the door. His whiskers twitch as he surveys everything, tail thrashing uneasily.

"Killian, why don't you wolf out? You tend to find things faster that way," Cat calls as she holds Not-Rodan's hand.

"Because I don't want to scare the mortal," I growl.

"Honestly, it can't be any worse than what he's already endured," she says while patting the poor sap's hand.

A low growl emanates from behind me, and I turn to see Ryker glaring into a chest. He slams it closed, looks over at Cat, and growls again. I smother a grin at Ryker's possessiveness.

"Focus on the keys, man; if she sees you getting all possessive, she's gonna kick your ass," I say before I go wolf to search. I sniff the air for any hint of Jade or Rodan, but gag at the putrid stench in the room.

We scour every inch and come up empty-handed. One cell has the faintest smell of ozone and rain, but the whiff is there and gone in a flash. Not-Rodan screams for Cat to hide and almost passes out when I emerge into view as a wolf. She calms him down somehow, and now he watches me with weary eyes.

I change as I walk up to his cage, and he swears as he puts two and two together. I walk up with my hands raised. "Do you have any clue where the key might be? How do they feed you? You must have seen something."

"I–I never saw a key. There's a girl who comes down here once a day, or at least I think it's once a day. In the mornings, when the torches light back up." He tries to explain.

Wait, what? "Describe the girl."

"She's blonde, pale skin, big blue eyes...full lips—really pretty girl. Always dressed nicely, like a movie star. But she's insulting and has the personality of a cactus."

I scratch my head as I try to figure out who he's talking about. Cat shrugs when I glance at her.

Not-Rodan looks forlorn as he tries to remember more details. "She wears white. I've only ever seen her in white. I thought she was an angel the first time I saw her, thought I was saved." He turns and scowls at the floor.

I understand how frustrating this must be for him. There has to be a way to get him out. "Did she say anything to you?"

"She mostly just brings me food and talks about how gross mortals are. Once, I asked her for some water to clean myself with, and she handed me a bucket of ice and left."

"Beatrix," Cat says so low I almost miss it.

"Gods," I breathe. "Ryker, melt the floor, the iron. I don't give a shit; just get them out. Grum, get my mother and apprehend Beatrix for questioning. Go! Now!"

Grum bolts up the stairs as Ryker stands before the gate, concentrating on his power.

"I can't melt iron," he grumbles as he inspects the door. "The hinges have recently been reinforced on this door, same as Calazar's." He moves his attention to the floor as stones start to crumble and move. Ryker digs deeper into the dirt to make a path large enough for the man to fit through.

Not-Rodan looks on with wide eyes at Ryker's display of power. He inches closer as the opening gets broader and deeper. Ryker stops when it's sufficient for one of us to shimmy through and walks over to Calazar's, beginning the same process under his door. This is not ideal.

"Oh, shit!" Ryker bellows as he stumbles backward. "Shit, shit, shit!"

Cat and I watch in shock as a titan set of mandibles reaches out of the dirt, and legs pull the creature from the hole. It rears up, slamming down onto the ground. The monster, three feet long and a foot wide, keeps coming, getting longer and longer. Legs protrude from its sides as it slithers towards Ryker, who is still stumbling backward while trying to pull his hammer from his belt.

I push a fire shield between Ryker and the centipede as he turns and runs for us. A single look from him has Cat going all giant crazy scorpion monster again.

The colossal centipede bullshit thing rears up and changes course right for us. Mandibles pinch as its now fifteen-foot body skitters across the floor.

Ryker throws his hammer, narrowly missing as the thing dodges, the hammer clattering across the floor. Its many legs tap the ground as it slithers towards us.

Cat frantically stabs with her stinger, leaving great gouges in the stones but missing the ridiculously colossal bug.

I throw a stream of fire at its legs, and they burst into flame as the thing thrashes and screeches a horrible sound. Barbecued bug mixes with the rancid smell permeating the air. The three legs crumble beneath it as it convulses and then whips its head towards us again.

"Cat, grab it with your pincers to hold it still," Ryker yells as he beats the wiggling form with his hammer, trying to break through the hard shell. The thing swings around and shoves Ryker into the wall with its long body.

Cat hisses in response. I'm pretty sure that was a fuck no. I don't blame her.

The centipede whirls around to bite Ryker as he thrusts his hammer into its face. Cat's enormous pincers grab it by the neck, and a large crack sounds as its head thumps to the floor.

Was that a neck? Do they have necks?

The body continues to writhe. It grabs hold of Cat's pincer arm, curling up, wrapping itself around her arm, circling tighter and tighter as she hisses and flails, screaming. She stabs wildly at it with her tail and stumbles through the room. Her massive form crashes through cell doors and crushes the metal table in the middle of the room.

Ryker jumps out of the way, face wild with panic as we try to figure out what to do. My palms sweat as I stare in terror. There has to be something we can do that won't hurt her.

"Get small and run, Cat!" I yell.

She shrieks as she morphs into a tiny house cat with scales and bolts as the centipede thumps to the floor. She limps on her front leg as she gets behind Ryker.

The look on Ryker's face is murderous as he faces down the beast. The ground rumbles as rocks float into the air and shape into sharp stakes.

The monster uncurls from the ground and rears up again. As another set of mandibles pushes through the severed body, reshaping into a head once more, Ryker lets the stones fly.

Sickening cracks reverberate as each stake finds its mark, nailing down each segment of the fifteen-foot creature. A spark ignites within me as I flambé the still-wriggling creature. Each leg turns black before crumbling away into dust. Small thunks ring out with every stake that falls to the ground as the body is reduced to embers.

Facing Cat, she sits on the floor, breathing hard and cradling her arm to her chest. Ryker rushes to her side and inspects the gashes on her arm with a delicacy I didn't know he possessed.

"The doors are open," she breathes as a tear slips down her cheek. She gives me a half-hearted smile. "Sorry if I almost flattened you."

"Well, that was certainly one way to do it." I grin.

Turning back to the cell Not-Rodan was in, I see the door is indeed lying bent and broken on the floor. He looks out bewildered, but doesn't step out. Calazar's door also lies smashed, but he hasn't moved from the cot.

Footsteps thunder down the stairs; Warrick runs into the room, sword drawn, followed by Suff, three other fae guards, and my mom.

Warrick rushes over to Cat and crouches down to talk with her and Ryker, no doubt to get an update and heal her.

My mom lets out a small gasp as she takes in Not-Rodan. Her face contorts with misery as she realizes he is not her son. "Who are you?" she whispers.

"Jin Yoon," he says as he looks at her and bows his head, clearly terrified.

"Why do you look like my son? What sorcery is this?"

"No sorcery, Miss. I just want to go home. Please, just let me go home," he begs.

I move to my mom's side and hold her hand. "We need to get him washed up and fed. Let Lorelai have a look at him." I tell my mom before turning my attention to him. "I understand you've been through a lot, but we have questions that need answering before we take you home."

"Jin, Killian is correct. No more harm will come to you, but we must ask you some questions before we return you to your world. I am Queen Aleena of Amara, and you are now under my protection." She turns and sweeps her gaze around the room. "Guards, please carry Calazar upstairs to the healers. Inform me at once if he awakens. Killian, you and your friends will go straight to my chambers. We have much to discuss before we interrogate Lady Beatrix."

Chapter 7
Rodan

"You can't just take a hiatus when your career is peaking!" my agent yells. His face flares like a tomato as his eyes nearly bug out of his head. His dark suit is getting more disheveled by the minute as he paces the office. He is a stark contrast to the antiseptic white of the room. Ever heard of an interior decorator? Maybe some color would calm you down.

My manager's brows furrow in disapproval as she stares out the floor-to-ceiling windows at the cityscape below. She had warned me yesterday that they would react this way. The producers are going to have a fit, and it's their job to smooth everything out. I probably should care more, but I can't bring myself to.

"Well, I just don't feel like myself yet. You said I could take as much time as needed after the accident. I'm taking that time," I say, lifting a brow.

"That's not what I meant! I can only keep the media frenzy at bay for so long; you haven't been seen publicly for almost a month. Production has already been postponed for a full week. They are talking about replacing you," he says, seething.

Indifferent, I shrug. "I don't know what to tell you; I'm not feeling it. I need a break. Things are still pretty hazy."

Michelle rises from her chair by the window and stands beside me. "Mr. Choi, I believe it is in our best interest if our client is in his right mind before returning to work. We do not need him to have a meltdown like a certain k-pop star I won't mention." She smirks down at me as Mr. Choi turns maroon.

"Never speak of him in my office! I made that boy, and he spits in my face." He slams his hand down on his desk.

I wonder if his head will pop if all the blood keeps going there. I smother a grin, covering my mouth with my hand as I picture his brain bits sliding down the glass. It would definitely add some color to the space.

This meeting has been happening for an hour now, and I just want to go home and curl up with a good book. Nothing has felt right since the accident. There are considerable gaps in my memory that won't fill themselves. Partial amnesia, they call it. How the fuck am I supposed to keep working if I don't remember how to? I've seen the TV shows and movies I star in, but I can't recall doing it.

So here we are, discussing more time for me to get my head right again. I lounge on the couch with my feet crossed on the coffee table as we discuss my future. Michelle and Mr. Choi continue to argue over the loss of income my hiatus will cause. Michelle understands and wants what's best for me, but Mr. Choi only thinks in dollar signs.

Perhaps I can nap while they debate my future. I honestly don't care if I get replaced. This industry is dog-eat-dog, but my fans are loyal. It's not like I won't get hired again. My social media presence is blowing up all over the world. I don't know what he's concerned about.

Chapter 8
Killian

"I didn't do anything," Beatrix whines like a petulant child.

"Talk," I growl. I swear this fae is driving me crazy; she just pouts while I glare at her. Warrick stands behind her with his fingers firmly in place at her temples, eyes closed in concentration.

She lets out a huff of frustration and crosses her arms, staring straight at the stone floor of the cell. The soft glow of the lights highlights the messy tangle of blonde hair framing her face. Her eye makeup streaks down her cheeks in dark rivers as her lip trembles.

"Talk," I growl again. "Where is Jade?"

"The mortal? How should I know? I don't understand why I'm down here. You have no idea who I am. I want to talk to the prince." Her defiant glare bores into me.

A lazy smile spreads across my face. "You are."

Her skin goes pale as the blood drains away, eyes growing wide with realization.

"I can have my father interrogate you if you prefer, but his methods are less...pleasant." It's an empty threat, but she doesn't have to know that. "Let's start easy, then. Why were you feeding the man in the hidden cell? Don't lie; we know it was you."

"I don't know; I just had to do it. You've seen that place, saw how gross it was. You think I would feed that filth willingly?" Her face morphs into disgust.

"Why did you have to?"

"I don't know," she spits out.

I look up at Warrick, who gives a swift shake of his head.

She's lying.

"Well, if you will not tell me the truth, I guess I'll have to start biting off fingers. I gotta say, it's not my favorite." I run my hand through my hair, musing on the idea, and look at the white walls as if actually contemplating it.

"You can't," she breathes. "I–I'm–"

"You're?..."

She growls in frustration. "I'm Princess Beatrix of Light, daughter of King Cornelious. If you hurt me, my father...will start a war," she blurts.

"Princess? I thought you were a lady."

"You hid your identity; I did the same."

"To what end?" I say, looking up at Warrick, who nods as he monitors her truths.

"To marry the prince and merge the kingdoms," she mumbles.

I laugh as I continue to pace the small cell. Around the corner, out of sight, I can hear my father's low chuckle and the thunk of my mom shushing him. I knew Beatrix was a throne chaser, but this is too much.

"So why would you kidnap a mortal and hide him in the hidden dungeon?"

"I didn't. All I know is that it was my job to make sure he got food." She glares at me.

Warrick nods his confirmation of her story.

"So, who *did* kidnap him?"

"I. Don't. Know," she spits.

"Okay...why?"

Her mouth snaps shut, and I know she is working hard against Warrick's magic to conceal some truth as sweat beads on her forehead.

"Why?" I growl again.

"I–My father wanted insurance. He said if I couldn't get the prince to marry me, he had other plans in place to ensure he achieved what he desired," she says. Groaning, a tear slips down her cheek; she must really be fighting Warrick if she's in pain. "He wants Amara for his own. But I don't know what his backup plan is. I only knew he had one because he thought I would fail!" She sobs, her face contorting in misery.

Mom's footsteps recede up the stairs, no doubt to deal with this new revelation.

"Who is involved? Who showed you the passage? Who is working with your father?"

Beatrix's expression goes blank, and she stares ahead, saying nothing.

Warrick furrows his brow. "There is a hole in her memory here, like a wall went up, and she can't access those memories. I cannot break through."

Great. Okay, a new tactic. "What is the plan for the mortal in the dungeon?"

"I don't know."

"Why did he look like Rodan?"

"I wasn't allowed to know." She looks at me pleadingly.

My patience is wearing thin. "Where is Rodan?"

"I'm not sure; I just know he was important for some reason."

"Are the attacks like the dragon related?"

She gasps in pain as Warrick smirks, his golden eyes gleaming.

"Yes!" she shrieks.

"You know, if you would just tell me everything, the pain would stop. It only hurts because you're fighting it." I smother a smile as I watch her heaving breaths, like she's drowning.

"I'm a princess! You can't do this to me! When my father hears about this, he will make you pay."

I wave away her protests; he is already a problem, and we will deal with it.

"Who sent the dragon?"

Her breathing grows heavy as she tries to resist. "A sorcerer," she sobs. "He was exiled from Eneara and has been one of my father's advisors my whole life. He wants to help Light build an empire."

Words almost escape me; we were on the right path, but this is much worse than just a sorcerer. The King of Light is working with one? Wanting to build an empire and hiding in plain sight all this time.

"Now, why would he want a cursed kingdom?"

She screams in pain as her eyes roll back in her head. I glance at Warrick, who shrugs. She is really fighting hard to keep her mouth shut. "Why, Beatrix?"

"Because he knows how to break the curse!" She screams and slumps forward, sobbing.

My heart stops. He knows...I take a deep breath, my mind reeling. Shadow cursed us because they blamed us for their curse. Does that mean...

"Did your father place the curse on Shadow?"

"No," she squeaks, not looking at me.

"Is he responsible?"

"Yes," she whispers.

"Is Scarlette a part of this?" My heart thunders at the prospect; I like the fiery female.

"No." She sneers. "She is as good as a commoner."

Okay then, and here I thought they were friends. At least I don't have to lock up Scarlette; I think Corsac would murder me. I'll still have questions for her, but I'm at peace with it for now.

"Who is the sorcerer?"

Her face goes blank again, and Warrick shakes his head. "Someone has wiped her memory. There are impenetrable walls around certain information. I'm surprised they didn't do it with the details surrounding her father's involvement."

That's a good point. Why remove some knowledge and leave equally incriminating information about others? Unless whoever this sorcerer is wants the King of Light to take the fall for all of it. But if they were working together, why would he set him up? Every answer leads to more questions.

"Where is Jade?" I ask one more time; she had nothing to do with any of this.

She sneers. "The little gold digger is gone."

My blood boils as I look at her and nod to Warrick to let her mind go. He stands beside me as I look down at Beatrix. "Well, have fun in your new room," I say, glowering at the cell door as my father opens it, taking in Beatrix. We step out and flank my dad's back.

"You have brought war to my doorstep, child," Dad says as he locks the door. "I have no pity for your plight. Perhaps your family is no longer fit to rule the Kingdom of Light. I'm sure the other kingdoms will agree with me. Until you tell me who the sorcerer is, you will live here, *Princess*. But speak ill of my son's intended again, and I'll make sure your stay is not a pleasant one. I hear a lord of the bog is looking for a new wife. He ate the last one a little too quickly, if you ask me." Dad turns and winks at me as Beatrix's face goes pale.

"Bog lord." I snort, shaking my head, and leaving the room.

Wait, would Dad really do that? Shit, I honestly do not know. Sucks to be you.

"Jin Yoon is from the mortal world—Seoul, Korea, to be exact. Warrick, you are to escort him through a portal to return him." Mom states calmly as she pours Not-Rodan a cup of tea.

The guy has cleaned up; the healers have helped him and clothed him. He looks even more like Rodan in his clothes. My heart aches for my brother. It's too bad the poor guy didn't know more, but leading us to Beatrix was more helpful than he will ever know.

"Killian, now that this new information regarding the King of Light has been brought to our attention, we've decided you will accompany them. There is a slim chance that Rodan may be in the mortal world. But seeing how Jin looks strikingly like Rodan, I'm hopeful it was a simple changeling swap." She takes a deep breath and sips her tea. "Ryker and Cat will also accompany you."

"Mom, I know I must find Rodan, but with war looming, is it a good idea for me to leave?"

"Killian, we already had knowledge that you were a target. Hiding you in the mortal world for a few days may be advantageous. You will focus your hunt for Rodan and Jade there for now. The war council has been called for this evening. The King of Decantous, Lyra's father, has arrived and offered his aid. Apparently, Cat told her everything?" She lifts an eyebrow at me.

Oops, I forgot to tell Cat not to tell the girls...

"That said, we also have delegates from Selk, Lupos, and Tomarapos set to arrive within the hour. The Queen of Marapor has extended any assistance we might need in exchange for our backing in expediting the trade agreement with Eneara." She dismissively waves her hand. Mom would never disagree about something that important. "As it stands, Light doesn't know that we are aware of their plans, which gives us an advantage for the time being."

I let out a sigh of relief that so many countries would come to our aid like this. But leaving doesn't sit right with me.

"Scarlette has been cleared; she was cooperative and rightfully horrified. However, she has been ordered to stop all communication with Colire for the time being," she says.

Thank the gods, I can't imagine how Scarlette must feel right now.

"I want you to know we did not make the decision to send you away lightly. You are the future of this country, and so is your brother. We will explore every avenue to bring him home and find your girl." She puts her hand on mine. "Warrick will drop you off and check in every few days."

Mom pulls out a small box and opens it, revealing a deep burgundy stone wrapped in silver with a matching chain. "Wear this, and Warrick will be able to find you no matter where you are. Hold it, push your fire into it, and he will know you are in trouble. Regardless of the circumstances, save a spark of power within you for the amulet. Do not forget that your power will not recharge within the mortal realm." She smiles as she clasps it around my neck, the weight as heavy as my heart. She pets my cheek before grabbing my hands in hers again. "You will find them, Pup. Now go get ready, and be safe. Your father and I will take care of things here."

I stand and pull her into a hug and hold her tight. Tears prickle my eyes as the knot in my throat lodges itself deeper. "I'll find them, Mom."

Chapter 9
Jade

Ace paces the pale blue room, exasperated, running his hands through his curls. Every crunch of his shoes on the dead flowers and drywall causes me to flinch. Vases lay scattered across the floor within the graveyard of roses.

Sinking deeper into the soft mattress beneath me, I curl my arms around my knees. Shivers wrack my body as I struggle to piece myself back together, wishing I could disappear. The headboard presses into my spine, the furthest I can get from him. My gaze fixates on the fist-sized hole in the wall. The storm has passed, and the tsunami's fury—dispelled.

I take a deep breath, not bothering to rub away the tears drying on my face. My lip throbs in time with my heartbeat, every part of me aching. His fingerprints pepper my skin; I feel them blooming like wildflowers all over. An overwhelming need to wash his touch from my body creeps up my spine. Scald the memory from my flesh. Get his scent off of me.

"You force me to be this way. I only hurt you because you hurt me first. You have unpleasant memories of our marriage, but I know what really happened. I just want things to go back to the way they were before," he says.

With a heavy heart, I gaze at the bathtub, where the shattered

TV lies on its corner. The shower at least remains functional in its separate space. But my only escape from this hell is now lost; a chilling numbness engulfs me.

"You never deserved the things I did for you. You're so selfish; I give, and you just take." *Says the man who drained my savings and demanded that I do everything. The man who thinks he owns me.* A huff of a laugh chokes out of me as I return my gaze to his face.

He doesn't seem to notice as he continues. "No one will ever love you like I do," he pleads.

"I'm okay with that," I mumble.

"I'm sorry, okay? What more do you want me to say?" He contorts his expression into one of misery. The old me may have fallen for it, but now I can't bring myself to care as I school my features into an impassive mask. The dull thud in my chest is now a mockery of the life I'm living.

His eyes fill with tears as his face crumbles. "I miss you. I miss us." He sniffles and takes a deep breath before sighing. "Please, Jade, I love you. I know I've made my share of mistakes, and I promise I'll never do it again. This time apart has made me realize what a fool I've been to ever let you go. I'll never give up on us; I'll spend the rest of my life showing just how much I love you and how great we can be together again."

You don't know what love is.

I've heard all this before, but the only difference is that I can't walk away now. I look back at the small black TV, the cracks splintering across the screen- cracks, exactly like the ones splintering across my life.

This is my nightmare; if only I could wake up.

Chapter 10
Rodan

It was a ridiculous train wreck of a day. First, I got chewed out by my manager, then my agent, and then the producers called me personally to raise hell. For fuck's sake, what do they expect me to do? Magically, remember how to act? We tried that. It was a disaster. I couldn't recall my lines, whatever the fuck a mark was, or how not to stare at the cameras. Apparently, all of which are important.

Who knew?

I finally got off the phone and called Suji's. Gods, I love that place. Suji snickered when, for the millionth time, I attempted to order her hottest spice level: cry. Once again, she convinced me to go with a level two because I'm "a candy ass." She's right, but I love making the old woman laugh. The little restaurant on the corner has been a lifesaver since, apparently, I also have no clue how to cook.

How can I remember important things about my life, such as my parents, my name, and my manager, but cannot recall all the small things, like how to turn on the blasted stove?

I groan in frustration as I open the takeout box, and the titillating aroma of vegetables and beef calms my nerves. Japchae has got to be one of the best things to exist. I wonder if this was my favorite before I got hit upside the head. There is no way of knowing because I cannot recall that kind of information.

A month ago, I woke up slumped against a dumpster outside the movie theater on opening night, and my memory has been spotty ever since. The police say the camera footage went down at the exact time I disappeared, and it was my manager taking a call in the alley who found me. I had a headache for two days, and my chest has been aching nonstop. I still do not know what the hell happened. Of course, the doctors say I'm in peak health, idiots.

Oh well.

I turn on the TV to watch more of this fairy and demon show that I'm hoping will jog my memory. The guy is kind of a bastard, but I'm intrigued by the story. I don't understand why the fairy is so enamored with the fairy prince, but it's hilarious to watch the demon try to help her win him over. The demon still hasn't realized he's in love with her, poor sap.

I dig into my food, enjoying the unique texture of the noodles. Lights twinkle across the night skyline through the walls of windows in front of me. The black leather couch creaks as I settle back to get comfortable. I don't have a lot of furniture and no knick-knacks to be seen. Honestly, I don't know why I haven't thought of putting up some bookshelves, at least. I don't even know when I last read a book.

The hair on the back of my neck stands on end, and a strange sort of sizzling sound radiates around me. I pause the TV, but the peculiar sound continues. It's not coming from my speakers. The lights in the minimalist apartment flicker, casting bizarre shadows across the walls. The white wall warps as fog curls out of the ripple, and five figures walk through my wall and into my living room.

What the fuck!

I drop my food as I jump off the sofa. "What are you doing in here?" I shout at the intruders as I try to wrap my head around what just happened.

"What are you doing in my apartment?" a man yells as another holds him back.

Moments ago, I was tired, but now I feel as though I've run a marathon, my blood pumping hard through my veins. What the hell just happened? How?

"Rodan?" A man with long blonde hair steps forward out of the mist and cocks his head to the side. He's about my size, but his clothes remind me of a western renaissance festival. The man's eyes water as his mouth grows into a frown.

"Who the hell are you? What are you doing in my apartment? Get out!" I point to the door, still unbelieving of what I just witnessed. How do people just materialize through a wall? Especially an exterior wall on top of a skyrise. Am I hallucinating?

"Guys, guys, calm down. Do you speak English?" A tiny girl steps between all of us and looks at me pleadingly. Her long, reddish blonde ponytail swings slowly as she moves forward.

I take in her slight frame and look at the first man who spoke. The dark-haired man understood me perfectly; he spoke Korean just fine. The fog clears, and I take a step back. It's like staring into a mirror. His nearly black hair hangs around his face, framing his alabaster skin and dark eyes. He could be my twin were it not for his frame, which is not as muscular, and his eyes–brown instead of green. My heart thunders in my chest. I take another step back and glance towards the front door. Do I have a chance of running? Finding the police? I quickly peek toward the kitchen. My phone is charging on the counter, which is too far away. I don't think I can take on all five of them. Anger radiates through me. How could this scenario even happen?

"He doesn't know us," says the blonde as his face falls. He turns to the man behind him, whose golden eyes and bright smile set me on edge. His dark skin crinkles around his eyes as the blonde man whispers something. He laughs silently and nods once, never taking his eyes off of me.

These must be the people who knocked me out in the alley, come to finish the job. Who else would barge into my home? My palms grow sweaty as the girl takes a tentative step towards me with her hands up.

"We just wanna help. Don't worry; we are the good guys." She smiles hesitantly.

Bullshit.

Hands grasp my head from behind, and I about jump out of my skin; my breath leaves my lungs as I realize the man the blonde was talking to is now gone. But how? I took my eyes off of him for only a second.

I will myself to fight him off, but I can't move as pain sears through my brain. There are soft murmurs, and then the man who looks like me rushes into the kitchen and yanks open the freezer. The other three people close in on me as I sink to the floor, my vision darkening around the edges.

Why can't I move? What is happening?

The agony is so overwhelming I can't concentrate. The world goes blurry as darkness creeps in. A feeling of calm washes through me.

"Don't worry, Rodan. Warrick will fix you," says a gruff voice, and my eyes fall closed.

Who the fuck is Rodan?

"Do you think Jade is like this too?" the girl asks.

"We won't know until we find her," says the man holding my temples.

Jade?

Jade...

I groan as I wake from a terrible dream. "What the fuck was in the wine last night?" I grumble. Everything is hazy as I pull the ice pack from my eyes. I feel drained, not a lick of magic left in my veins. What the hell happened?

"Rodan?" Killian asks.

"Who the fuck else would it be?"

"To be fair, you've been Jin Yoon for the last month, so—" Cat pipes up unhelpfully.

"Ha, ha. You guys are hilarious," I deadpan as I open my eyes and push myself off the floor. Killian wraps an arm around my back for support, which is weird. I know he gets all touchy-feely sometimes, but everything feels off.

I focus on the surrounding room; the windows looking out onto an unfamiliar city full of skyscrapers, and my heart sinks. "Killian, tell me we just had a bender in the mortal world and that the last month was a dream."

"Gods, I've missed you!" Killian says as he wraps me in a hug, throwing me on my back again.

No, no, no.

The past month plays through my mind with surprising clarity. I reach for my ears and find their familiar pointiness returned. I don't know what kind of bullshit illusion was placed on me, but I'm going to kill whoever did this.

"How did you get here? How did this happen?" Warrick's booming voice comes from above me. Things are so fuzzy, I'm not sure how to answer.

Killian jumps to his feet and helps me stand. Cat sits on the sofa beside a man who looks shockingly like me.

Oh, no. You have got to be kidding me.

"I was changeling'd? Are you serious?" I growl.

"Is that a word?" Cat asks.

"Cat..." I warn, fixing my gaze on her

"Seems so. Pretty fucked up if you ask me. We found that poor sap in a hidden dungeon beneath the castle. Almost died trying to save his ass." Ryker says while digging into a takeout container.

I rake my hands through my hair. "I remember being in the woods and hearing the most beautiful music, and then I woke up here." What the hell happened?

"What about Jade?" Killian asks.

My heart stops, and a cold sweat chills my spine. "No, no, no. Oh gods, Jade. Is she okay? I left her in the tower."

"We were hoping you knew." Cat looks down, worrying her hands in her lap.

"Bravos attacked her–" My blood boils at the memory.

"We know; we don't know what happened to her after you took her to your tower," Killian says, brow furrowed. "I caught her scent in that secret passage, in some strange laboratory. But–" He takes a deep breath. "We can't find her. Honestly, we only found you because we were returning the mortal home. Kind of a lucky break."

"I can't believe I let her down like that." Pain lances through my chest at the thought of her alone somewhere, with whoever did this. "You don't have any idea where she might be?"

Killian shakes his head, his eyes growing shiny.

A sharp pulse in my heart takes my breath away. I stumble back, and Killian steadies me as I grasp my chest. A steady thrum of power radiates through me, pulling, trying to guide me.

The bond.

"I know where she is..." I whisper.

Killian's eyes widen as he grabs my shoulders. "Where?" he demands.

"I'm not sure. I just know I can find her." I look at him as if he might hold an answer I cannot find. The bond is faint but unmistakable. "She's here in the mortal world."

"Where?"

"I don't know. Far? Very far from here." I can feel her. She has to be in this world, but I don't even know where to start.

"Do you think she went home?" Cat looks hopeful as she walks to Ryker.

I shrug. "It's as good a guess as any. We need to go."

"Cool, you guys go. Thank you for the ride home and the rescue.

I hope I never see any of you again," says the real Jin Yoon. I can't say I blame the guy; he's going to be pissed when he finds out how I cocked up his job.

"Anything is worth a shot," Killian says. "Warrick, you got enough power to take us to Cat's house?"

Warrick nods. "I'll have to go home after that to recharge my power, though. You'll be on your own for a couple of days."

Killian nods and shoots a glance towards Jin. Warrick is on him before he even has time to register it. Holding his head in both hands as he concentrates. Poor bastard will wake up tomorrow with a nasty headache, having lost the last month or so of memory. But at least he will be able to continue his life, having no idea he was kidnapped by fae.

I'm coming for you, Trouble.

Chapter 11
Killian

"There was so much blood, she was gonna die." Rodan puts his head in his hands. "Her powers started manifesting, and she was freezing herself and the room. I should have been there sooner."

Cat passes us cups of tea as we sit on her purple sofa. Her apartment feels small, with the four of us occupying all the space. Bookcases line every available wall, even behind her couch. She really should be a book dragon. Ryker leans against a pile of books under the window, while Cat bustles about, trying to find blankets and pillows.

Warrick was once again spot on with his portal simply by having Cat think about her apartment. His mind powers get scary sometimes. It's a good thing he is on our side because I never thought about the implications of those abilities. I've never been so grateful for them as when Rodan looked at me with familiarity.

"I killed him. I killed Bravos," Rodan whispers. "I was so angry I couldn't stop myself. Then I didn't know what to do. I didn't know who was involved, so I took her somewhere I thought was safe."

"You couldn't have known," Cat says.

"I should have shadow-walked us back to the castle at the first sign of trouble. I never should have left her side. Why didn't I listen to her?"

I shake my head, looking at the golden tea as it swirls in the cup, steam wafting in the air. I don't disagree. It's puzzling to me why he didn't return immediately. But I wasn't there, and I can't help but think I'd have done the same. "It's not your fault."

Rodan continues to tell us everything he remembers. Exhaustion weighs heavily on all of us. Cat settles herself between Ryker's legs as we debate our next move. She orders a heavenly food, which I've read about in books, but recreations in my world do not hold a candle to *pizza.*

Warrick left us with large bags of mortal clothes to blend in. The T-shirts are comfortable, and the sweaters are cozy. The jeans feel less flimsy than the slacks. Cat grumbles about pockets, but the pair I chose have great pockets, so I don't know what the problem is. I think we come across as quite striking, if I do say so myself. Although the illusion to hide the points of our ears makes them look funny, I still look damn good, though.

I don't know how Rodan seems to know where Jade is, only that he knows she's close now. He won't explain, but considering no one discloses all of their powers, I guess I'm not surprised. I just want to get to her. We are so close to rescuing my fair maiden; I feel it. Finally, some happiness slipping into my soul. If I weren't so tired, I'd be bouncing off the walls in excitement.

"She's not at her apartment, and her parents haven't heard from her. Her mom is furious that she just disappeared on them. We may need to do damage control after we find her. I might have promised that all of us would spend the weekend at their house." Cat looks down at the floor sheepishly.

Ryker and Rodan glare at her, and I flash her a half grin. With every lead bringing us nowhere, the mood has been sullen. We sat outside her ex's place for a while, and there was no activity. Cat said that he hadn't been home in a while, judging by the amount of letters in his box, whatever that meant. She drove us past a building and pointed out his car, explaining that he was at work. Her face has been scrunched in thought all day, puzzling things out.

Rodan grumbles, closes his eyes, and slowly turns in a circle. "I should have thought of this sooner." He points towards a wall of books. "She's that way." He clutches his chest as if in pain and steadies himself on the bookshelf. Now is not the time, but he will have to teach me how he's doing that at some point.

"South?" Cat's brows knit. She pulls out her phone and brings up a map. The technology here is super handy. "No one we know lives that way—oh. Oh no," she breathes, looking up at me, panicked. "We've gotta go! I know where she is!" She turns in frantic circles and snatches her keys off the table. "Ace's dad has a ranch about an hour from here. God, I hope I'm wrong. Rodan, I hope whatever you're using to find her can guide us because I don't know the exact address, but I can get us close. Please let me be wrong." Silver gleams from her lash line as we all run for her car.

Rodan is pale as we get in the backseat. My frenzied heartbeat is the only thing keeping me grounded. Cat's panic means things may be so much worse than I imagined. At least when I thought she might be here, I convinced myself she'd be safe. After finding Rodan, I hoped it would be simple: find her, give her the memory antidote that Warrick gave me, and then, yay, happy reunion.

"Can you go faster?" Rodan growls.

"Not unless you wanna waste time on a speeding ticket. Can any of you do the mind-wipe shit Warrick can? No? Then shut it," she barks as she merges onto a freeway and punches it.

Chapter 12
Jade

I ran out of food yesterday. After our last fight, Ace took off and hasn't returned for two days. With nothing to do, I chug another glass of water, hoping to trick my stomach into thinking I'm full. God, what I wouldn't do for some actual food.

Any food really, but protein bars, as my only source of nutrition, is awful.

Ace must think it's the most incredible diet ever. I have never been so thin. I've always been curvy, but my hourglass is suffering. With every fight, he's brought me less and less to snack on. He insists that eventually I'll eat what he makes me. Maybe that's his plan: starve me until I have no other choice but to eat his drugged food.

Drug me until I wake up pregnant? No, I don't think so. Not that the alternative is much better.

I wish he hadn't smashed my only entertainment. I sit on the floor, watching the trees sway in the orchard. Birds flitter about, mocking me with their freedom.

I tense as the door lock clicks open, but I don't bother turning around. "I'm out of food."

He sighs audibly. "You have to come with me. We need to go."

I roll my eyes. "Why? Did the cops catch on to what you're doing?

Oh, wait. That's right. They already know."

I hear his hurried footsteps behind me. His hands land on my shoulders, and he attempts to turn me around. Nausea rolls through me at his touch.

"Jade, come on. We have to go," he pleads.

"No, I'm comfortable right where I am. Unless you're letting me go, don't touch me." I shrug his hands off my shoulders in a sharp movement. Glancing behind me as I stand, he paces back and forth across the room, pulling at his hair.

He's freaking out. This should be good.

I sit on the side of the bed with a sick satisfaction racing through me. Something has rattled him; maybe someone has finally figured out what he's doing. Or, it's another manipulation...

Shit. Almost fell for it.

"Come on, Jade, we have to leave. Right now," he says.

I lean back, cross my legs, and dangle my chain loudly. "I'm happy to leave, but I have a bit of a problem."

He lifts a glass of orange juice that I didn't notice he had brought in. My stomach growls at the sight of it.

"Oh, no. Not a chance," I say, crossing my arms.

"Please be reasonable, Jade."

"Reasonable? You want to drug me to move me to some other fucked-up prison. Fuck you." I can't believe the audacity of this man. I mean, anything he does at this point shouldn't surprise me.

Ace flushes red in fury, his upper body tenses, and his stance changes. Everything about the way he's looking at me is intimidating. I feel the cold sweat dripping down my back, and the color drains from my face. I keep my eyes trained on him as I take a deep breath and try to hide the trembling in my hands.

He turns on his heel and storms out the door, returning a moment later with something in his hand. It's hidden partially behind his back as he marches forward. "You leave me no choice. I didn't want to do this."

Heart hammering, I scramble back on the bed, grabbing the chain to pull it along with me. "Then don't!"

Ace leaps on top of me, pushing me down as he brings a syringe up to his mouth and pulls the safety cap off with his teeth.

Not again.

Oh, please, not again.

I struggle underneath him, screaming in defiance. I flail my free arm, clawing at his face. Growling in frustration, he puts down the needle and yanks my arms straight against my sides. His weight is pinning me to the bed as he moves to straddle me, trapping my arms down with his legs.

He leans forward, face inches from mine. "You did this to yourself."

I seize the chance to slam my forehead into his nose as hard as I can. My head swims as pain rattles my brain. Warm liquid drips down instantly as he screams in surprise. He jolts upright, holding his face, blood pouring like a faucet through his fingers.

"What the fuck, Jade? I think you broke my nose."

I take advantage of his distraction to free my arms, grab the chain, and punch him with it. His head flies backward as he topples off the bed. Pain flares in my hand; that hurt a lot more than I thought it would. Movies lie. Note to self: do not punch someone with chains wrapped around your knuckles.

All I see is red as I scream and leap off the bed on top of him, slamming my fists into his head with all my strength. He struggles to protect his damaged nose with his hands while trying to get me off of him. He wails as I land another blow to his broken nose. Every hit is retribution for a sour word, an unearned accusation, or a touch without consent.

"Fuck you..." My fist slams into his face.

"Wasted my life on you..."

Thud.

"This is for every." Thud. "Time." Thud. "You gaslit me..." Crack.

"My apartment..."

Thud.

"These fucking chains!" I screech, putting everything I have into the hit.

I grab him by the hair and slam his head to the ground. My ears ring, the world moves as if underwater, and I'm only somewhat aware of screaming, but it could be me. I don't know how to stop what I've unleashed; only so much rage still needs to be released—justice for myself and every other unsuspecting victim of his.

Ace is bleeding everywhere; his movements become slow and sluggish as my adrenaline wears off, and my hits aren't coming as fast as before. I feel as though all my energy has been zapped, leaving only pain in my hands and a headache.

Panting, I raise my gaze to the door. Three people stand there dumbfounded. As my eyes come into focus, I see the demon staring at me with something like pride on his face. He's handsome and remarkably tall, with his dark hair framing his face. The blonde man from my dreams stands next to him, smiling widely. He's just as towering, but even broader than the first. My heart skips a beat. This can't be possible. Have I started to dissociate fully?

"Great, now I'm hallucinating," I grumble.

Chapter 13
Rodan

I can feel it; she's inside.

Killian steps beside me. "This house reeks of fear."

The sprawling orchard surrounds the house. It's a modern mortal build painted a cheerful pale cream, hiding the monsters within. Cat stares up at the large house with a furrowed brow, Ryker following closely behind. Their footsteps crunch on the gravel driveway.

"Not exactly the murder house I was expecting. I thought it would be a rundown shack with a creepy cellar," she says.

The bond in my chest tugs incessantly. What manner of hell is this place? Why would Trouble be here? This house is twenty miles from the nearest town. Is she hiding? None of this makes sense. Surely, she would have contacted her parents when she returned.

I walk up to the bright blue door and bang loudly. "FBI, open up!" I yell as Cat giggles behind me. "This is the FBI. Open up; we have a warrant to search the premises." I glare at Cat, who has buried her face in Ryker's chest as she tries to muffle her laughter. My efforts are met with silence, but I can hear movement inside. This is trying my patience. "I thought you said he'd open the door if we yelled this shit."

"I overestimated his intelligence." She shrugs.

I consider knocking again when a muffled scream breaks the silence. Shoving open the door, I race toward the screams as they grow louder, our footfalls thundering across the wooden floor.

I reach the room in the back of the house just in time to see Trouble's forehead connect with a man's nose and stop dead in the doorway.

"I told you no one ever sees the headbutt coming," Killian whispers beside me.

"Do we stop her?" Ryker whispers.

"No, she needs this," Cat says, crossing her arms.

Stunned, I watch the brutality of every hit as Trouble beats the man senseless. She looks pale and thin; tears and blood streak her face, and violet halos her eyes. But as frail as she appears, she doesn't let up until the man stops trying to fend her off.

Rose petals litter the floor in various states of decay. Holes mar the walls in an otherwise barren room. This room speaks of untold horrors; each one layered upon the last.

Breathing heavily, she drops her bloodied hands to her sides, and her eyes connect with mine. The bond swells within me, and pride fills my chest.

I found you.

"Great, now I'm hallucinating," she grumbles.

I exchange a look with Killian, brows furrowed. Does she think we are not here?

Cat steps forward. "Ya good?"

Trouble's gaze snaps up at her friend's voice, and tears fill her eyes and begin to spill over. "C—Cat? Are you really here?" she whispers as the man groans, his head moving. She looks down and punches him in the temple again before crawling off him. She stands and kicks him in the head, jerking it to the side.

Tears pour down her face as she looks at Cat.

"I'm really here. Are you okay?" Cat says, holding back her emotions as she rushes into a hug.

Hiccuping a sob, Trouble buries her face in Cat's shoulder. She trembles violently as Cat pulls her away from the man. A strange rattling follows them, like metal rubbing on metal. Cat stops walking and stares down at Trouble's foot; she sucks in a sharp breath as her hand flies to her mouth.

A growl escapes me as I see the chain locked to her ankle and leading above the bed. "He chained you to the wall?" I seethe. This man is lucky I don't have my powers right now.

Killian tenses beside me. His fury—as palpable in the air as my own. "This one we kill."

"Cat...who are they? Don't get me wrong, I'm grateful for the rescue, but..." Trouble looks at Cat. "There *are* three guys standing in the doorway, right?"

My heart collapses, and Killian lets out a low whine as his shoulders slump. She doesn't know us. It will be okay, though. Once she drinks the potion, it will undo the locks on her mind.

"Yes. These are our friends. They came to rescue you. Sorry, it took us so long. We didn't know where you were. Killian, can you get the chain off her? Ryker, I want you to drag his sorry ass outside. She doesn't need to see what I'm gonna do to him." Cat glares at the floor behind her, at the man I will destroy.

Trouble looks unsure as she's handed off to Killian, who has her sit on the corner of the bed. He kneels in front of her to inspect the chains. She keeps looking at me bewildered, and my heart aches to fix it.

Cat grabs my arm. "She will be fine. Killian will get her the potion. In the meantime, you can help dispose of Ace."

"Ace?" I growl, glaring at the unconscious man on the floor. "This man—the man holding her hostage—was her ex-husband? Gods, she said he'd never let her go, but this..." I gesture around helplessly. I should have guessed it was him; it's his father's house, after all.

Cat regards me. "She told you?" Her eyebrow arches as she looks between us. "Huh, she pretty much never talks about him to anyone."

"Well, she told me everything," I growl defensively.

Cat raises her hands. "I'm just surprised, is all. I didn't realize you two were so close that she actually opened up. I don't even know half of what he did."

Nodding, I observe Ryker dragging the man out by his foot. Catching one last glance at Trouble as Killian tries to help and calm her. I know how scary it can be when you don't know the people who show up to help you. She's been through so much and has no idea who we are. Fury rises through me. This should never have happened to her.

"Ugh, this is the worst trope," Cat groans, following behind Ryker as he drags Ace out the back door.

"What?"

"The whole memory wipe thing. I hate when this happens in books."

"This isn't a book." I roll my eyes.

"I know; that's what makes it worse," Cat whines.

"Tell me about it; I was an actor, for fuck's sake."

"Were you any good?"

I laugh, "Not at all. I didn't get those memories. That Jin guy is in for it. Don't worry; that potion will fix her right up. It's even stronger than the magic Warrick used to destroy my mind. And less painful." I wince. Bastard could have given me one of those instead of frying my brain cells.

We walk out to a clearing right before the treeline starts behind the house. Through the window, I see Killian leading Jade out of the bedroom.

"What was with all the holes in the walls?"

"His fragile masculinity was showing." Cat kicks at Ace.

"Ryker, do you have any stored power? I'm tapped since I've been in the mortal world too long," I say.

Ryker grins like the devil, and vines snake their way around the body like a python. Within seconds, the coward is cocooned in foliage and pulled up to stand. Ryker nods at Cat to let her know it's safe to approach.

Glee shines in her eyes as she steps towards the fucker, and then slaps him. "Wakey, wakey, asshole," she coos.

He groans again but doesn't wake. Blood drips from his nose, covering most of his face. Trouble really did a number on him. Satisfaction at that thrums through me. I'm glad she finally fought back; he deserved every blow.

"Hey, asshole, wake up," Cat barks.

His eyes flutter open and focus on Cat. He sneers and then flinches, probably just recalling that he has a broken face. Panic brightens his features as he struggles, at last noticing us standing sentinel behind Cat.

"Let me go. Do you have any idea who my father is? Cat, you know better than this. I'll have all of you locked up for assault, including Jade. Oh, she will pay for what she just did."

The fuck she will. He won't be doing anything to anyone ever again. We will make sure of that.

"Shut the fuck up," Cat seethes. She paces before his mummified body, growing tenser by the minute. "No. You will do nothing else to her. I've had to stand by and watch you take the light out of her eyes for far too long. You are a terrible human being who deserves what's coming. Rotting in hell would be too good for someone like you. Also, stop with the threats; no one is ever gonna find your body, so fuck you."

As she paces back and forth, her arms flail wildly. I think she needs this as much as Trouble did. Ryker and I stand by, arms crossed, as we watch Cat verbally rip into him, listing off all of his offenses. She's not even breaking a sweat or slowing down. Every time Ace tries to say something, she just steamrolls him into silence. Her anger builds by the second, and I can smell the steam coming off of her.

Ace seems to be crumpling in on himself, his face going

increasingly sallow by the minute. The lines on his forehead are more pronounced–oh shit.

He *is* going sallow.

Ryker seems to notice when I do, and we both step forward. It's like he's becoming more skeletal by the second. My eyes grow wide as I realize what is happening.

"Sweetheart..." Ryker says.

"What?" she snaps, whirling around.

He walks over to her and wraps her in a hug. "Okay, don't get mad. But you need to calm down and let go."

"Are you fucking kidding me!" she shrieks and tries to get out of his hold.

I chuckle at the terrible choice of words, but decide to spare the poor guy the fate Ace is experiencing. "Cat, what the dunderhead is trying to say is you are killing Ace. He's going to be jerky soon."

Her face goes pale as she turns to look at Ace. "H–how? I...that's not me?"

"Afraid it is, sweetheart. Neither of us has water magic, and you are sucking it right out of him." Ryker grins. "So, deep breaths and let go. Let Rodan finish the job, okay?"

She nods, still staring at Ace, inhaling deeply as Ryker whispers in her ear. I guess it's not too surprising, considering Trouble has some sort of frost power. And they both descend from the same Ice fae, but this is royal-level power...and a problem for later.

"I'm so glad we finally got to meet," I purr as I walk around Ace. He smells of fear and loathing. A shallow man, a coward. "I once told Jade I'd make you suffer greatly before I kill you." I lean in and whisper in his ear. "Looks like I get to make good on that promise."

I slip the knife from my pocket, some little thing Cat had lying in her apartment. Ace cringes as he hears the click of the blade locking into place. His rasped scream pierces the air as the blade slides into his lower back. I believe his kidney is around there somewhere. He lets out a hoarse screech as he flails his head and wiggles his constrained body.

"I think that's a pretty shit place to get stabbed; what do you think? Does it hurt?" I muse, circling to face him. I lock him in my glare, wanting to see the fear in his eyes. "It's not fun being penetrated without consent, is it? You see, you will have a quicker death than I'd like today, mostly because I don't have the time. But if I did, I'd torture you in the dungeon for months. Since you did unspeakable things to Jade for years." I turn the blade and push it slowly between his ribs. Right around here should be a lung.

His eyes bulge as he tries to scream, but whatever Cat did to dehydrate the shit out of this guy is making it a paltry attempt. Gasping for air, he rasps with each breath.

"You think you can treat women like that, and there will be no repercussions? You may be a monster, but I am worse. I'll haunt your afterlife. I'll destroy your soul. You made a big mistake taking her and doing what I can only imagine. You miscalculated." I lean into his ear so only he can hear me. "She's mine."

I pull the knife from his chest with a sickening squelch, dragging it down to his abdomen and slowly driving the blade back in. I watch every jerk of his body and flinch on his face. "You didn't answer me. How do you like having something shoved in you without your permission? I imagine this is what it felt like to every woman you took advantage of," I growl, knowing this would never be enough to fix what he broke.

"We should finish up here and go check on Jade. I enjoy torture as much as the next guy, but I think I'm done. Just rip his junk off and bury him under a tree already," Cat says.

I glance back at Ryker and grin at his little hellion. "As the lady wishes," I say, removing my blade and wiping it on him. I pat his cheek and nod to Ryker.

Cat's wish is granted with a sickening creak of the vines and Ace's final gurgling scream. The shrieking abruptly stops as Ace either passes out or dies from blood loss. I don't give a shit which. I turn, heading inside, looking back to see the roots of a tree reach out of the dirt and roll Ace up into its gaping maw. Soon, the ground is settled; the body is gone, and all the blood has soaked into the grass. No trace left of Ace to be found—everything as it was before we arrived, like we were never here. Who would think of looking under an established tree?

I cross into the kitchen to see the carnage that is Trouble stuffing her face, packages of food scattered across the counter. Carelessly, she tosses a box onto the floor before picking up another. Despite bandaging her bloodied knuckles, red speckles still decorate her beautiful face. Orange liquid puddles on the floor as she tiptoes around broken glass. Killian sits across from her with his head in his hands.

"Hi, sorry. I haven't eaten since yesterday morning," she says between mouthfuls. I gape at her; she is in shock. "That, uh, potion? Didn't work. How do I know you?" She wipes her hands on a towel before extending it to me.

I stare at her extended hand, my heart falling to the floor. I shake her delicate hand and look at Killian, who has tears in his eyes. "That shouldn't be possible," I breathe. Her body trembles as she puts on a brave face. I want to pull her into me and tell her everything is okay now, but I am rooted to the floor. She doesn't remember. A hollow feeling envelops my chest as I take in her split lip and the faint bruise on her jaw. Violet and green marks speckle her arms with fingerprints I couldn't protect her from.

She cocks her head and looks beyond me, face lighting up. "How the hell did you find me? I never brought you here."

"It was a hunch. Rodan was somehow able to track you. You know these guys and their crazy powers," Cat says, walking up to Trouble and hugging her again. Glass crunches under her shoes. I wince at Trouble's bare feet in the mess of glass and orange liquid. She seems unfazed by the disheveled kitchen; I assume she's had some fun being destructive in here.

"I have no clue what you're talking about; I'm just so glad you found me. Please get me out of here before Ace regains consciousness or his dad shows up."

I don't think now is the time to tell her he won't be waking up.

Cat looks over at Killian expectantly.

"It didn't work. She doesn't remember." Killian's expression goes slack. He crosses his arms on the counter and puts his head down.

"No," Cat's voice is barely above a whisper.

I don't know what to do. If she doesn't remember me, if she doesn't remember our bond, what will that mean for us? We will never know what happened to her or how she got here.

Fate has taken her from me.

An empty void consumes me, all those hopeful stars winking out amongst the black hole that devours them and everything I love. Maybe I didn't escape the curse on Shadow. What if I am the curse?

Trouble leans in close to Cat, trying not to be heard. "Why is the demon here? Like seriously, did you become friends with the actor while I've been gone?"

Her earnest question pulls me back from my raging thoughts. My lip quirks into a grin. She doesn't know about fae hearing. "I'm not a demon, but I can be if you want."

She flushes scarlet as her eyes snap to mine. Her mouth drops open, then promptly shuts. I don't know that I've ever made her speechless before. Interesting.

"Okay...let's get you out of here. You're going to have to sit between these two." Cat points at me and Killian. "The three of them would never fit in the back together. Also, I kind of promised we'd stay at your mom's for the weekend." She says the last part in a rush as she speeds towards the front door.

Trouble shrugs, grabs a small wedge of cheese, and tiptoes out of the kitchen. "Wait. What?" She yells after Cat.

Killian rises from his seat, glancing briefly at me with red eyes that I'm sure match mine. Ryker claps me on the back as he passes, following Killian and the girls.

A knot lodges itself in my throat as she walks away. "I'm sorry I failed you," I breathe.

Chapter 14
Jade

"What do you want for dinner?" Mom asks before we've even made it through the door. I'm so relieved to see her, I almost burst into tears as she pulls me into a hug. Her blonde hair tangles across my face as I squeeze her.

Once I was in the car, it hit me all at once like a fucking sledgehammer to the face—I'd escaped. Then, the uncontrollable tears came. Rodan had pulled me into him, wrapping me in his warm embrace. He smelled like rain before a storm; breathing him in had a calming effect that I melted into. Killian had rubbed slow circles on my back. His touch, a soothing balm to my soul, telling me I was safe. Rodan whispered to let it out as I soaked through his navy henley. I'm not sure why I collapsed onto him, but I just needed someone to hold me. Before we reached my parents' house, I was able to gather myself.

I groan, thinking about real food as I hug her. "Hamburgers. No, wait-lasagna and milkshakes. Oh, and french fries! And pie, god, I miss pie." Really, I miss food that doesn't come in a wrapper.

Mom laughs, kissing my forehead and ushering all of us in, eyeing the guys with an approving stare. "Is that all?"

"Yes, maybe? I don't know."

Mom bustles about setting us up with drinks in the living room while she prepares the lasagna. My mouth is already watering at the thought of it. She puts in an order at a local fifties diner for fries, milkshakes, and pies, and I could just kiss her. I'm so happy.

Cat whispers in the hallway with the Viking-looking dude she calls Ryker. Are they dating? I've never seen her like this with anyone. She stands close to him, winding her fingers through the ends of his sandy blonde hair. Worry etched all over her face, the same concern all the guys seem to share since I took that vial of pink liquid that tasted like water. I wasn't sure about taking an unknown drink, but something about that Killian guy made me trust him. Plus, Cat wouldn't have brought dangerous guys to rescue me or to my parents' house.

Cat gently pulls on Ryker's beard and guides him into a kiss, and I look away. I guess I was spot-on. They promised to explain everything over dinner, so they didn't have to explain it again to my parents. I'm so out of the loop, and sitting here between these two men is killing me.

Did I somehow manifest the guys from my dreams into reality? It took me the entire drive here to put it together. Killian is the blonde I dreamed about, with his sweet words and smile. This Rodan guy is apparently the demon from my dreams who got me all flustered by his flirting. The resemblance is uncanny. God, I need answers because this is super awkward. These men had saved me, and I'd sobbed all over them. I'm an absolute mess, but I'm so relieved I could soar.

I stare down at my beer, a strawberry marshmallow concoction from a local brewery that my dad picked up for me when he heard we were coming. It was very sweet of him, considering he hates sour beers. Honestly, if you drink beer, it may as well be one you like. The tang of the beer assaults my tongue as the subtle fruit scent washes over me. The guys are sipping a dry mead that my dad gushed about on his way out the door to get the food from the diner.

A fire keeps the space cozy; an amalgamation of all the places my parents have visited decorates the room. Bright mosaic tapestries hang between shelves of knick-knacks. Rich woods play against the soft velvets of jewel-toned furniture. A crocheted rainbow throw covers the back of a crimson sofa. A bright satin blanket embroidered with an elephant lies across an emerald chair in the corner. Golden curtains contrast against teal walls—the space screams of eccentric color and coziness all at once.

"I don't know how to express how grateful I am that you guys showed up today." I stare at the floor and see both men jolt at my voice. "I had no plan. No way to escape the chains..." and it goes without saying, he probably would have killed me if he had woken up.

"Emerald, we'd always come for you." Killian smiles as he takes my empty hand and kisses my knuckles.

Blood rushes to my face as I give him a shy smile.

Rodan lets out a heavy sigh. "If I'd protected you as promised, this never would have happened."

I take another drink of my beer, feeling a bit lightheaded already. What the hell did I get myself in the middle of? Did Cat and I join some weird cult?

My fork drops with a clatter. "Whoa, whoa, whoa. We were kidnapped, and you expect me to go back? You've been stalkholmed." I can't believe what Cat is telling me; all of these guys just stare down at their plates as my parents nod along to this ridiculousness.

How are my parents just taking this in stride? They only gaped once when the guys dropped some *glamor* that hid their ears. Dad promptly stood up and inspected them one by one with an awed expression. Mom giggled like a damn schoolgirl.

I guess that's better than the tears that came when we explained what Ace had done- the abridged version. Rodan had to pull my dad aside to explain that Ace would no longer be a problem, since Dad was ready to murder him. Granted, I still don't know what they did to him. I don't fully trust that he will never be a problem again.

"Well, technically, you got stalkholmed first. I was ready to go home after a monster ate our friend, but *no*, you wanted to stay," Cat says, pointing her french fry at me across the table.

My heart slams in my chest. "Ate our friend? Do you hear yourself? I'm not going."

"You are. You loved it there. And I'm not going alone."

"So don't go." I fire back but notice Ryker bristle at my words.

"I haven't fully decided, but you did. Maybe your memory will come back if we go. Plus, your lover boys will probably caveman you back if you try to stay." She winks as they both look at each other in confusion. "Shit, I guess the cat's out of the bag. Yeah, pretty sure you're both in love with her."

Killian looks at Rodan, surprised. Rodan purses his lips and looks away.

"Wait...no. Rodan, you knew how I felt about her," Killian says, his brows pinched.

"You don't love her, you don't know her, you love the idea of her." Rodan glares at Killian.

"You think you know her? You avoided her." Killian says incredulously.

I watch the back and forth in shock. Are they fighting over me? Me? I glance at my mom, who is still grinning like a schoolgirl over a crush. So, she definitely won't be the voice of reason here.

"Fuck...She's my mate," Rodan whispers, shaking his head.

I almost choke on my food. *Your what?*

"What? That's impossible," Killian growls, standing from the table and stepping up to Rodan. "She can't be because she's mine." The look in his eyes is predatory as his posture stiffens.

"That's impossible, Killian, and you know it–" Rodan growls.

Killian's fist connects with Rodan's jaw, and Rodan falls backward out of his chair with the force. He rolls onto his knees and rubs a spot of blood off his lip with his thumb.

Holy shit, what the hell is going on? I stare, gaping at them, unable to move. The look in Rodan's eyes is murderous and, honestly, rather hot. What is wrong with me?

Mom stands abruptly, her chair squeaking against the wooden floor. "Rather than fight like heathens over my daughter, why don't you two work to make her remember the relationships you had? Let her decide. Or find a way to both have her. I don't care either way, but I won't have bloodshed in my house." Her stern tone makes both guys hang their heads while Dad chuckles.

What the hell is happening right now? Both have her? What the fuck, Mom?

"But she's my mate," Killian breathes, his shoulders falling.

"Explain what you mean by mate," Dad says. "And sit down before Clair has an aneurysm." His dark brows are furrowed, but I can see the grin he's hiding behind his hand. Does he think this is funny?

"It's fate. Someone meant just for you. There is an undeniable bond, like a string linking two souls. If you pay attention, you can feel it. Sometimes, it's immediate, and sometimes, it takes time to strengthen. And I never heard of it happening with two people." Killian gives Rodan a sharp look.

"I felt it the moment I met her," Rodan says.

"And I feel it now, like a tangible thing..." Killian says as his face falls.

"Apparently, the way your bond works, both of you shouldn't feel it. So?" Mom muses.

"So what does this mean?" Killian looks at Rodan, who shrugs.

"Do I get any say in this?" I ask, my voice not nearly as authoritative as I'd have liked it to be.

Both guys' eyes snap toward me. They look at a loss for words as they open and close their mouths and then nod. They've been so sullen since my memories didn't come back, and now they are fighting over me. It's all too much.

"Mom, Cat, can we talk outside?" I lift my milkshake and motion toward the back door.

Leaving the table without another word, I head out the sliding glass door. I don't know how to process any of this.

"Looks like you fellas are in the doghouse tonight." Dad chuckles. I can't help but grin as the door closes behind me.

The small deck with a wrap-around bench is just how I remember it, surrounded by my mom's lovely garden. Even in the dark, it's beautiful with the little string lights that illuminate the railing in a warm glow.

Mom and Cat talk in low tones as they stroll onto the patio. Cat purses her lips, sitting on a bench. "They were friends, but I think Kilian is in love with her."

"So you think both of them are?" Mom asks as she settles on the bench beside us on the porch.

Cat nods as she sips her milkshake. I stare through the window. The guys get up and move to the living room, where Dad is putting on a movie, and Killian is bouncing on his toes with a big smile on his face. I hide my grin behind my glass as I look at Mom.

"Well, I guess we'll see how round two goes. Maybe one person can be fated to two people." Mom smiles.

We'll see how it goes? I glare at my mom, piercing her with daggers, but she pays me no mind.

Cat shrugs. "At this point, I think anything is possible."

Mom looks at the sky. "Why have one boyfriend when you can have two? It's not that unheard of these days." She rolls her gaze over to me, amusement written all over her face.

"Mom, I don't even remember these guys." I laugh as she wiggles her eyebrows at me.

"Well, Cat seems to think things were going well with them." She winks.

Of course, Cat thought things were going well; she's always

trying to set me up. "They aren't even human," I say. This may be my weakest argument yet. But of course, this is the point of contention I decide to focus on, not the fact that I'm a wuss.

"Apparently, we aren't completely human either. Honestly, you need to be more open-minded. If what Cat says is true, this is amazing."

"I don't know them," I grumble. I don't know why I need to win this. Everything is so overwhelming. To be honest, they are so attractive, it's maddening.

"It will be fine," Cat says.

"Well, maybe if you tried to get to know them, you'd feel different." Mom pets my hair and looks through the window at the boys. "Are they watching Beauty and the Beast?"

"They don't have movies." Cat giggles.

"And *that's* what they decided to watch?" Mom rolls her eyes.

"Killian is obsessed with fairytales; that one is his favorite," I say absently, leaning back.

"How do you know that?" Cat's eyes go wide as she looks at me.

I rack my mind, trying to figure out where that information came from, but I come up empty. So I go with the only explanation I can think of: "They may have starred in a few of my dreams. I don't know...I just think it's true." Stammering, I glance at the guys all watching the movie.

"Jade, I'm going to level with you. I think you were just as in love with them as they are with you. You were so torn between them that you refused to make a decision. You wouldn't even acknowledge that you liked Rodan, but I know a lot more happened with him." She grins, and my face heats.

"Like?" Mom giggles, crossing her legs. Great, she's gone into gossip mode.

"They definitely got it on in a magical cave."

"What?" I shriek. I look at Rodan, make eye contact, and flush an even brighter red as he smirks at me.

Oh, my god.

"Can they hear us?" I whisper.

"Probably." Cat snorts as I bury my face in my hands and groan. Mom rubs circles on my back and laughs.

This is mortifying.

"It will be fine," Cat says.

"You always say that," I grumble.

"And it always works out fine." She grins.

Sighing, I turn to Mom. "You don't find this all really weird, Mom?"

"I see weird every day. I pull tarot cards and walk people through past lives. I see the horrors of this world in the news. This is magical—strange, yes, but magical. The kind of adventure one can only dream about. So yes, it's weird, but in the best way. So, Cat, tell me about Ryker." Mom has always been so levelheaded about the strangest things. I doubt anything could faze her. Mom fucked a fae once, didn't she? Or Dad's actually a centaur? At this point, I wouldn't be surprised.

"There's nothing to tell," Cat says, inspecting her milkshake with the intensity of a scientist.

"Oh? Because that boy is smitten, I don't think you will be able to prise yourself out of his grasp. He's very attentive, quiet, but always watching. Not in a creepy way. That boy adores you."

"You know I don't do relationships," Cat whines.

"I think you're getting a bit old for that rule. Not everyone's relationship ends up like your parents. They were toxic to each other and everyone else in their lives. It doesn't have to be that way. Look at Rey and me."

Cat looks down at her hands as she fidgets with her straw. "I'm scared. I think I really like this one."

"So don't write him off until he gives you a reason to. That one is a keeper; I feel it. And you know I'm never wrong about these things," Mom says. "So tell me more about these powers you mentioned."

"Oh, my god! This is the coolest part: I can turn into an animal. Like any animal, except I struggle to turn into just one at a time, so it's usually a weird mutant, but I'm getting there. And Jade is an otter shifter, like the cutest little white otter you've ever seen."

I spit out my drink. "I'm a what? Seriously?" Of all things, a cute otter? Why couldn't I be something ferocious, like a tiger?

Mom clutches her belly while she laughs. "I always thought she'd be something aquatic; I didn't see that one coming, though." She wipes a tear from her eye while I glare at her.

Of fuckin' course, I get otter.

"We also have these crazy powers, but mine only just came up today...it was scary...But I think it's water-related. Rodan said Jade got her power just before she went missing, and it was some sort of frost, so also water powers."

I sigh; of course, I get cartoon princess powers. What else would I get?

Mom nods as if any of this makes sense. "So Elemental. Got it. I'd love to learn more once you get the hang of it. This is very exciting."

We sit outside in the cool night air a while longer, talking about everything Cat knows about fae. Mom and I are full of questions, and I just can't wrap my head around any of this. I curl up in my mom's arms and enjoy the comfort of her embrace.

Yawning, I go inside, shower, snuggle up in clean clothes on a familiar bed, and cry.

Chapter 15
Rodan

"Again?" I ask Killian as he pushes the button to replay the movie for the third time. "There are other movies listed right under it. Look." I point to the pictures of other fairy tales.

Trouble's mom silently laughs as she sips her tea and reads a book. Clair is a taller version of Trouble. Silver strands lace her dark blonde hair, and years of knowledge faintly line her eyes. She had been shocked by Trouble's appearance initially. I guess she had covered her silver hair for most of her adult life. Rey is a large man compared to the girls with short, dark hair. He reminds me of a more subdued Killian, a friendly person overall. I can't say I expected them to take the truth about where the ladies have been so well and how easily they accepted we were fae. Especially after they found out we'd kidnapped their daughter. They took it way better than Cat and Trouble did.

Trouble went to bed hours ago; she was exhausted. I don't blame her. She's been through a lot. Then we dumped all of this on her. I'm still trying to wrap my head around the fact that we are preparing to go to war with Light.

I demanded we return, but Queen Aleena apparently ordered us to stay in the mortal realm until further notice. Warrick returns tomorrow. Cat and Ryker will go back to her apartment to meet him.

Clair has already insisted he come for lunch before returning to the fae realm, which is impossible to argue with. Now I see where Trouble gets it.

"But I like this one," Killian pouts. "Fine, we'll watch the Ice Princess one next." He carefully pushes the buttons to navigate to another movie. Not that it matters; I will have the music stuck in my head for the next week.

"Don't you think we need to talk about this?"

"The movie? Did you want to pick one?"

I scrub my hand down my face. "Jade."

He stiffens and clenches his jaw. "Did she accept the bond?"

I look down at the floor; my chest tightens. "Yes, but after...She still had feelings for you. She was seriously torn up about what to do."

"It makes no sense. If your bond solidified...why do I feel the thread? Gods, I wish we could talk to Mom about this. Maybe she knows what's going on. Jade should have had eyes only for you after the bond snapped into place. And I certainly shouldn't feel the bond." Killian takes a deep breath. "Sorry I hit you."

"Knocked me right outta my seat." I chuckle.

"Call it payback for the time you thought I stole your textbook." He laughs.

"Your legs went over your head," I say through tears in my eyes as I try to breathe. I remember being so heated that I cold-clocked him off a stool during our tutoring session.

"Good lord, you two really are brothers, aren't you?" Clair snickers. "I'm glad to see you getting along again. I'm going to bed. Stay out of trouble."

I try not to smile at the innuendo in my head. Gods, I'm a child.

"Hey, Clair?" I look at her as she steps away.

"Yes." She stops, turning back towards us.

"What happens if she has nightmares? What should we do?" I ask.

"She still gets those?" Clair's brow furrows.

"Yes."

She looks thoughtful. "What did you do before? I mean, there's not much you can do."

"I, uh...slept next to her in my panther form, and she either wouldn't have them or would settle if she woke and found me there. Sometimes, I just put my head on her."

"That's cute." She smiles. "Do that."

"I can't change here, and I'm afraid she will get scared if she wakes next to me." Granted, she freaked out when I was a panther, too. I didn't think that plan through very well.

"I'm sure you'll figure it out. I'm going to bed." She turns and pads down the hallway on light feet.

Killian looks at me with sad eyes. "She has nightmares? I didn't know. She never said anything. Maybe you do know her better than I do."

"Let's not fight about what we do and don't know. If she has nightmares, we both go in there and try to soothe her. I don't know what else to do. If you still feel the bond pulling you, I can't just push you out of the picture." This is such a mess.

"Do you think two people can be bonded to the same mate?"

"I have no idea. For now, we need to work together to try to bring her memory back. When we get home, we'll ask your parents."

"They're your parents too." Killian smirks.

"I know. It's just been a long time since I haven't had to hide that they raised me."

Killian snorts a laugh. "Gods, it would totally figure if we had the same mate."

I can't help but laugh with him. "You're not mad? I mean, anymore? That shot at my face spoke volumes about how you felt earlier."

"I think I can forgive you if you watch Beauty and the Beast with me again." He wiggles his eyebrows as I choke a laugh out. "Plus, she doesn't remember us. Which means our first impression was saving her instead of kidnapping her. It will be so much easier to win her over this time."

I wake with a crick in my neck on the couch. Killian is passed out on the floor in front of the TV like a child. The credits for The Little Mermaid scroll up the screen. I don't know how far he got. I fell asleep sometime after the Ice Queen movie, and now I understand why Trouble was so annoyed. Gods, it will be fun to use that movie against her—my little Ice Queen.

Clinking from the kitchen catches my attention. Trouble is holding up a baking tray and a frying pan. She crinkles her nose and then lets out a silent laugh. I walk into the space, lean against the doorframe, and hear low murmuring coming from a phone on the counter. Two guys are discussing some movie they hated. I can't help but notice how often they get sidetracked into other conversations that make Trouble giggle as she reads the side of a tube.

"Hello, Trouble."

She jumps and spins around. "Oh my god, Rodan, you scared the shit out of me. Don't creep up on people."

"I didn't creep up on people—just you. And I like it when you jump," I purr as I approach her. Her silver hair sparkles in the morning light coming through the window over the sink. I want to take her in my arms and claim her right here on the counter; that primal urge is almost uncontrollable. She needs time to remember, or I need to win her over again.

I can do it right this time around.

I see her throat work as she swallows. "Do you need something?" she squeaks out.

"I need a great many things, but for now, just to help. And to know what that is?" I point to the phone.

"The podcast? It's Streaming Wasteland. I think the guys are funny. The episode is almost over. I was about to switch to music while I cook."

"Last time I saw you in a kitchen, you looked rather lost."

"Oh? Well, I'm sure there was a reason. I know how to cook. Here, you can open these." She hands me a cardboard tube with metal caps. "Just pull the paper off and separate the cinnamon rolls; you'll see where they come apart. Put them in that glass dish and then open the other one."

It seems simple enough. I nod as I pull the corner indicated. The paper slowly pulls off to reveal brown cardboard.

Pop!

I drop the damn thing on the counter as it explodes in my hand. "Fuck." My heart hammers in my ears as I try to calm my breathing. I stare incredulously at this horrible tube with dough oozing out the sides.

Trouble bursts into a fit of laughter, keeling over, holding onto the kitchen counter for balance. She takes several deep breaths as I glare at her.

"You did that on purpose."

She laughs even harder, wiping tears from her cheeks. "No. I–I forgot to warn you." She slumps to the floor as she continues to laugh. "I'm sorry; I forgot you wouldn't know. But your face!" Laughter rolls out of her, and I fight the grin pulling at my lips. It's nice to see the light coming back into her eyes.

"I'll cook the bacon. You deal with your little dough bombs." I step over to her cooktop and investigate the sizzling pan and package of bacon. Thankfully, it's already lit because I have no idea how to use this thing. That was definitely a problem when I was Jin. I'm used to eternal fire ovens, not whatever the fuck this shit is.

She nods and looks up at me, smiling. I offer her my hand and pull her up, her body sliding against mine. Her breath hitches as she makes eye contact. The bond thrums lightly in my chest, electrifying my body in a happy melody. I run my fingertips down her arm, and she shudders. I can feel her emotions run hot through the bond- her mind has gone to a wicked place. The air around me is thick with the scent of cinnamon, and I don't know if it's her or the dough still sitting on the counter. "It's dangerous to sit on the floor in a kitchen, Trouble," I whisper in her ear. "I could mistake you for something I want to eat."

Gods, I want to kiss her.

Her heartbeat ramps up as she tries to compose herself and school her features. "Why would you eat something off the floor? That's so unsanitary." She rolls her eyes as she turns to the dough bomb.

There's that spark.

Chapter 16
Killian

"The queen is thrilled you found Jade and Rodan, but asks that you stay here for a few more days while the war council is occurring. Ellis and Sorrel have worked as dignitaries with the other delegates to discuss further courses of action against Light. As it stands, they have not gotten a majority rule to see the King of Light dethroned." Warrick stands with his hands behind his back, giving me the official report. His formality is out of place in the dining room of Jade's parents. "How is she?" he asks, dropping his arms and formalities.

I sigh. "The potion didn't work. She has no idea who we are."

"Fuck." Warrick sits and picks up the beer Clair put on the table for him before she gave us some privacy. "You want me to try...the not-so-fun way?"

"It's up to her. I'll ask her if she's willing." I grimace; Rodan said it's awful. "Do you think we are going to war?"

"The evidence is damning. That laboratory you found was full of some pretty dark stuff. We found ledgers full of incriminating evidence about the king and letters written in his own hand. Beatrix had an entire box of letters under the floorboards in her room from her father, detailing some pretty heinous stuff. There were also notes in the box, giving her meeting places and times within the castle. Honestly, I can't believe she didn't burn the documents."

"She isn't the brightest candle on the chandelier." I grin.

With all that evidence, I'm surprised any of the other kingdoms would object to putting another ruler in charge of Light. Sure, it would disrupt trade agreements for a time, but this is pretty serious.

"Why are the other kingdoms opposed?"

"I think they want the Kingdom of Light for themselves. It's also possible that, as allies, they worry the war council could turn against them in the future. It's why wars happen; power and greed fuel them. What concerns me is that the sorcerer lives under our noses and still moves undetected. That's the reason your mom wants to keep you away as long as she can. Unfortunately, it will raise too many questions if you are gone for over a week. The delegates are already growing suspicious that your parents are up to something." Warrick takes another long drink from his beer.

"My absence screams impending war. In their eyes, any number of schemes could be going on—hiding me away, spying, infiltrating, dead..." My mind reels with the implications of my disappearance. There is not much I can do unless I defy my parents' wishes. I'm sure they have everything under control. Mom has always been good at political maneuvering. It's kind of unsettling how her thoughts operate.

"True. I brought you guys some more mortal clothes since it appears you'll be here for a while longer. How are things with Rodan? Cat says you punched him?" Warrick chuckles, his honey eyes alight with mirth.

I look down at my beer. "I may have overreacted..."

Warrick rolls with laughter, smacking the table. "I wish I could have seen it. His face must have been priceless."

My shoulders shake with the amusement I try to suppress. "We're good. I just don't know what to do about the situation. Have you ever heard of a person having two mates?"

He shakes his head. "I'll ask your parents about it. But I have to say I'm not surprised. I saw the way you both looked at her. Take her out, let her show you her world. Stop being so cautious and demonstrate to her what she'd be missing without you." He winks and takes another drink. "I need to get going, but I'll check in tomorrow. I should go thank Clair for lunch." He stands and smiles. "Try not to fight Rodan while I'm gone, or at least wait until I can watch."

We walk along the pier. The city lights glitter over the water like their own city lit beneath its depths. Wooden planks creak, withered, and rough with age as the salt clings to the air. The slow ripple of waves is a song on the wind. What a lovely place to have our first mortal realm date. The tables are turned for once, and I get to experience the magic of Jade's world. Bundled up in a puffy lilac jacket, Jade stares out at the bay. Her loose strands of hair play in the breeze as I admire her in the soft light.

"I dreamed of having dinner with you in a glowing garden." She says as she shrinks in on herself.

My heart jumps at the admission. I snap my attention to her and smile wide. "Our first date. I took you to the bioluminescent garden. Do you remember?" This could be wonderful news. She's been so unsure of us, but I appreciate her giving us a chance. Honestly, I'm surprised she even agreed to go to dinner with us after what her ex-husband did to her.

"It's hazy. I remember talking about our childhoods and how beautiful and magical everything seemed. I also had a dream where you were training me to fight, so let's not put too much stock in my dreams." She giggles.

I stop and pull her to face me, happiness filling my chest. "I *did* teach you to fight." Gods, I want to hug her. "I don't understand why those memories bled into your dreams, but I'm so glad they did.

What else do you remember?" I need to know; I don't see how this is possible, but somewhere in her mind, the memories are there, locked away. Somewhere.

"I used to have dreams—well, no, not dreams—recurring nightmares. They were always of things that actually happened. It was like reliving them over and over again. So maybe this is like that, but not so unpleasant." She blushes and looks down. "Dreaming of you and Rodan was all that got me through; it was an escape...It's also why I thought I was hallucinating when I saw you. I saw bits and pieces of stuff. I know I don't remember everything, but I think I remember enough." She sighs.

"Thank you for agreeing to come out with me tonight. I feel like I have a lot of ground to make up with you."

"Why is that?"

"Because it's my fault you are in this predicament in the first place." The weight of it is heavy on my shoulders. All I wanted was to find my person and make them happy. Instead, I caused her so much pain; I was naïve and selfish.

"You know, Ace would have probably still kidnapped me even if you didn't. God, that's a statement, isn't it? Anyway, who would have saved me if I hadn't met you? So thank you." She reaches out and laces her fingers through mine as she turns to walk again.

Butterflies dance through my chest as I walk with her. This is even more nerve-racking than the first time we went on a date. I was so convinced everything would play out perfectly that I didn't stop to think about anything. My brother and I are in love with the same woman, and I can't find it in me to stay mad about it. All I can do is worry that both of us will walk away from this broken-hearted.

"Did we–"

I look at her, confused. Her whole face turns bright red, and I can't help but laugh. "No. We were taking things slowly. It's my fault, really. You made it very clear you were interested." I feel my face heat.

"But I did with–"

"Yeah." I sigh and squeeze her hand.

"I don't know what to do about all that. I have a hard time believing I was dating both of you."

Stopping her, I turn and cup her face in my hand. "You don't have to do anything about it. Something is going on with all three of us; fate is meddling." I huff a laugh. "Please don't feel bad. Just give us a chance to win you over. I'm here whether you pick me, him, or both of us. I just don't want to live without you any more than I already have."

Her eyes go round as a shy smile spreads across her face. "That has got to be the most romantic thing I've ever heard." She sighs, looking into my eyes. She reaches her hand up and tangles it in my hair, pulls me down, and slants her lips against mine.

I suck in a sharp breath and, with shaky hands, caress her cheek. She is warmth and light, filling me with elation. Time slows as I tease her mouth with mine, holding her delicate face in my hands. My erratic heartbeat is sure to end me at any moment, but I'd die happy. Her hand slides behind my neck, pulling me in closer as she flicks her tongue at the seam of my lips.

I growl, sliding my hand around her waist and backing her into the railing, deepening the kiss. Her rich vanilla scent has cinnamon dancing along the edges. I want to be entwined like this with her forever. She runs a hand down my chest and groans, the sweet sound sending messages to my cock that she's not ready for.

I pull away and look into her eyes. "You are magnificent, you know that?" I kiss her again before I turn and walk with her firmly tucked under my arm.

"Still taking things slow?" Her sultry voice makes me second-guess everything.

"Wouldn't be much of a gentleman if I didn't. Plus, Rodan is waiting at the restaurant. We don't want to be late. It was only supposed to be a short walk." I laugh as the butterflies dance happily in my chest.

"So what, you two are just going to trade me off? Spend a little time with you, then go spend time with him?" She laughs.

"And time with both of us together. Don't forget about that." I smile and almost trip when the scent of cinnamon on her intensifies. She's aroused? I wasn't insinuating anything; I meant dinner. However...Rodan and I may need to have a chat.

Chapter 17
Jade

While I'm glad everyone talked me into going out with Killian and Rodan, this is weird. When we arrived at the restaurant and got our table, Killian whisked Rodan away to the bathroom. They are worse than girls. Hopefully, my kissing Killian won't cause any problems.

A part of me feels like this is all moving too fast, but it also feels strangely right. My palms sweat with the anxiety this is giving me. What if I'm different from how they remember me? What happens if Ace comes for me again? I guess that won't matter if I return to their world with them. God, what am I thinking?

I'm just so relieved to be out of that house, away from Ace. I never thought he'd hold me hostage. He agreed to the divorce, had a girlfriend, and moved on. I don't even want to know what changed. Believing I was going to die there has made me grateful to be free. I can't believe I fought him off; for once, I didn't just freeze in fear. Something is definitely different about me; maybe Killian is correct, and my memories are returning somehow.

It's been ages since I've been to this restaurant. It is in an old warehouse on the pier, San Francisco's finest hidden gem, at least to me. The industrial decor of iron and wood, mixed with the low lighting, makes the place casual and perfect for dates. The booth in the corner is cozy, and the view of the bay is gorgeous. I plan to get a ridiculous amount of fish tacos because this place has the best.

Mom encouraged me to take the guys out and show them around. We took the train from Dublin into the city since it's beautiful at night with the fog rolling back in. The guys were fascinated by our mode of transport, having only read about trains. I'm still unsure where they got the suits from, but hot damn. Rodan walked out with his hair tied back, wearing an all-black suit. Killian followed in a charcoal ensemble with a white button-up. The jerks came into the living room with their jackets slung over one shoulder like they were walking a damn runway.

I pulled a cute dress out of my mom's closet, a little red number I paired with black tights and heels. My outfit clashed horribly with my lilac jacket, but options were limited, and I didn't feel like freezing my ass off.

My phone buzzes on the table, pulling me out of my nervous thoughts.

CAT: Ryker and I are going to my place tonight. And your parents may or may not have gone on a mini-vacay for a couple of days. Love you.

JADE: What?!

CAT: Have fun!

CAT: Relax, it will be fine.

JADE: I hate you.

CAT: Love you too!

JADE: I'm changing your name in my phone, FYI.

TRAITOR: LOL! Don't blame me. It was Warrick's idea.

JADE: WTF!

TRAITOR: Lol. It will be fine.

JADE: They've been in the bathroom a long time...

TRAITOR: Together?

JADE: Yes...

TRAITOR: Lol. Too bad they don't have phones, or I'd have Ryker investigate.

TRAITOR: Off to dinner…I better not be listed in your phone as traitor again…

Serves her right. I smile and tuck my phone away. The guys leave the bathroom, and my heart lurches into a thundering crescendo. Suddenly, it's sweltering in here. I grab the glass of water in front of me and gulp it down.

Rodan pins me in, sliding into the booth beside me with a smirk as Killian sits across from us. My face flushes as I pick up the menu and pretend to peruse it.

"Trouble, are you trying to avoid us?" Rodan shifts, sliding an arm across the back of the seat, boring his gaze through me.

"No, I'm deciding what I want to eat. Do you need me to read the menu to you?" I bat my eyelashes at him.

He chuckles and picks up his menu, shaking his head. We sit in silence until the server comes and takes our order and my barricade from me. Killian regales me with tales of the dates we had in his realm. Parts of his stories bring back vivid memories from my dreams, and I feel some of the tension melt off me.

"You were pretty adamant about going home and just taking the money until we found out you were part fae," Killian says.

"How did we find that out?"

"That happened on your date with me at the beach. There was a dragon attack," Rodan says. "Up until then, it was a great date."

Killian puts down his drink, his excitement palpable. "I wanna hear about the date. You never told me." He grins from ear to ear as Rodan scowls at him.

I nod in encouragement, as Rodan has been pretty quiet through the exchange. He tells us about everything from the horseback ride to the beach and how we ditched to a cave when everyone else showed up. It sounds like a nice day, but he clams up at the cave.

"Why'd you stop? What happened in the cave? Did you two fight again?" Killian asks.

"She *really* liked the cave," Rodan says, taking a drink of beer.

"That's it?" Killian whines.

I crack a smile and look at Rodan expectantly, raising an eyebrow.

Rodan turns to me and leans in close, just inches between us. Out of the corner of my eye, I see Killian leaning in. "I made you see stars in that cave," he says in a low tone.

I gape at him, unable to speak. The implications of what he's said and...oh god, Cat said something about me and him in a cave. I squirm in my seat as heat rushes to my core. Blood floods to my face as Killian laughs.

"I knew something happened on that beach. But I thought- no, Rodan isn't into her. Damn, and here I was taking it slow."

"There's nothing wrong with slow Killian," I squeak out, still pinned down by Rodan's intense stare. I clear my throat. I can't help but imagine what it must have been like. Heat pools low in my belly as I wonder what Rodan's hands roaming my body would feel like. He looks muscular. Does he have tight planes of muscle under that shirt? Or is he chiseled and solid like a statue?

The heat in Rodan's eyes intensifies, and I look pointedly at the table. "Do we need to find somewhere private, Trouble? Or are you picturing things right here in public?" He smirks.

I flush scarlet. The amused look in his eyes tells me he knows exactly what I was thinking about. The idea of them bending me over this table right in the middle of the restaurant is obscene, but now the idea is planted- Rodan's hands moving up my skirt while Killian kisses up my neck...I blink away the thoughts and focus on the scorched wood grain of the table.

"Anyway, what do you guys do? Like in your...kingdom?" I squeak.

Killian just about bounces out of his seat. "Well, you can't tell anyone because I'm kind of the target of some really freaky sorcerer, but I'm the prince of Amara and will be taking over the throne when my parents retire. My parents adopted Rodan when he was little because his entire kingdom was cursed." He shoots Rodan an apologetic look.

"I guess that makes me the prince of Shadow." Rodan shrugs. "Please don't repeat this information to anyone. Killian is in danger, which is why his parents don't want us to return yet."

I almost choke on my cider at their declarations. They are both princes? I gathered they were pretty much brothers, but *princes*? I should have put it together with Warrick being a royal guard, but it's been a lot to take in, and I may have missed some details while freaking out about others. So I was okay with that? They are set to rule kingdoms, and I'm dating them like guys who work standard nine-to-fives?

"Well, Cat knows," Killian says, a bit sheepish.

"Seriously?" Rodan groans.

"You're the one who fried Bravos and left him all..." Killian crosses his eyes, sticks out his tongue, and puts his hands on his throat. I cough out a laugh as Rodan rolls his eyes. I have a feeling I don't want to know.

Our food arrives and interrupts the conversation, and I grin as a large plate of street tacos arrives in front of me. I'm sure my eyes were bigger than my stomach, but I don't care. Ten glorious tacos line the plate, and the fried fish is nestled in a purple pickled slaw— the most heavenly combination. Killian smiles at me across the table as he digs into an enormous burrito. Rodan looks down at the tacos before him and back at me as if contemplating the life choices that led him here. Serves him right for not reading the menu and ordering what I got.

Rodan takes a tentative bite, and his eyebrows raise in approval. I catch him staring at me as I eat, and my heart does a brief flutter. After taco number eight, I'm beginning to understand the look he gave me; I think he knew it was too much food. Although I attempt to power through, my stomach is so stuffed that I don't believe I can eat another bite. I forgot how your stomach shrinks when you don't eat enough. Damn it.

"Need a little help, Trouble?"

"No," I groan. "Why do you call me that? Actually, why do you both call me weird nicknames?"

Rodan cracks a grin, putting his tongue in his cheek. "Because I knew that's what you were from the moment I met you."

I feel my face go scarlet again. Damn it, why do they do this to me? How did I manage this before? Was I this big of a mess? Probably.

"And you? Why Emerald? Tell me it's not because it's green," I say, trying and failing not to squeak.

Killian's eyes shift back and forth as he gives me a shy smile. "I mean, that's not the only reason..."

I laugh, shaking my head. Of course.

Rodan leans towards me and rakes his hand through my hair. "We really missed you. I really missed you." My heart thuds in my ribcage, and the urge to lean into him floods me. I want to trust what everyone is telling me, to trust myself in this, but how can I when I messed up so horribly the last time? For fuck's sake, look at where that ended–me chained to a wall.

"How is this supposed to work?" I whisper. I wring my napkin in my hands and look down. Maybe it would be better to cut things off now before I develop more feelings for either of them. Pressure builds behind my eyes as I contemplate everything. I take a deep breath and wait in silence for one of them to tell me. Why does the idea of not being with them bring me so much heartache when I don't remember them?

Killian reaches across the table, and I slide my hand into his as Rodan moves closer and wraps his arm around my shoulders. "So long as you are happy, so am I," Rodan whispers in my ear. "Plus, we might have some ideas for making things work." He nips my ear, and I take in a sharp breath. Heat floods my core, and I pinch my thighs together. "Don't look so worried; we don't bite...hard."

"Rodan..." Killian growls.

My stomach does a little flip, and I do my best to slow my breathing. Good god.

I straighten and look at Rodan and his self-assured, smug smile. "You can't seriously think lines like that will work on me," I say, flashing him a sardonic grin.

His eyes darken, and his smile broadens, revealing sharp fangs. "You didn't complain when I bit you the last time."

Holy hell. My body is molten with want, every nerve on fire with need. The fresh scar along my inner thigh flashes through my mind, and my jaw drops. "I have no idea what you're talking about." Truth. Except now I'm curious. Damn him.

The server comes with the check, saving me from where this conversation was going. Killian pulls a credit card from his pocket and hands it over. He explains that Warrick has them to pay for stuff in our realm, and he's borrowing one.

"I can't wait to show you your favorite spots in our realm." Killian smiles. "I want you to see everything. The gardens are so beautiful, and the library. You loved it there. You had all these notebooks filled with stuff you learned from our history books. Oh, I should ask Warrick to bring them so you can read them. Maybe it will help your memory."

"That's a great idea." I beam.

Killian continues telling me about the castle and the things we did there. He holds my hand and strokes his thumb over the back of it. Rodan sits so close I can feel the heat coming off his body, his arm draped across the backrest. He plays with my hair casually but doesn't fully invade my space by pressing into me, leaving a few inches between us.

A familiar voice catches my attention, causing me to look away from Killian. Just over his shoulder, a tall blond man in his fifties makes eye contact with me. My heart thuds to a stop, and the world slows. Sweat trickles down my back as my hands begin to shake. As little spots form, walls close in around my vision, blocking out the world around me. I'm drowning in a sea of fear.

A calloused hand caresses my face and guides my eyes to a dark green abyss. "Hey, talk to me. Breathe, Trouble," he coaxes. "Breathe. Focus on me. What just happened?"

My mind whirls as I try to take a breath; my throat constricts as my heart beats erratically into my ribs. Rodan places my hand on his chest. "Breathe with me," he whispers, pulling me into his arms and placing his palm over my racing heart. "Long, slow breaths. That's it, Trouble." I pull air deep into my lungs and glance over Killian's shoulder again. The man grimaces, moving towards us. I push down my panic, trying desperately to compose myself.

I drop my hand under the table to hold Rodan back. "Don't say anything," I hiss.

"Trouble if you want to do that; this is hardly the right place." He chuckles.

Confused, I look down and see my hand firmly holding his dick down. I snatch my hand back and flush red. Shit.

"Hello, Jade. I'm surprised to see you here." Mark's contemptuous smile makes me want to hurl. *What you mean to say is I'm surprised to see you out of my son's little dungeon kink, you sick bastard.*

I give him a feral smile as I try to muster up the confidence I don't feel. Killian holds my hand in reassurance, and Rodan squeezes my leg. "Yeah, long time no see. Guys, this is Mark, my ex-father-in-law." Killian's smile falters briefly as Rodan's glare deepens at the man.

Mark lifts an eyebrow, the cruelty in his gaze so much like Ace's. "Who are your friends?"

I open my mouth to speak, but Rodan cuts me off, extending a hand. "I'm Rodan, Jade's husband, and this is Killian, her boyfriend. A pleasure to meet you–"

"What?" I hiss so only he can hear me as my jaw drops. I glare at him, growling under my breath that he's crazy.

"What? It's the truth," Rodan smirks.

"It really is," Killian says, amused.

Mark's glower grows vicious as he sneers at me. "I guess congratulations are in order. This is truly surprising news. I'll have to pass it on to Ace. Speaking of, have you heard from him lately? He hasn't been answering his phone."

"No, but I've been busy with all the getting-married stuff," I say flippantly, gritting my teeth. I take slow, shallow breaths, holding on to the scraps of composure I can.

"I see. I must catch up with my date, but I'll be seeing you around, Jade. I'll tell Ace you said hi."

Fuck me.

"Good luck with that," Rodan says under his breath once Mark is out of earshot. "Let's get you out of here. Go back to your mom's house."

"Don't forget the ice cream place around the corner from the house. I think Emerald needs it," Killian says, holding my jacket up for me as we exit the booth.

"No, *you* want it." Rodan gives him a pointed look as he pulls me toward him, zipping my jacket. "Don't worry, we'll protect you."

Chapter 18
Rodan

"Oh, my gods, this is the best thing ever." Killian groans as he takes another bite of the uncooked cookie ice cream.

"You didn't have to get six pints." I laugh.

"I couldn't decide, and Jade said I could. All the flavors looked so good. I mean, I'd only ever had that chocolate milkshake, and come to find out so many flavors existed. Six was seriously narrowing it down."

I roll my eyes as I sit on the sofa. Groaning as Killian flips through the different animated movies he hasn't watched yet. I'll never admit to him that they are entertaining.

Jade went to bed a while ago. We talked for a long time about what had happened to her after she came back here. Killian and I were ready to kill Ace all over again. I think she's hiding how overwhelmed she is with everything. She puts on a brave face and laughs things off, but I feel her agony through the bond. She's barely holding it together.

Hell, I'm barely holding it together. I spent the whole night wanting to wrap her in my arms and tell her everything would be alright. But how is it supposed to be okay when everything has gone to shit?

Killian picks another princess movie; the girl's family treats her like a slave, and a prince has to choose a wife immediately. Of course.

Jade's scream has us up and running for her door. She thrashes wildly on the bed, crying out for help. Killian breathes heavily as he darts into the room, searching for the threat. Moonlight shines through the window across the small room. The navy blanket looks almost black in the low light. She seems so tiny, nestled in the large bed in the center of the room. Drawings are haphazardly attached to the wall above a small desk. Underneath the window is a dresser painted in swirls of color.

Was this her room when she lived here?

I quietly pull Killian to her side and sit next to her on the bed. She whimpers as I run a hand down her arm. She feels like ice under my fingertips.

Realization flashes across Killian's face as he nods and moves to her other side. I carefully slide beside her, ensuring I do not jostle the bed. Killian follows my lead on the opposite side. Taking a deep breath, I lay my head next to hers. She's on her side facing me, but as I stroke her arm, she calms and curls into my body.

Killian wraps himself behind her, and a low whine escapes him whenever she twitches. His arm wraps protectively around her middle, and she relaxes. Something about this clicks into place; it feels right somehow. Her hand drags up my torso and clings to my shirt as she burrows her face into my chest. Content, I close my eyes.

Fuck, I hope she doesn't freak out in the morning.

"Oh shit," Trouble whispers, pulling me out of sleep. She has her head on my chest and a leg resting on top of mine. I crack my eye open to see Killian tense, panic in his expression. He is fully draped across her back, pinning her between us.

"Please don't freak out; you were having nightmares, and we just...wanted to help." Killian's voice cracks, groggy with sleep.

"Maybe you wanted to help. I wanted to wake up like this." I smirk.

Please don't be mad. I could spend the rest of my life waking up like this, but last night, I only wanted to ease her suffering.

Trouble smacks my chest but makes no move to get up. I snatch her hand and pull it to my mouth, planting a kiss on her palm. "Good morning to you, too, Trouble." I don't know if I've ever slept this well, and I do not want to get up anytime soon.

I place her hand back over my heart and rest mine on top of hers.

"So, you guys plan to keep me pinned like this?"

"Yes," we both answer in unison.

She giggles and reaches behind her for Killian's side. He jolts as she tickles him, and he laughs, batting her hand away. His squirming leaves an opening that she leaps for, but I close my arm around her and flatten her on top of me. Face down on my chest, she squeals as I hold her in place.

She howls with laughter as she tries to wiggle out of my hold while Killian tickles her sides. She's entirely at our mercy. I laugh silently as she struggles and heaves for air through giggles. Her eyes are bright and full of mischief and glee. It takes everything in me to keep myself under control as she grinds against me.

Killian sits on her feet to stop them from kicking wildly as her shirt rides up, exposing her ribs. He slides his hands up her sides to the exposed skin, relentless in his revenge. She screams and thrashes, gulping down air between laughs. Killian grins and flops on top of her, sandwiching her between us.

Her giggles continue as she wheezes, "You're. Crushing. Me." And she goes into another round of laughter.

Killian rolls to the side, pulling her with him. I prop myself up on my elbow as I face them. She's sprawled across him, heaving breaths, staring up at the ceiling with a giant smile painted on her face. Killian is gleefully nuzzling her hair with his arms draped across her stomach.

An overwhelming urge to strip her bare and kiss her from head to toe comes over me. To bury my face in her pussy right there in Killian's arms. Gods, she is so beautiful. She's glowing with happiness.

What Killian told me in the bathroom last night plays through my mind. *She got super turned on when I mentioned both of us together with her. That wasn't even what I was talking about, but...but...maybe one day.* Gods, I need to stop thinking about this before my dick bursts through my pants.

"I think...I can breathe again." She twists her head around to look at Killian; at least, she tries to. "I think I should see what's in the kitchen for breakfast."

"Can't I just eat you?" Killian purrs.

Dude. My eyes widen at his brazenness.

"Killian!" She laughs as she smacks his wrist. He winks at me as he releases her, and she climbs out of bed—the scent of cinnamon and vanilla trailing after her.

Killian's eyes widen, and he jumps off the bed. "I'm getting ice cream." He runs out the door and down the hallway.

"Ice cream, it is. Oh, there is still pie; maybe I'll have that." She muses as she moves toward the door.

"What, no dough bombs this morning?" I crack a smile as I stand.

She smiles broadly as I stop next to her. "No, it will never be as funny as the first time," she says.

I cock an eyebrow and scowl at her, then move to walk past the little smart-ass. She puts a hand on my torso, stopping me. I see a sparkle in her eyes as she quickly reaches around my neck and pulls me down into a kiss.

My heart thunders as I wrap my arms around her. Her soft lips press into mine. I feel her need, want, and desire course through the bond, mirroring everything I'm feeling. She shoves me against the doorframe as she glides her tongue along mine. Her vanilla and sugar scent overwhelms my senses, as the spice of cinnamon almost brings me to my knees.

You don't know what you do to me.

She breaks the kiss and stares up at me. "Wow," she breathes and bites her bottom lip.

I have no words as I stare at her.

"Let's get out there before Killian wonders where we are." She grins and saunters down the hall, leaving me dumbstruck by her.

Chapter 19
Killian

How is this so hard? Push the button and steer the stupid little car. I growl as my car spins out again on a stupid yellow banana peel.

"Sorry," Jade says through a giggle as she speeds past me. Again.

"You are a dirty little cheater," I say through gritted teeth. This is the sixth round we've played. Her little cartoon princess is speeding around the track as my giant turtle with horns throws up his hands in defeat. I know I'm getting better at this as I play, but damn, she has to be cheating.

She sets down the controller and stretches her arms over her head, revealing a sliver of her stomach. I avert my eyes, trying not to think about how soft she had felt under my fingers.

"He's out cold," she says, gesturing towards Rodan, who is indeed still passed out on the chair.

It's getting late, and Warrick hasn't shown up for his daily report. I'm sure everything is fine; the day probably just got away from him. I mean, I have nothing to worry about, right? Running my hand through my hair and taking a deep breath, I try to calm my nerves. I'm sure everyone is fine.

I nod as I stare at the screen with furrowed brows.

"How about we pick out another game? I have a few more in my room." Jade gets up and motions for me to follow her.

"But I want to beat this one." I'm unsure why I need to win; it's just infuriating that I can't beat her.

"Hey, at least you weren't playing with Cat; she would have mopped the floor with all of us," she says, pulling my hand away from the controller. "Come on, I have other games we can play together and beat up bad guys."

Earlier, she suggested we play these games to help her get her mind off things. Rodan was content to watch me get stomped and didn't want to play; then he passed out. I was just happy to see the tension melt off Jade. She opens up in little bits and pieces before she shuts down again. The game was a good distraction, but I wish I knew how to help and make her feel better. I guess only time will heal what's happened to her.

"Killian?"

"Oh, sorry, yeah. I'd like to see what else you have." I follow her into her room. Light shines through the window, illuminating the lavender walls. The space is colorful but more subdued than her parents' living room. Rodan's room comes to mind when I see the dark midnight blues and silver thread work on the bed. Pictures of her and Cat when they were younger adorn a mirror on the wall, while old sketches are artfully arranged over the desk. It's like getting a peek at who she used to be. Her bed is still messy from this morning's antics. I smile, remembering her laughter and her sprawled across me, breathing heavily. My hands touching the soft skin beneath...

"You looking for a round two?"

I whip my head around to look at her, shocked. "What?" I croak out, my voice cracking. Well, if she didn't know what I was thinking about before, she does now. My face heats as I clear my throat. "What?"

"You were staring at the bed rather intently." She smirks.

"I...I was just thinking about this morning," I say honestly.

She cracks a smile, and then her face goes thoughtful. "I had another dream with you last night...I'm curious if it's real or not." She rubs her hand down her arm.

I sit on the end of the bed and pat the spot next to me. She doesn't move. "What happened? I hope it wasn't the nightmare that had you screaming. Unless those were good screams." I grin and wiggle my eyebrows.

She laughs and pushes my shoulder. "Umm, we were in a library, reading...and then we were kinda making out?"

"Oh, really? Tell me more." I reach forward and pull her towards me.

"Killian!" She playfully bats at my hands but sits straddling my legs. "Well, it was kinda like this." She laughs.

I run a hand down her spine, and she arches her back. "Yeah, that happened." The wolf inside me growls for domination as I attempt to keep myself in check.

"And—how did it end?"

Her breathy voice is causing my blood to heat. "I kissed you, and then you went to bed. Nothing else happened." I shrug, giving her my most innocent look. Gods, I'd wanted to do so much more. I'd wanted to claim her as mine. And with her sitting on me like this again...

She shimmies up my lap until her breasts press against me. Her arms wrap around my shoulders as she buries her face in my neck. "Being cautious is the last thing I want to do right now. I'm so tired of being scared of everything." I can feel her heartbeat thundering in her chest as that intoxicating spicy scent fills me. Again, the wolf thrashes against its leash, wanting to claim her, mark her as mine.

I take long, slow breaths, trying to calm myself. She can't possibly mean...she couldn't want to...no, I need to keep it in my pants. She's been through too much, and she's only just getting to know me again. Shc doesn't remember. I need to take things slow; the fates said so. My body calms as rationality keeps my nature in check.

"I know I don't remember. Not enough, but I feel safe with you. And I'd like to know what it's like to be with you before you leave." She doesn't move. I don't move. I'm struck dumb by her quiet admission.

"I...why would I leave?" Does she think I'd leave without her after everything I did to find her again? I wrap my arms firmly around her, pulling her as far as I can against me. "I'll never let you go, not so long as you want me."

"But what if I don't go back with you? You can't stay here."

"I'd move the heavens to stay with you. I'll work every day to remind you how much I..." My heart stalls in my chest. I don't know how to make her see, to make her understand. "I don't know how to go on without you. As soon as you vanished, I felt as though I had lost a part of myself, becoming a faint reflection of the person I once was. Because I didn't want to rush you, I took things slow. I wanted our love story to be perfect, like in the stories, because you are perfect to me."

"God, why do you have to say such wonderful things?" She groans. "What about Rodan? How do I reconcile all of this? I am so confused." She slumps into my arms and burrows further into me.

"I mean, we kinda grew up sharing everything...why can't we share you?" I smirk as I poke her in the ribs, eliciting a squeal.

Cinnamon floods my senses as she shifts in my lap. "That's crazy. And unfair to both of you." Aw, look at her, trying to be thoughtful when the mere mention of both of us together gets her all hot—it's so cute.

"Unfair is you not giving us a chance, because we are not letting you go. Now stop shifting because you're giving me ideas, and I'm trying to be a gentleman." I tell her as sternly as I can muster. The wolf inside is pacing, and it's getting extremely hard to resist her.

She giggles and wiggles her hips. Gods, help me with this woman.

"Maybe I don't want a gentleman right now."

Chapter 20
Jade

His body tenses beneath me, posture going rigid. I lean back to look into his bright blue eyes; they dilate as they meet mine. "I want to live. Like really live my life and not be afraid of everything. Not just coast through life like it's happening to me. I thought I was going to die, and I will not squander this chance to truly *live*. So please, Killian, shut up and kiss me."

One second, I'm watching his eyes dilate to almost black, and the next, his lips consume mine. Butterflies combust into fireworks in my chest as I match his hunger. I run my hands through his hair, frantic from the feel of him against me.

His hands glide down my sides, slipping under my shirt, the heat of his touch on my bare skin igniting me. Roughly, he pulls the hem of my shirt over my head and discards it on the floor. With the same grace, my bra is gone in a moment. He pauses, staring at me with a predatory gleam in his eyes. A low growl rumbles through his chest as he wraps his arms around me. A chill runs down my spine as his hands caress my bare back.

"I don't know if I can be as gentle as you need if I let my wolf out to play. Say the word, and I'll stop."

Heat ignites in my core, and curiosity about Killian's animalistic side sparks me to life. "I want to play." I pant.

Running his hands down to my ass, he lifts me and flips me onto the bed like I weigh nothing. He looks down at me, standing between my legs, with a smirk. In one swift motion, he tugs his shirt off.

And oh dear god.

Holy wow. Like, wow, how does he have so many muscles? Absentmindedly licking my lips, I take in the sheer spectacle that is Killian. I knew he was muscular; I could feel it through his shirt. He's like a mountain. The—I want to scale it—kind of mountain. The—I want to lick my way up to the peak—type of mountain. It feels almost forbidden to look at him the way I am, but I can't look away. Corded muscles flex as he strips. How had I not jumped him before? He's like sex on a stick. Great, I'm objectifying my...boyfriend? Is that what he is? I lock eyes with him, and his knowing smirk brings a blush to my cheeks that I feel down to my core.

"You keep looking at me like that, and I'm not gonna be able to control myself," he purrs.

Yep, I'm wet. And about two seconds away from begging for it. The black skin-tight boxer shorts he's down to are bulging, and I gasp as he reaches down and pulls on the waistband of my leggings. He cocks an eyebrow at me in question. I nod as goosebumps freckle my skin. I'm really going to do this. Nervous excitement fills me as I'm laid bare for him.

"You're sure, Emerald?"

"Yes," I whisper, never having felt more sure of anything.

He growls as he comes down on top of me, enveloping me in a kiss. The longing within me is finally being met. His hand roams down to my breast as he tweaks the nipple, sending a shot of pleasure through my nerves. I can't help but run my hands over the planes of his chest and down to the ridges of his abs. He shudders at my touch, and his length grinds into me. A slight moan escapes me at the contact; I don't know if I've ever felt this turned on.

A small voice in the back of my mind tells me this is right. This is what I've been waiting for. I feel it in every kiss, in every touch. There is an undeniable magnetic pull that is driving me closer to him, with an intensity that is hard to resist.

He trails his lips over my neck, licking and nipping his way down. He makes eye contact with me as he takes my nipple in his mouth and sucks, letting go just before the sensation turns painful. A playful tilt to his lips precedes a nip to my side that has me squealing and trying to buck him off. He firmly grips my hips and silently laughs as he trails down further. I have zero regrets about where this is going.

On his knees, he splays me before him, gently pushing my thighs further apart. I'm so on display, a blush stains my cheeks as he looks at me like a feast. I want to squirm and close my legs under his scrutiny.

Before I can move, he dives in, and his tongue strips me of my sensibilities. One long lick right up the center before he devours me, and I'm at a loss for air. It is so abrupt I couldn't even brace myself for the impact. The precision with which he works is bewildering; I squirm as I gasp. It is all sensation, riding the wave.

His finger starts circling and barely dipping into my center, teasing me as he gives a slight nip to my clit. "I couldn't resist a taste; you were already so wet for me." His eyes rake over my body. "But keep squirming like that, and I definitely won't be able to control the wolf in me." His fingers thrust deep, and he groans as I clench around him. "Something tells me you don't want me to control myself. You're dripping for me."

I blink at him. I can't believe my sweet Killian would talk so dirty.

The pressure building in me has me delicious with need. The slow strokes of his tongue, in tandem with his fingers, have me delirious. I gasp with every thrust. Then he curls his fingers into a spot that has that tension almost ready to burst.

"Come for me. I want to give you my cock so bad, but I'm not giving it to you until you come for me," he growls before sucking hard on my sensitive bud.

That command pushes me over the edge. I come so intensely, my whole body shakes as my thighs clench around his head. The shock of it leaves me breathless, and a low moan escapes my lips. Every inch of me goes into spasm as he licks and rings every last ounce of release from my folds.

Smiling savagely, he slides his arms under my back, lifts, and tosses me further up the bed. I bounce as I land and laugh. He smirks as he drops his shorts, and his dick springs free; my mouth goes dry at the sheer size of him. I'd seen dicks like this in porn but never in real life, and I have to say, I'm a bit intimidated.

He leans forward and crawls on top of me, resting the head of his cock against my entrance. He gently cradles my face in his palms, his lips pressing against mine in a tender kiss. It's slow and sensual as he glides himself up my center, coating himself in my release. I moan with every pass over my sensitive clit. Grinding against him, as the need to feel him inside me intensifies.

"Don't worry, I'm spelled against procreation." He murmurs on my lips.

"Huh?"

He pulls away from my mouth but continues slowly rubbing his cock up and down my center, making my brain go all hazy. "I can't get you pregnant or anything like that," Thrust. "We have spells and potions for such things. Just figured I'd let you know." Thrust.

Christ on a cracker. My IUD took care of that, but did I really forget?

"Like your world's condoms, but a thousand times more effective," he says as he kisses along my neck. Thrusting past my clit and sending shudders through me. "You're still sure?" he whispers in my ear, chuckling at the torture he's putting me through.

I am going wild inside; the pressure in my core is building again; I need him inside me. "Please, Killian." I whimper.

"Thank fuck," he groans as his lips meet mine.

He stops his maddening teasing and lines himself up, pushing slowly into me. As he slides in, the intensity of the stretch builds, and I can feel every inch steadily rocking in. I'm so wet he's not meeting much resistance, and what I thought would hurt feels amazing. His body shakes as he works himself at an agonizingly slow pace. He watches our bodies meet as I envelop him.

"Oh, fuck," he gasps.

I rock on him, urging him further, wanting all of him. I run my hands up the stiff muscles of his back, every inch of him rigid as he takes his time. We both gasp as his hips meet my own, and his eyes flick to mine, dilating to almost black as he stills and kisses me. He doesn't move, kissing me languidly as my body relaxes around his girth. Everything feels so right; I feel grounded in the world, like this was inevitable. Under his touch, my skin feels electrified. And I can't help but believe that somewhere deep down, I have powerful feelings for this man.

He gives a shallow thrust that has me moaning and arching my back. Then his kisses turn savage as he moves, picking up pace as I feel myself growing more and more wet for him. The pressure is intense, as if I'm right there at the peak and nearly ready to fall over once more. Every time I think I can't bear it anymore, he slows his pace, only to increase it and push me back to the edge. He can read my body and see exactly what he can do with it. He plays me like an instrument, and whenever I think I'm at the crescendo, he lulls me back again.

I may burst if this keeps building this way. He wraps his arms beneath my back and lifts, pulling me up until we are both kneeling on the bed. He continues to rock within me as he pulls my leg around his waist. As he thrusts forcefully into me, my arms encircle his shoulders, my head falls back in ecstasy, and I moan.

"Mine," he whispers. My heart clenches as he declares this, some primal part of me wanting to claim him. His fingers move between us, and he strokes my clit as he thrusts hard again. The pressure builds as he slicks his fingers in my folds and continues to circle my sensitive nub.

I feel it coming. It builds like nothing I've felt before. I explode with the next hard thrust, screaming his name as he groans so loud I'm sure we shook the house. He bites my neck with a snarl, and there's a slight prick of pain before I climax again, clamping down hard on his cock as I shake around him. I see stars as it rushes through my body. Slamming down on his dick as it fills me, I tremble through the orgasm. The world melts away as I feel myself become one with him. I take him fully within me again because I can't control my body as I ride wave after wave of euphoria. Something in me settles like a missing piece slotted into place. He is mine.

"Oh shit, shit, shit," he hisses out as another wave overtakes my senses. It feels like he's swelling, filling me more; he's hitting some spot that has me grinding against him, and with each jolt, I'm thrust over the edge again.

I'm whimpering as he lays me down underneath him. He smooths my hair around my face and looks at me with big puppy-dog eyes. "I'm so sorry." He kisses and caresses me with tenderness.

I stare at him and lift a very tired brow—god, my eyebrows are worn out. "For what? That was...amazing. I've never felt like that, not that I can remember, anyway." I pet his beautiful golden hair as I lie there.

"No, no, not for that, never for that." His head drops to my shoulder. "It shouldn't be possible...Not if you're mated to...It only happens with your mate-"

"What are you talking about?" I pat his head, totally confused. There is nothing wrong here from my perspective. I take a deep breath and try to bring myself back down to earth.

"I knotted," he groans. "I bit you and I knotted."

I have no clue what that means. I didn't mind the bite—shit; it was seriously hot.

Laughter fills the silence, and my whole body turns red as we both take in Rodan leaning in the doorway. "How? Did you seriously manage to mark my mate? Fuck, this might be sad if it weren't so funny. Are you really stuck?"

Huh? Like, huh? Okay...Rodan doesn't seem too upset finding us...like this...and god does he look good. What is it with guys just casually leaning that instantly makes you want to touch them? What am I thinking? I've got Killian inside me, and I'm turned on that Rodan saw us. This is so fucked up.

Killian sighs and pulls my face to his. "So because you're already mated and marked by Rodan...I didn't think I could–didn't think I would–shit, I didn't even give you a choice," he groans and plants his head in my chest. "I just marked you as mine, and now I've knotted, and we are stuck like this for like an hour," he says in a rush.

I'm still not following.

Rodan closes the door and walks over to the bed, smirking. "Trouble, any strange marks on your body? Like new tattoos?"

"Yeah, between my shoulder blades. What does that have to do with anything? Maybe we can talk about this without Killian inside me...this is kind of awkward." Not to mention that the way he's looking at me makes me want to grind on Killian more.

Rodan smacks Killian's ass, causing him to thrust into me again, and my body to hum with pleasure. Oh god, not with Rodan right here. I turn bright red as I pant. Rodan pushes Killian's hair to the side and whistles. "Well, shit. Looks like you have two mates, Trouble."

"What? Seriously, Killian, can we get up and put clothes on before we have another talk about mates?"

"Killian is stuck–like, really stuck. You two are going to be there a while," Rodan says, sitting in a chair and propping his feet on the desk.

What the fuck are they talking about?

"Don't be mad, but he's right. I'm stuck. It's a wolf thing; at the base of my cock is an area that swells up and locks it in place, a knot. It only happens once a mate has been marked. I didn't think I could mark you since you've already been marked. I kind of lost control and bit you, and by the time I realized my knot was swelling...you kind of slammed yourself over it. So now we have to wait for it to...deflate, as it were."

I don't even know what to say about all of that. He's stuck. His dick is legit stuck inside me. While it's a bit concerning, all I want to do is grind against him. My head is fuzzy with everything warring for my attention. "So we are mates now–"

"Yes," Rodan says, his face stoic.

"And you're not mad about it?" Should I be mad about this? Just looking at the two of them together makes me want to go again. What is wrong with me? Rodan sitting there is getting me all needy again.

"Nope, honestly, this is pretty hot." Rodan's eyes darken.

I flush and squirm, but the slightest movement sends jolts through my body, and the need to move on Killian fills me. The tiniest moan escapes me as I clamp my mouth shut. Now that I concentrate on it, I can feel what he's talking about. It's like a lock keeping him from pulling out; I'm filled almost to the point of discomfort, but it has me desperate to move against it.

"So, what do we do?" I breathe, trying not to shift, but my walls flex against his shaft. I shudder and close my eyes, trying to concentrate.

"Put her out of her misery, Killian. She's going to need friction until your knot goes down."

A wicked smile passes between them as Killian grinds into me, and I lose all sense of the world. Rodan's hand lazily strokes down his stiff length through his pants. The sight sends even more ideas through my head. I squeeze around Killian, and he curses. Excitement flutters through me. I want this. I want them. Both of them.

"You good with this, Emerald?" Killian asks.

I moan as he rocks me. "Yes."

Rodan rises from the chair and comes over as Killian rolls us so I'm on top, and I moan at how deep he feels as I grind into him. Rodan's hands snake around my middle as his teeth graze my neck. Although not as muscular as Killian, he still has the physique of a god. Of all the things I thought I'd do, this is not one of them, but I can't stop myself as I lean into him. The rough fabric of his jeans presses into me, his hard length against my back.

Killian's abs flex as I watch his golden skin glisten between my thighs, warmth flooding through me. Strong arms wrap around my waist, giving me goosebumps as Rodan plays with my breasts.

"Next time, I'm watching. I wanna see Rodan spread those pretty lips over his cock and lick you while he does it," Killian growls.

Killian's words leave me speechless as I rock harder on him. I had no idea his dirty words would make me this hot. Rodan's hand trails down between my legs and pinches my clit, sending my body spiraling over the edge; I buck wildly as I explode on Killian again. Everything about this feels like it was always meant to be this way, like I belong in both of their arms. I feel wrung out, but every time they touch me, another wave rolls through my core.

Rodan moves to my side and kisses me deeply, exploring me. I unzip his pants and free his erection. Reaching for his dick, I run my hand up and down in time with his thrusts. Killian watches with rapt fascination as he rolls his hips, causing my eyes to flutter shut and another wave to roll through my body. His knot keeps me right at the peak, where the slightest pressure sends us over.

I stroke Rodan as I come apart. Rodan groans with pleasure as his release drips down my hip. He kisses me long and deep, like he's making up for lost time. I think I could stay in this bed forever with them. Maybe not knotted in place, though.

I feel it as the pressure lifts, and Killian is able to pull out. With a sigh, I roll to his side as Rodan moves to lie beside me. I'm surprised that Killian is a bit more domineering in bed. I was definitely not expecting the dirty talk or the encore with Rodan in the mix, either.

"I—um—I wasn't expecting to-" I stammer.

"That was just the beginning, Emerald. Unless you're mad, in which case I am so sorry I marked you."

A laugh bubbles out of me. "How could I be mad after that? I don't think I could be anything after that. And you, were you watching the whole time?" I turn to Rodan, trying to glare and failing miserably as I grin at him.

"Not the whole time. I was standing there before you started fucking, though. Honestly, thought it would make me jealous, but fuck, it just made me want you more."

"Perve."

"You liked that I watched."

Gaping like a fish at him, I decide to switch gears. "Anyway... what is the deal with the tattoo you asked about? Why did you look at Killian's back?" I ask.

Rodan sits up and sweeps his hair to the side, then turns his back to me, revealing a near replica of the tattoo on my back. The only difference is that where mine had weird gaps, his has golden flames wrapping around the snowflakes with the smoke. I graze it with my fingertips, tracing the intricate details. The bed shifts behind me, and Killian turns his back and pulls his hair over a shoulder, displaying the exact same tattoo.

"Wow, it's beautiful," I breathe.

They both turn towards me, and Killian runs his hand down my spine. "Yours is the same."

"The bond is complete," Rodan says. "The blank spaces were meant for Killian, so it appeared incomplete. We were all fated to be together. That's...intriguing."

Killian smiles and wraps his arms around me as he tackles me to the bed. "Now you have two husbands."

My breath catches. Oh god, what have I gotten myself into?

Chapter 21
Killian

Warmth radiates through my bones in a wave of contented excitement. I glance down at the beautiful creature asleep in my lap, sliding a strand of hair out of her face. I don't know how things ended up this way, but I know she somehow remembers the feelings she had. When the bond snapped into place, I felt it—the sense of her being exactly where she's supposed to be. As Jade drapes herself across us, I sink further into the couch, savoring its plush comfort. Rodan absentmindedly strokes her ankle.

Her parents and Cat are due back soon. We cleaned up and collapsed onto the sofa to wait. Putting on another movie that Jade recommended, I find myself watching her more than anything. Her soft breaths as her chest rises and falls, her rosy pink lips parted ever so slightly. I'm captivated by her. She is my everything.

Memories or not, I will spend the rest of my life trying to make her as happy as I feel in this moment.

"Could you stop with the mental tail wagging?" Rodan says.

My eyes snap to his. "What are you talking about?"

"I can feel it. You're sending all your feelings down the bond to her...it's like a damn trumpet in my head." Rodan cocks an eyebrow as my mouth drops.

"It's not like I can turn it off." I shrug. That's like trying to stop a waterfall from falling.

Hot lust races through me, and all the blood rushes to my dick as flashes of what we did earlier come to mind. I take a sharp breath, not understanding where this came from. The beast in me opens its eyes and blinks. I want to ravage Jade more than anything right now. But she's sleeping and needs rest; for fuck's sake, I'm still exhausted. I feel like a damn teenager. What the hell.

The sensation dulls and winks out as I find myself again, closing my eyes and exhaling slowly.

"See. If I can turn it off, so can you." Rodan smirks.

"That was you? Gods, do you ever think about anything else?"

"Yes. I was proving a point. You need to work on that mental shield because your feelings don't seem to filter when she's asleep. I'm sorry, but I can't take it. At least when she's awake, she seems to have her walls so thick that I barely sense them. But damn, I don't want unfiltered Killian blasting through my head all the time."

Well, shit, I knew I could feel what she was feeling if I focused. I didn't realize I could feel Rodan as well. That's...complicated. It's also the best thing ever. Now that the bond is complete, we are all connected—one big happy family. I stroke Jade's hair again, careful not to disturb her. My heart swells in my chest.

I found my mate.

Rodan groans, shooting me another glare. I smile because nothing can bring me down right now.

"It's been three days; something's wrong," Rodan says, pacing the back porch. Our eyes are fixed on Jade as she sips coffee and talks with Clair. She has tears in her eyes as her mom cries. We decided to give her some privacy to have this conversation. Nevertheless, I can hear her muffled words through the window. She's finally telling her mom the whole story about what Ace did to her. I have to fight the urge to hold her, but I think talking about it will help. I can feel her agony of making her mom cry coursing through the bond.

"Killian, something is wrong. Are you listening to me?"

"His full attention is on Jade," Ryker says from the bench.

I shoot them both a look. "I'm listening." I take a deep breath. "You're right. Warrick was supposed to check in with us, but maybe he just got busy." The alternative is that he doesn't have enough power to reach us right now, or worse. "I've only got dregs of power left in my veins to activate the crystal, and I don't want to use it unless I have to."

"So there's nothing we can do but wait?" Rodan growls.

I nod and direct my gaze towards the clear sky, the color so unlike the crystalline blue of home. Taking my cup of coffee, I sip its warm bitterness. I don't think I like it, but it's growing on me. Rodan and I have been glued to Jade's side since the bond was completed. She is still unsure of everything but is trying to go with the flow. I want to possess her, hold her, never let her out of my sight, but I keep the wolf at bay to let her find her way.

Rodan riles her up constantly; they bicker like an old married couple. I'd be jealous if I didn't find it so endearing. Aside from kissing her, we haven't been back in her bed except to sleep. She's pretty shy about how things went, and we will do things in her time. I'm content to be near her.

She's my moon, and I exist to orbit her.

Our attention is drawn to the garden as a wave of power sweeps through the air, revealing a swirling cloud of white smoke. Warrick stumbles out and collapses to his knees as the portal closes. Blood drips from his temple; his clothes are covered in dirt and gore. The reflective surface of his armor has dulled to a rusty bronze. He heaves a breath as his golden eyes flick to us, and relief fills his features.

"Shit, Warrick," Rodan says as we take in the sight of our friend.

Rodan reaches him first, helping him to his feet as I drag his arm around my shoulders and help him limp to the bench. Ryker hands him a cup of coffee.

"Are you okay? What happened?" I ask.

Warrick shakes his head, gulping down the coffee. He scrunches his nose and glares at the mug, offended. With a long exhale, he sets the cup down. His hand scrubs over his face, wincing when he runs over the cut on his temple. "You have to come back."

"Obviously," Rodan deadpans.

Ryker paces while we wait for Warrick to collect himself. What the hell happened? Why is he covered in blood? Why didn't he heal himself before coming here? I draw a deep breath, trying to calm my thoughts of all the what-ifs.

"Oh my god, Warrick, are you okay? You're bleeding!" Cat shrieks from behind us. We all turn and take in her pale face.

"Who's bleeding?" Clair runs through the door behind her. She takes one look at Warrick, and I see mom mode take over. "Help him inside; let's get you cleaned up before the interrogation I can see brewing in this one." She looks pointedly at Rodan, who lifts his eyebrows in innocence. I put my tongue in my cheek, trying not to smile at him getting called out so perfectly.

Warrick raises an eyebrow, and I shrug; I don't think he's getting out of this. Resigned, he agrees to get cleaned up before we talk. We need information before we rush into action, and Warrick needs to regroup from the looks of it.

We help Warrick inside. Clair runs him a bath and makes him a cup of tea, ordering us to give him some space. She inspects the cut on his forehead and cleans it before sending him off to clean up. From the living room, where we've been ordered to stay, I see Jade and her mom swipe his clothes and put them in the washer, leaving him with some of mine. Both of them rush around, trying to help the most fearsome warrior in my kingdom. Once satisfied, Clair wipes down the metal armor with a rag and sets to work polishing it, a concerned expression crossing her features. I know that look; when you don't know what to do, so you find any task to keep yourself occupied.

Cleaned up and settling on the sofa, Warrick leans forward with his elbows on his spread knees. He looks down at the floor. "I failed them. I failed you." His shoulders fall as my heart ramps up.

Cat sits on the floor and looks up at him, touching his knee. "Start at the beginning. What happened?" She asks as Ryker absentmindedly strokes her hair and watches Warrick, his troubled expression matching mine.

Clair hands out tea as we sit around the living room, tense.

Warrick takes a deep breath and makes eye contact with me, his face near breaking. "Your parents went to make their morning tithe to the orbs, just like every morning. Since you left, they've been going daily, funneling fractions of their power in instead of draining themselves once a week. They didn't want to get caught off guard.

"Everything was going as usual, but then the orbs turned bright purple, and they both just collapsed. I was right there; nothing was amiss or out of the ordinary until that flash. I attempted every possible method to wake them, but none of them worked. Lorelai and I drained ourselves, attempting to rouse them. They are trapped in an enchanted sleep. Somehow, the orbs were tampered with, but I don't know how; none of the wards were broken."

My chest hurts as I try to take in a breath, head spinning.

"By the time we realized it was an ambush, it was too late. The army arrived in the middle of the night. If you can call it that, disturbing grotesque things with no heartbeats. The smell alerted us before we saw them, unnatural creatures from our worst nightmares. Their flesh didn't quite stay on their bones, eyes black as midnight, just devoid of life."

Rodan and I make eye contact. "Like the constructs that attacked us in the forest," he breathes.

A chill runs down my spine as I gape in horror. My parents, the most powerful fae in Amara, are down. An army of those monsters attacked the castle. Nausea crawls up my throat as he continues.

"It was all calculated." He shakes his head, shrinking in on himself. "While the guards defended the castle from those monstrous things, black sludge appeared throughout the castle." He looks down, breathing heavily. "It targeted the queen's cats; they couldn't escape it. It was a valiant effort, but..." he closes his eyes, turning his gaze to the ceiling, pain etched over his face.

Cat's sharp inhale precedes tears as she crumples into a ball. "No, they were my...Suff ...Grum." Her voice cracks as she says their names, my heart breaking with hers over their loss. Ryker scoops her off the floor and pulls her into his lap.

"I'm sorry," he whispers.

I swallow the lump in my throat as Jade tightens her grip on my hand. I hadn't noticed her sitting between Rodan and me or taking my hand. My parents are incapacitated, and the queen's cats, whom I've known my whole life, are just gone. The pain on Warrick's expression says there's more, so we wait for him to continue. A numbness creeps through me, cutting off every emotion, blocking the true terror that I can't deal with right now.

He takes a drink of tea, swallowing hard. "We were overrun so fast; nightmares came to life in every corner of the castle. I got out as many as I could once I saw we were fighting a losing battle. Lyra, Scarlette, and Corsac were with me when the initial attack happened; I got them out first. Lyra's father managed to escape, but they already had all the other delegates and councilors by the time I realized what was happening. A small group of us escaped, but it's taken days to regain enough power to get to you, and right before I portaled, I was attacked."

"Fuck, how could this have happened?" Rodan stands and paces the room.

"It was Ellis," Warrick growls.

My eyes widen in disbelief, mirroring Rodan and Ryker. Everybody in the room freezes in place. Silence fills the space where disbelief has taken root.

"In an attempt to gather information and identify any potential survivors, we dispatched scouts to assess the scene. They reported that Ellis was calling himself king and Beatrix his would-be queen, uniting Amara and Light under one banner," he says with disgust. "He has the councilors and dignitaries that survived in the dungeon hooked up to some machine involving the orbs, siphoning the power out of them. He has some of the most powerful fae in the realm down there."

"My parents?" I feel the blood draining from my face as my heart thunders in my chest.

"They are still unconscious in their chambers, but protected by the wards. The entire continent is in chaos. If this continues, all the Seelie courts may fall. They've been infiltrating us for decades, hiding who they are. Thank the gods no one knows who you are, and that you weren't there. We have to come up with a plan. No one stands a chance if he gets a foothold on the whole of the north."

"He has a foothold," I breathe. "He's taken the castle and united with Light. The Unseelie sorcerers are in Auburnigh. The Great War is happening. Only they've made their stand here this time. They were right under our noses."

"What are you gonna do?" Jade's soft voice cuts through the panic filling my head.

"We have to go back." My shoulders slump, and I turn to her. Pink stains her cheeks as she scrunches her face. "Warrick needs to rest, and we need time to think before we return." As much as I want to spring into action, that will only get people killed.

She lets out a long breath and nods, silver rims her eyes. She is trying so hard to be strong; it's adorable. But the weight on my shoulders just became so overwhelming that all I am able to do is lean back, stare at the ceiling, and watch the fan make its slow circle.

I don't know what to do.

Chapter 22
Jade

I blink at the morning light, sitting on the tree swing my dad built for me when I was seven, slowly rocking myself as I sip my coffee and look up at the wispy clouds dotting the sky. It's quiet and peaceful, with birds chirping their morning songs and the streets calm. I forgot how nice it was to just sit in nature—well, as much nature as the suburbs get.

The click of the door behind me draws my attention, but I don't turn around. Somehow, I know who it is. His presence sings to me like a balm to my soul. Rodan quietly sits on the grass beside me, steam wafting from the mug in his hand.

"You can't hide from me," he says.

"I wasn't hiding."

"Good. Because I will always find you."

I open my mouth to retort, but stop myself. My face heats, and I can't help the giddy smile I make.

We sit in companionable silence in front of the house until my coffee is long gone and neighbors start moving about their days.

"Would you like more coffee?" he asks.

"That's like asking if I'd like more air."

He chuckles silently as he stands and takes my mug. I watch him walk in the front door; he looks exhausted and defeated. The guys were up all night talking after Warrick fell asleep. My heart aches to see him so broken; he was so lively when I met him. I guess I met him before, and it kills me that I don't remember all of these people I was supposedly friends with. It's terrifying. The truth is insanity, yet it's painful not to remember.

Everything in me says not to let them leave without me, but that's also the screw that is totally loose in my head. Or is it this attraction? Bond? Thing? I feel towards Killian and Rodan. Which is crazy, in my mind, we just met a few days ago. I was also a hostage recently, yet somehow, I just feel safe with these two. I need to talk to a therapist because there is definitely something wrong in my brain. This is not normal. But then again, they have fangs and pointy ears; nothing is normal anymore.

I take a deep breath and look up into the tree branches again. A bird flits about, jumping from one branch to another. The green of spring is well underway, and tiny buds sprout from the barren limbs.

Rodan hands me my mug, the rich aroma invigorating. Standing beside me, he absentmindedly runs his fingers over my shoulder.

"Thank you," I murmur.

He nods as he sips from his mug. The other night, he filled me in on things he'd told me in the past. I guess he was a jerk when we met, but eventually, he came clean with his feelings. It's strange to have someone lay themselves bare for you; his past is heartbreaking. It tears me up inside that I remember so little, like peeking through cracks in a wall. I can see it in his eyes; he hides how this affects him, but it's there—the sorrow of his broken heart like a siren call to my soul.

Now, his home world is in shambles, and they have to go back, but I don't know what I will do. Do I stay here and try to rebuild some semblance of a life? I'd forever be looking over my shoulder for a threat hiding in the shadows. Or do I try going with them, following this pull I feel towards them? If things go wrong, I may not be able to come back. Can I trust myself to make the right decision here?

"Talk to me; what's going on in that head of yours, Trouble?"

"Nothing."

Liar.

Gripping my hair, he gently pulls my head back until my eyes meet his. He narrows his eyes at me, and my stomach flips a little. "What's wrong, Trouble?"

"Everything?" I squeak out. "My psycho ex held me hostage. Apparently, I'm practically married to two men, and your country is under siege. Let's see, my best friend staged a coup to set me up with the guys who kidnapped me. And I think I will need a bigger cup of coffee."

He lifts an eyebrow. "Maybe you've had enough coffee if all that is running through your head."

I gape at him. "Never."

A grin tugs at one side of his face. "Maybe I should distract you so you stop worrying so much, Wife." He leans down, breath tickling my lips.

My pulse quickens as I inhale sharply. "Don't call me that." My voice is breathier than I intend it to be.

He huffs a laugh before claiming my mouth. Wrapping his hands around my face, his kiss is devouring, deep, and delicious. My head spins as my body responds to his touch.

He pulls away almost as suddenly as he began, with a self-satisfied smirk. He turns back towards the street, like nothing ever happened, while I try to calm the thunder in my veins.

Damn him.

"Why is a cop parked down the street? It wasn't there when I went inside." Rodan's brow furrows as he looks at me.

I glance down the road, see the familiar vehicle, and shrug. "Maybe someone called them, maybe they live around here, maybe they are taking a break. Who knows? I wouldn't worry about it."

A low growl rumbles through Rodan's chest, and I look up at him, a little alarmed. "What did you say your ex-father-in-law did for a living?"

No, he wouldn't…Panic sears through me, and I tremble as I stand to get a better look. It is not a local police unit, but that doesn't mean they don't live around here. Movement catches my eye in the driver's seat as sunlight glints off blonde hair and the unmistakable San Francisco Police Department logo as the door opens.

The world goes silent, and ringing fills my ears. I can't get enough oxygen to fill my lungs. My insides turn hollow as my stomach drops.

"No," I whisper. On shaky legs, I spin and trip over a tree root in my attempt to run. Rodan catches me before I smash my face, sweeping me into his arms and carrying me inside.

Chapter 23
Rodan

She clings to me for dear life as I enter the living room. The sour scent of fear is so potent I can almost taste it. I'm torn between comforting her and destroying the person who's put her in this state.

Clair puts down her coffee, a crease of concern across her brow. "What happened?"

Trouble sniffs as silent tears run down her face. "Ace's father is outside." Her heart is racing as I hold her close to me, panic written all over her features. "I don't want to talk to him again. I don't think I can hold it together." Her breathing turns rapid as she attempts to pull in air.

"Rodan, go sit down with her; I'll handle Mark. Not every day needs to be a strong day, honey. It's okay to fall apart sometimes, and it's okay to be scared," Clair instructs.

I open my mouth to protest, but she glares and points to the sofa. Do all moms have that look? Because our mom looks exactly the same when she's not going to put up with our shit.

I sit as instructed with a huff and hold her tight. "Breathe Trouble, focus on my voice and breathe. I won't let anything happen to you. If I didn't think your mom would murder me, I'd just kill him for you."

A muffled laugh escapes her. She pulls away from my chest and looks up at me with watery eyes. "My mom won't murder you."

"But she could, and I know not to pick battles I can't win."

With a very distinct eye roll, she turns her face back into my chest, inhaling deeply. I hate that she's been so tortured by this world that she feels this way. I want to smooth away the panic and take it from her. She's strong, though. I've seen her swallow and stuff down the anxiety, but today, I'll help bear the burden. I'll take any reason I can get to hold her like this. She is my star in the darkness. I only wish I were the same for her.

There's a hard knock on the door. Clair smooths down her shirt as she moves to open it, but a shirtless Killian bolts out of the hallway, grinning from ear to ear.

Fuck.

He puts his hand on the doorknob before Clair can stop him and yanks it open, leaning against the doorframe. "Why hello there, nice to see you again."

This is going to be a clusterfuck.

Clair clears her throat and lifts a frustrated brow at Killian. "What do you want, Mark?"

"Hello, Clair. I need to speak with your daughter."

"Yeah, that's not going to happen. So thanks for stopping by," Killian says with that cocky grin playing across his mouth.

I almost snort a laugh. Mark's face stays neutral but turns a little pink. Be careful, buddy; that one has anger issues.

Clair sighs. "As you well know, Jade and Ace are divorced now. I see nothing else that would warrant her attention. Please stop harassing her and leave my family alone."

"I want to talk to her. That's all." Mark's tone gets annoyed, and anger simmers under the surface of that calm facade.

"Nope," Killian chimes in. "She doesn't have to talk to anyone, least of all you."

Trouble shakes a little in a silent giggle. I think she might be enjoying this. Thankfully, she's hidden enough by the back of the couch that Mark can't see her, but I sure can see him from over my shoulder. The red is creeping up his neck.

"I thought she'd like to know that Ace is missing," Mark growls, raising his voice.

No shit.

"I'm sorry to hear that; thanks for letting us know," Clair says.

"I know that little girl, and these assholes have something to do with it. I'm taking her in for questioning. Now let me in."

Fuck.

There went that calm demeanor; his patience snapped. He will have to prise her out of my cold, dead arms; even then, I won't let him touch her. Jade curls up tighter in my lap, shrinking in on herself. I tighten my grip on her and stroke her hair.

"Mark, unless you have a warrant and proof, you will do no such thing. Now, please get off my property and stop harassing my children." Clair keeps her tone calm, but her posture is stiff. I have to admire the way she sticks up for her family.

"Nice to see you, Mark. Don't hesitate to drive off a bridge before your next visit." Killian smiles as he slams the door in Mark's fuming face.

Clair smacks at Killian's arms as he dances away, calling abuse. "You think she's trouble? What about him!" She looks pointedly at me, and I shrug.

"Ace is missing? God, how dumb do they think I am? It's just another manipulation to draw me out." Trouble grumbles as she sits up, shifting in my lap.

I scratch my head and look at Killian; his grimace says everything. "So about that..." I start, my heart rate ramping up. Fuck me. "He's missing because he's dead. I mean, they'll never find him. But..."

Her eyes grow wide. Ah, shit, she's not happy. We may have fucked up.

"Oh. Okay." She blinks.

Killian and I wait with bated breath while Trouble and Clair process this bit of information.

"You can't stay here. Mark will never let this go," Clair says, sinking into a chair. "He knows you were the last person to see him alive in that terrible house." A tear slips from her eye as she turns to Killian. "You bring her back for Christmas and birthdays. I get those." Her resolute tone leaves nothing for discussion.

"Mom!"

"I'm serious. You have to go. He'll have you locked up with planted evidence. I can't bear to let that happen to you again."

Thunder pounds through my ears as I wait, not daring to speak or breathe.

"There are four of you; you can protect my girls. Here, I'm powerless to protect them from Mark. I trust that even in war, they will be safer with you. Am I wrong?"

"Seriously, Mom?" Trouble gets up and paces, running her hand down her face. That spark of fire ignited in her that I love so much.

"Yes. Do you want to go to jail?" Clair glares.

Trouble stops, the wind knocked out of her sails. "No." She whispers as her lip wobbles. I want to kiss that wobble away, but she's still looking a bit stabby.

Killian pulls her into a hug and nuzzles her hair. "It's okay. I was planning on kidnapping you anyway." She attempts to push him away with a scowl painted across her features.

I plant my face in my hand, shaking it. "You weren't supposed to tell her." I don't have to look up to know her ire is pointed at me now. *I'll take your fire, Trouble, even if it guts me.*

"It's not exactly kidnapping if you already have the parents' permission. Kind of a gray area, really." Clair muses. We'd discussed this with her parents, who agreed that she should return with us. Mainly so we could find a way to restore her memories, but also because I'm a selfish prick who refuses to leave her side.

"Oh, so you're all just deciding everything for me now? This is ridiculous. God, I have the worst taste in men!" Trouble breaks free of Killian and stalks down the hallway. Killian's low whine mimics my sorrow. He slumps into a chair with a look of despair.

"Don't worry, she'll come around." Clair gives us both pitying looks.

It was the last thing we wanted to do, but we didn't want to leave her behind. With Mark sniffing around, she isn't safe here anymore. I just hope she can forgive us.

Chapter 24
Jade

Son of a bitch, that sucked.

I lay in the cool grass, trying to get the nausea to settle and the world to come back into focus. Branches stretch towards the unnaturally blue sky. I'm momentarily awed by the enormous moon framed by trees. From this vantage point, I assume we landed in a forest, but who knows? Cat dry heaves on her knees beside me, her wavy hair puddling on the ground.

Killian kneels beside me. "Are you okay?" Concern creases his features as he looks down at me, tentatively pushing strands of hair from my face.

"You are a traitor."

Cat laughs dryly as she stands on shaky legs. "Don't worry. I've been labeled that many times and come back from it."

"You're still on my shit list, missy," I groan as I bat away Killian's hand and try to sit up.

Killian gives me a weak smile and steps back. Guilt washes over me; none of this is really their fault, but I'm salty I wasn't left with any other options. Once again, I've been dragged here against my will. While curious, I would have liked to have made the decision myself. Mom wasn't wrong. I was up shit creek without a paddle, and this was the best solution, but they don't need to know that. I refuse to be a pushover anymore, so I'll let them think I'm more pissed about this than I really am. Am I scared shitless? Abso-fucking-lutely.

Rodan stands on the opposite side of Killian with an infuriating smirk on his face. Warrick and Ryker look off into the woods, swords slack at their sides. The small circle of trees blocks the view of where we are, not that I would know.

Cat snickers as she pulls me to my feet. "I don't think I'll ever get used to those portals. When we returned to the mortal world, I didn't feel sick at all. Stupid portal."

"Where is the camp?" Rodan glances at Warrick quickly, keeping his eyes on the surrounding forest.

"I need to ensure no one has discovered us; then I'll lead. Ryker, are you able to transform?" Warrick asks.

Ryker gives a curt nod before feathers burst into existence, and a beautiful speckled black-and-white falcon flies above us. I gasp, and my jaw hangs open as I try to make sense of the large man becoming so compact. By no means is he a small bird, but the math isn't mathing. He soars above the canopy of trees, graceful and majestic, breathtaking.

"Cool, right?" Cat says in awe.

"Holy shit," I murmur. We are definitely not in our world. My doubt about their stories has just gone up in a plume of feathers. A low growl behind me has the hair on the back of my neck stand on end. I slowly turn, and a whimper escapes me. Bright green eyes blink at me from midnight fur. I suck in a breath and pull Cat's arm into me.

A nearby howl has me frozen in place. I don't take my eyes off the panther. We are deep in the woods with god knows what wild animals surrounding us, and now we will be lunch. What the fuck was I thinking coming here?

A golden wolf catches my eye right before it collides with the panther, taking it to the ground with a huff. They snarl and roll as they each fight for dominance. It's a blur of black and gold as their heavy paws clash with each other's faces.

Cat giggles as she watches. "I think they are happy to be home. I didn't realize Rodan was a panther; he's so cute."

Scanning the clearing, Warrick looks as amused as Cat, but Rodan and Killian are strangely absent. I let out a deep breath, jarred by the realization. They are wrestling. They aren't trying to hurt each other. I guess I wasn't ready to see them this way. I should have known after Ryker turned that Rodan and Killian were telling me the truth, but hearing it and seeing it are two completely different things. "They definitely left out the part that they are enormous."

Cat bursts into laughter. "Not sure how you'd miss that when they rocked your world."

Warrick's booming laugh follows as my cheeks heat. Yeah, I walked right into that one.

Rodan and Killian stop their tussle and lock eyes with me. The golden wolf tilts his head while he lies atop the panther. I feel my flush spread down my body under their stare. There's no chance they missed that, huh?

Killian stomps on Rodan's stomach and then prances over to me, sits, and looks at me with big puppy eyes as his tongue lolls out the side of his mouth. It's endearing how puppy-like his wolf is.

Rodan's graceful movements are those of a predator. He makes no sound as he slinks up next to me, rubbing his back against my side, and wraps his tail around me. Was I used to this? Because I just don't see that happening. I mean, a guy I had sex with a few days ago is a wolf right now. I'm not going to think about what that makes me. Granted, I'm supposedly an otter, so how does that work? Nope, let's not go down that rabbit hole.

"You could have warned me before you turned...instead of scaring the shit out of me." I chastise Rodan.

He looks at me with innocent eyes as he snaps his teeth together, so close to my hand I feel his hot breath ghost my fingertips. I pull my hand up and watch his fur twitch and shake across his back. Is this motherfucker laughing?

I sneer at him and lean down to pet Killian; his eyes light up, and before I can stop him, his tongue laps up the side of my face. Yep, should have known better.

I laugh, "Seriously, Killian?"

"Stay between them on the path. Their heightened senses in this form should keep us from getting ambushed. Ryker just gave me the signal that it's all clear. Cat, I don't need any of your crazy animals right now, so please stay huma-fae," Warrick says, giving us pointed looks as he leads us deeper into the woods.

"Another portal?" I whine. Something about this place gives me a strange sense of déjà vu.

"It's the only place we can't be tracked. The wards around this clearing make it nearly impossible to find us. If anyone were following us, the magic of this place would lead them on a wild-goose chase. However, we are not fully safe until we enter the Grove of Fate. It's thanks to you and Killian that we even found the portal. Your notebooks had just enough for us to follow." Warrick says, walking up to the oval mirror-like structure.

Notebooks I don't remember writing, but Warrick read? God, I hope I didn't put anything embarrassing in them. Knowing me, I did.

"We get to see the Fates?" Cat's excitement is palpable as Ryker lands on her shoulder.

"It's not as great as you'd think; they are...eccentric, to say the least," Warrick says.

"You mean they only speak in riddles," Rodan growls as he slips a hand around my waist, making me jump in surprise. I was getting used to his silent presence behind me, the predator stalking my steps these last few hours. I stiffen my spine in my best attempt to stop myself from melting into his warm embrace.

Killian makes a yip sound before barreling through the portal, disappearing into its mirrored surface.

"Every damn time," Rodan grumbles.

Warrick extends his hand to Cat as she goes up the three steps, guiding her through and leaving me alone in the clearing with Rodan. Dusk is fast approaching, and I hope this means we are almost there.

"You act like you don't like it when I touch you." He purrs in my ear. The heat of his breath sends shivers down my body.

I pull away from him and saunter toward the portal, pushing down the queasiness that fills me as I look at it. I'm not very fond of portals. "Well, I don't really like guys who kidnap me so—"

His hands encircle my waist, spinning me to meet his smoldering eyes as I lose my balance in his hold. He slowly lays me down on the stone step, filling my vision with only him—my pulse racing as he consumes all the air around me. The shock of cold rock beneath my back contrasts with the warmth he radiates as he hovers above me. I gasp as he pins my hands to my sides.

Leaning into my neck, his breath tickles my nerves as he inhales deeply, and an overwhelming desire to pull him closer overtakes me. "You always protest what you want, but your body doesn't lie. Not to me." His low, sensual voice resonates through my bones. He leans back, capturing me with his mesmerizing gaze. Gently, he pulls my arms above my head, pinning them with one hand and causing my back to arch over the steps. His other hand traces down my arm and side, almost tickling with its delicate path, landing on and gripping my hip.

All I can do is breathe and try to glare at him, but god, I don't want him to stop. His eyes dilate as he watches me, and his grin grows vicious, a hint of one fang sparkling in the dying light.

"You seem awfully sure of yourself," I chide, or try to. It comes out much breathier than intended. Damn him.

"I don't see you fighting it."

And...he's got me there. I am not fighting it. At all. It would take nothing to break the light hold he has on me. I should hate this, but I'm so turned on by it, I don't know what to do. How does he do this to me? He did this in my dreams, and I woke up hot, bothered, and just as confused as I am now. I still don't understand why my memories feel like hazy dreams, glimpses of my past through frosted glass.

My lips part to protest, but nothing comes out; all I can think about is the man on his knees between my legs, holding me down. How did I even end up in this position?

His mouth presses firmly into mine, and my racing thoughts turn to smoke. Every nerve in my body is alight as we connect. He tastes like sin and danger, like a terrible decision waiting to happen, and in this moment, I'm here for it.

A growl rumbles through him as I try to arch into him, his firm grip on my hip holding me down. He is the calm before the storm, the smell of ozone before the rain, and the lightning that crackles through my veins. He deepens the kiss as I fall into the oblivion that is his touch. I want to feel his body pressed against mine. I arch again, furious that I can't have more.

Breaking the kiss, he lets my hands go and stands, holding out a hand to help me up. I lay across the steps, bewildered, as I stare at his offered hand. "What the hell?"

"Just wanted to prove a point. Come on, we don't want to keep them waiting."

With a huff, I scowl at him and pull myself to my feet, pushing his hand away. I smooth down my hair and take a deep breath as I turn to face the portal. I guess if I ever want to see my backpack again, I need to go through it; damn Killian for running ahead.

I step into the swirling vortex of doom and get shot out the other side, stumbling to my knees onto grass overlooking a cliff. The sky is clear and sunny, hours from the dusk we left behind. Is it another realm? Dimension? I'm so lost.

"Come on, Trouble. They must have gone ahead of us. It's not far from here." His arms sweep under mine and lift me onto shaky legs. I stumble across the small clearing to the path in the trees, looking like a baby deer learning to walk. Yeah, I hate portals.

The cobbled path leads us into more trees, mushrooms popping up every so often to enjoy the dappled light. Rodan, to his credit, remains infuriatingly silent as we walk.

A squeal has me stop dead in my tracks as a beautiful brunette woman comes careening out of the trees and crashes into me, wrapping her arms around my shoulders. My face collides with her collarbone, softened only by the burgundy scarf that drapes down from her head. She pulls away, keeping her hands on my shoulders, her deep chocolate eyes alight with glee. "Oh heavens, sugar, I didn't think I'd ever see you again." The bright smile on her face brings a shy smile to mine. "Oh, pardon, I heard you don't remember nothin', but we were great friends, and I'm sure we will be again." She grabs my hand and pulls me along after her. Shock has me following her like a lost puppy. "So much has happened since you left. It's downright terrible. Home was a'callin' my name, but I couldn't just let y'all fend for yourselves. It's been like a wolf at a raccoon party round here."

Lyra eventually introduces herself and prattles on in her southern twang, which I did not see coming. Her long, coppery gown flows around her lithe legs as she walks. She is exactly what I'd picture Princess Jasmine to look like in real life.

"Why would you stay if things are so dangerous?"

"Let's just say my father's council would just bury their heads in the sand and pretend nothing was happening if I returned. Then, they'd act surprised when that dishonorable sorcerer appeared on our doorstep."

"So you're holding yourself hostage?"

She laughs and grabs my hand, squeezing it. "It's what Arlin would have done. She was to me what Cat is to you. Always wantin' to help people and have fun doin' it. It's why I stayed after...She would have wanted me to keep going, for her." She sighs. "I miss that girl, but every time I think about going home and throwing in the towel, I hear her telling me to fae up and stop being a baby."

I lift an eyebrow. "Mourning someone doesn't make you a baby."

"Of course not, sugar. But stopping your life when they'd want you to continue isn't healthy. She'd have told me not to be afraid to live my life. So here I am, living it. I get so tired of always being afraid of things. But Arlin, she was brave and, if she saw a way, would dive in head first...I want to be more like her."

"I understand that."

We reach the end of the path to a large clearing filled with small tents and the tallest trees I've ever seen shading the area. My breath catches as I see the trees move, and I take in the details. They are not trees, not really, but very naked, very attractive women. Well, that's something you don't see every day.

Lyra pulls me over to a fire surrounded by women, one of whom is teal. I find Cat in the mix and focus on her, so I don't gawk. Cat makes room on a log for Lyra and me to sit beside her. As I'm introduced to everyone, sadness and pity reflect at me from their faces. I feel exposed; all these people I'd known are strangers to me now.

"The pixies should be returning soon with more news of the castle," Corsac says, her voice tinged with anticipation. She has short, curly hair that reminds me of milk chocolate. Freckles dapple her rich brown skin. Scarlette sits between her legs and entwines their arms. Her long red hair cascades down her shoulders as Corsac nuzzles into it.

"I should have known Beatrix was up to something. I hate that she spelled me into forgetting she was the princess. She's such a rotten person," Scarlette fumes.

The teal woman, Yudoku, sneers, showing off pointed teeth.

"Let's not forget that freshwater scum that helped orchestrate this bullshit." Her shimmering, light teal hair falls around her face as she pulls at the grass in front of her.

"I'm still not convinced you had nothing to do with it." Scarlette mumbles.

Yudoku's head snaps up as she levels Scarlette in her glare. "Says the one from the same kingdom as Beatrix."

"Enough," Corsac interjects. "We can go around in circles on this all we want, but I don't think anyone here is helping Ellis. We all barely escaped with our lives. Shit, Jade just got back and has had her memory completely fucked by whatever he did to her."

Yudoku stands grimacing. She brushes dirt and grass from her lavender skirt and looks at me. "I'm going to the pond. Glad to see you are alive, Jade."

The chatter continues as I watch the dejected woman push her way through the circle of men talking at the other end of the clearing. She hisses at them as she walks. I slip away from the chatter and follow her, keeping a wary eye on the three tree women watching me with interest, their stares making the little hairs on my arms stand on end. The fates are unnerving, but I guess if they are allowing us to stay here, they must be nice. Just beyond them are some tiny cottages. A little farther off is a small pond that ripples in an unnatural breeze.

Yudoku sits and puts her feet in the water. "What do you want, mortal?" She doesn't look my way as scales rush from her waist down her legs. Within seconds, her lower half is a beautiful array of teal, violet, and black scales. I hold back the shock and keep my face impassive as I watch the mermaid sun herself on the shore before me.

"I'm not sure," I say honestly.

She grumbles something under her breath. "Well, come on, get in."

I sit on the edge of the water beside her, pulling off my shoes and rolling up my pant legs. "I'm sorry. I don't know why I followed you."

"To answer your questions- no, we weren't friends. I keep to myself. I never wanted to come here in the first place. Yes, I'm a siren."

I keep my features neutral as I listen, a little shocked by her curtness. "Okay, I'm super overwhelmed by everything. My ex-husband kidnapped me. Now I'm mated to two fae I barely know, who also just so happened to kidnap me. I just walked into another realm, knowing there is a war happening, and met a siren."

Her eyes crinkle into a genuine smile. "I like you better when you are honest with yourself."

"Do sirens actually lure sailors to their death?"

"Yes, if they are in our territory. Not the scrawny ones or the young. Usually, we drag down the strong ones who think too highly of themselves. I like to watch for the moment when the light leaves their eyes, and they realize they are not as powerful as they think."

"Morbid."

She laughs and splashes her tail in the water; the spray hitting me as laughter bubbles up. "Come on, Otter, let's go for a swim."

"I don't know how to change. I don't remember." It's so frustrating that I had this whole life here that I only know bits and pieces of. How am I supposed to make decisions based on dreams?

She sighs and gives me some elementary and ridiculous instructions before diving into the water.

"You're not gonna eat me, right?" I ask as she surfaces.

Flashing me a devilish smile of razor-sharp teeth, she dives deep. Yeah, I'm going to be mermaid chow; I just know it.

I focus on the things Yudoku promised would make me change, my eyes squeezed shut. I don't know what I'm feeling for, but a small rush of sensation passes through me. Upon opening my eyes, I let out a squeak at the sight of furry, white paws instead of my hands. I am never going to get used to this.

Swimming is invigorating, the fur blocking out the cold as I cut through the water. Yudoku chases fish as I enjoy the feel of the cool pond.

When I climb out of the pond, I lie exhausted on the grassy shore and stare at the cloudless sky. When I return to myself, I'm dry except for my hair. My leggings and shirt are only slightly damp from the wet grass. Yudoku sits on the shore, sunning herself, her tail trailing in the water listlessly.

"What do you know about mates?" I ask.

"The fates weave two souls together, threads connecting them to find each other and fall in love. It's rare for someone to have two." She glances at me, her mouth in a tight line. "The only stories I've heard about two rarely have happy endings. Fae are not inclined to share."

"They don't seem too upset about sharing—"

"I heard Killian punched Rodan."

News travels fast around here. I pull my legs into a crisscross position and pick at the grass, shredding it in my fingers. "Yeah, that's true."

"From what I've observed, they are thick as thieves. Killian is naïve, a bit sheltered, and immature. But that's expected of young fae men. Rodan is a prick that I wouldn't hesitate to drown. I won't, but he's far too cocky for my taste." She wrinkles her nose as she looks out at the glittering water.

"What do you think I should do?"

"Let them in, open yourself to the bond. You'll be able to feel what they are feeling. Once you let down all the walls, you can learn to communicate down the thread. Perhaps take a few days to think it over; let them squirm a bit." Her devious smile spreads. "However, if you are apart for too long, the bond will urge you together. I've heard it can be quite unpleasant."

"Is that what that hollow pain was? It felt like my chest was burning, and then they showed up, and it stopped. I thought it was just relief from being rescued."

"Probably." She shrugs.

"Why do the others avoid you?" I ask tentatively, not wanting to upset her.

Her tail twitches in the water as her body grows tense. "Owari betrayed them, that freshwater caulerpa. She's the other siren from Illa who came here. Even though we are from different kingdoms, we are from the same country. Now, they distrust my motives. Like I'd help that Unseelie scum; we have enough problems in court without getting involved with sorcery."

"Well, I believe you, for what it's worth."

Her scales fold back into her skin, and she stands. "One of your idiots is coming. I'm going back to camp. Swim with me tomorrow after training. The fish here are rather dull to talk to, and I don't hate your company." She glides into the trees as gracefully as she swims, disappearing behind their thick trunks.

I watch the still water as the scent of rain washes over me. I don't turn as I sense Rodan approaching. He doesn't need to know about the butterfly frenzy going on inside me.

"You shouldn't be out here alone." He says as he comes to a stop next to me.

"I wasn't alone. You scared off my company with your ego." I say, examining a flat white rock.

He sits gracefully next to me, looking out over the water. "Do you plan to start a fight every time I talk to you?"

"Do you plan to kidnap me at every opportunity?"

"Yes." He grins.

I gape at his audacity. He is so absurd I almost laugh. "See, this is why Killian is the better choice; he wouldn't do that."

"I've already told you I'm never letting you go. I'm just waiting for you to catch up again. As for Killian, it was his idea the first time and the second that we brought you here. My hands are clean on that front, Trouble."

Of course, Killian is responsible. My heart swells at his words, but I tamp it down deep. I'm not letting him off the hook that easily. "Stop calling me that."

"Never." He smirks. "Unless you prefer I call you wife? That has a nice ring to it."

"No," I growl.

I understand we had something—have something I can't deny. Then I rushed things with Killian because I wanted to forget my problems for a little while. Now, I'm utterly confused.

"I know you think I'm a jerk most of the time. I show my dark side, but Killian keeps a tight leash on his."

"What do you mean?"

He sighs, raking a hand through his hair. "It's in our fae nature. We are not exactly inherently good, and he is better at hiding it. He's a wolf. He has worked hard his entire life to keep it leashed. When he bit you, that was his control slipping. The wolf inside needing to claim what's his."

"Like he has two personalities?" I raise an eyebrow.

He laughs. "No, not at all. He just fights his instincts and occasionally loses the battle. I don't fight mine. Well, except when it came to you, I did fight that for all the good it did me." His face falls, and he throws a rock across the water. "Killian has a heart of gold and wants everyone to be happy. He is so determined to fix everything that his wolf nature gets in the way. So he keeps it locked away. But with you, the wolf comes out. He is just as possessive as I am."

"And with everything in the kingdom going to hell..." I muse.

"He's losing his battle. I understood it when we were kids: the wolf was volatile and dangerous. But now I think he needs to learn to embrace his fae nature and let it be a part of him."

"Do you really intend to share me? Wouldn't that go against your nature?"

"Do you have a better solution, Trouble? Want to make us duel for your hand?"

I giggle at the ridiculous idea. "No, that's not necessary. You have bad choices written all over you. Killian is the kind of guy I should be with."

He lifts a brow and leans in to me so close his breath tickles my lips. "Is that so?"

"Yes," I squeak out.

"Tell me how you really feel." His gravelly voice sends shivers down to my lower stomach. "Or let me worship you. Fuck, let both of us. I don't care. I'll be here whether or not you ever let me touch you again. You're mine, and I'll let the whole world crack and burn for you if that's what it takes." His eyes darken as they peer into my soul. It takes everything I have not to melt into him. How can I possibly be falling for this man when I hardly know him? My heart thuds so hard against my ribs, I'm sure he can hear it.

"I just need space to think," I say, straightening my spine and looking towards the water.

"Then I'll give you space and something to think about."

I look at him with my brows pinched as his hand snakes into my hair and pulls my head back. His lips find mine, and I gasp. The cells in my body light up, and the bond thrums with approval as his tongue finds mine. I greedily kiss him in return as my mind goes blank and I fall into the moment.

He releases my hair and leans away with a self-satisfied smirk. My back is on the grass again. I pant as my chest heaves for air, and I ache for more.

Damn him.

"Find me when you're ready for more."

He walks off toward the camp as I pull myself back together. I stand, clutching the smooth rock in my hand. I fling it at the water and watch it skip across the surface, leaving ripples in its wake.

God, it's like he has two modes: sweet and infuriating. And some sick, twisted part of me is seriously attracted to both. I throw up my hands in surrender and vow to avoid both men until I figure my shit out.

Chapter 25
Killian

It feels great to have my powers back; I hate running on so little. It's been a week of planning and letting the injured heal from the battle at the castle. So few escaped the onslaught. Scarlette and Corsac mourn Fennec, who is unaccounted for. Lyra's bodyguard, Darius, has barely let her out of his sight. Yudoku has mostly kept to herself, but seems to have warmed up to Jade, as much as that unnerves Rodan and me.

The fates rarely speak to us, just observing our comings and goings. They shrink down at dusk and disappear into their small cottages, only to reemerge at dawn and stretch out to enjoy the sun. Gods, I wish they'd give us some clues. It's always *the path will deviate if interference is given.* Whatever the hell that's supposed to mean. They won't even tell me if I'm on the right path with Jade; they just smile and wink. I will take that as a good sign, even if Jade still seems distant.

I want to fix things so badly, but Cat says to give her space to process everything. I am trying, but I just want to hug her and cuddle the worries right out of her.

The pixies Juniper and Nucifera returned with news from the castle. Their small size easily went unnoticed by whatever creatures guarded Ellis. The pixies have lost their spark; misery taints their bubbly personalities.

Owari has been keeping the council under her spell while the Orbs drain them dry, day after day. Beatrix orders people around as if she were queen. Apparently, the two occasionally clash, but mostly avoid each other.

Ellis brings in more of his constructs every day, building his army. However, no one knows where he is creating them. Juniper managed to steal a notebook full of plans to take over the whole of Auburnigh. He plans to start by overthrowing Light and placing Beatrix there to hold the kingdom, which I don't get. She was already the crown princess, so why take it by force?

There are minor mentions of Shadow, but none of us can figure out why. The kingdom is dead. No one lives there anymore. However, the pieces are falling into place. Light was responsible for Shadow's curse, and in turn, responsible for Amara's. Thus, Ellis has been behind everything. But why? Why act now? After all this time, what is so different?

My parents stay locked in their tower, protected by the wards. The pixies were unable to get close but thought they spotted Lorelai through a window. At least someone is looking after them.

Gods, this is such a mess.

"I can't believe you'd drag me out to ask me that at dawn," Cat hisses as she stomps past my tent, pulling my attention from my thoughts. "You know how I feel about commitment."

Oh boy, here they go again. She runs so hot and cold on Ryker, it's almost comical.

"You can deny your feelings all you want, but you are mine," Ryker grumbles. "Or are you still hung up on finding a vampire?"

"Those were just books! Oh my god, Ryker, give it a rest."

"I'll give you a bite you won't forget," Ryker says. "See, you like the idea. I can smell it on you, and your heart rate just picked up." His tone has gone gravelly. "Come back to my tent, and I'll have you begging for it."

"Caveman," she says incredulously.

"If I were a caveman, I'd tie you up and keep you in my tent till you loved me."

"You...you—"

"Like that idea, do you?" he growls.

And I'm done eavesdropping. It's so obvious that Cat is in love with him, but he keeps pushing, and she's stubborn.

Jade trains with me again every morning, a routine I cherish, but still keeps me at arm's length. She fights the bond tooth and nail, which is adorable. I can see how hard it is for her to stay mad at me. Still, she's the bright spot in this bleak reality.

"Stop eavesdropping on Ryker. He's an idiot," Rodan grumbles as he turns over in his bed. Our sleeping arrangements are less than ideal: a pile of soft moss and blankets Juniper made. It's comfortable, but I miss my bed.

"I'm not." I glare at him.

"You are, and I can hear you stewing in thought. It's too early for that."

"I'm trying to figure out how a handful of us will win against an army. Dad would know what to do."

"First of all—" Rodan throws the covers off, getting out of bed. "We just have to kill Ellis. The army will fall if he does. Second, we keep spying until the pixies find a weak spot in their defenses. There is always a weakness to exploit."

"Ah, like yesterday when Jade threw a pine cone at your head? You were distracted by Darius, and she exploited that." I grin, remembering how good her aim was.

Rodan glares as blue sparks dance up his arms. "Trouble is a deviant and will be punished for that."

I laugh. He won't touch a hair on her head. The big baby is just embarrassed that she nailed him. I absolutely would never, ever put that idea in her head.

"Well, let's round everyone up. We need to discuss plans of

action before I work with Jade on her powers," I say. She may have accidentally frozen the pond yesterday while swimming with Yudoku. It's a good thing the siren had the power to undo it before Jade froze or drowned. I'm a little worried about what got her so frazzled that her powers surged like that in the first place.

"I still think you and me should simply go in there and kill Ellis. It'd be quick. I'd latch onto his nervous system, and you'd make him combust. Done."

I scrunch my nose in disgust. "That can be plan B."

Lyra makes a large arc with her staff as Darius dodges with grace. He is a tall, narrow man, but no less powerful than the rest of us. Sweat slightly slicks down his short-cropped hair as he weaves around her. She puts all the force of her rage behind the strikes that he narrowly avoids. The way they work together flows like water. I'm unsure why I never noticed before, but his presence near her is possessive. I guess it would be since he's her bodyguard and all.

Jade sips water from a stone mug as she watches them spar. Her gaze travels between Lyra and Cat. Cat is trying to learn to wield her water magic, but can only manage a small ball before she blinks it out of existence. Unfortunately, she's having much more luck sucking water out of things than manipulating it. A lizard was her first victim, and she was beside herself over it. Hence, the reason Yudoku and Nucifera are now assisting her.

Jade sneaks off with Yudoku every afternoon to swim. Yudoku snarls at anyone who tries to join them. I wasn't going to do anything; I just wanted to see Jade's cute little otter swim.

Warrick sits with Alvar, Juniper, and Ambrose, still trying to devise a plan. Alvar is all that's left of Warrick's guard unit. Ambrose was an accountant at the treasury. Fifteen of us against Ellis and his horde—the odds don't look great for us.

Scarlette throws knives at a makeshift target while Corsac stabs another with deadly precision with her ghostly tails. I did not know the fox was that fierce, and I am glad I'm not on the receiving end. They are both formidable fighters, and their skill shows. They break and embrace each other warmly. Scarlette pulls Corsac into a deep kiss, so I turn my attention. They are so affectionate; it's cute, but I think they'd be rolling in the grass if they were alone.

"I feel so useless; everyone else has trained their whole lives. I can barely swing a sword," Jade grumbles as she turns back towards me.

"That's why you have me, to protect you."

"But I want to help. There has to be something I can do. I can't just hide here forever."

"You're not hiding; you are training. Your ability to defend yourself is greater than you think. You got away from Bravos and beat the hell out of your ex."

"Who's Bravos?" she asks.

"You don't want to know. An asshole who deserved what he got." I beam at her as she takes a fighting stance. She may not remember, but her body does.

We go through the movements slowly, like a dance, as she gets used to the rhythm and anticipates my moves. She's improved so much since she stopped overthinking everything. My heart swells as I see her grow into herself. She perfectly times each jab and thrust, swinging and stepping with nearly perfect posture. Despite her captivity making her too thin, her muscles have become stronger. It's clear from her movements that she was working on staying strong. She is so beautiful.

Unfortunately, she still can't summon her powers at will. It makes no sense; they surge when she's stressed and then vanish like they never existed. Gods, I could really use Mom's advice.

Everyone has pitched in to explain how our powers work and how to wield them. She understands the concept clearly, but the well of power is just beyond her reach. She gathers all the information like a sponge, asks questions, and learns what she can. It's incredible watching how her mind works. She will undoubtedly be a formidable foe once she can grasp her power.

As Cat's powers continue to grow, it's becoming increasingly evident that she inherited a royal line of power. Jade being of the same bloodline and unable to control her powers is confusing, to say the least. That level of power will also need to be addressed when this is all over. I'm sure it will make some monarchs around Auburnigh uneasy. But as Dad always says: don't borrow tomorrow's problems for today, or something like that.

Jade lies in the grass, groaning that she can't move a muscle as I stand over her. "Take pity," she says. Her chest is heaving for air as she stares up at me. I'd love to take zero pity on her and kiss her senseless, but I'm not going to push her.

"Did you kill her, Killian?" Rodan says, patting me on the back.

I chuckle. "No, but she says she can't move."

"Is that so?" A dark look crosses Rodan's features as he looks at her stretched across the grass. He slides to the ground next to her, winking at me. I see the faint lines of electricity crackle along his arm before he runs his fingertips down her forearm and wrist.

She swallows and stares at Rodan as I kneel on the grass. Crawling over her legs, I straddle her thighs. Her eyes grow wide as we close in on her. The sweet smell of cinnamon dances through the air as I reach for her other arm and run heat through her tired muscles.

"What are you–" she stops and moans as we work the tension out of her body in tandem. We roll her onto her front, and Rodan switches positions with me. He releases the tight muscles of her back as I heat them into submission.

"You two are making it really hard to stay mad at you," she groans, melting into butter.

One day, she will forgive us for pushing her too fast and

kidnapping her. This is step one of my plan: get her so tired she can't move, and then we fix it as only we can. I'm still working on step two. And step three is a little sketchy, with this war looming. For now, I need her to stop being mad at us.

"Feeling better, Trouble?" Rodan says as he leans closer and licks her ear.

She sucks in a sharp breath and pulls herself forward and out from under Rodan. I chuckle silently as I watch her crawl on her belly and then jump to her feet. "Yep, thanks, guys. I'm gonna go...over there and see what's for dinner." She points to an area in the opposite direction from the food and tents. Pink flushes her cheeks, she spins around, and runs toward the actual camp.

"Damn it, she's still mad," I pout.

"No, she's not. She is trying to stay mad at us. It's damn cute to watch her try."

"Why is this so hard to fix?"

"Because she's scared. You would be too in her position."

I sigh, "True."

"If you're that worried about it, just kiss her and see how she reacts. It will tell you a lot."

"For the record, that's what the pine cone was for..." A long silence passes before we burst into laughter.

Chapter 26
Jade

"I don't know if I like this plan," Corsac says.

"Well, it's the only plan we've got." Juniper stirs the fire with a long stick. Alvar places another log and pulls the petite pixie into his lap. She is all sharp features on a tiny frame, with hair the color of evergreens. Alvar, on the other hand, is taller than Killian and just as muscled; his ebony skin contrasts sharply with Juniper's almost translucency. She cuddles into his warmth as we prep food for dinner. The fire crackles in the fading light. The cedar scent reminds me of camping with my parents and roasting marshmallows back when life was less complicated.

Amber light dances along the tops of the trees as the sun sinks below the horizon. Warm hues blanket the lush green field. The fire casts shadows across the faces of my friends as we contemplate the day's events.

I watch Yudoku carefully set up her blades to gut the fish we caught in the small stream that connects to the pond we swim in. The others observe her warily as she works. No one has given her much of a chance, and that Owari chick really screwed things up for her. She is pretty awesome once you get past all the walls she has up.

Cat strips rosemary leaves from their branches and drops them into the bowl for me to crush with other herbs. We're around the fire making dinner for the group tonight. It's such a mundane act that brings a sense of normalcy.

"We need to get as many out as we can. Even if we only manage one, it's worth the risk." Scarlette says as Corsac braids her long, red hair.

The plan is dangerous but sounds doable. Thankfully, I will be a lookout, so my part is tiny. A small group will break into the dungeon through an old tunnel. It is essential to rescue as many fae as possible during a very small window of time tomorrow night. Yep, it's totally doable. There is nothing *at all* to worry about. It's not like anything could go wrong, and we all end up imprisoned. Nope, it's totally safe.

If I keep telling myself that, maybe I'll believe it.

The discussion stops cold when the youngest of the Fates sits by the fire, smiling widely at us. Her relaxed crisscross position mirrors my own. The bark of her body is smooth and bends like skin. Vines of leaves cascade down her shoulders, puddling in her lap and into the grass.

"Hi." Cat breaks the silence with a squeak.

"Hello, wild one," says the fate.

None of the Fates have joined us since we arrived. Aside from inviting us to stay as long as we needed in their home, they haven't said much to anyone. They talk in a strange language to each other and weave their odd golden threads; occasionally, glowing orbs of light flit between them. I assume they carry on much the way that they always have.

"Hey, sugar, can I ask you a question? We've all been pondering, did Killian rattle ya sisters' branches?" Lyra smirks.

I gape at her; what kind of question is that? Curiosity gets the better of me as we all lean forward for the answer. Even the brooding Darius leans in after his initial shock aimed at Lyra. I glance quickly behind me to see if Killian is out of earshot. Thankfully, he is on the other side of the field with Rodan, Warrick, and Ryker.

The fates' smile broadens as she leans in. "He did not," the Fate says. Lyra slumps, and disappointed sighs ring through the space. "But he thought about it."

Laughter erupts from the group, and a pang of jealousy rings through me. I peek over my shoulder and see Killian staring at me with worry sketched over his brows—damn bond. I have to figure out how the block on my emotions works because they seem to slip through at the most inopportune times.

Strong emotion related to him equals: he instantly knows about it. I flush and spin my attention back to the fate.

"As I told you before, you need to give them a chance to prove themselves." Fate peers at me intensely.

"We spoke before?"

"Of course, and things are as they should be." The smooth bark of her face intensifies her smug look. After days of being here, I pretty much don't even notice that they are perpetually naked. She flips her bright green leaves over a shoulder. Her hair reminds me of the branches on a weeping willow tree. Does it flower in the spring? I can picture how her beauty would be magnified by little flowers covering her hair.

"Wow, that's comforting," I say, wildly unamused. If this is exactly where I'm supposed to be, then why is everything so screwed up? Why have Killian and Rodan lost everything that matters to them? It doesn't seem fair.

"Wild one, give in to your desires soon if you want your powers to bloom," the fate says in a singsong voice, locking eyes with Cat.

Cat's face flushes red as she plays with a seam on her pants, picking at it with the bare stem in her fingers.

"I thought you weren't allowed to interfere," I say.

"I can nudge. The time is near."

For the next few minutes, everyone in the group receives cryptic messages from the Fate. Her devilish smile is haunting. I doubt anyone really understands exactly what she's saying. For a while, we all sit quietly, contemplating.

"So when are you gonna stop torturing those poor boys? They've been walkin' on eggshells trying to please you." Lyra breaks the silence. I can't help but notice Darius stealing glances at her as he sharpens his sword. She says they are just friends, but the way he looks at her tells me he wishes they were more.

I take a deep breath. "I don't want to torture them. I'm just attempting to regain some semblance of control in my life." How do I explain this? "This has all moved so fast. I needed time to think."

Cat turns towards me. "Okay, I know it feels fast, but in reality, it's been months. And don't give me that; I don't remember B.S.—we both know you dream about them. The memories aren't completely gone."

"I know, but—"

"Otter, you'd feel better if you just gave in to your feelings. It would be one less thing to worry about. You are making it more complicated than it needs to be," Yudoku pipes in from my other side. The tray of scaled fish piles up as she cleans them for dinner. She has been a good friend to lean on; her no-nonsense approach to life is refreshing. My friends are right, of course, but I don't know what to do.

Yudoku still keeps her distance from everyone most days. She sits quietly in her loneliness. I don't know that she's ever even had a genuine friend. Hearing her speak up is surprising. Scarlette and Corsac give her curious looks.

"But—"

"They went all the way to the mortal world to save you, hun," Scarlette chimes in as she cuts up mushrooms on a wooden platter.

"She has a point," Yudoku says, giving me a pointed look. It's what she tells me every day when we swim together. Knowing she's not the only one who thinks that makes my skin flush with heat.

"No one knows what tomorrow will bring," Corsac says, feeding Scarlette a piece of fruit. "Well, except her." She nods towards the fate, who lies on her stomach, kicking her feet. She watches all of us with rapt curiosity. I get the feeling they don't get a lot of visitors.

My mind goes blank as I run out of excuses. They all have valid points, but I don't see why my love life is up for debate. Granted, the topic eventually lands on someone's relationship every night. I guess tonight was my turn. It helps alleviate the underlying dread of what is to come. We can't hide here forever.

The other kingdoms are in disarray, and Warrick hasn't been able to determine when help will arrive. It seems that facing an Unseelie sorcerer is cause for panic, and fae are holding their breath that it fixes itself before it lands on their doorstep.

A warm hand settles on my shoulder, and I just about jump out of my skin as I look up into Killian's troubled eyes.

How much of that did he hear? My heart skips a beat as I study the hard lines of his face.

"Can we talk?" He whispers.

I take his offered hand and set aside the bowl of herbs I'd been smashing, walking away into the trees with him. The sun is nearly gone, but small lights pop up along the path, illuminating our way. As much as everyone reassures me we are safe here, the forest is still slightly creepy at night without the lights. However, the glowing spheres make it magical.

"I didn't think about how having all control taken from you would make you feel." While we continue walking deeper into the woods, he confesses, "I saw myself as helpful, but I only deprived you of your choices. I thought I could give you the world, but I took it away selfishly because you are my world."

"Killian…" A lump lodges in my throat as I try to speak. I've taken this too far, and now I don't know how to fix it.

"I tried to give you space, but I don't think that's helping. How can I show you how much you mean to me if I'm not around you? Every night, I want to cuddle you and tell you everything will be okay. But it's Rodan beside me, and he gets all angry and broody when I do that."

I laugh despite myself; it comes out tearful and hiccuping. I want so badly to wrap him up in my arms, but he keeps his eyes forward and focused as he speaks. I ruined everything because I was afraid. This is it, the point where I must face what I've done to destroy it all. I may have still talked to him daily at training, but we kept the whole dynamic almost businesslike. Killian, ever the gentleman, fulfilled my wishes.

"I don't want to give up on you, but I can't deal with you shutting me out." He stops, pulling me to face his tear-filled eyes. "I didn't know things would be this hard. I was naïve to believe everything would be storybook perfect."

I trace his jaw with my hand. "Oh, Killian, I'm so sorry. Please don't give up on storybook endings. They always go through hardship before the happily ever after. Please don't lose that." A sob pushes from my chest as he leans into my hand, closing his eyes. "Please don't give up on me."

His hand comes to rest on my chest, above my twisting heart. I brace myself to be pushed away, closing my eyes. My legs are seconds away from giving out on me.

"I love you." He whispers.

My eyes snap open as my heart stalls. "What?"

"I'll spend the rest of my life proving it." He wipes the tears from my cheeks and cups my face in his hands. "I'm sorry I made you feel powerless. It was wrong of me to go behind your back and force you here."

"Thank you for saying that."

"We will never force you to do something you don't want to do again. Please give us a chance. I can't breathe without you; food tastes like ash, and I love food." He pouts, and I almost laugh at his puppy-dog eyes.

"I'm sorry I pushed you away. It felt like a mistake, but I didn't know how to stop once I started. It felt like condoning the behavior, and I didn't want to be controlled anymore."

"I never want you to feel that way, and we deserved it." His warm smile makes me lightheaded. I lean into him, pressing my face into his chest, and he hugs me. His foresty scent is so distinctive from the smell of the trees around us.

"Is Rodan mad at me?" I mumble into his chest.

"No, he said you'd come around. The stubborn ass. He said, to just kiss you."

"Did he learn nothing from the pinecone to the head?" I laugh.

"I think it'll take more than a pinecone. A brick, perhaps? No, not heavy enough...a horse?"

"I can't throw a horse." I giggle.

He pulls me in tighter as I wrap my arms around his waist. "Hmm, I'll have to come up with something because we have a long life ahead, and someone has to be able to knock some sense into him." I sink into him, letting the warmth flood my veins. My bond throbs happily in my chest, the weight pulling me down finally lifted.

"You wanna play a game?" Killian whispers, bouncing on his toes.

I sniffle, arching my neck to look at him. "What kinda game?"

"Well, I have an idea, but I don't know if you'll be up for it." Killian looks bashfully down at his feet. He mumbles something I don't quite catch; I stifle a giggle and arch an eyebrow at him. "I wanna play Little Red Riding Hood with you."

"You want to stalk me in the woods and eat my grandma?" I laugh.

"No, I'd be Red. I can't have you being the bad guy. You get to be the hero."

"What? You lost me. Red is the girl. The bad guy is the wolf," I say.

"No, the wolf is the hero. You must have heard the story wrong."

"Then please enlighten me." I grin.

"Okay, so Red was visiting her grandmother in the forest. Deep in the woods, she runs into a kindly wolf who offers directions to her grandmother's house. But Red is mean and throws rocks at the wolf. The wolf is scared that Red will get lost, so he travels ahead to make sure she's safe from predators. Little does he know, Red is now hunting him.

"Red, of course, gets lost and takes hours to find her grandmother's house. While the wolf waits, he gets scared that something happened to Red, so he knocks on the granny's door to tell her to go look for Red. But when the grandmother opens the door, she sees the wolf and tries to kill him with a butcher knife. She tells him she's going to eat well tonight.

"The wolf gets scared and eats the granny before she can kill him. This was purely self-defense. He didn't mean to hurt the little old lady, but he panicked. He quickly cleaned up the mess and tried to hide all the evidence, but then Red appeared. Freaking out that there might be a misunderstanding, the wolf put on the grandmother's clothes and hopped into her bed. You do crazy things when you're scared.

"So Red marches into her grandmother's house and eats all the food her granny had put on the table. She made a massive mess of the place before she even tried to check on her grandmother, who hadn't made a peep since she arrived. She was so inconsiderate.

"Anyway, Red barged into her granny's room and gaped at her. She started insulting her granny immediately. Which is very rude. 'Oh, Granny, what big eyes you have,' she says. Feeling a bit self-conscious, the wolf tells her, 'The better to see you with, my dear.' Red continues to scrutinize her granny. 'What big ears you have.' The wolf lays his ears down flat, not feeling very good about any of this. 'The better to hear you with,' he sniffles. 'Oh, Granny, what big hairy hands you have.'

"The wolf is truly starting to think Red is just a big jerk and pulls his paws under the covers. 'The better to hug you with,' he grumbles. Red walks further into the room and gets right in the wolf's face. 'Oh,

Granny, what big teeth you have.' This time, the wolf just can't take it anymore. 'The better to eat you with!' he snarls and eats her all up."

I laugh at Killian's antics as he acts out the story.

"So the woodsman shows up, and the wolf is already feeling so dejected. When the man asks the wolf what happened, he tells him the whole sordid tale over tea."

"They just have tea?" I deadpan.

"Yes, the story is about a wolf's terrible day."

"You do know that the story is actually a cautionary tale to little girls to beware of lecherous men."

Killian steps back and clutches his chest. "No, it's not."

"Did you just clutch your pearls?" I laugh.

"This is serious. That story is not about perverted men."

"It really is..." I grin.

"Then the mortal version is just wrong."

"Anyway, how exactly do we play this game of yours?" I ask.

"Well, I play Red, and you play the wolf...and I hunt you down."

"That makes no sense; you're a wolf."

"I know, but Red is the one who chases the wolf, and I really wanna chase you." He bounces on his toes.

"You want to chase me...through the woods...and what do you get if you catch me?"

"I get to eat you up." His eyes darken as he looks me up and down.

"I still think you are the wolf in that case–"

"In my story, Red is the hunter. I'm Red, and you may want to run, little wolf."

The gleam in Killian's eye tells me he's not joking, and I know he's faster than me. I turn and take off away from the camp at breakneck speed. I jump and dodge bushes and fallen trees as I try to put space between us. The breeze pushes past me, throwing my hair wildly behind me. The sun has all but disappeared from the sky, and shadows cover everything in my path as I distance myself from the little balls of light.

I hope Killian finds me since I'm getting myself thoroughly lost. Adrenaline pumps through me, excitement warring with curiosity. I don't know what he will do when he catches me, but whatever it is, I want it. The forest is quiet except for my breathing and leaves rustling under my feet. I dodge a tree leaning over the path and veer to the left, hoping to throw him off my trail. I reach a small stream, run for a log a short distance away, and slowly balance my way across it, jumping onto the other side before I pick up my pace again.

Far off, I hear a wolf howl, and all the hairs on my arms stand on end. He must have given me a head start, but that means he will find me soon. I may think I'm clever and can evade him, but I know he can probably track me on scent alone. Damn cheating fae.

The further I go into the woods, the darker everything seems to get, and a sense of foreboding comes over me. He wouldn't have suggested this if I could get lost or hurt, right? I mean, the worst thing that could happen is I trip, fall, and bust my ass, right?

An owl hoots nearby, and I jump. The feeling of being watched settles over me. My pace slows while attempting to take in my surroundings and catch my breath. The canopy of trees blocks the moons, and everything is quiet as I do a slow circle, trying to gauge which way camp would be.

A crack sounds from somewhere to my left, and I whirl around, peering into the darkness. Slowly, I back up, bumping into a tree and nearly letting out a startled yip. I keep backing up, maneuvering around the tree, finding myself in a small clearing with the moon shining down on me like a damn spotlight. I roll my eyes at my great self-preservation skills.

Excellent job hiding.

Another snap ahead of me trips my heartbeat as I continue backing into the clearing. I pant, trying to catch my breath as rustling noises seize my attention behind me. I whip my head around, struggling to see into the dense trees; the shadows are still as leaves flitter on my right. Either Killian or my imagination is fucking with me, or there's something out there, and this was a terrible idea. I don't dare make a sound as I frantically seek out movement in the darkness.

A dark silhouette emerges from the tree line, hidden beneath the shadows of the trees. I suck in a sharp breath as he stalks forward, his eyes glinting in the moonlight.

I take a tentative step back, trying to hide my trembling hands.

A low growl breaks the silence. "My, what big eyes you have," he says as he prowls into the clearing. Killian's eyes are dark with promise as he rakes his gaze across me.

The loud thrumming of my heart is an ocean of waves as I take another step back. "The better to see you with," I whisper, fighting a grin. My palms sweat as anticipation rushes through me.

"What big ears you have," he says, taking another tentative step forward, a slight grin playing on his lips.

"I do not."

His brow lifts, and another growl rumbles in his chest.

I huff and roll my eyes. "The better to hear you with," I say, taking another step back into something hard. I don't dare take my eyes off the predator in front of me as I stop.

"Oh my, what big teeth you have." He smirks.

An arm wraps around my shoulders from behind, and I jump, my heart leaping into my throat as I squeak.

"The better to eat you with," Rodan's smooth purr whispers across my ear.

I freeze, held in place by Rodan and staring into the eyes of the hunter in front of me, trapped in their snare. Killian continues his slow prowl towards me as Rodan's hand glides over my waist. His ozone scent, mixing with the heady forest, makes me lightheaded.

"You cheated," I pant.

Killian's eyes darken as he leans into me, eliminating the few inches between us. "I never said I wouldn't use the woodsman to help." He winks.

Rodan trails his lips lightly over my neck. I melt into his embrace as heat floods my body.

"So, Emerald, my love, do I get my prize?" Killian's eyes drag down my body as he runs his fingertips down my arm.

I flush as I try to hold eye contact with him and nod.

"Use your words, Trouble," Rodan says, continuing to lightly drag his mouth along the sensitive parts of my neck.

"Yes," I breathe.

Killian closes the space between us, caressing my cheek as he delicately brushes his lips across mine; my eyes flutter shut. Heat pools in my core, a heady mixture of adrenaline from the chase and anticipation. Hands drag the hem of my shirt, their mouths only breaking contact with me long enough to get it off. Their skin is hot against mine as their calloused hands skim my bare skin.

Sinking to his knees, Killian moves to pull my leggings off. Rodan grabs my chin, turns my face to his, and kisses me fiercely, claiming me and making my knees weak. He holds me tight as I step from the final confines of my clothes, my bra dropping to the forest floor with the rest.

"This little wolf needs to be taught a lesson," Rodan growls against my lips. Digging my fingers into his hair, I pull his lips onto mine. Butterflies dance through me, sending shivers through my core.

Killian sheds his clothes and pulls me into his embrace, kissing me slowly and taking my breath away. My pulse slows as I run my hands across the plains of his chest, the bond between us almost tangible. Rodan's heat presses into my back, his now bare chest warm against me. I feel his hard length pulse against my backside as he captures my wrists, pulling me into him.

I open my eyes as Killian trails his mouth down my body. "Remember what I said last time?" Killian says between kisses.

I shake my head as he nips at a ticklish spot on my side. Rodan groans as I wiggle against him.

"I said I wanted to lick you while he fucks this perfect pussy."

I gulp as his eyes move to that sensitive area, his hands running over the inside of my legs. My breathing quickens as the idea fills my head.

"You good with that?" Rodan whispers.

"Uh-huh," I nod, unable to form coherent sentences as Rodan wraps his arms around my waist and breasts, stabilizing me as Killian pulls my leg over his bare shoulder. Butterflies dance in my belly as he looks at me like caught prey. A shiver runs down my spine as he nips at my inner thigh.

"Are you wet for us, Trouble?" Rodan says, nipping my ear.

Killian's eyes darken as they flick up to mine. "You're practically dripping, little wolf—"

A moan rocks through me as Killian glides his tongue up my center. I lean my head back on Rodan's shoulder. I wouldn't be standing if he weren't holding me up. Rodan pulls my face over to his, and his lips find mine as I fall into the sensation of them.

I lose myself to him as my hand tangles in Killian's hair.

Something soft ghosts across my waist, slithering down my leg, and I pull away from Rodan and watch tendrils of shadow in fascination.

"Relax, it's just me," Rodan says.

The shadows crackle with blue electricity, popping along my skin, waking up every nerve. My breath hitches as Killian sucks hard on my clit, and one shadow slips inside. Rodan groans as his power fills me, hitting some spot that amplifies what Killian does with his tongue.

I'm so close, the pressure within begs to be released. I feel like I'm coming apart at the seams. Killian pulls away and grins as the shadow tortures me from inside. Very undignified sounds escape me when the shadow pulls free and wraps around my leg, leaving me empty.

Killian stands as I glare at him for leaving me on the edge. My leg is still held aloft by the shadow; he kisses me and runs his hot fingers over my clit. Rodan aligns himself, his cock nudging my entrance. I almost beg him to hurry, needing the release they teased me with. He slams into me with force, taking my breath away.

And oh god, if that isn't the sweetest feeling.

A growl rumbles through him as he pulls out achingly slowly and slams into me again. The intensity of it sends shivers of pleasure through me.

"You take him so good, little wolf," Killian purrs.

Killian's eyes bore into me as he sinks to his knees and licks me again, causing me to clench down hard on Rodan. I don't know why I ever thought sex sucked; they wash away every touch from my body with their own. They claim me in a way that makes me feel loved and wanted. We both moan as they send me over the edge, and I see stars. Literal fucking stars. I cry out as something shocks my clit into another wave of pleasure before I'd even come off the roll of the last.

A shadow fills me from behind, but I hardly notice as another wave crashes over me. I can barely breathe as I ride Rodan's cock through each climax. That damn shadow adds another unknown element to the pleasure that I'd never experienced.

Killian smirks as I finally come down panting, wondering what the fuck these guys just did to me.

Rodan holds me tight, nibbling on my neck. "Good girl."

Heat floods my core at his words, and I clench down on his hard cock that he has stopped moving.

Killian steps forward and brushes my hair out of my face, leaning in to kiss me. "I'm nowhere near done with you, but I promise not to lose control this time."

A thrill runs through me, and Rodan groans as he gradually pulls out of me. He readjusts his hold. I feel the shadow pull free before the head of his cock replaces it; he rubs something wet across the tight hole. I suck in a breath as fear takes hold. Inch by inch, he slowly works himself in, slick and meeting little resistance. It's a strange feeling of being full but not unpleasant; his shadows must have worked some real magic on me. His head rests on my shoulder as he shakes, trying to move slowly into me.

I gasp as he fully seats himself and gives me a minute, leaning into Killian to adjust. Gently, Killian pushes me into Rodan's arms, positioning himself. I suck in a deep breath as he pulls my leg up and gently moves into me. I grip Killian's shoulders, holding myself still as they fill me.

The stretch is intense and incredible. Panting, I claw at Killian's back as he moves.

I have never felt this level of fullness; I can't believe I'm doing this. Fully suspended between them, they move slowly, finding a rhythm that has my eyes rolling back in my head and the pressure building inside me like never before.

"Fuck," Rodan gasps as he bites my shoulder, suppressing a moan.

A light breeze tickles my skin, causing my nipples to harden against Killian and a chill to run through me. Sweat gleams across Killian's chest; he breathes heavily as he moves.

Killian is gentle as he rocks into me, holding me to his body and supporting all of my weight. The crackle of electricity runs over my leg as the cool shadow slips between us. I gasp as it circles my clit. I can't help the sounds I make when it shocks my poor, over-sensitized bud over the edge.

"Come for me, little wolf," Killian growls. "Yes, just like that."

The world explodes around me as I scream in ecstasy. Rodan roars his release as Killian picks up his pace, sending them both over. In the surge, I swear, I can see the bond between us tighten and solidify, shimmering golden in the darkness. Every muscle in me shudders as I continue rolling through each climax, bearing down on the cocks still buried deep inside of me.

As if in sync, both of them slowly drop to the forest floor before Rodan pulls out, nearly collapsing with the effort. Killian unsheathes gradually; his knot swelling at the base of his cock. He tilts my chin and meets my eyes, kissing me gently as he lays me down on the grass.

"I made sure I didn't put the knot inside this time. Figured that Rodan didn't want to get locked in." Killian smiles as he picks up his shirt and starts carefully cleaning the mess between my legs.

"I don't know how you form complete sentences after that." I giggle.

"That was a complete sentence. Are you saying we need to try harder?" Rodan rolls on top of me with a wicked gleam in his eyes. Killian's eyebrow arches as he moves to my side.

"What? No!" I shriek. "I can barely move, and I'm going to be so sore tomorrow as it is."

Rodan quirks an eyebrow, tracing his eyes down my body. I try to push him off, but I'm met by shadows holding me down. They wrap like snakes around my wrists, ankles, and waist. My eyes grow wide as a nervous giggle escapes me.

"Have mercy." I squeak.

"Never." Rodan smirks, and his hand trails between my legs, cupping my sex. Warmth spreads through the area, and all my muscles relax as I feel the healing magic pulse through me. Even muscles I thought would be sore feel normal again. Now, that kind of healing is handy; granted, being deliciously sore has its merits, but I probably don't want to be walking like Bambi tomorrow.

Pressure builds quickly like a wave slamming into the shore, and I rock with the climax before I even know what's happening, screaming out in shock as much as pleasure.

What the fuck? He barely touched me.

Rodan gives me a self-satisfied smirk when I look at him, surprised. "Did I forget to remind you I can make you orgasm without touching you from across the room?"

"What? Rodan, come on, let me up." I pull at my bonds as Killian lies down beside me, running his fingers down the inside of my arm.

"I want to see that. I like the shocky shadows. It's amazing to be inside her when she's completely lost to it." Killian has a mischievous smile, and I pull harder at the shadows.

Rodan's eyes darken as he stands and walks a few feet away.

Oh god, "I don't need a demonstration, I believe you, but I couldn't possibly–"

Rodan snaps his fingers, and I feel warmth rush through my core as another wave crashes through me. I pant as my back arches and my body begs to be filled again.

"That's not fair," I pant.

Killian's eyes darken as I look at him, lifting my hips as the last of it rocks through me. He rolls on top of me, kissing me deeply as he lines himself up with me and thrusts hard. My eyes roll back into my head as he bottoms out. His quick pace is unhindered by how wet I am. They fit my body as if we were made for each other. He growls as I rake my nails down his back.

Rodan stands stroking himself, and as I make eye contact with him, I feel myself grow even wetter under his deep gaze. Heat fills my veins as every sensation fills my being. My back arches as I fall again, and Killian growls deep in his chest, collapsing on top of me and kissing my collarbone.

I heave heavy breaths as he rolls to my side, pulling me into him, the shadows releasing their hold on me. Rodan's healing magic thrums through me again as I relax into Killian's hold.

Killian nuzzles into my hair. "I love you," he murmurs as Rodan wraps himself around me from behind.

"You have no idea how much," Rodan says, kissing my shoulder.

I melt into their embrace. "I don't know what to say."

"You don't have to say anything, just don't give up on us," Killian says. "I'll wait for you to catch up."

"Okay." While I can't imagine going on without them, I can't bring myself to tell them how I feel. Maybe I don't want to believe I could fall for them so fast, especially since there are two of them. I'm not that girl. Jumping into things isn't something I do, and I definitely don't fall for two guys simultaneously. How did this happen?

My heart thunders; it's just the mind-blowing sex. I need to clear my head of the crazy hormones before I try to figure out what all this means. But I can't deny that we just seem to fit, that it only seems weird when I make it weird in my thoughts. Maybe it's just me who can't seem to work this all out because they are perfectly at ease and in sync with each other. Maybe being in love with them isn't as bad as it seems in my head.

Chapter 27
Rodan

Cat and I creep through the damp tunnel, listening for any movement ahead. The rocks beneath my feet are slick with moss and sludge, I don't want to know the origin of. I scan the craggy boulders as I leap from one to the next, using my claws to keep from slipping. No light touches this place, but my sight is unhindered in this form. The tunnel is narrow, and the air is thick with a musty smell. Every step is a risk, as the ground could give way at any moment.

Cat holds onto a tuft of fur near my ear, her tiny body barely noticeable as I traverse. She shifted into some sort of fly, but in true Cat form, she has the head of a feline. Her wild shifting allows her to communicate with me in the silent language of felines. We all agree she is best suited to help me sneak into the castle. She can get small enough to open locked doors from the other side.

Of course, Ryker was against it and wanted her at his side, but we needed him for aerial support. However, her flying abilities leave something to be desired.

I crouch down to assess a small recess in the rocks leading to a bigger cavern beyond. I haven't been down here since I was a child, and Killian accidentally caved in the tunnel. It used to serve as an emergency exit for royalty, but they abandoned it when they built new exits.

Crouching down on my belly, I wiggle through the opening, trying to be mindful that I don't bump my head into the rocks and squish Cat.

"Don't you dare," Cat hisses at me.

"I would never." I chuckle as I pull myself through. The boulders dig into my sides as I contort my body. I growl with frustration as my leg gets pinned behind me, and I lose the leverage to push myself.

Cat flies off my ear and returns to her fae form, sighing as she grabs my arm and pulls. "You know you are smaller in fae form." She says through clenched teeth.

I growl at her, baring my teeth. Letting go, Cat throws her hand up in defeat and glares at me.

Returning to my fae form, I huff as I dislodge my hips and fall from the hole in a graceless heap. I glare up at her as she wipes a smile from her face and shifts back into the tiny fly. She bounces around as if she's drunk, occasionally bumping into the wall and rebounding into a rock.

Trying to stifle a laugh, I close my eyes and take a deep breath.

My panther bursts forth again, and we continue on as I wrap us in shadows. It may seem like overkill in this dark tunnel, but if anyone comes through who doesn't need light to see, it should protect us. Up ahead, the passage opens up, the stone walls becoming smoother as the floor levels out.

"Do you think the others will be okay?" Cat whispers.

"They will be fine; they will cause a diversion big enough to allow everyone a window to get in and out." At least, we hope it gives us ample time. Killian and Corsac are using a newer tunnel to get in, which was built after we destroyed this one.

"I'm worried about Jade." A pit forms in my stomach as Jade fills my thoughts. I don't like that she got roped into helping, but she refused to be left behind. This morning, I didn't want to leave her side. I'd woken with a peace I'd never felt before, with her arms wrapped around me. She'd finally slept in our tent last night, dreading what tonight's plans would bring.

"Yudoku will keep her safe. No one will expect them to come in through the water; it's a good place to keep a lookout and gather information. Plus, Yudoku is ridiculously strong when she is in her element. I would not want to cross her." I shiver at the thought. "There's a reason why no one dares to challenge sirens."

"Why?"

"You think this is the time?" I grumble.

"I'm a little freaked out, so yes, distract me. It's not like anyone can hear us."

I sigh as I continue down the long tunnel towards the castle. "Sirens have dominion over water. They are calculating in everything: how they take mates, passing their powers down to more powerful sirens. They are cunning and dangerous. As they mature, so do their forms. Older sirens can grow wings, similar to harpies. Their songs are hypnotic, and most fae are charmed by it. It's like mind control. Think of every mermaid story you've ever heard, the good and the bad; it's all based on some truth. They can be vicious and won't bat an eye about killing."

"Is the mind control what Owari did to you and Jade?"

"I believe so, which is why we will stay in shifted form as much as possible. It's harder to charm us this way."

Cat goes quiet as we round another bend, and an iron gate lies ahead of us. I approach on silent feet, inspecting the metal bars and the tunnel beyond.

"On the far wall is a lever that opens the gate. You'll need to fly to get to it. Do not touch the bars."

She flies off my head, bobbing and weaving. She almost makes it through the opening in the grate when she suddenly dips hard and slams into the iron.

Fuck.

She tumbles over the other side and spins to the floor, shifting back into fae, swearing like a sailor, and holding her arm. A large, angry red welt runs from wrist to shoulder, and I hiss, knowing that burns like a bitch.

I theorized that the fae blood in her veins would take over if she were in our realm long enough. I was correct, since iron would have had no effect on Cat a few months ago.

She takes a deep breath and stands, bolting for the lever at the other end of the corridor. Slamming her weight into the mechanism, she thrusts it up with a grunt. The grate ascends, creaking and groaning, the gears rusted with age. When the gap is large enough for me to pass under, I run to Cat, who has slumped to the floor, catching her breath.

I leave my panther form and pull on my power to heal her. Light forms along my palm as I press into the angry red of her arm. Cat sighs in relief, the burn only slightly pink.

"Thank you," she whispers.

"Warrick will have to heal you the rest of the way. Hopefully, that helps for now."

"I'll take light sunburn over third-degree burns any day."

I shake my head; no point in reminding her she shouldn't have touched the iron. I could be a dick about it, but it's not her fault she still sucks at flying. She did exactly what I needed her to do, because we are in.

Down the corridor to our left is the secret door panel. It leads to the hidden passageway we used to play in. The passage runs through the royal wing of the castle, connecting our bedrooms to multiple wings of the estate.

Once Cat has caught her breath, we sneak through the door and return to the shadows in our shifted forms. Small orbs of light dance in the old passage, illuminating cobwebs and dust collected in this unused hall. I reach my shadows ahead of us, snuffing out the lights as we walk.

"That's creepy as hell. It's like being the monster in a horror movie. Although it's interesting to see it from the monster's perspective. You know, instead of the lights down the hall turning off towards you, all creepy-like. We are the shadows extinguishing the light."

"Stop rambling, I need to listen," I growl.

"You're no fun," she huffs.

"I will be even less fun if someone gets the drop on us."

"Noted."

The ground shakes, and the walls rumble around me, dust raining down as I struggle to maintain my balance. This is our chance. A deafening boom echoes in the distance, and I quicken my pace, navigating the labyrinthine hallways. I reach a stairwell and descend into the dungeon, my determination driving me forward despite the chaos. As I approach the bottom, I slow my steps, my senses on high alert for any sign of movement.

Soft murmurings come from behind the wall, muffled by the stone. The hidden door is up ahead. Hopefully, whoever is guarding the dungeon has been pulled to help with the chaos raining down in the enchanted garden.

I press my ear against the door, listening carefully for any indication of the guard. I'm ripped out of my panther form, the shock of the transformation causing me to collapse under the weight of Cat. My head slams into the unforgiving stone, and she rolls off me, a curse escaping her lips. We stare at each other in disbelief. She's in her fae form, and my panther is unreachable.

What the fuck just happened? The lights in the passageway suddenly illuminate. White dust floats in the air around us, clinging to her hair and my arms. I stagger to my feet, using the wall for support, while my head swims with dizziness.

This isn't right.

Something is wrong.

I can't shift.

Cat's eyes meet mine, and sheer terror crosses her features, confirming what I already know.

This is a trap.

"I told Ellis you weren't dumb enough to come this way, but I guess I was wrong."

I whip around to see Hunter leaning against the wall behind me. He casually inspects his nails, and I sneer at him. His red hair, blazing under the glow of the lights, makes him look like the pompous ass he is. How the fuck was he able to sneak up on me? Lightning crackles down my arms; I let it fill me as I prepare to strike.

"Ah-ah-ah." A feminine voice tuts behind me. In my periphery, I see Cat staggering to the side with a knife at her throat. "Wouldn't want the poor mortal to die now, would we?" Beatrix giggles as she comes into view.

Fuck.

Where the fuck did they come from?

Cat lets out a little squeak as a drop of blood traces down her neck, pooling in her collarbone.

I growl as the lightning continues to crackle through me, ready to lash out.

"You killed my brother." Hunter seethes.

"He had it coming," I say, keeping my face stoic. I can't let them see me rattled.

Hunter bristles and steps forward, snarling.

"Down, boy!" Beatrix snaps. "Ellis wants him alive."

"Yes, down, boy. Be a good little pet for the parasitic princess." I wink at Hunter, loving the fury written across his face.

Beatrix clears her throat. "It's interesting to find you here with her, though. I thought you liked the other one. But I guess that was Killian. You both have wretched taste, half-breeds, honestly." She grimaces. "I was shocked when Ellis told me you were the prince. I can't believe the one set to inherit the throne is a bastard. That's right, my Ellis figured it out. It makes sense why the queen didn't want anyone to know who the prince was. Who would want to marry a bastard born of a shadow whore?" She giggles.

I'd laugh if this situation weren't so precarious. Where the fuck did Ellis get that idea? It's probably a good thing; let them think I'm the crown prince. Killian is safer that way. I guess the cat is out of the bag about my shadow abilities.

"Is it because Killian is a bit dim? I never talked to him much, but he seemed rather excitable. Although he really had me going in the dungeon, so maybe he isn't a total waste. What's more disgusting is you falling for some half-breed. When a pureblood like me was right in front of you."

"Is there a point to your ramblings?" I drawl.

She stiffens and glares at me.

"Lock down your powers and come with us, or I kill your precious pet," she snaps.

I keep my eyes pinned on Hunter as he takes a step forward. Vines whip around my legs, and my heart leaps into my throat as I throw my power at him. Blue light sears through the air, crackling out and hissing as it connects with his eyes. He screams and clutches his face, his body convulsing; he hits the ground. Smoke rises in rivulets off him.

Oops.

Beatrix cries out, and I stumble over the vines as I spin to face her. Cat stumbles away, clutching her neck. Aside from the slight scratch, she looks okay.

Beatrix's hands cover her mouth, and her eyes are wide. The dagger is still clutched in her hand, only tipped in blood. Her expression grows dark as she looks at me with pure loathing. Ice creeps around her, covering her skin and the wall behind her. Cat scrambles to get away, but the ice crawls up her leg, and she screams out in pain.

I pull on my power, letting the lightning show through my eyes. I want her to know what I'm capable of. I feel it crackle through me, electricity washing over me, shadows flickering with the eerie blue light.

I see some of the fire leave her as her arms go slack, and a tear trails down her face. "You're a real bastard, you know that." She whips out a glass vial that crashes at my feet. Crimson smoke tendrils snake around me, and my power dies in my veins, winking out like a candle flame. I look up in horror to see a smug smile cross her lips before red engulfs me.

Chapter 28
Killian

Corsac and I race through the woods, the moon at our backs as our paws hit the soft forest floor. She is a blur of motion beside me, her ethereal fox coming in and out of focus. I'm pretty jealous of her form; imagine how cool I'd be if my wolf were a ghost.

We reach an unassuming mound of rocks on the side of the mountain. Corsac spins her nine tails, and a blast of air throws the boulders from our path, opening the hidden tunnel beyond. I race ahead, ensuring I can keep the way clear. Her shield wraps around us as she winks us out of sight from our enemies.

We need to reach the courtyard with the orbs, free as many fae as we can, and get the hell out. The pixies reported that some of the high councilors were chained to the orbs, being drained of all their power. I don't know how they got overpowered, but if we succeed in getting them back, we might stand a chance of keeping our heads above water until aid arrives.

All of this is a big *if*, and I really hate it. I wanted to go after my parents, but until we figure out how to wake them, they won't be of any use. I sigh as I bolt around a corner, scenting the air for danger. The fae lights cast down here years ago illuminate the tunnel, but everything is still dusty and murky. I ignore the cobwebs as I barrel through them because there are definitely no spiders down here, just like there certainly was no giant one hidden beneath the castle.

A shiver runs through me, and I focus on the task at hand. Scarlette will start the diversion at any moment, and the volcanic explosion in the enchanted garden should draw most of Ellis' horde away from us. Warrick and Ambrose are waiting in the forest to help anyone we manage to save, keeping the portal up and protected.

My girl is with Yudoku, whom I still don't trust not to eat her. They are gathering intel from the water system in the central saltwater pond in the night garden. Yudoku is strongest there, and the fish can give her a lot of information we can't get on our own.

The ground shakes as dust rains upon us, and a sound like thunder rocks the castle. I barely catch my footing as the earth sways. Corsac gives me a wide-eyed look, and then her teeth gleam in the faint light.

That's her girl up there. She's a badass.

Finally reaching the staircase leading up, I take the steps two at a time. It is imperative that we close as much distance as possible before they figure out our plan. Thankfully, this passage is in good shape since Rodan and I weren't allowed to play in it when we were pups. I may have lost control of a fireball in the one Rodan is going through and collapsed part of it. Rather than fix it, my parents decided to block it off and build a new one that wasn't so close to our bedrooms. Let's just say it was epic, and I only roasted Rodan a little.

We reach the landing, and I return to my fae shape to open the door and peek into the dark, empty hallway. I signal Corsac to follow as we creep into the shadows. The tingle of her shield surrounds me as we pass a mirror, the distorted reflection showing me what others would see. We are like a phantom that you catch a glimpse of out of the corner of your eye before we vanish entirely.

I lean down and whisper, "You have the coolest power ever."

She snorts and shakes her head, moving down the hall.

Reaching a tapestry of a valiant wolf, it stands on a mountain roaring to the moon. Next to him is an armor-clad white cat with defiance in her eyes-my parents. I swallow the lump in my throat and open the panel hidden behind the fabric.

I'll figure this out. I'll come back and save you both.

The panel makes a small snick as it shuts behind us, and we run for the end of the corridor. We pass multiple doors leading to all the principal rooms on this castle level. Down at the end is a heavy wooden door with large metal hinges that leads to the courtyard. A trellis of roses hides the other side with razor-sharp thorns. Attempting to enter the passage from that side is seriously not fun.

"This is it. Don't let the door close completely, or we won't be able to get back in," I whisper.

She sheds her fox, shaking out her short, curly hair. "Just melt the locks, and I'll get them through."

I want to ask how this tiny fox plans to do that, but at this point, I know better.

When I crack the door open, the orbs and a handful of fae come into view. Four orbs glow brightly, illuminating the courtyard in vibrant colors. Fire swirls in copper and molten gold. Water casts shades of aqua along the walls that blend with the bright carnation-yellow of air. Together, they create greens that harmonize with the rich browns and emeralds of earth. It's a kaleidoscope of lights that dance across the walls.

The fae lay bound, their ankles and wrists cuffed in iron. The one closest to me is Maysant, her long, dark, corkscrew hair spread out over the ground around her. Her bronzed skin is ashen and pale. Just beyond her lies Oberon; large gashes and bruises ravage his body. He did not go down without a fight. The other fae are too far for me to make out, but none are the high council members.

My heart sinks. Where are they?

I sneak from the doorway and move to Maysant, forcing fire into the chains' locks. They melt away, leaving the cuffs. I work quickly, pulling them off and swearing as the iron burns my fingertips. Freed of her bindings, Corsac pulls Maysant on a gust of wind into the tunnel.

I lift an eyebrow and nod my approval. Because, holy shit, that was impressive.

I move over to Oberon, repeating the process to free his bindings.

I cry out as a lash of pain rocks through my back, falling to my knees before Oberon. Breathing heavily, I snap my head around, searching for whoever attacked me. My veins freeze within me. A glowing leash of power has attached itself to me from the fire orb—my power draining like a faucet left on full blast.

What the fuck!

I stagger to my feet, trying to break away from the pull of the orb. What the fuck did they do to it?

Typically, I have to touch the orb and open my power to it. I let as much flow out of me as I want, and then I can simply walk away. This is not how they are supposed to act; this is violating. I stumble to my knees as my eyesight begins to blur, dizziness taking over, and black spots beginning to form on the edges of my vision.

A gust of wind shoves at me, pulling me away from the orb. I cry out as the tether on my power jerks taut. My fire winks out as the leash snaps. I tumble into the razor roses, slicing my arms through my shirt. A giant thorn stabs into my thigh, and I hiss out a string of curses. This could not be going worse.

Cold hands wrap around my arm, pulling me through the door. There's a faint click, and the smell of roses assaults me as Corsac's face comes into focus.

"What the fuck happened?"

"I–I don't know. That's never happened before. It drained me." I shake my head as I sit up. "I'm tapped." Not an ember remains, chilling me to the bone.

A moan pulls my attention to Maysant, who pulls herself to a sitting position against the wall. Her bronze wrist is red and blistered from the iron. "It was a trap for the prince." She lets out a heavy sigh. "We were the bait. Good thing he sent you instead, because that psycho has some pretty twisted plans."

I glance at Corsac, who raises a brow. "Who does he think the prince is?"

"Prince Rodan. At least that's what I overheard before I got dumped by those fucked-up orbs. What is wrong with this kingdom?" Maysant coughs.

"They didn't used to be that way. I don't know what Ellis did to them," I say.

"Ellis? You mean Sorrel. He's the one who did this to us. Him and that bastard Calazar planned this whole thing."

I shake the last of the haze from me. "Well, now we know who's working with Ellis." I meet Corsac's eye. She looks murderous.

"What do you mean?" Maysant asks.

Corsac sighs. "So Ellis is an Unseelie sorcerer; looks like Sorrel and Calazar joined him."

"Damn it." Maysant leans her head back on the wall.

"Yeah," Corsac says and looks away.

"We need to get you out of here. With my powers gone, I think we are out of luck. Hopefully, the others manage to save more fae than us."

"I'm not leaving. The others are still here. You go. Thank you for helping me out of that, but if these passages do what I think they do, I'll be fine from here."

"I don't want to leave you here." I give her a pointed look.

"Once I find a place to rest for a bit, I'll be fine. I am a basilisk, after all; I can get small enough not to be noticed and large enough to swallow fae whole. They won't get the drop on me again." Her eyes blaze with fury.

"When this is over, I'd like to see you in action. Not the eating-fae thing. That's kinda gross." I wink at her.

She smirks. "Yeah, I don't recommend it. But I'll be fine now that I'm free. Now go before you can't get out."

Corsac goes all crazy-tailed ghost fox again, brushes one of her tails over Maysant's ankles, and the burns seem to wipe away. She repeats the motion over her wrists, and the fae visibly relaxes.

"Thanks, girl," Maysant says.

Corsac smacks my hands in irritation with her tail, melting away the pain. I block my face as she whips her tail across my arm and leg, healing my wounds. I huff as both of them snicker.

"Why you gotta smack me around to heal me, but she gets a gentle touch?" I laugh.

Corsac shrugs.

"Maybe because you rush headlong into danger." Maysant smiles.

I grin, "I wouldn't be me if I didn't." I run down the hall, leaping into my wolf.

The ground shakes again, and I know we are running out of time. I can't believe I had all my power drained like that. She said it was a trap for Rodan. A shiver runs down my spine. How many traps are laid out? I pick up speed, needing to get to the forest and call everyone back.

When we reach the end of the hall, I feel a tingle like my leg being asleep rush through my body as Corsac shields us again. I turn fae and open the door, peeking out into the dark before we creep out and make our way to the tunnel.

A soft song floats in the air, and I find myself in a hallway. Swaying to the most lovely melody I've ever heard, I stand confused. Why am I in this part of the castle? I must have been trying to find that amazing music.

Pain shoots through my hand, and I look down, sucking air through my teeth. A blue fox has its teeth sunk into my palm; blood drips down her muzzle as she pulls me toward a wall. I reach for my fire but find it empty. What the fuck? I pull, but pain flashes through me as she bites down harder. What the fuck, you rabid banshee?

The song fills my head, and I no longer feel discomfort. My emotions float on a cloud of happy feelings I long to reach. Promises of serenity and calm entice me.

Agony rips through me as the fox bears down harder, snapping the fragile bones in my hand and yanking me through a doorway that slams shut behind us.

The world goes silent.

The fox lets go of my hand, and I clutch it to my chest as warm blood pours down my arm, dripping off my elbow. I tilt my head, shooting daggers at my broken hand as I try to regain my train of thought.

Corsac turns fae and stands, glaring at me with her hands on her hips. "You still wanna get brain fucked by Owari? Or do I need to break your other hand?"

Squeezing my eyes shut, I shake my head, concentrating on the pain. My skull pounds from the song. "We need to get the fuck out of here."

"No shit." She turns and starts running down the tunnel; I follow, hot on her heels. I don't ask her to heal me. The pain will keep that siren out of my head, at least partially.

Now I understand why Rodan told me I was an idiot to invite sirens.

Fuck, Jade...

When we reach a fork in the path, I tell Corsac to keep going and to spread the word to run. We need Ryker to warn who he can. I split off down the other tunnel.

I need to get to Jade.

Chapter 29
Jade

"It's too quiet," Yudoku says as we emerge from the water. The eerie beauty of the bioluminescent garden is captivating. It casts a cool glow over her pale teal hair; the surrounding leaves cast purple and pink light across the strands. Illuminated by the glowing saltwater, we attempt to hide in the shadows along the edge. "It was too easy to get this far." Her body is tense as she surveys the garden.

I watch the doors to a ballroom; the glass reflecting the glow of the trees. The room is dark, and there is no movement from within. I train my eyes up to windows that emit a gentle light. The ancient castle is beautiful: gray stone stacked to the sky, tall towers, and balconies. Various glass doors and windows line the sides, mirroring the night sky.

"Maybe we should check the other garden," I whisper.

She huffs. "I'm supposed to keep you safe."

"Get the information you came here for and let's go. I'm not just gonna sit here while everyone else is doing something."

She smirks. "Sure you're not part siren?"

Part of me goes all warm and fuzzy at the compliment. My mouth is braver than I am, but sitting in an empty garden feels wrong.

She dives under, circling into the depths in search of the fish that she can interrogate. Hopefully, they have knowledge that we don't.

Apparently, fish are busybodies and live for court drama.

Who knew?

Movement on the third-story mezzanine catches my attention. As I submerge into the water, the shadows envelop me. A lean man with shaggy brown hair and glasses leans over the railing. He casually drapes his forearms over the edge, a wine glass dangling from his fingertips. A smirk of disdain tugs at his lips as he surveys the castle grounds.

My heart ramps up, and an icy chill runs down my spine. I don't know who this man is, but every molecule of my body wants to retreat from his presence.

The water shifts next to me, and I throw out my hand, halting Yudoku's head before she surfaces. Submerging completely into the pool, I make eye contact with her and shake my head, pointing towards the balcony. The saltwater burns my eyes, but her quick nod is all I get before she latches onto my arm and pulls me down.

Swimming with her has taught me to just go limp and allow her to drag me. She swims so fast I could never keep up; it was terrifying the first time. Being dragged by a siren is like being flung onto a roller coaster in the dark. We twist and turn through the deep tunnels that connect the ponds throughout the castle grounds. She speeds through gracefully, never skimming either of us against the rocks lining the walls.

When we surface in the enchanted garden, I gulp down the air as I try to calm the thunder in my ears. The area is gloomy, and the pond looks like ink. Trees loom over us like monsters in the night.

"What did you see?" she hisses.

"A man looking over the garden. He was lean, wearing glasses–"

"Ellis." She casts her eyes to the sky. "That's not great. Thank you for warning me."

I nod. "Did you find out anything?"

Her eyes look haunted as she nods. "We'll discuss it later. I'm afraid it's nothing good."

A falcon flies past us and circles a small hill across the garden. The ground roils and moves where he circles, building up onto itself. I clench my teeth at the sound of rocks grinding against each other. The falcon soars back into the sky and out of sight.

A soft rustling nearby has me sinking further into the water and feeling for the daggers lining the fighting leathers along my ribs. The weight of my clothes and blades feels much more cumbersome in the freshwater pond. Thankfully, Yudoku brought me to a spot where I can stand. Interestingly, the saltwater doesn't mix with the fresh through the tunnels.

Fire erupts from the mound of dirt and rock. The water shifts violently as the ground rolls around the garden. Trees rise on hills before sinking down again; some fall over in the tremors. Water rushes over my head, and I latch onto a root at the water's edge before I get cast deeper into the pool. Yudoku's grip on my arm turns biting as she's tossed in the waves.

The mound explodes, the percussion causing everything to go quiet as Yudoku pulls me under. Flaming rocks rain down around us, fizzing out in the water as I sink.

Holy shit.

The night sky turns bright with fire. Trees burn overhead as more fire pummels down. Rippling distorts the brilliant light, but that explosion lit up the world.

My lungs ache; I didn't have a chance to take a breath before we dropped. I pull toward the surface, looking at Yudoku. Panic takes me as she refuses to let go of my arm. I tug and try to prise her hand off me.

Her brow furrows as she looks at me and glances at the blazing world above. Giving me a quick shake of her head, she pulls me towards her. Her other hand wraps around the back of my head. My eyes widen as her mouth collides with mine, and air fills my lungs. I stare into her eyes, my body relaxing as the ache in my lungs eases. She holds me there, pressed against her, easing the burn in my chest.

I take a deep breath, and she pulls away. Shock has me frozen in place, staring at her.

"Air magic, remember?" She smirks as her hair floats around her.

I just got kissed by a mermaid. I'd laugh if I didn't need the air in my lungs. Jealous of her ability to speak underwater, I can only touch my lips where her touch lingers.

The water stills again, and we emerge into utter chaos.

Scarlette stands like a goddess of fire on a tall tree surrounded by flames. She pushes away the fire from the tree she's perched on, her crimson hair flying wildly around her. Her path of lava is direct as it splashes onto grotesque-looking creatures flooding the garden.

Juniper swoops out of the sky with a spear, its tip glinting in the firelight, and dive-bombs a large man. The spear pierces the man through the chest, leaving the man like a shish kebab bent backward. His arms flail as the spear sticks in the ground behind him. His hand grabs the end of the lance, and he pulls himself, sliding his body up the shaft. My mouth drops as his legs straighten, and he stands, leaving the spear at a forty-five-degree angle in the dirt. His black eyes scan the battlefield, and goosebumps freckle my arms.

"What the fuck," I breathe.

Alvar runs to the large man, dropping to the grass and sliding past as he sets him alight. Surprising the man, he appears behind him and wraps his arms around his neck, snapping his head off in one clean motion.

My stomach rolls as I watch the head drop, and the body goes up in flames. I almost choke as I realize the man's skin is sickly and drips from the heat. These are not normal fae.

An unnatural wind carries the stench of burning flesh and rot across the garden. Nausea hits me, and Yudoku goes pale, her eyes going dark. The water churns around me. I take this as my sign to get out of the pond or fall victim to her wrath.

I pull myself to shore, sliding a dagger from my thigh.

Don't freeze. You can do this.

Nucifera zips past me on a breeze; she says something to Yudoku. I watch as they whip up a flurry of fog that rolls over the ground. The mist surrounds a group of fae as they run into the fray. Nucifera disappears into the haze as Yudoku pushes it through the garden.

The tail of the giant cobra that is Lyra slithers into the gloom, and screams erupt. As I creep closer to the wall of mist, I see her gargantuan hooded head rear up out of the fog, and acid erupts from her as her hood flutters.

My breath gets caught in my chest as I watch.

What the fuck am I thinking, getting closer? Even my friends are terrifying.

You can do this.

A shrill scream rings out, and the mist drops like water, sloshing to the ground. A tall man with long white hair, a few steps away, holds Nucifera in the air by her neck. She kicks and struggles in his hold as he laughs.

"Sorrel...no," she wheezes. "Please—"

Lyra turns her golden eyes on the man and hisses. Something hits the side of her face, and powder explodes around her head. She collapses onto the grass immediately, looking up in horror from her fae body.

Darius cries out for her and shoots a stream of fire at the woman who flung the powder at Lyra. The woman's black eyes are devoid of life as she screams, flailing wildly. Darius runs to Lyra's side and helps her to her feet. Together, they retreat into the trees. They leave a trail of flames in their wake as Darius sets whatever lurks in the woods on fire.

My steps are deliberate and cautious as I approach the man holding Nucifera, mindful of every crackle or crunch that could give away my presence.

"Why, Sorrel? Why are you...helping him?" She rasps.

He reaches for his sword, and my heart stops. Damn fae and their hearing. Quicker than a blink, a flash of silver and Nucifera's bone-rattling scream shakes me to my core. Her wings float lifelessly to the ground, like petals from a flower.

I hold in a horrified gasp as my jaw drops.

She goes slack, and he throws her away from himself, chuckling.

Don't freeze. I can do this.

Don't think about it; act.

You belong to me. Your body is mine. I blink away the memory and the voice that haunts me.

Red.

All I see is red.

My vision narrows on the fae. I refuse to stand by while another girl gets brutalized.

I throw myself into his back before I can think better of it. The sound is sickening as I slam my knife between his shoulder blades. He roars in pain, his back bowing. I quickly drop to my knees, pull another dagger from my vest, and slice across his Achilles tendon. I roll away as he collapses, using the maneuvers Killian drilled into me. Standing in front of Nucifera's frail, limp body, I sneer at him. Breathing heavily, I stand my ground, unable to believe what I've just done.

I didn't freeze.

"You," he rasps. "The fucking mortal–" he coughs, struggling to sit up. Blood trickles from his lips as he takes rattling breaths. His eyes are surprisingly sharp and steely gray, not black like the others. Blood splatters his face; it drips down his front like crimson confetti.

"Would you just die already?" I growl.

"I'll make sure to torture you real slow. Unless you like it rough, Princess."

Gross.

God, why can't he just bleed out? I need to get Nucifera out of here. I stand with my blade ready, guarding my friend.

Screams ring out all around. A roar fills the air, a clash of fae and monster, and the crackle of powers colliding. The ground rumbles as another explosive sound causes me to cover my ears and curl in on myself, searching for the danger around me.

The white-haired man laughs. "You should have just agreed to be a slave because what he has planned for you will be far worse."

Anger flashes through me, boiling my blood. I sneer at him as I throw a dagger at his chest. "Fuck you." I'm so over guys like this.

He rolls and catches it in his arm. Snarling, he pulls it out. Fire blazes in his eyes as his entire body tenses, and fear trickles down my spine.

He's going to roast me.

Of course, this asshole is a fire elemental.

I pull frantically on that little well of magic I can barely feel in my chest. Ice frosts my fingertips and then melts away.

Come on. Why can't I use it?

I reach for another dagger.

He is yanked backward by teal claws wrapped around his throat. He pulls at the claws that draw blood, rivulets drizzling down his chest. His feet kick wildly, legs scrambling for purchase. Yudoku drags him along the ground, a wicked smile playing across her jagged teeth. Her body moves quickly in a serpentine motion. With a yelp, she drags him to his watery grave.

I rush to the edge of the pond, worried he might still roast my friend. They are gone; only the ripples in the water remain.

Well, that's a shit way to go, but he deserved it.

Turning back to the petite pixie, I look around helplessly for someone to help me pick her up. I carefully scoop her featherlight wings up and place them on her. Lifting her shoulders, I drag her towards the treeline. I catch Scarlette's eye, and she puts a river of lava between the other fae and us. With my hands under her arms, I pull her as fast as possible in the direction of the meeting point.

"Fall back!"

My head snaps up at the voice.

"It's a trap! Ryker! Fall back!" Killian yells through the garden—panic written across his face, his hair a disheveled mess around him.

The falcon makes a screeching noise that causes everyone to run. Killian rushes in my direction, cradling his hand to his chest.

"Yudoku is still underwater!" I yell back.

"Just go! Run, Jade!"

I keep pulling the unconscious Nucifera, watching as walls of earth and fire erect to slow down our pursuers. The others break away to run for the forest.

Yudoku rises out of the water, and her tail vanishes. Her air power glides her to the grass as she sprints towards me.

I let out a relieved breath.

Killian catches up to me and picks up Nucifera, tossing her over his shoulder. I take her wings as we sprint through the trees, Yudoku close behind.

The ground rumbles again, and I trip, stumbling into the dirt. Killian is thrown off his feet and tumbles next to me. He winces as he catches himself on his forearm. Yudoku lies behind us, groaning. I glance over my shoulder to see a giant white dragon land in the garden. It towers above the trees. If not for the gruesome burns taking over half of the body and the black eyes, it would be beautiful. Its roar is deafening and rough, like it's pulling it from the depths of its soul.

My heart stalls in my chest. Flashes of a stunning white dragon on a beach flicker in my mind.

Yudoku stares in horror. "We killed that thing," she breathes.

Great...zombie dragon, that's just what we need. My mouth is dry as I take in the sight. Bones protrude from its sides where the scales have rotted away. Part of its skull is showing on its muzzle. My palms grow damp as my throat closes.

"Ah, come on. You've got to be kidding me. Fuck!" Killian says, scrambling to his feet.

With a burst of energy, Yudoku and I stand. It's only a little further.

A blur of green flashes by the dragon, and my stomach drops. A spear lodges in the dragon's eye as Juniper speeds toward us. The dragon's roar turns piercing. Its head swings back and forth as it charges at her. Trying to avoid the beast, Juniper bobs and weaves. Fluttering her wings like a hummingbird, she retreats in a flurry. Teeth snap down, and the pixie vanishes behind pearly whites.

Screams flood my world. My throat feels raw, and I can't breathe. The screaming won't stop. Choking on the bile that rises up my esophagus, it takes everything in me to stay on my feet, but I'm rooted to the spot in wide-eyed horror.

Vines burst from the dragon's neck, twisting around and around. Flowers spring from its nostrils as thorns bore through, stitching themselves along the skin. It wildly thrashes, engulfed in greenery like a macabre topiary. The dragon shrieks, its roar shrill and deafening. Thorns expand, moving down its body, growing to epic proportions. The dragon's scales split apart as the vines pierce it from the inside, while they continue to cut into its neck.

Then everything stops, the vines stop moving, and the dragon drops to the ground with a crash that rumbles the earth.

Someone is pulling me, and I stumble backward as I wait for the pixie to emerge. I know I'm moving, but I feel like stone, like everything is going in slow motion.

A person is talking behind me, and then I'm lifted into a warm embrace. I keep my eyes on the dragon over his shoulder. "She could still be alive." I whimper.

Killian doesn't say anything. He just runs into the portal, and the last thing I see is Warrick dragging Alvar through before the world tilts.

Killian sets me down in the grass, the clearing filled with fae in various states of despair. The world moves at a crawl around me. Warrick works tirelessly to heal Nucifera, her wings lifeless beside her. Corsac holds Scarlette, and tears stream down her face as she talks. Ambrose applies pressure to a gash down her leg.

Alvar kneels in the grass, staring into the trees. The pixie he loved is gone from this world, and a husk of a man has been left behind.

Lyra sits silently on the steps to the portal—the portal that has vanished. The swirling vortex is now a hole within a frame. Darius bows before her, his head on her knees, as she absentmindedly strokes his hair.

I'm numb; I should be feeling something, but I feel empty.

"Where the fuck is she?" Ryker booms.

I turn my head, trying to focus on Killian and Ryker. They stand behind Warrick, who is going pale. The light in his honeyed eyes has gone out.

"They didn't come back?" Killian asks, with a hint of panic in his tone.

Ryker holds Killian's bloodied hand in his, lavender light sparkling around the wound. He flexes his fingers as the bite mark closes.

Ryker's eyes flit over everyone in the clearing, his jaw feathering with tension.

I will myself to get up, my body feeling like a lead weight. I'm lightheaded as I move towards them on shaky legs.

"No. I waited. There was no sign of them." Warrick's face is sullen as golden light flares around the stubs on Nucifera's back. His hands gently apply pressure to stop the bleeding.

I walk to Killian, placing my hand on his arm. "Rodan and Cat?"

They all look down, not meeting my eyes.

My entire world cracks.

No.

No.

No.

"Where are they?" Panic floods me. "Oh god, no, this is all my fault. Cat wouldn't even be here if it weren't for me."

"This isn't on you, my love." Killian's hand cups my cheek, wiping away a tear with his thumb.

I shake my head. This can't be possible. I refuse to believe this. Rodan is too strong. They would have come back if something wasn't right. They were supposed to hide in his shadows. Cat can get so small that she could slip away from any trouble. This can't be real.

"We have to go back!"

Ringing fills my ears as I try to breathe air that feels like water.

I pull on Killian's arm, imploring him to look at me.

A tear slides down his cheek, and he takes a shuddering breath. His shoulders fold in; my wolf looks so small. A piece of me breaks away and turns to ash.

Ryker drops to his knees, his arms limp at his sides.

No, we don't have time for their logic or their planning. They can't just give up. I tremble, bordering on hysteria, as I ball my fists.

"We have to go back for them! We can't leave them there!" I turn to run for the treeline, but Killian's arm wraps around my waist, stopping me. He pulls me into him, holding me tight as I thrash. Screaming, I push against his chest, frantically trying to escape.

My throat begins to close as spots dance around the edges of my vision.

"Please." I rasp, sinking as my legs give out. Killian embraces me, dropping to the ground with me.

Pain sears through my chest, and I crumple in on myself as a sob racks through me. Killian holds me tight, his stuttered breath causing a chasm to split me down the middle. A flood of tears breaks through.

"Killian, please. We have to go back."

"It was a trap," he whispers. "We walked right into it. I thought it was a weakness in their defense. We fell for it." His grip around me grows tighter as tears slip down his face.

"It can't be over. We can't just leave them."

"We're not just going to leave them. We need time to regroup." Warrick says.

"What if they don't have time? Cat can barely defend herself," I say.

"She can defend herself." Ryker's low growl makes me flush with shame. He folds over his knees, pounding his fist on the ground. He cries in anguish to the gods. The tidal wave of emotion drags him under, our world collapsing around us.

Corsac and Scarlette settle on either side of him. Tears stream down their stoic faces. Corsac rubs small circles over his back as his whole body shakes with sobs. Scarlette lays her head on his trembling back—the man who rarely seems rattled by anything, broken.

I bury my face in Killian's shoulder. His head rests on mine as the fight drains out of me silently, one tear at a time. Sorrow washes through me, salty tears washing away a bloody battlefield. I'm drowning in grief and regret. The pool so deep that there is no hope of ever seeing daylight again.

I lost a man I love and my best friend.

This is the truest heartbreak and exactly what I deserve.

I'm a terrible person. I pushed Rodan away out of fear. Even when he constantly showed me, I had nothing to doubt. He holds me together when the world wants to break me. Even when Ace took me, Rodan somehow kept me going, bleeding through my dreams, my smallest ray of hope.

I convinced Cat to stay and encouraged her to go with Rodan because I trusted he could keep her safe. And now—

And now...

I can't feel him.

Pressure fills my skull as fresh tears spill through the busted dam. The ache in my head and chest is so profound, I welcome the tunneling of my vision as the black turns everything to a pinprick. The anguish that fills my chest spasms through me as I struggle to breathe.

Falling into the dark void of my mind, I accept silence and let it swallow me. I curl into a ball and let the tears spill.

Chapter 30
Killian

What have I done?

I let down my entire kingdom.

I let her down.

There's an emptiness within the bond that I fear can never be repaired. Where do we go from here? I'm suffocating with the need to do something, anything.

Nightfall drapes the clearing in a melancholic veil, the sky blushing a somber shade of orange. The moons ascend, and the broken orb of light is a grim reminder of how shattered I feel. The mountains rise above on all sides, their jagged peaks casting shadows across us. Thick evergreens encompass the secluded area hidden away from the world.

Jade shivers, sitting between my legs as I hold her. She stares into the fire, catatonic.

Ryker has retreated into himself. He sits against a tree on the far side, gaze fixed to the sky. He blames himself for what happened to Cat, but this isn't his fault. It's mine.

The fire pops and crackles as Darius turns the spit, roasting some small birds. No one is hungry, but we need to keep up our strength. He knows Lyra won't eat unless he pushes her to; I can only assume the same is true for Jade.

Scarlette and Corsac huddle around Nucifera, who hasn't stopped sobbing since she awoke without wings. Warrick broke down when he realized he couldn't reattach them. He folds in on himself, keeping his distance from the pixie, blaming himself.

Yudoku strokes Jade's hair, her eyes downcast. "Killian?"

I shift my focus, taking in the siren.

"I need to tell you something." She takes a deep breath. "The high councilors attacked us in the garden with those monsters. Their eyes were black, but I recognized a few of them. The fish said they were all puppets now. Sorrel was out there, too."

I furrow my brow. That explains why they weren't near the orbs. We can assume at this point that anyone with black eyes has been turned. The dragons and monsters all had black eyes; it must be something Ellis did to them. I rest my chin on Jade's head, tightening my arms around her.

The blows just keep coming. I close my eyes, concentrating on my breathing before I have a complete meltdown. I'm right on the edge, teetering and terrified. My stomach rumbles as my insides collapse upon themselves, the stress eating me alive, or perhaps the guilt.

My parents would never have screwed up this badly. I still can't believe they got caught so off guard, but with what that orb did to me, I understand now. The embers of my power have barely started stirring after being drained. An empty pit sits where my light used to be.

"Sorrel? Were his eyes black, too?" Lyra asks.

Yudoku slowly shakes her head. "I'm sorry. I don't think he was under anyone's control."

"Son of a bitch," Lyra grumbles. She wraps her arms around her knees as she looks around the small circle.

"Sorrel cut off Nucifera's wings. I stabbed him," Jade murmurs.

My heart stops, and my spine stiffens. I blink a few times, wondering if I heard her correctly. "You... stabbed him?"

"I just lost it. He had her by the throat and...when he...I didn't think; I just moved. I did it like you showed me, then dropped to the ground and took out his ankle. I thought he was gonna kill me, but Yudoku dragged him into the water."

Yudoku nods as I make eye contact with her, flashing her jagged teeth and wiggling her eyebrows.

A huff of a laugh bubbles out of me.

Shit, I wanna be mad at her for putting Jade in harm's way, but I'm impressed. She was supposed to stay in the night garden, closer to Warrick and away from the fighting. I'm proud as hell, but Rodan is gonna kill her.

If he's still alive.

I take a deep breath.

I can't imagine everything going through Jade's head right now. I should have realized how fierce she was when she beat the tar out of her ex. I shake my head as I put my chin back on Jade's head. Comfort washes through me as I feel her breathing against me. I'd get under her skin if I could.

I love this woman.

Lyra sighs. "And you think you have poor taste in men. I could teach a lesson in wicked men, Sugar." She winks at Jade.

I guess Jade didn't fully fill her in on everything that happened to her in the mortal world. Just the thought makes my eyes burn and my blood simmer.

Darius smirks, shaking his head.

"Don't believe me? Once, I dated this gorgeous man. He was a fox shifter. Long white hair, dreamy eyes, muscles for days. Have mercy; he was fine." She fans herself, and I feel Jade's body shake with a slight giggle. "It turned out he had a snake fetish, if you know what I mean."

"He liked men?" Jade asks in almost a whisper.

"No, darlin', nothing like that. A *snake* fetish. Like he wanted to do the deed with my cobra." Her face is serious as everyone erupts into uncomfortable laughter. "Honey, no! Get your sword away from my scales. This form is sacred." She smooths down her pants, flashing a weak smile.

"Want me to drown him?" Yudoku giggles.

"Oh, that would just be peachy." She winks, and we all laugh. "I guess Sorrel will have to be added to my list of failures. Arlin would have been losin' her shit about this; she kept sayin' there was something off about him. And let's face it, he did not keep the best company. Anyway, what about you? Any juicy stories? Ya never really said much about yourself, and I'm dying to know more about the murder-maid." She trains her full attention on Yudoku.

Yudoku's eyes widen, and her mouth opens in surprise. She collects herself, scrunching her brows in thought. "Umm." A slow, devious smile spreads across her face. "My mother tried to arrange a marriage once. The man was a toad. Seriously, he shifted into a toad. In case you missed it, I'm a *sea* siren. That wouldn't have been such a big deal if he wasn't an absolute prick." She sighs.

"You see, his earth powers were out of this world. My mother thought he would be useful, seeing as earth powers are rare in my queendom. So, I agreed to go on a date with him on land. Big mistake, he got handsy in the first ten minutes. I'm not exactly strong on land." She winces. "Anyway, after, I got him close enough to the water to drag him under. I fed him to Larz."

"I'm sorry that happened to you," Jade says, putting her hand on her friend's knee. A pang of sadness runs through everyone. My heart falls as I realize just how sheltered from the world I have been. I didn't know people could be so cruel. Maybe Rodan was right long ago when he said I should get my head out of the fairytales.

Lyra's eyes are wide with sympathy. "Who is Larz?"

"A shark shifter." She smirks, giggling. She chomps her teeth and smiles widely.

Everyone laughs, but I can't help but wonder if that's why she didn't pursue anyone while she's been here.

"So, Mother was pissed, but not because of what the toad did. Which, fuck you, Mom. She was mad because rumors spread like plankton that I would bite off any prick that got near me." She laughs maniacally, snapping her teeth again. Darius, Warrick, and I all exchange a look. I shiver at the thought. "Now, no one will come near me. That's how I ended up here."

The women erupt into laughter, even Nucifera. She wipes tears from her eyes as she tries to catch her breath. So this is how the girls decompress and lighten the mood. I should have figured it would be this or taking out aggression on something. I'm glad to see some smiles light up the group.

As the ladies keep talking, no one wants to breach the subject of what happened today or who's missing anymore. What else is left to say? It hangs over us like a shadow. Haunted eyes meet across flames; we all feel it.

The loss.

Everyone takes turns telling random stories, sharing the burden of distracting ourselves. Ryker eventually comes to sit by the fire. He doesn't say anything; he doesn't have to. Halfheartedly, he eats with the rest of us; the food going down like ash. At least, that's how it feels to me.

Alvar still sits where we buried Nucifera's wings and said some words about Juniper. It was a less-than-ideal way to mourn her, but what else could we do without a body? We all feel her loss. Nucifera brings him a plate of food, and they sit staring at the dirt, plates untouched.

With the portal to the Fates Grove gone, we find ourselves stranded in the mountains, vulnerable and desperate. Our priority now is to return the ladies to their kingdoms and hope for a miracle. Once Warrick has enough power, he will open the portal and get everyone out of Amara.

Gods, how did things go so incredibly sideways, so fast?

Jade shifts in my lap, turning to gaze at me. "He had moments before he died when she pulled him under." Her eyes look into mine, pleading, searching. "I was so angry."

My heart clenches for her. She will bear the burden of that scar, even if the prick deserved it. The look on her face breaks me; I did this to her. I was selfish and so stupid. Who did I think I was? That I could just rush in, save a few people, and take back the castle together. They believed me...I believed me...That might be the worst part.

"You saved Nucifera, defended her. I'm proud of you." I caress her cheek, and she leans into it, closing her puffy, red-rimmed eyes. "You did well today, my love."

"I don't know what to do."

I lean down, brushing my lips against hers. My chest is heavy, and my ribs are too tight around my lungs. I don't say anything because I have no words to make it better. No way to fix things, no plan.

I can't think straight without my brother.

I toss and turn on the hard ground, but I'm not the only one who can't sleep. In the dim firelight, Jade stares up at the sky. Her chest rises and falls on shuddered breaths as tear tracks glisten into her hairline. She and Yudoku huddled against the side of the steps to the broken portal, keeping the night breeze off them. I roll towards Jade, running my hand across her abdomen.

"Can't sleep?" I ask.

"No, I'm afraid that if I close my eyes, I'll just relive what happened."

Yudoku rolls over, looking at me from Jade's other side. Her pale eyes gleam with sorrow.

"You weren't even supposed to be in the enchanted garden," I say, glaring at Yudoku.

"We couldn't stay in the night garden. Ellis was there, and I figured you'd want her as far from him as possible." Yudoku levels me with her stare.

My heart jumps in my chest.

Shit.

I don't even try to wipe the look of shock off my face. I feel like a jackass for even bringing it up now. As much as I want to protect Jade from the world, I need to learn to trust her intuition. I wish they had told me sooner, just for my own peace of mind. Knowing that would have also kept me from putting my foot in my mouth with the siren who still might eat me.

"I also saved her from the destruction of Scarlette's volcanic explosion," she whispers.

"It's true, we had to dive under the water, and I would have drowned from how long we had to stay under if she hadn't kissed me and given me air." Jade turns her head and gives me a weak smile.

Wait, what?

She what?

My body tenses, and I grip Jade harder. Trying to rein in my temper and the possessiveness of my wolf, I take a deep breath. "You kissed her?" I growl at the siren.

Yudoku cocks a brow and silently laughs, mirth washing across her face.

Jade's brows furrow as she looks at me like I just grew a second head.

I take another deep breath and try to keep my tone even. "You have air powers. You could have just put a bubble around her."

"Where's the fun in that?" Yudoku quips.

I level a glare at her and flex my fingers out of the tight fist I'd been making.

"Wait, you didn't have to kiss me to give me air?" Jade says with a quiet giggle in her voice.

Yudoku laughs, and I narrow my eyes at the little vixen.

"I had to see what all the hype was about," she says simply, rolling onto her side away from us.

Shaking my head, I pull Jade to my side, giving in to my nature to possess her. She settles her head in the crook of my arm and closes her eyes.

On my other side, Darius is chuckling. Apparently, he's awake and also thinks this is hilarious. Sharing her with Rodan is hard enough, but at least that makes sense. I am not sharing with anyone who isn't her mate. Thankfully, almost everyone else is asleep in the circle of the fire. We are all so devoid of power after that fight, but hopefully, everyone will get a much-needed recharge. I still feel only the barest of embers within me—the tension is like a dragon perched on my chest.

Warrick sleeps soundly next to Nucifera. He hasn't let her out of his sight since she awoke. Corsac and Scarlette stay huddled together, keeping each other warm. No one left the ring of the fire when night fell, and sleep came for us. Safety in numbers is our only ally.

The dark trees around us rustle in the light breeze. The shadows of branches dance across the ground around us. Soft skitters of animals chitter through the underbrush. Clouds glide over the moons, casting gloominess across the land. The shattered moon peaks out between the heavy gray haziness, a firm reminder that nothing has been right with the world in a century.

The light from the moon winks out as the clouds close in and block out the last of the light. The world around me fades into darkness as the shadows in the treeline grow darker. An ominous silence falls around us. Cast into pitch-black as the embers of the fire snuff out, darkness creeps towards us. The slight breeze has stopped, and the ruffling of animals has ceased.

I listen, holding my breath.

This has to be just my imagination playing tricks on me.

I reach into myself, trying to find the barest ember to form a spark, but there is still nothing. My heart beats erratically as I try to steady my breathing. There is no need to scare everyone if I'm just paranoid.

But I can't see a damn thing.

Fire flickers next to me as Darius sits up and sucks in a breath.

Slowly, I rise from the ground, and a wave of dread comes over me as I take in the wall of shadow surrounding our small group. It swirls and pulses with blue crackling light, and smoke-like tendrils weave in and out of the cylinder we find ourselves in.

"What in the blue blazes?" Lyra whispers, sitting up.

I stand, casting my eyes quickly to Jade and Yudoku, huddled together with wide eyes.

The dark wall is unsettling; I've never seen anything like it. Trepidation settles in my bones. The blue light that flashes through the smoke is so similar to Rodan's. This is beyond anything he's ever done with his shadows, though. The wall seems alive and writhing like a pit of snakes.

I reach into my well of power again, hoping to find something there, but I can't reach it.

Ropes of shadow shoot out all around us. Screams rip out of people as they are yanked from sleep. The tendrils wrap around legs, pulling every fae in a different direction. They scramble, flailing their arms as the tentacles drag them across the meadow, disappearing into the smoke. It is so sudden, I don't even have time to take a breath of surprise. The screams die out as fast as they came. The forest goes silent again.

I spin around, searching for an assailant, but find none.

In one swift move, all that's left is Jade, Yudoku, and me, protected by the steps at our back. Did the steps stop the shadows from grabbing us? I don't know what to think.

The girls rise to their feet, tiptoeing behind me as we stare into the rolling darkness. Their small bodies press into my back, vibrating with fear.

"What the fuck is that?" Jade whispers.

"I do not know," Yudoku hisses.

Thunder claps overhead, and lightning flashes across the sky, illuminating the empty clearing. The women jump and huddle closer to me. Only the sound of our labored breathing remains. The scent of ozone hits fast and hard before the sky opens up and dumps a deluge of water on us. Instantly soaked in freezing water, the sky flashes again as thunder rumbles the ground, sending my frayed nerves into overdrive.

I search the wall of shadows for any signs of movement through the downpour. With every flash of lightning, the thunder rumbles, and the wall of smoke writhes. I don't see a way out. A pit forms in my stomach as my pulse spikes with every crack of thunder.

A figure catches my attention as it steps from the shadows. The darkness seems to melt off the figure, pooling in clouds of smoke at their feet. Lightning flashes, and my heart drops as I take in the pitch-black eyes glaring across the clearing.

No.

Jade sucks in a sharp breath, and I feel her lunge before stopping mid-step.

Light illuminates the sky again, and the cold black eyes devoid of white, my worst fear imagined. Rodan stands before us, his shadows wisp off him like smoke. The ominous blue light is unquestionable as electricity crackles across his arms.

"What are you doing?" The deafening roar of rain drowns out my shout. Water drips into my eyes, rolling over me like a waterfall. I stare into the darkness as the man I call brother looks at me like a stranger.

His face morphs into a cruel smile that has the ladies shrinking behind me.

"What's wrong with him?" Jade whispers.

"His eyes are black. We've lost him," Yudoku says, her voice going gravelly.

No.

He wouldn't do this to us. This can't be happening.

"Rodan, think about what you're doing. This isn't you," I plead as my chest cleaves open.

His head cocks to the side, his smile growing wider.

A shiver runs down my spine. For the first time in my life, I'm genuinely terrified of the man who stands before me. The way he moves is unnatural, almost mechanical. The power he's exhibiting is like nothing I've ever seen. My brother may be lost to us.

"Rodan, you can't do this to me!" Jade rushes past me. Panicked, I chase her and pull her into my chest, only a few feet from him. Holding her like a vice, she pushes at my arms and screams, desperate and pleading. The rain conceals her tears, and her hair becomes plastered to her face. She shivers as she screeches, slipping in the mud under her feet as she tries to free herself. "Come back to me! Fight it! Whatever it is, fight it, you asshole!"

Rodan's smile falters as his body stiffens.

"I will never forgive you if you leave me this way! I'm sorry, okay! I'm sorry I was so slow to come around. I'm sorry I pushed you away! I'm sorry, I don't remember!" Jade continues to scream and thrash in my arms as I watch on in horror. I pull her, kicking and screaming, away from him. My chest aches from the betrayal I feel down to my bones. Her sobs grow more ragged, and my heart cracks. A deluge of emotions overwhelms mine, a suffocating whirlpool of hopelessness dragging me deeper into an abyss of despair. I'm so wrecked, I can't put up the walls around my mind to stop the connection with Jade. A mournful wail escapes me, tears streaming down my face as my vision blurs in a haze of sorrow.

This can't be goodbye. This can't be how this ends.

As if he's taken all the air, I gasp for oxygen, unable to stop the ache in my chest. Jade shakes in my arms, an icy chill taking hold of her. I can't bear to watch her suffer this way.

"Come back to me. I love you," she whimpers as she goes limp in my arms.

His face scrunches, and he clutches his head as if in pain. A scream roars out of him, and he looks at me with pleading eyes, green glints off the crackle of power encircling him. "Run—" he gasps, buckling over.

The shadows recede around us, gathering around him, forming a wall but leaving the way clear behind us. Resolute, I nod at my brother and drag Jade backward.

"No!" Jade screams as I pull her towards the forest.

Rodan's voice booms, "Run, Trouble. I can't stop..." His tone turns desperate. "I need you to run because it will destroy me if you don't. I don't want to hurt you...Please go...Don't come back for me." He screams in agony as he sinks to his knees.

I reach the treeline, the dense forest looming before us, and look back with a lump in my throat as I watch my brother regain his footing. He glances at us with resignation, turns, and walks in the opposite direction.

Chapter 31
Rodan

White.

Solid white walls rise above, encapsulating me.

One singular window breaks up the white; it is tall and rectangular, but there is not a single door.

Beyond the glass is a solid sheet of black.

Where the fuck am I?

It's been hours, and as much as I go over the last things I remember, I still can't figure out where I am. I sit against the wall, exhausted from trying to break the window. I stare across the room at the impenetrable glass.

I can't feel the bond. Emptiness consumes the space in which it once resided.

I can't feel my power.

I don't know what happened to Cat.

Gods, Cat.

Running my hand down my face, I peer at the darkness beyond the glass. The light in the room is so bright that there is no escaping it, not even with my eyes closed. It permeates from the walls themselves, like I'm in a cube carved of incandescent stone.

When I get my hands on Beatrix, I am going to strangle the life out of her. Then, I'm going to kick-start her heart and do it again.

I hope Killian fared better than I did. If he managed to save the high council members, he might stand a real chance of saving everyone. I don't want to think about what would happen if he failed.

Darkness falls over me, the light snuffed out.

The window reveals a forest moving past.

What. The. Fuck?

The rustle of footsteps and crunching of leaves surround me. I can smell the forest, the dirt, and the rotting smell of decay.

I crawl forward, settling in front of the window, trying to see where the fuck I am. Everything seems wrong; the scale of the world is too big.

Where the fuck am I?

My heartbeat picks up as I see the melted and charred constructs weaving through trees in the distance. Red flashes to the right, and the world goes silent as if the sound has been cut from my prison.

"No!" I bark, slamming my hand on the glass.

I need information. I need to know where the fuck they are taking me.

The world outside the window stops. Shadows swirl and writhe, snaking out fast and filling everything as far as I can see.

My stomach drops.

Pressing myself to the glass as my world collapses, I watch in horror as my power encircles a clearing—lightning crackling in the smoke like storm clouds.

How?

I feel the blood drain from my face.

I'm not in a room.

This is a prison of my own mind.

My body is merely a puppet being pulled by someone else's

strings.

Nononono.

I stand banging on the glass, throwing my weight into it.

I can't see anything beyond the wall of smoke, but the knot in the pit of my stomach tells me what is about to happen.

Screams ring out as sound returns, and fae are dragged through the wall.

Warrick roars in defiance before a beat of power silences him. My power.

Everyone falls silent at once.

Ryker, Scarlette, Corsac...

Please, please don't let them be dead.

My arms fall slack as I watch high counselors and constructs load my friends into a wagon. The rise and fall of Lyra's chest gives me the slightest bit of hope. My window shows me every single person my power reaped through the wall.

Four faces are missing from our group.

My body walks into the mist as the last of them are loaded into the wagon, no doubt to ensure they got everyone. Fucking assholes. Thunder claps overhead as rain pours, drowning out the clearing with my hopes.

Killian stands in the middle, with his back to the portal—or what's left of it. My heart sinks as I take in the circle perched on stone steps. All the magic of the gateway has been removed. I can just make out Jade and Yudoku standing behind Killian through the downpour.

If they needed confirmation of who could do something like this, they just got it. I don't know how I formed a cylinder of shadow around the entire clearing, but I have a feeling Ellis is behind it. He must have tampered with my powers somehow.

With renewed vigor, I thrash against the walls of my prison. I have to save them. I have to save them from me.

"...You can't do this to me!" Jade's voice cuts through the din of the rain and thunder. She fights like a wildcat, trying to release herself from Killian's hold to get to me.

I scream in rage, slamming my fist into the wall.

"I will never forgive you if you leave me this way! I'm sorry, okay! I'm sorry I was so slow to come around. I'm sorry I pushed you away! I'm sorry, I don't remember!" Jade pleads.

Her broken voice tears me apart. I want to destroy everything that puts that look on her precious face. Again, I roar and slam my fist into the wall, and a faint line appears, a hairline crack. The faint pull of the bond thrums to life. Unbearable sorrow engulfs me, as if a heavy cloud has settled upon my chest, weighing me down with each agonizing breath. Her despair is nearly debilitating. I feel her heart breaking, crushing my own with it. Consumed by grief, I beat at the wall with everything I have.

I can't do this to her.

"Come back to me. I love you."

Her pain rips through me, and I feel the bond pull taut. Crashing through the box, pain sears through my brain as rain soaks me. I clutch my head, struggling to steady myself. Threads of light pull at my consciousness, yanking me back towards my prison. I grit my teeth, trying to hold on as long as I can. Gripping my power, I pull the shadows to myself, opening a path behind them.

"Run—" I gasp as the threads pulling me grow stronger.

Jade thrashes, screaming as Killian pulls her away.

I look up into those midnight blue eyes. "Run, Trouble. I can't stop..." I plead, "I need you to run because it will destroy me if you don't. I don't want to hurt you...Please go...Don't come back for me." Panting, I fall to my knees, the searing pain ravaging my body as a roar breaks free. I tremble as I keep my hold on the shadows; betrayal fills me with how they fight.

I want to tell them more, but I can't hold my power back and regain control of my speech again.

When they reach the edge of the clearing, I manage to pull

myself to my feet and meet Jade's eyes. I want to tell her: I don't think I can be saved. That she should run away with Killian, take him back to the mortal world, and have the life I couldn't give her. That I failed her. Again. That I'm sorry. That I love her with every fiber of my being. Instead, I turn and walk through the shadows, giving them time to escape before I lose control.

"I am very disappointed but also impressed, Prince." Ellis sneers from across the room, where I am tied to a fucking chair. "No one has ever broken through my enchantments before."

I find that hard to believe.

After I watched my reason for living escape into the forest, I lost my momentary control and was shoved back into the white box of my mind. I looked out of the window as we traveled back to the castle. My friends were dragged out of the cart and into the recesses of the dungeon. I hate feeling this helpless, but at least Jade and Killian escaped with the siren.

Now I sit, drained of power but allowed to inhabit my mind again. However, I once more find myself stripped of my panther. I don't know what the fuck that powder is, but it's bullshit.

"Let's see. How should I punish you?" Ellis muses.

"There must be a better way to control him; my song only goes so far," Owari says, dancing in the corner of the room. Her lavender hair swirls around her pearly pink skin. She always looks so ethereal, even in a madman's lair. The walls are stone, but rougher than the upper levels of the castle. Across from me lies a table strewn with old books and manuscripts. Cabinets full of glass vials in various hues wink at me in the dim light. This must be the hidden lab; probably the one Ryker said had a giant spider guarding it. I'd give anything to see the look on Killian's face when he found it. I've never seen anyone as afraid of spiders as that man.

The wall of books undulates with power. Occasionally, they move of their own accord, as if switching seats to sit next to a long-forgotten friend. It's creepy as shit.

"Yes, it seems my normal methods don't make him quite the puppet I was hoping for. Alas, the puppet I had in mind is back in the mortal world. The human was so much easier," Ellis says, flipping through a large black book. "It's no matter; now that I have you, I'll find a better way to use you and keep you on a leash."

"Why are you doing any of this? Power? Control? Why take Amara?" I keep my tone even, devoid of feeling.

Ellis looks at me and lowers his glasses. He has that evil scientist crap down. I wonder how much time he spent in the mortal world watching movies, because this is uncanny. While I continue to keep my stoic expression intact, the urge to laugh grows as I envision him studying those films like gospel. I may have watched far too many movies while at Jade's parents' house.

"I want to finish what my father started so long ago in Eneara. Seeing how we were run out or imprisoned, I fled to Auburnigh. There have been challenges, but I find that if you plan long enough, you can make things happen. I've already got Shadow exactly where I want it, and now Amara is falling in line."

Well, that confirms what I needed to know about Shadow, but how does that tie into the Kingdom of Light? Unless he already controls Light, which means he's taking over the country from the top and working his way down. Perhaps he already has things in motion in other countries that no one is aware of.

Fuck.

"Why send me to the mortal world? Why not just kill me?" I glance around the room. There has got to be a way out of this.

"You were Plan B, which I now need. At first, I thought Killian was the prince, as he bears a striking resemblance to your father, but then I realized you are. As unconventional as it seemed to crown the bastard heir, I figured it out with enough digging. You are the more powerful son, and the queen adored you. Sickening really. I had originally planned to replace you with the human puppet; they are so much easier to control, but your brother botched that plan. I'm really impressed. I thought him a bit too dim to do it. But now I've figured out how to use you and your powers to my advantage." He shrugs.

"And Jade, why send her away? Why keep her alive?" I have to keep this guy talking; distracted. The binds holding me to the chair look ornamental, but the frayed ropes are not strong enough to hold me this well. How the fuck am I supposed to escape magical bindings? This is ridiculous.

"Collateral."

"Why wipe her memory?"

Owari spins to a stop and looks at me, her face alight. "Oh, did it stick? I didn't think it would. Her soul was a wreck, all jagged, frayed bits." As much as I'd like her to think her bullshit didn't work, I think I'll keep the fact that Jade remembers more than they'd like to myself.

"Because I liked her better when she was broken, weak, more pliable. If I need to use her, I'd prefer she has no memory of her fae heritage or powers. Granted, you've already messed up that plan. How are her powers coming along? No problems, I hope?" He smirks.

The menacing look on his face has my stomach bottoming out. "What did you do to her?"

"I was just testing something. We'll call it a contingency plan. I don't need another powerful fae actually learning to wield against me." He moves to a cabinet, pulls a notebook out, flips a few pages, and writes furiously. "That block I put on her would be pretty hard to break through. Granted, if her memories are breaking through, I suppose she could also have some slips of power. Am I correct? I'd like to know for my notes." He looks up expectantly. I train my eyes to the floor, refusing to give him anything. "Not going to say? No matter. She will be here soon enough for me to study."

I grind my teeth, subtly twisting my wrists in their binds.

I am going to murder this fucker.

"You will be my finest achievement once I get you under control. The King of Light was a fine puppet, barely put up a fight." He smiles wistfully and looks over at Beatrix.

She stands in the corner looking bored and annoyed, shuddering at the dust on a shelf. "Is this gonna take long? I have things I want to be doing."

Ellis rubs his temples. "No, this won't take long. Come over here and keep my puppet company, won't you? I grow tired of his questions. I'll have him fixed in no time."

A wicked smile spreads across her face as she saunters over, twirling her long blond hair. If she weren't so vile, she would be pretty. She brings to mind the fashion dolls they advertised to small girls on mortal TV. But the way her hips sway in that over-exaggerated way just reminds me of a drunken dog. "I always wanted a prince as a plaything," she purrs. "Owari has dibs on Ellis till she gets pregnant. I'm seriously tired of sharing, but it's all part of the plan." She walks around me and trails her finger across my chest; a low growl rumbles through me as I watch her.

"Oh, I like them feisty. You, my dear, will pass on your lovely powers." She smiles as she plops down into my lap, straddling me. I nearly choke on the jasmine perfume cloud that surrounds her. Gods, woman, people need to breathe. Did she bathe in the bottle?

I am going to give this woman an excruciating death.

"Just think, your dark hair..." She runs her hand through my hair, and I turn my head, trying to look anywhere but at her. "My blue eyes. Lightning and shadows, or maybe ice and shadows. Who knows! But they will be so powerful and hold a place of power after Ellis and I retire. I'm sure I'll have many children with Ellis once we are married, but the one you and I will make will be so powerful."

I really hate the direction this has taken.

"Just fucking kill me."

"No! You are my gift. Why would I kill you?"

Fuck me.

Wrapping her arms around my neck, she sways as she prattles on. "One day soon, I will be queen of all of Auburnigh. Then, we will take over Eneara as well. And you will be by my side as my first of probably many powerful concubines. We will breed a perfect royal fae lineage with only the most powerful fae."

Nausea flips my stomach at the picture she is painting. The fact that she is spilling the plan means they believe there is no chance I will escape. Whatever comes next is endgame for me.

Beatrix grinds down on my lap, and revulsion rolls through me.

"Ah, here it is," Ellis calls, holding out an open book with a smile. "Now, bear with me. The instructions are rudimentary at best, but they seem pretty straightforward."

"What are you gonna do, Elly?" Beatrix perks up.

Hopefully, get her the fuck off me. Scrub my brain clean of this memory. Maybe I'll get lucky, and he will fuck it up and blow himself up.

"Seeing as how he'd make a better ally than foe, I just need to turn his mind and emotions into something useful. Strong emotions are such pesky things." He sets the book down and rummages through the cabinet of vials. "You see, my queen—his bond, his love— it's all a problem for us. But his hate, rage, bitterness—those can all be used for our purposes."

"So you can make him like me?"

Ellis scoffs. "Nothing so trivial but I'll leave you his lust. Sound good, Pet?"

"Oh yes, that will do." She smiles, turning toward me and stroking my head like a god-damn dog. I jerk away, and she frowns.

"I believe he will be more pliable if I remove most of his emotions. Then, with a little help from Owari, we sway him to our cause. He won't have anything to fight after that. If this works, I can use this as the blueprint for the other kingdoms when we move on to the next phase."

Sweat drips down my back, and my hands go clammy as I listen. No doubt, part of his plan is letting me know precisely what is coming and knowing there is nothing I can do to stop it. My breathing grows shallow as my eyes dart between them.

Maybe this is why Jade has two mates, so she wouldn't be alone. Records gave me the impression that it never ended well when a person had two. In the end, only one came out on top. If I'm right, it's not because the mates fought, but because one died.

Take care of each other. I may have failed us all.

Hopefully, Killian is long gone with her. If they make it to another kingdom, someone will help them.

Gods, why are none of our allies here yet?

Ellis dumps vials into a big glass cauldron over the hearth. The air is thick with dark magic, and its potency stings my eyes. I thrash my shoulders in their bindings, rocking the chair. Beatrix screeches as I try to buck her off me.

The cutting tip of a dagger to my throat stills my movement. Her eyes gleam in triumph. "Save that energy for later. Or I'll stick the tip in *you* instead of the other way around."

I sneer at her, leaning into the blade; it has a sharp bite as it slips into my skin. A warm trickle runs down my neck as she pulls the knife back and looks at it in disgust. "Ew, you have weird kinks," she mumbles.

"You're the one who wants to enact your rape fantasy."

"No. I don't want that."

"You want me to fuck you. I don't want you. That's rape, Doll."

"But you *will* want me," she huffs, bristling.

I've struck a nerve. Maybe if I piss her off enough, she will just end me. If not, perhaps she won't want anything to do with me. "Say what you want; that's what it will be. Because I don't want you, Doll."

"Stop calling me that!" she hisses.

"But that's what you will be to me—a toy. A doll. That's what your precious *Elly* will turn you into, *Doll.*" I learned some fun things in the mortal world: this pet name is definitely getting under her skin.

Her face flames red as she abruptly exits my lap and storms over to Ellis.

Owari continues to dance to music that only she can hear in the corner, occasionally smiling in my direction. Ellis drops more and more things into his pot, which now sits on the table and emits red vapor. The pit in my stomach grows as I watch him mix his concoction. For a moment, I thought it was stupid of him to tell me what he's planning. But I have no way of stopping him, and the psychological torture he intended is working. I can barely breathe; my lungs feel so tight.

"Stand back and don't move. I need to concentrate to control where it goes," Ellis tells Beatrix and Owari. They both duck into a corner and watch with rapt attention. Ellis starts chanting some strange ancient language that I don't recognize. His tone becomes increasingly urgent as the crimson cloud pulses with light.

I take a deep breath.

The swirling mass judders and swells towards me with unnerving jerky movements. Ellis continues chanting; his hands outstretched as he directs the vapor. As it moves closer, the head of a viper takes shape, and it opens its wide jaws, hissing.

My heart sinks as it takes every ounce of strength in me not to panic. I pull on my bonds again, to no avail.

The red smoke snake rears up, and I snap my eyes shut as I feel it engulf me.

My chest is on fire.

My heart is going to explode.

Agony rips through my rib cage, and I roar in pain.

I don't know whether it's been minutes, hours, or days. All I know is anguish.

"Hello, lover." A woman purrs.

I open my eyes to find Beatrix perched on my lap. "Well, hello there," I purr. I'm surprised I'm not rising to attention as she grinds on me, but my interest in the woman is lukewarm at best. I can't tell if the foul odor in the room is her or something else. Overpowering floral notes mixed with the acrid stench of fear is bothersome.

She squeals with delight and plants her lips on mine. My stomach turns, and revulsion flows through me. This woman would be adequate if not for the fact that I feel repelled by her mere presence. She seems attractive enough, but my head is still a bit fuzzy. I must still be groggy from sleep.

"Glad to see you're doing better. I had to restrain you for a bit there." Ellis says, writing in his notebook.

"Why?" I look down, but the only restraint is the woman straddling my dick.

"Some fae tried to curse you, but we got you back to your normal self. Good timing, too, because we have a lot of work to do, and I still need your help."

"Looks like we will have to play later, Doll." I grin.

Beatrix groans, climbing off my lap. "Ugh, why did that stick? I hate it when he calls me that."

"Well, I took away the love; that's probably related to lust or anger?" Ellis shrugs, unconcerned. He turns to me. "How do you feel about Jade and Killian?"

"Manipulated. Do you have to ask?" I deadpan. Their names bring a hollow feeling to my chest, like my last fuck to give just expired.

I feel disoriented; memories of Jade float through my mind, and disgust and anger cloud my thoughts. Whatever she did to me made me weak and pathetic. I'd gone soft; how could I have acted the way I did if not under some spell? My memory feels hazy, but I suppose it would be after an enchantment is lifted.

How long has it been going on? Did the queen place something similar upon me? My blood boils, and my lip curls. I've been made a fool of.

They will pay. They will all pay.

"See, it worked." He kisses the back of Beatrix's hand. "My queen, will you put away that jar with the metaphysical heart, please? Owari, go open the safe so she doesn't drop it."

Still pouting, she picks up the jar, undoubtedly another one of Ellis' experiments. It glows bright red, pulses, and resembles a snake coiling in a large specimen jar. The women huddle next to a wall in the corner.

"Glad to have you on my side." Ellis slaps me on the back, and I follow him out of the room. "Let's get you caught up on what we're doing."

Chapter 32
Jade

The forest is dense and dark as I stumble my way through. It's been hours, and since my initial breakdown, I am fuming. What kind of mind-fuck, dumbshit bullshit is this place? I am so disillusioned with magic. Fuck this shit.

I've replayed the last twenty-four hours in my mind, trying to make sense of it all. What the fuck happened to Rodan? Somehow, I got through to him, but I have no idea how. Killian has been quiet, lost in a storm of emotions, somewhere between devastation and rage.

The rain stopped almost as soon as we exited the clearing. I don't remember much of the run; it's a blur of tears and heartache.

Fuck the fates and their games. They knew exactly what would happen and let us fall into a trap.

"Jade, slow down. Maybe we should stop and take a breather," Killian says, his tone placating. I shrug him off when he tries to place a hand on my shoulder. I need the rage that fuels me right now.

"No."

"Do you even know where you are going?" Yudoku chimes in.

"South," I grumble.

"How can you be sure?" She asks.

I stop and spin around to glare at my friend. "Do your moons rise in the east and set in the west?"

Killian looks a little uncomfortable. "Yes, but where are you going?"

I sigh. "You have allies. They would be south of your kingdom, correct?"

Understanding fills their features, so I go on. "We can't just stay here. That sorcerer's magic is bullshit. We need help. He has obviously been one step ahead of you this whole time; maybe it's time for a change of tack. We planned to get the hell out of Amara anyway, before everything went sideways again."

"We could probably make it over the border into Lupos in a couple of days; ask them for help," Killian says.

"I don't think that's such a good idea," Yudoku says. "Ya know, with one of their princesses being dead and the other having her wings amputated...and possibly—"

"Good point," Killian says. "We can go to Marapor. As far as I know, their ladies are still alive. We could probably cross into Lupos and follow the border over."

"Okay then, let's go," I say, growing impatient. I'm running on adrenaline and wrath; I need to do something, and just standing here is making me antsy.

"When we get there, I'll find you a portal master to take you home—"

"No! Absolutely not, Killian." Ice chills my veins as I glare at him.

"I'll figure out how to keep Ace's dad away from you."

"Not my point," I growl. "Listen, for the first time in my life, I didn't freeze when I was scared. I fought back. I am not just going to run away, not when Cat is still out there." Not when Rodan is...whatever he is.

"We don't know if—"

"Don't! I'm not leaving her or anyone else. Rodan was alive, and we all saw him fight whatever was done to him. He is still in there. That means there is hope for Cat, too. I will march into whichever kingdom I have to and demand help from the people who are supposed to be your allies. I don't care what political bullshit they need to hash out. People are dying, and it's not just your people; it's theirs, too. I need to do something, or I will fall apart. Do you understand that?" I poke his chest slightly harder than I mean to, but my point is made.

"See, there's that siren energy. I agree with this plan." Yudoku flashes her jagged teeth at me.

Killian steps towards me and takes my hand. "I admit this is a better plan than mine. Let's hope they notice us crossing the border and send a portal master, because if not, that's a long walk."

We continue our trek with renewed vigor. Killian holds my hand but lets me hold on to my anger.

Leaning close, he whispers, "Is it bad that that kinda turned me on?"

"Huh?" I raise an eyebrow, a little concerned he's losing it.

"I like your assertive side; it made mine want to come out and challenge you."

I crack a smile despite myself and shake my head.

"Okay, wolf boy." I roll my eyes.

"Just past this ridge is the border of Lupos. We should be able to cross here and follow the border down to Marapor. We might be able to borrow some horses along the way once we are on the other side of the mountains," Killian says.

The trees are thinning as we round a bend in the mountain. Flat grasslands stretch to the west. Morning light shines through the trees at our back. My feet ache from the last few days of walking, but the idea of horses or even a portal sounds amazing. Since the Faeglo Forest nobles don't know their princesses' fate, we should be safe traveling the Lupos border—at least safer than traveling within

Amara.

We've only stopped for a few hours here and there to hunt, eat, and sleep. Not that any of us get much rest. It's like the camping trip from hell. It makes the camp in the Grove of Fate look like a five-star resort. I couldn't care less. God only knows what conditions Cat is living in. I still won't let myself think about what could have happened to her. Maybe she got lucky and escaped and is hiding, or they locked her in a lovely room with a warm bed.

Sure, yeah. They just locked her in a lush room as opposed to the dungeon.

Killian and Yudoku have discussed the many intricacies of court politics and how they plan to proceed once we reach the Marapor capital, Dialigh. Most of it is over my head. Apparently, we can't just storm in and demand aid. However, they believe we can arrange their help quickly since they already know some of what has happened.

Yudoku plans to portal to her queendom and amass what she can there. I guess the siren has a powerful army at her disposal, but she's hesitant to use it.

"Why is asking to use the army going to be a problem?" I ask.

Yudoku gives me a long, suffering look. "A siege from the sea would be ideal; I get that. But I will owe my mother a favor. Right now, I think it would be of the marriage type. Even if the threat here would eventually reach our shores, she would just use it as an opportunity against me. I can't imagine what she will ask of Amara." She turns back to Killian, and they continue their discussion of a plan going forward.

"Is your kingdom not an ally?" I interrupt.

"We have trade agreements. But no, they are not exactly allies." Killian says, glancing nervously at Yudoku. "Maybe you and I can fix that. You know, after we save my kingdom." He tries to laugh, but it is half-hearted. He's struggling. At night, when we stop to rest, he lets his wolf fully take over, getting aggression out as he hunts. But his usual positive attitude is suffering; it's plain to see he is holding on by a thread. We all are.

As we reach the bottom of the hill, Yudoku spots a lake beyond. Relief floods her features as she runs towards it. I imagine it's like a piece of home that she misses down to her bones. At various points along our route, we have paused near streams, allowing her to stretch her fins and enabling us to replenish our water supplies. However, we have yet to find a stream big enough for her to swim in fully. Five minutes in a stream doesn't compare to submerging in a large body of water.

She glances nervously around as she nears the edge of the trees, then sprints toward the lake.

Killian and I follow behind her, smiling at the tiny bit of happiness provided to the siren.

"I never thought I'd see someone so happy to see a lake," I say.

"She lives in an undersea kingdom; I doubt she's ever gone this long outside water. It is beautiful."

Plush, deep green grass surrounds sky-blue water that shimmers in the light. Sparse fruit trees bursting with a rainbow of colors stand like temptations around an oasis. Everything is so vibrant, it looks fake. Until now, I've only seen what looks like a typical forest and the strange gardens of the castle. This is the surrealist version of a lake, described by a child.

Yudoku passes a low burgundy shrub spotted with bright cobalt blueberries.

She bounces backward and falls to the ground, groaning.

What the hell?

It looks like she ran into a wall, but nothing is there.

Killian rushes to her side and helps her to her feet as we stare into the distance, searching for what knocked her down.

Stepping forward tentatively, Killian reaches his hand out and places his other hand on the hilt of his sword. Passing the burgundy bush, he stops, his hand going flat against a surface.

"No," he breathes.

"What is it?" I ask, catching up to him.

"Some kind of ward. No, like a barrier." He drops his arm and leans his head against the invisible wall. With a growl, he slams the side of his fist on it, and for a split second, I swear it shimmers.

"Fuck me, that hurt," Yudoku says, rubbing her nose as I approach her.

"Are you okay?"

"Fine, I just...fuck." Yudoku says. "This is bad. We can't get out, which means no one can get in. This explains why Lyra's kingdom hasn't sent help yet."

"So you're saying we should have left when we still had Warrick?" I ask.

"We don't know when this went up. You all might have portaled in right before this barrier was set."

"We don't know that it covers the whole border..." I look around helplessly.

"If you put up a barrier, would you leave openings?" Standing, Yudoku walks back towards the bush.

"Damn it, I was trying to be optimistic."

"That time has passed." She sighs and sinks into a crouch, inspecting the strange blueberries on the ground. Popping one into her mouth, she chews tentatively before gathering a handful and handing them to me. "They aren't poisonous."

"How do you know?"

"I'm immune, but can taste it if they are. You have no idea how many things in the sea are poisonous to eat. How else would sirens survive? Thankfully, it means we don't have to worry about people trying to poison us. It's also why other kingdoms hire us as food testers."

Nodding, I pop a berry into my mouth. Juice explodes on my tongue, and I'm reminded of the taste of strawberry Starbursts. Their damn fruit tastes like candy. I pick at the handful of fruit, contemplating how interesting sirens are while Killian walks, running his hand along the barrier.

"What do we do now?" I ask.

"No clue." Yudoku sweeps her long teal hair into a ponytail, making her look even younger than she already does. Part of the allure of sirens is their youthful appearance; she barely looks older than a teenager. The gauzy material of her top sparkles as she moves. It's a bit battered from days of travel, but she still looks beautifully put together.

I can't imagine the state of myself. After traveling and rinsing in streams, my hair is tinted brown in spots. I take the unexpected break to braid it.

A mournful howl resonates through the air. We both look into the distance to see Killian's wolf. Golden fur ripples as he walks towards us, his head hung low. I feel his sorrow through the bond and know in my bones he hasn't found a way through. This must be what Yudoku was telling me before about being able to feel his emotions through our connection. It's getting stronger; finding the thread between us is becoming natural, like stretching a muscle.

As I watch Killian walk towards us, I feel down the bond and try to find Rodan. The bond leads to an empty hole that I can only describe as utterly black. My heart sinks; I can't feel him anymore. No matter how many times I check, he's just gone. I pull back and focus on Killian again, feeling his agonized hopelessness flood me.

I wipe a tear from my eye as I take a deep breath. There has to be something we can do.

"I know it's a long shot and super dangerous, but what if we attempt to get to Killian's parents?"

"Even if we could, we have no way of waking them up from whatever curse is on them." Yudoku sighs.

Killian's head perks up, and his ears lay flat; even from a distance, I hear him growl.

Yudoku spins around, getting to her feet and hisses, baring her teeth. Her claws elongate as she takes a defensive stance.

The hairs on the back of my neck stand on end as I slowly stand and turn, looking into the trees behind us.

The stench hits me, making me almost lose my lunch. Rotting death assaults me as I cover my nose with my hand. Taking shallow breaths, I unstrap a dagger from my ribs, watching for movement.

A tall fae man steps out of the trees, flanked by two truly horrendous-looking...things? People? These things are so much worse in the daylight than they were in the garden. Their flesh seems to melt off their bodies as they stagger forward. The stuff of nightmares stitched together like Frankenstein acquired his parts from zombies.

Flashes of these things run through my head: by a lake, Rodan and Killian decapitate monsters, and then they explode.

My eyes grow wide as the memory comes back to me.

Shit, shit, shit.

"Black eyes," Yudoku hisses.

The grass behind me crunches, and I whip my head to see Killian slowly approaching. He snarls as he moves in front of us, his back bristling.

Another fae appears to our left as more gather on our right, each flanked by the creepy monsters.

Yudoku moves behind me, pressing her back into mine. "When I say, you get on Killian's back and run like fucking hell," she whispers.

Killian's ear twitches, the only sign that he hears her as he watches the enemy slowly surrounding us.

"What about you? What are you planning?" I whisper.

"I can reach the lake with my power. I'm going to take them out. But if you two don't run, I'll take you down, too." Her words are strained as she moves her arms, and I feel the wind pick up around us, and the sky begins to darken.

I peek around Yudoku towards the lake, and my stomach plummets.

The water swirls towards the sky, snaking upward in a giant funnel.

A siren with air powers, holy shit. To say I had no idea of her true capabilities is an understatement.

I grip Killian's fur and hoist myself onto his back, holding on for dear life with my thighs. He stares down the fae as they come closer, contemplating an opening between them. He glances back at Yudoku and whines.

"Yudoku, you didn't say how you were gonna get out of here?" My stomach sours as I look at my friend and the waterspout that has covered the entire lake. Grateful, I tied my hair back; the shorter hairs whip around my face. The trees sway violently as the monsters stumble, slowing in their pursuit.

Killian locks eyes with her. An unspoken agreement is made, and he nods.

"No, I didn't," she says, almost sympathetically. Panic sears through me. "Go! Now!" she shouts, and Killian takes off, weaving to the side and between two groups of fae before dodging in another direction. Flames erupt from his mouth, setting a group of monsters aflame as he burns his path through. I hold on tight as I glance back.

We pass more monsters, each burning with Killian's fire.

The waterspout moves forward at an incredible speed, ripping trees from the ground and spinning them into the sky. It crashes through Yudoku, who seems immovable; her arms are wide as her hair falls from her ponytail and whips around her. She is a goddess, and this is her wrath.

My jaw drops as I watch in awe at the magnitude of her power. The black-eyed fae and monsters are swept from the ground and into the torrent of the tornado. Flashes of power crackle through the streams of water.

We reach the tree line, and the battle becomes hard to see, coming in and out of focus through the foliage—a flash of red, a flare of purple. Sparks dance along the swirling water.

No.

How are they still fighting?

Killian continues running through the forest, climbing higher up the hill we came from. He rounds a bend, and I get another unobstructed view of the meadow. The top of the tornado is murky and dark, but the bottom is like crystal clear water. Yudoku kneels in the dirt, one arm outstretched as she holds her ribs with the other.

"Killian, she's hurt! We have to go back! We can't just leave her!"

Killian shakes his head and presses on, climbing up the rocky cliff-side where we found ourselves. Rocks crumble beneath his feet as he slips and pulls us. I pull myself up his back and grip around his neck, careful not to choke him. His claws dig into the dirt and rock, but I can't tear my eyes away from Yudoku.

The wind stops as the water plummets to the ground, splashing wildly. Water floods in all directions. Four fae slowly descend to the ground like fucking superheroes.

You have got to be kidding me.

I search the area for Yudoku and take a sharp breath. She lies in a heap between the fae. She struggles to move as they close in on her.

"Yudoku," I want to shout, but my lungs close, and it comes out as a rasp.

Dragging herself away from a fae man closing in on her, she pulls herself with one arm, the other still holding her side.

No.

Flames engulf her.

The world slows.

A sound I've never heard comes out of me as I scream.

Killian howls as he pulls us over the edge of the cliff; I bury my face in his fur.

A shrill sound of shattered glass and a cloud of dust engulf us. The soft fabric of Killian's shirt replaces his fur. Wrapped around his back, I look up through watery eyes to see black eyes staring down at us. Killian sneezes as we climb to our feet, bewildered.

I step back towards the cliff, and something jagged pokes me in the back. I suck in a breath and turn. Razor-sharp icicles grow at my back, curling up the cliff face and pushing me forward.

"Oh, don't want you falling off the cliff now, do we?" A blonde woman steps forward, looking like the cat that caught the canary. "Hello, Prince."

"Beatrix." Killian strangles out. His body is tense as he surveys our predicament.

The woman's eyes are a striking blue, so I assume she's not like the fae that surrounds us.

My friends.

Black eyes bore through us with zero recognition of who we are.

Warrick stands behind Beatrix, with Ryker flanking her other side. His face is devoid of the person I know. A smear of blood through his hair tells me he put up a fight. Scarlette faces Killian, lava dripping from her palms as a river of it sways between them. A quick glance shows me Corsac, Darius, Lyra, and Nucifera, who all share the same blank look and black eyes devoid of light.

This is it.

They have us.

Because they know we won't hurt them.

"We can do this the easy way or the hard way." Beatrix smiles at Killian, batting her lashes. "But...after what Rodan did, I don't think I'll give you the chance." Her smile fades as she launches something at us. Killian throws up a wall of fire, but the small object shatters at his feet, and deep crimson smoke billows out of it. It swirls up Killian's body like a snake coiling around its prey, and he drops to the ground.

Ice slices into my back, and I wince as I stare at Killian, my heart thundering. My eyes snap to Beatrix just in time to see another vial sailing toward me. It shatters, and more red smoke pours out. I take a quick breath, and then everything turns red.

No, no, no.

Please don't let Yudoku's sacrifice be for nothing.

I feel it as my body hits the dirt, pain searing through my knees, then my head as it collides with the ground. I fight to hold on to my consciousness, groping for any control of my body before it all goes black.

Chapter 33
Jade

Groggily, I roll over on the hard ground. My head feels like a jackhammer is having a bachelor party with a bunch of frat boys. Groaning, I open my eyes to a gray stone ceiling. Wonderful.

I need water and to not drink so much.

I sit up and look out a set of bars that face a room with cells on the other side. The room is dimly lit, with a single torch flickering in the corner. Three walls of my cell are solid gray stone, cold and damp to the touch.

That's right; it's not alcohol-related this time.

"You have got to be fucking kidding me. Again?" My head hurts too much to be thoroughly outraged, but if I could, I would. "Fuck." I groan, drawing out the vowel. I drop onto my back and throw my arm across my eyes. It's just so unbelievable; it's almost comical.

I know exactly where I am. Well, maybe not precisely where this dungeon cell is located, but who cares? I remember everything, and I don't know what I should be feeling: grief, panic, anger, sadness—the list goes on and on. It's a confusing mix of emotions that I can't seem to untangle.

Perhaps it's all just too much, and I've finally cracked. Because the only things I'm feeling are numb and frustrated. I guess being frustrated is a step in the right direction. But seriously, come on. I'm locked up again?

Do I have 'kidnap me' written across my fucking forehead?

Fuck me.

"She's awake." A woman's voice drawls.

Sitting up, my head pounds, and the world swims as I take in the lavender hair of a strikingly beautiful woman. I blink, clearing my vision.

"Wonderful," a man's voice says. Heavy footsteps precede the arrival of the shaggy-haired man I saw on the balcony in the bioluminescent garden. He cleans his glasses on his shirt, slips them on, and smiles at me. "How have you been?"

I gape at this man, who must be Ellis, cock an eyebrow, and look exaggeratedly at my confines. The threadbare blanket is tossed over a flat mat on the floor. A bucket sits in the corner, and a tin cup is near the bars.

"Ah yes, well it's a necessary evil, isn't it?" He raises a clipboard and flips some pages before pulling out a pen. "How much do you remember from before your return to this realm?"

I blink at him.

What the hell?

"I should clarify. Do you remember me? Do you remember your time here?" His smile is disarming, but from what I've witnessed, this man is bad news. His white button-down is slightly skewed. Despite appearing put together, it seems like he's been in the same outfit for a few days.

He's the reason my memory is messed up. Everything that's happened to me since then is his fault. I clench my jaw and avert my gaze.

"I just need to know for my notes..."

Warning bells go off in my head, but I don't have the energy to fight him. I sigh. "Only what I see in my dreams. It's disjointed and incomplete."

"See, I told you it would bleed through," the woman groans.

Ignoring her, he writes something down. "Interesting." He leans forward, pinning me under his stare as his face turns contemplative. "Your bond? How is that going?"

My heart thunders. I take a shaky breath and scoot back against the wall. The rough ground scrapes the palms of my hands, loose pebbles lodging in my skin. "I can't feel it anymore." I don't know how much he knows. The less I say, the better.

He hums, jotting something down. "Now, now. I feel like we are past lying."

"I'm not." I scowl at him.

"But it's not the entire truth, is it? You have two mates. Which is fascinating."

How the hell does he know that? I try to school my features, but give up and drop my head to my knees.

"Begin with Rodan. How's the bond?"

"I told you, I can't feel it," I mumble.

"I suppose that's to be expected, but I wasn't honestly sure," he murmurs, and I hear the scratch of his pen. My stomach drops as tears burn my eyes.

What does he mean by that?

"And Killian? Gotta say, this was a shock to me. Two mates are very rare; it is a bad omen. But I've never gotten to study something like this." His tone is borderline excited for someone so clinical.

"It's fine. I feel it."

"Elaborate."

I swallow the lump in my throat as I reach down the line.

"It feels calm, like he's asleep."

"Wonderful. Circling back, I'd like you to tell me more about your bond with Rodan."

"I can't. It's gone, a void," I choke out.

"Perfect. This is better than I expected. How did the bond feel when you were in the mortal world?"

"Painful," I say. I hate this guy. I don't want to tell him anything, but deep down, I know if I don't, I'll regret it.

"Wonderful. I believe that will be all for today on that topic. Now, I was hoping you could tell me how your powers are developing. From past experiments, I know that occasionally, they sporadically overflow their binds. How is that going for you?"

"What do you mean?"

"I'm working on a method to bind powers, but in previous experiments, fae found they would intermittently have power erupt from themselves. Is this true for you as well?"

He bound my power? "Is that why I can't control my magic?"

"I'll take that as a yes." The scratching of the pen continues. "No bother. I believe I've at least perfected the spell against being broken. You would not believe the hassle of having my binding broken. Finally, I have figured out the flaw that caused that. Do tell me if you feel anything besides a random surge of power. I believe that is all for today. Killian is in the cell on your right. Don't abuse the privilege. I'd like to monitor you both thoroughly. I know, you are so close yet so far."

"Why are you doing this?"

"This has been carefully planned for decades. Now, I'm studying my opponents for future conquests. Understand this is nothing personal, aside from your being a thorn in my side. So maybe it's a little personal." He chuckles as his footsteps fade into the distance.

Ellis really has that evil scientist thing down. It would be comical if I didn't feel so helpless.

Yudoku sacrificed herself for nothing. Despite having incredible power at her disposal, she was still taken down. A tear slips down my cheek. Why did she do it? Why didn't she run? At least if she'd run with us, there'd be a chance of her being alive right now.

The floodgates open, and I let myself cry. I sob harder when I think of Cat. I think the not knowing may be worse than knowing.

I search for my bond with Rodan, wanting the comfort that would provide, but it's empty, vacant, gone. It's the same way it's been for days. Where once it felt tangible, it's like it never existed.

I wrap my arms around myself. The harness that held my knives is gone. A whimper escapes me; I don't know what I expected.

I put my hand on the floor and will my power to come to me. Feeling for the well inside my chest, but it's just out of reach. I groan. This is hopeless.

"Well, well, well. If it isn't the witch." Rodan says, and my head snaps up.

I stand and rush to the bars. When I touch them, it's like picking up a hot coal. I hiss and take a step back.

"Iron's a bitch, isn't it," he muses, his eyes back to their rich, deep green.

"Rodan. You're alive. You have to get out of here before they see you." Panic swells in me at the prospect of him getting caught again.

His face is impassive as I take him in—his jaw ticks. "I'm free of the curse you put on me. You can drop the act, witch."

What?

Why does he keep calling me a witch?

Bewildered, I take a step back. "Rodan, I—what are you talking about?"

He leans closer to the bars. "I'm no longer under your thrall. How much clearer can I be? Oh, drop the act and wipe that heartbroken look off your face. And don't think for a second I won't get my revenge for what you did."

"What?" I squeak, my heart shattering on the floor.

"I'm going to enjoy watching Ellis break you and your prince. What you did to me was far worse than anything I could imagine. You stole my life. They stole my birthright."

Oh, for fuck's sake.

Tears slide freely down my face. I grind my teeth, not wanting this bullshit to continue. I am so done with Ellis and his games. God, how does he do this shit? Why? What does he stand to gain by warping Rodan's mind like this?

I'm starting to understand why some women get a little stabby. Because I definitely want to stab Ellis right now. It takes everything I have to keep my breathing calm and my voice even. "This isn't funny, Rodan. Stop. They're controlling you. And you're being an asshole."

He betrays no emotion as I talk to him. His eyes flick to mine. "No one is controlling me, not anymore. I know the truth. My eyes are finally open. Love is a bullshit concept that doesn't exist, and with your curse on me removed, I can finally see clearly. Why should I hide away in the shadow of another when I was born for greatness?"

Does he hear himself?

I open my mouth, but nothing comes out. My ears ring, and my chest throbs. A sharp pain strikes through my ribs, and I take a shuddering breath, shaking my head.

This can't be happening.

"What have they done to you?"

"Freed me." He spits.

Chapter 34
Killian

Waking up in the dungeon where we found Rodan's doppelgänger is disorienting. Hearing the words Rodan spits at Jade is infuriating.

What is wrong with him?

I'm going to rip Ellis' head from his body and roast it.

How did everything get this bad so fast?

I growl as I stand. The world tilts, and I steady myself on the wall, moving towards the barred door. Gods, they just had to use the creepy old dungeon instead of the one that is actually humane enough to have toilets. So glad to see they fixed the floors and tables that got destroyed since the last time I was here. Probably put more of those damned centipedes in the floor too.

Power radiates from the metal gate as I approach. Determined, I test it, putting my hand through the bars, yanking it back as soon as more bars materialize. I'd read about this kind of spell; the iron will replicate to make escape impossible, even for small shifters like Jade. Her otter would just get caught between the metal.

Running my hand through my matted hair, I listen to Rodan spout madness. Leaning against the wall, I take a deep breath.

Rodan steps in front of my cell. "I see you finally ended up where you belong."

"Don't worry, man, we'll figure out how to un-brain-fuck you again." I roll my eyes, not looking at him.

"No thanks, I'm done having my brain messed with. Ellis will fix my kingdom; then I will take back what is rightfully mine. Amara will be left in Ellis's capable hands as soon as you relinquish it to him. Your parents hid you so well that he believed I was Amara's heir. Don't worry, I set him straight."

"You are just his puppet. He will never give you back your kingdom." I sigh.

"Keep telling yourself that. You will either break or become this puppet you speak of. Although you're already *her* puppet, I don't know if your brain could handle much more tampering."

"Why don't you say that to me without bars to keep you safe, brother?" I sneer. Maybe I can beat the sense back into him.

Gods, this is shit.

He chuckles and walks away. My heart plummets. What the fuck did they do to him?

"Killian?" Jade's voice squeaks.

I slide down the wall, my boots scraping the gravel covering the floor. "Don't worry, Emerald, I'll figure this out."

"His eyes aren't black anymore."

"Something else is wrong; Owari probably brain-fucked him again," I say, taking a deep breath.

"Can they change his memories, though? He knows the truth, or he did. His face was so vacant of emotion, it was strange. This isn't like my memory being removed. I was still me. He was different."

Something is different this time. He even smells foreign. Something is fundamentally wrong, like part of him is missing.

"Who knows? Rodan's always been an asshole. So it's hard to tell." I sigh.

Her feet crunch the gravel on the other side of the wall. She shuffles around, and her voice becomes closer. "Okay, so we need to figure out how to escape, fix Rodan, and find the others..."

"Are you okay?"

"Peachy," she grumbles.

I close my eyes and shake my head as a grin pulls at my lips. Despite the seemingly insurmountable situation, I am resolute in my mission to bolster Jade's spirits. I refuse to let her succumb to despair; I am determined to be her beacon of hope. "What do you want for dinner?"

"Why? You got a kitchen on your side?" she says with amusement.

"Oh yeah, I got everything you could possibly want. Name it, and I'll make it happen."

"Pizza."

"Well, damn. I'm fresh out of dough. But maybe I can put in a call to the castle kitchens; they can bring one down."

She sighs. "So, this is the castle dungeon?"

"It's an old hidden one, not the official dungeon. Trust me, that one is a lot nicer."

"What do you think they are gonna do to us?" she asks.

"Ellis needs me to transfer my royal powers to him to take over officially, so I imagine I've got some unpleasant days ahead of me."

"And me?"

"I wish I knew, my love. But I'll do everything in my power to protect you."

"He bound my powers... that's why I can't use them. I also can't find my otter; it's like the doors have been locked since we were up on that cliff." Her words shake a little, and I wish I could wrap her in my arms. This wall between us is infuriating.

I reach for my wolf and come up empty as well. The powder they threw at me locked away my ability to shift. Fire flickers in my veins, but it's depleted. At this point, I may as well be mortal.

"We will figure this out." I try to reassure her. I'm not sure how.

The fae we faced in the forest were some of my parents' most trusted advisers. I grew up with them. How do I fight people I can't bear to hurt?

The siren saved our asses, only for me to run right into a trap. Gods, I didn't want to leave her behind, but she clearly knew what she was doing. She was giving us a fighting chance.

A knot in my chest twists.

She screeches, and metal clangs. I jump to my feet, wanting to help her, placing my hands and forehead on the wall, feeling down the bond. Anger radiates around defiance.

She is all desire for destruction and pain.

"I can't believe I'm locked up again!" she screams.

Let it out, baby.

"I'm so sick of this shit! You know what?"

"What?" I ask.

"We can let bad people destroy us or beat them at their own game. If I'm going to die anyway, I may as well raise hell about it. I'm so sick and tired of being taken advantage of. I'm tired of taking the high road or just being afraid. Fuck all of this. I'll answer their questions like a good girl, but anything else, I'm fucking done."

"Sounds good." A smile spreads across my face. She always had a spark in her eye, but she's finally letting that inferno out to play.

Maybe it's time mine came out to play, too.

I wake, yanked out of a dream and my cell simultaneously. Invisible bonds hold my arms trapped at my sides. The room is still dark from when the torches went out hours ago. In the gloom, three figures stand; two drag me towards a table. A third person walks a short distance away.

"Get the fuck off me," I growl.

"Killian!" Jade shouts.

My stomach rolls as I'm hoisted onto the table, face down. Whatever they are about to do, I can't fight.

No, no, no.

Lights flicker on, and I blink several times, adjusting my eyes to the sudden brightness.

Jade's wide eyes stare at me from her cell. Her hair is a mess, and dirt smudges her face. She is still the most beautiful woman I've ever seen.

"Stop! Let him go!" She grabs the bars and screams.

"Don't touch the bars, my love. I'll be fine." I say, as my heart pounds in my chest. Panic runs ice through my veins.

She lets go and sinks to the floor, tears streaming down her face.

"She must really love you to hold on to those bars like that; it's like she didn't even feel the pain," Owari says from somewhere in the room.

"Strap him down to the table," Ellis says.

Hoping for the invisible bonds to drop, my heart thumps wildly as leather straps hold me down. The bonds never loosen. I swallow the lump in my throat.

Ellis walks between me and my view of Jade. He holds a small knife in his hand. "Do you think she will feel your pain through that bond of yours? Listen, I could tell you this will only pinch a little, but your pain is part of the process, and I'm hoping hers will make it more potent. But then again, this is all just theory. No one has ever tried to steal power this way."

Oh great, he's experimenting on me.

Shit, shit, shit.

I struggle in my bonds, but I can't move a muscle. Ellis slices off my shirt, and someone tugs my hair aside from my back.

"Close your eyes, Emerald. You don't need to watch this," I say, pushing all the calm and love I can through the bond before blocking it off. I'll shield her from my pain as long as I can. I know she can feel my emotions. I don't want her to feel this.

I don't want to feel this.

She curls up next to the wall facing me, her face pale beneath her silver hair.

"I'm here, Killian."

Searing pain rips through me as Ellis starts cutting into my back. I clench my teeth and groan, trying to be strong for Jade, but eventually, I crack.

She never breaks eye contact with me.

Chapter 35
Rodan

I sit in the main dungeon, babysitting—Ellis's control over the fae here has waned. Most of them are resting, slumped in their cells, subdued.

A black orb, a mesmerizing nexus of power, pulses in the center of the room. Violet tendrils whip out, draining the fae of their essence. It's a spectacle that captivates, yet it's disturbing.

Next to my book on the table is a smaller orb. One touch from me causes the power drain to stop. It's ingenious. Between that and the powder that makes shifters unable to shift, these fae are helpless.

My memory is a patchwork of fragments—a testament to the silver-haired witch's betrayal. Ellis revealed that she had conspired with the queen for years to ensnare me.

Make me weak.

Fuck that.

Ellis will find a way to break the curse over Shadow, and I'll take back my kingdom.

"Hey sexy, what are you doing?" Beatrix purrs, sauntering up beside me.

"Babysitting," I grumble. "It's late. Go to bed, Doll."

Flinching at the nickname, she slides into my lap and tangles her fingers in my hair.

"I was hoping you'd come with me."

I'm seriously not in the mood; even my dick doesn't respond to the idea. "No."

Her lower lip pouts out, and she looks at me with lowered lashes. "But I can make you happy."

I blink at her.

She huffs. "Gods, did he remove that, too? Don't you feel anything?"

"No." Should I? I shrug and slide her out of my lap. The emptiness within me doesn't stir. This is freedom from all that held me back.

"I thought you said we'd play later." She spins and puts her hands on her hips.

"I've got to make sure none of them can fight us. Ellis wants all of them drained." It is my duty to this country to ensure people like this never take power again. Honestly, I don't understand why Ellis is keeping them alive. The smart move would be to kill them all. Perhaps he is going soft, which could be a problem in the future.

"Can't he just do the black-eye thing to them again?" Her impatience is getting on my nerves.

"Said something about it wearing off and needing to make a new batch of potion."

She groans, "Yeah, if only it worked as well on fae as it does on his monsters. I guess the stronger the will, the harder they are to control. Sad, really, considering how powerful some of them are, it would be great if we could use them for more than a day or two at a time."

A jolt of something hits me. I'm momentarily disoriented. I feel something on my cheek, swiping at it, my fingers come away wet.

What the fuck is this?

Ellis fixed me; tears should no longer be possible. He'd agreed: A *ruthless leader has no need for such things.*

"Well, this isn't all of the prisoners." She looks around the room, keeping a safe distance from the orb.

Shaking off the strange feeling, I focus on Beatrix. "I know." Jade and Killian are in the cells by the lab. I watch the king's councilors, or what's left of them, being drained of their power. Across from them are the fae who took part in the dating bullshit. It was just a parade of weakness.

"No, I mean, we have another prisoner somewhere else."

I lift an eyebrow in question, waiting for her to continue.

"He has someone else he's monitoring separately."

Annoyance floods me. "Spit it out."

Beatrix leads me to a small room behind the lab. It's probably meant for storage.

I stand in awe before the glass box that houses an enormous scorpion. The cube, a staggering ten to twelve feet across, barely contains the monstrous creature. It's curled up with red armor plates down its back and legs, ending in a coiled tail—the tip is a menacing sight, dripping venom.

"What the fuck is that?"

Beatrix leans against the wall, crossing her arms. "Catria."

That name is so familiar. The tiny strawberry blond flickers through my mind. The thought of the half-mortals with their witchcraft and curses makes my blood boil.

I shake my head. Why keep her separate from the others?

"Why doesn't he dose her with the powder again?"

"Because she's built up a tolerance to it," Ellis says, walking into the room.

I cock an eyebrow; he has blood splattered across his shirt and running down his hands, and his hair is a mess.

"I'm unsure how, but she can flush it out of her system. I'm studying her. I had to cage her in here because she was destroying every cell I put her in. So far, this is holding."

"Rodan won't come to bed," Beatrix pouts.

"Darling, Rodan is still getting up to speed. I need his help going forward. Let Rodan work," he says.

Beatrix moves towards the door, swaying her hips. "Then you come to bed. Wash off and join me, or I'll be a brat all day tomorrow."

She's already a brat.

Ellis shakes his head, following her to the door. "Rodan, I put more books and notes on my desk if you'd look them over. We can discuss ideas as we advance our plans in the afternoon. I've got Warrick under control again." He pinches his brow, grimacing.

Warrick had come out of the dark magic just long enough to punch Ellis in the face and cast a portal. Thankfully, my shadows got him before he could escape. Now, we don't take chances with him. He has muscle, so he doesn't need his power—not yet.

Ellis continues, "My latest batch of constructs should be ready in a few days. I can't believe how many that siren took out."

He leaves the room, and I eye the monster behind the glass.

"Well, if it isn't the other mortal." I drawl, tapping on the pane.

Her head whips up, and the cat-like eyes widen, shifting into a girl before me. Strawberry hair fluffs out around her tear-streaked face.

"Rodan," she says almost breathlessly.

I sneer at her.

"Oh, for fuck's sake." She slams her hand on the glass before spinning around. "Let me guess your team, Ellis, now. God! I should have known. What did he do? Use Owari to wipe your memory again?"

She prattles on and on about books and evil scientists.

I lift an eyebrow and watch the feral girl screech and rant.

"Where is Jade?" She levels me with a glare.

"Around," I say. Jade's face flashes in my mind, and I ball my fists. I keep my face placid, but I can't get that woman out of my head. Just hearing her name stirs up the rage within me.

"You son of a bitch. I hope she kicks you in the balls."

"My, my, that's not very nice."

"Hasn't she been through enough? First Ace and now you?" She throws her arms up in exasperation, reminding me of a child throwing a temper tantrum. "I'm assuming you have Killian, too, or is he like you? Fuck!"

Jade is crumpled in on herself in a clearing, crying. I crouch down, ready to kill whoever did this to her. She lunges into my arms, surprising me. Holding her, she trembles and cries. My heart is cracking as anger floods me. "Who hurt you?"

I stumble back a step and clutch my chest. Hollow pain radiates through my ribs.

What the fuck was that? That minute flicker of emotion unsettles me. She must be casting another spell over my mind.

Glaring at her, I turn to leave, wanting to get as far from this witch as possible.

"Oh, don't like facing the truth? Just wait until I find a way out of this box, too. I'll find Ryker and Jade, and she's going to kick your ass for abandoning her. She might be fun-sized, but it won't feel like that when she castrates you."

Chapter 36
Jade

Killian has been passed out for hours. Without windows, I have no way of knowing what time it is. I just know it's been hours.

Whatever Ellis was trying to achieve didn't work, so he left angry. Warrick and Owari dragged Killian out of sight and into his cell.

Ellis carved some kind of sigil into Killian's back. A circle covered his entire back with strange markings inside that I couldn't make out through the blood. He poured potions on the cuts, which had Killian screaming bloody murder; he didn't go limp until Ellis threw an empty bottle across the room.

I sit up against our shared wall, feeling through the bond, waiting for him to wake up.

My stomach growls, yet nausea has sweat beading across my forehead.

Painful burns line my hands and fingers. They are dark red in the flickering light. I wasn't even thinking when I grabbed the bars. Didn't feel the pain until Killian was back in his cell.

Witnessing everything they did to Killian was sickening. He put a wall around his emotions, so I sat there helplessly. I kept eye contact every agonizing second, so he knew he wasn't alone.

My hands throb as I clench and flex them.

I reach for my power again. It's like trying to grab a glass of water that your fingers just brush. If I could call on the frost, it might ease the burn or make it worse. Wishing for relief, I have no idea how to channel it into healing magic.

As I concentrate, I can almost feel the power tipping towards me. It's like a wild horse, eager to be ridden, and I'm the inexperienced rider. It wants to be used, and it's ready to overflow.

Ice floods my veins, a sensation both exhilarating and terrifying. It pours out of me in furious streams, like a river breaking its banks.

Oh shit!

In seconds, the entire cell is covered in crystalline frost; it sparkles around me, creating a blue-and-white wonderland.

"Shit, shit, shit." I hiss.

My breath fogs like smoke as frost falls from my hands like snow. I shake them, willing it to stop, flinging ice that clatters against the iron bars.

Panic overcomes sense as the frost starts sealing the gaps between the bars. A surge of energy rushes through me. I flail and duck.

"No!" I scream as my power floods out. Covering the ceiling with long icicles.

Steam wafts off my skin, and as suddenly as it began, it stops. My power is entirely out of reach again.

"Damn it!" Why does everything have to be so complicated? Oh, that's right, because Dr. Frankinfucker fucked everything up!

Now, my whole cell looks like a blizzard stopped by to say hi.

"Emerald? My love, did you just freeze your cell?" Killian groans.

"Maybe." My face heats. Well, this just got ten times more embarrassing.

He chuckles softly.

"It's not funny," I grumble.

"It's a little funny." I can hear the smile in his voice and feel his amusement down the bond.

My adjoining wall with Killian drips as the frost melts away. I huddle next to the stones, feeling warmth radiate through them.

"Are you doing that?" I ask.

"Warming your icebox? Yeah. I pulled fire from one of the torches. It's not a lot, but enough to heat the wall."

"Use it to heal yourself. Don't worry about me." I shiver and rub my bare arms. Leggings and a short-sleeved top are not ideal for this.

"I'm fine. I think they healed my back before they threw me back in my cell."

"But you were dripping with blood when they dragged you away."

"It's healed," he says, sounding just as perplexed as me.

I lean the side of my face against the warm wall, wishing it were him.

"Killian? I'm scared."

"We'll get through this."

"How?"

"Did it feel hopeless when Ace had you chained up?" His soft voice comforts me. I turn, leaning against the wall and tipping my head back.

"Yeah. It did. I thought I'd die in that room."

"What kept you going?" He asks.

"I kept dreaming about these two guys. Almost every night, they were an escape, a comfort, a fantasy of a better life. I watched that damn tv show with that actor who looked exactly like Rodan." I laugh softly. "Knowing now that you were both real, that I just disassociated reality to be with you, it's kinda funny."

"What about us helped you?"

I flush. I guess there's no reason to hold anything back now. Who knows what tomorrow could bring?

"It's like he holds my broken pieces together while you mend them. At least, that is how I see it from my dreams. Rodan kept me from completely giving up; half the time, I was so caught up in arguing with him or beating him that I couldn't fall apart. The other times, he was just there when I needed him."

I smile, realizing how much I need that in my life. "And you were like my glue; even if I felt myself falling apart at the seams, you just swept in and made me feel better. Teaching me how to fight back, you reinforced everything inside me. You make me feel brave."

"You are brave. I just want you to see the fire inside you."

"Pretty sure I'm all ice inside."

Killian laughs. "Fair enough."

I startle when, out of nowhere, a plate of food zooms through the bars and lands next to me, followed by a tin cup of liquid. My stomach growls as the smell of rosemary and garlic assaults me. Roasted chicken and potatoes sit nestled in a brown gravy. Included is a roll with a pad of butter.

"Is this safe to eat?"

"Got a better idea?" Killian says, clearly set on eating. "Please don't starve yourself. I highly doubt they plan to poison us."

"It's not poison I'm worried about." I can't help but think about how Yudoku's power would be handy right now. I wipe a tear from my face and pick up the fork.

"Your dinner wasn't tampered with. It's just food. You should be grateful we're even feeding you." Beatrix sits on the metal table that Killian was strapped to last night. She swings her legs, studying me.

"Uh, thanks?" I take a bite, and the chicken just about melts in my mouth. From there, I swear I taste almost nothing as I inhale the food. I guess I was hungrier than I thought.

As soon as I finish the last swig of wine, the dishes fly out of my cell and land on a tray.

Beatrix glances off to the side; someone's standing just out of sight. Probably someone with air power, since I know Beatrix has ice, and I don't think she can make dishes fly.

"So, I know I didn't do that." She smirks, gesturing to the frozen wasteland decor I put up. "Did you have a problem with your powers?" She snarks.

Half of my cell is still covered in frost, snow, and ice. I'd be embarrassed if not for the colossal disadvantage I've been given.

"No. I just thought it looked pretty." I give her a saccharine smile.

"Whatever." She rolls her eyes, huffs, and hops off the table. "I've got shit to do."

I smirk. Getting under her skin is way easier than it should be. I wonder if we ever got along. Probably not.

Beatrix saunters towards the door. "Come on, Rodan baby, let's leave the riff-raff to their questioning." She smiles and winks at me as I grit my teeth. I am going to stab her. Rodan smirks and gestures for her to go first in a sweeping bow, making eye contact with me as he leaves. Was he standing there the whole time? Screw that, I'm going to stab them both.

Ellis appears, holding a stool. He places it in front of my cell, crosses his ankle over his knee, and pulls out a clipboard.

Great.

I lean my head against the wall again.

"What's your deal with her?"

"Who?" he asks.

"Beatrix, she seems rather... one-note. Thought you'd be with a smarter girl."

"She took years to cultivate into the perfect woman."

I scrunch my nose. That's disgusting. "Cultivate?" I already regret asking, but getting anything out of him could prove useful.

"From a young age, I shaped her into my ideal partner. Someone who understood my vision and wished to create a better world. She will do everything necessary to engineer the perfect royal line."

Bile crawls up my throat. So he groomed a Stepford wife with added crazy. I kind of feel bad for her now. Can that even be undone at this point? The creep factor on this is out of this world. And this guy thinks he should be in charge.

Can what he did to Rodan be undone?

"What did you do to him?" I drawl. Not that I expect him to answer.

"You'll have to be more specific. I've done a lot of things to a lot of people."

I roll my eyes; of course, he has. "Rodan."

"I removed his heart." He says this so nonchalantly that I almost lose my composure. "He has been an extreme case for me to control. Tell me, how did you break through my dark magic on him?"

Removed it? With creased eyebrows, I turn my head to look at Ellis. I feel the blood drain from my face as I gape at him. I can't have heard him correctly.

"You...what?"

Ellis sighs, clearly annoyed with me already. "Exactly what I said. There had to be consequences for his helping you in the forest." He removes his glasses and pinches between his brows. "How did you break my control?"

"I don't know."

He throws his clipboard on the floor as the stool screeches and tumbles back. Storming up to the bars, he glares daggers at me. "Liar! Tell me what you did!"

My heart thunders against my ribs as I stare him down, unwilling to give an inch. I gulp. "No." I wouldn't tell him even if I knew, and I'm used to dealing with guys bullying me.

His face turns red, and the bars of my cell fly open.

Oh, crap. That was a mistake.

He storms forward and grabs me by the roots of my hair before I can react. Pain throbs. I grab his hands, trying to lessen the screaming pull of my hair. I screech as I'm dragged from the cell, the cobblestones scraping my ass as I try and fail to gain purchase with my feet.

"Let her go!" Killian bellows.

Ellis slams my skull back onto the floor, and my eyesight blurs. Spots cloud my vision, and my head pounds.

"You son of a bitch! Get your hands off her!" Killian says in a rage.

"If you don't want to cooperate, then I'll make you tell me," Ellis says, strangely calm for how forceful he's being.

He sinks his fingers into my arm and yanks me up, pulling my back to his chest. His hand wraps around my throat, and he points my head towards Killian. His face brushes against mine, and I flinch. "You see him? I will have him whipped for every question you refuse to answer," he whispers.

My breath catches, my heart pounding in my chest. I grab his arm and throw all my weight forward and to the side. Ellis flings to the floor, his back hitting the hard stone. The air leaves his lungs as I stumble back, unable to believe what I've just done.

Oh. Shit.

"Run!" Killian barks.

His order breaks me out of my daze, and I turn towards the only door I see, hauling ass. Swinging around the corner, I take the stairs two by two and curse them.

I'll get help and come back for Killian. I won't leave him down there. All I need to do is find help.

Panting heavily, the twisting staircase ends, and I bolt through the next doorway I see. The hallway is long and lined with heavy doors. I stumble into the first door to my left and leave it slightly ajar so it doesn't make noise. My heart is pounding, and fear grips me as I press my back into the wall, trying to steady my breathing.

Of course, there had to be stairs.

My legs burn as I gulp down air.

The thump of footsteps thunders nearby, and I hold my breath, sinking into the shadows of the small room. From the corner nearest the door, I can just make out the light peeking through the opening I left. Ellis sprints down the hall, muttering.

When I hear a door slam at the end of the hallway, I let out a breath. I fold over, bracing my hands on my knees, feeling the desperate need for a moment's respite to gather my thoughts.

Now, what the hell do I do?

This is like the worst game of hide and seek ever.

Rustling catches my attention in the shadows on the other side of the room.

I straighten, trying to peer into the darkness. Something moves, and my heart skips a beat. Sliding slowly towards the door, I try not to make a sound. It rises, and its shadowy figure nearly touches the ceiling.

A cold chill runs through me, and my palms begin to sweat.

I slide closer to the door, reaching out for the handle blindly.

Glowing yellow eyes snap open and land on me.

Fuck that!

I bolt and pull the door open, skidding through and slamming it shut behind me to the sound of a roar. The door shakes, and dust rains down around me as the beast slams into it. I turn and run to the room across the hall. Pushing it open, I see bookshelves and tables lined with what looks like lab equipment.

Looks safer than the monster room. I quickly take in my surroundings, feeling a sense of déjà vu.

There must be a good place to hide in here, at least until I figure out my next move. I can't afford to waste a second. Maybe there are weapons in here. I search through a cabinet full of colorful vials, my hands shaking with adrenaline. I look in every chest, but they are filled with scrolls and books. Spotting a door off to the side, I run for it, my heart racing.

Dashing through the door, I close it behind me and sigh. The air is cool and musty, a sharp contrast to the warmth of the other room. Turning around, I see nothing but an enormous glass box at the far end. It's illuminated, and its glow lights up that end of the room, casting eerie shadows on the walls. A thick and palpable darkness shrouds the rest of the space. Aside from a small bird circling inside the box, there is nothing else in the room—no place to hide.

"Fuck," I groan, slumping against the door.

"Jade?"

I snap my eyes to the box. Cat stands in the middle, her hair wild around her. Her dark leather pants are dusty, and her black tunic is torn, but otherwise, she looks unharmed. I take her in, unable to believe what I'm seeing.

I rush to her and press my hands to the glass. "Are you okay?"

"Yeah, I'm fine. Look, no black eyes." She opens her eyes wide and turns her head from side to side. "A lever by the door will drop the force-field on the box. Get me out of here."

Rushing to the wall, I search for it. This side of the room is dark, so I run my hands over the dusty stones. A corner of cold metal brushes the side of my hand, and I pull down on what feels like some sort of lever. The resistance of it feels unyielding. I yank and pull, and it gives a little. Determined, I put all of my weight into it. Hanging from the lever, it finally snaps down.

The light from the cube flickers, and a crackling resonates through the room.

"Yes!" Cat whoops.

I stare in horror as my friend morphs into the most enormous scorpion I've ever seen, growing into the glass. She continues to grow larger until the glass splinters. Cracks form and grow like lightning, spreading through the box. I duck and cover my head with my arms. The box explodes, glass shattering to the floor.

Arms wrap around me, and I uncurl to see Cat's hair draped across my face. Breathing in the lavender scent that lingers on her hair, I rise, pulling her fully into a hug.

"What were they doing to you?" I ask.

She steps back and grins mischievously. "That powder shit they use to stop shifting didn't work on me long term, and I kept breaking out of their cells. I got it down to five minutes. I don't know why, but I can just focus on the powder in my system and flush it out." She shrugs. "So, I think this was their last-ditch effort to lock me up. I couldn't break out with that damn force-field up. Ellis wanted to do his coo-coo experiments on me. Thank god you found me. How did you escape?"

"How did you know I got captured?"

"Rodan as much as told me without telling me," she huffs. "I don't know what Ellis did to him, but it's like any trace of warmth is gone, ya know?"

"Yeah, I noticed. Ellis said something about taking his heart. I have no clue what that's supposed to mean. But we need to get the hell out of here before someone finds us. I may have bolted when Ellis was down, so it's not like we have the advantage of time."

"Quite true; you lost the advantage the moment you ran into this room."

Cat and I jump and spin around at Rodan's voice. He steps from the shadows, his eyebrows pinched in anger.

"Well, fuck," I breathe. Of course, he's in here. My heart wants to sing a happy tune at the sight of him, but my head wants me to run. "I hope you came to kiss and make up. Although I should warn you, I'm still feeling a little stabby after that show you put on with Beatrix."

Shadows snap out of the darkness and coil around us so fast I can't even take a breath before the air is squeezed from my lungs. He glares down at me as I struggle in my bindings. I want to claw his beautiful face, but I also want to wipe that smug look off him and kiss his brains out. This is complicated.

"Last time I was wrapped in your shadows, it seemed hotter. Are we going to play again? Because this isn't really working for me, Rodan baby." I try to sound sultry, but my voice is strained and tight.

His eyes darken, and his jaw ticks.

He wrenches the door open, dragging his shadows and us behind him. I struggle, and Cat whips her head back and forth. She locks eyes with me and winks, a sly smile dancing on her lips. Rodan opens the door to the hallway. Cat dissolves into the smoke tendrils. A hummingbird bursts from the shadows and darts through the door. She is a blur of motion, then she's vanished.

Rodan stops, stunned. He turns, looking back at me and the empty shadows beside me. Wrathfulness reflects in his eyes, and he sneers. I smile at him, batting my eyelashes as I shrug.

Chapter 37
Rodan

"You let her escape?" Ellis drawls.

"I didn't *let* her do anything. You let the other out, and she freed the feral one." I lean back in my chair. "Sounds like a failure on your part, not mine." This guy is obviously more incompetent than I gave him credit for—even more reason he shouldn't rule this kingdom.

Ellis glares at me. "Should I be questioning your loyalty? Or do I need to show you why I'm in charge again?"

"This was your failure." I take a drink of my wine. "I honestly give zero shits. Jade is back in her cell, so what if the other one got out? They are harmless, worthless half-mortals."

"With royal blood!" he shouts.

I shrug. "And? What are they going to do? Talk you to death? You have Killian; soon, he will break, and you'll have his power. Are you really letting mortals stop us from taking what's ours?"

It's amusing that Ellis truly believes I'll let him have this kingdom. I'm more powerful than ever and free with the curse of love lifted off my shoulders. I'll take back my kingdom and this one, too. He's convinced he's got me under his thumb, but he will be easy to crush once everything is said and done. Like anyone, he has weaknesses; I plan to exploit those when the time is right.

"Keep your eye on the prize," I say, flicking my eyes up to meet his.

He sneers. "And what if Killian doesn't break?"

"Break the girl, break the man," I say simply, setting down my wineglass. I frown as my eyes burn, and a single tear drips down my face. I wipe it away, furrowing my brows as I stare at the wetness on my fingers.

Ellis watches me with curiosity. "Does that happen often?"

"Once before," I grumble.

"Intriguing. I need to go check on something." He rushes out of the lab, the door slamming behind him.

Footsteps thunder down the hallway, followed by low murmurings. I turn my head, listening.

"What do you mean, the orbs are malfunctioning? Turn them back on immediately. Are you truly so incompetent, Calazar?" Ellis growls.

Sounds like someone is going to be in deep shit. I settle onto the couch as a grin pulls at my mouth.

"No, sir, but other strange things have happened. Things keep going missing..."

"Being an absent-minded fool is not my problem. Get down to the dungeon and make sure those fae are drained. No excuses. I don't want to hear another word about my orb malfunctioning. My potion to control them still needs a week to become active. If you hadn't been such a blundering fool in the first place, I wouldn't have had to use the entire stash to capture the princes. Now, I can only keep them subdued until I can puppet their powers again. Get the orb working."

The conversation stops, and I hear the clicking of shoes going in opposite directions.

I down the rest of my glass of wine and then another. I need to find his weakness. His plans to take over the continent are good, but his execution leaves much to be desired. His dark magic has more limitations than I'd believed when he first brought me to my senses.

I can see the drain on him; dark magic is slowly killing him physically, which must be why he's so desperate to take Killian's powers. He knows I'm much more useful to him as an ally than an enemy, so he will tolerate my opinions without too much questioning.

But what if I took Killian's powers, perhaps the mortals too? If Ellis can figure out how it can be done, I can take them for myself. Then, nothing could stop me. Ellis does not realize how freeing it has been to have the curse lifted from my shoulders. It's like I can see clearly for the first time.

Not one kingdom lifted a finger to help Shadow when it fell. I think it's time the rest of the world suffers like my people did.

Fuck them all.

I want to see the world burn.

Chapter 38
Killian

"You should have seen the look in his eyes; it was like he's not even in there anymore." Jade sniffles.

I scowl in the darkness, my back against the wall. Draping my arms across my knees, I listen to Jade recount the events of her near escape.

"At least Cat got away. Maybe she can get help." Holding on to my last sliver of hope, I feel for my power, but there's nothing left. They drained me again after Jade was thrown back into her cell. There's a hollowness that comes with being drained by the black orb. It's unnerving in the way it rips power from your soul. It was so unlike the gentle euphoria that the orbs used to provide.

"I hope so. I'm so sorry. I tried to hide. I—tried to get away." The sorrow in her voice breaks me.

"I know. You did well, Emerald. You should have seen Ellis' face. It was priceless."

A thunderous boom resounds as a door flies open, and the room illuminates, making me jump to my feet as Ellis storms in. He stops in front of Jade's cell, and my heart drops.

"What did you do to Rodan?" he asks through clenched teeth.

"What are you talking about? I didn't do anything to him," Jade says, a slight quiver in her voice.

"Why are your emotions affecting him? I need to know. You cry, he cries. Why? You said you can no longer feel the bond."

Looks like someone isn't as smart as he thought he was.

"I have no idea. Maybe your bullshit magic got fucked up. How the hell am I supposed to know?" she growls.

I lift an eyebrow at her tone; my girls got teeth.

"I see—" Ellis' face is stormy as he walks past me, his shoulders stiff. The clatter of metal makes my spine stiffen. This can't be good. "If you won't tell me, I'll simply have to find out for myself."

Resuming his position in front of Jade's cell, he whips open the door, and she shrieks. Pulled along the floor by invisible bonds, she wiggles and thrashes.

"Don't you dare touch her!" I slam my shoulder into the cell door, and the bars sizzle against my skin as I watch helplessly. "If you hurt her, I will kill you." Seething with rage, I glare at Ellis. Every cell in my body is on alert, the hair on the back of my neck standing on end.

He pulls Jade onto the metal table and straps her down. With her arms pinned to her sides, he tightens the straps and secures them around her back. Metal cuffs lift from the side of the table and close over her wrists and ankles. I growl and pace my cell, rigid, clenching my fists. I need to get out.

There is nothing I can do.

Panting, Jade stops screaming and looks around wildly. "Why are you doing all of this? At least tell me what all of this is for. Let me understand," she pleads, her voice trembling with a mix of fear and desperation.

I scoff, knowing this asshole will only tell us what he wants to. I don't want to know how his twisted brain works.

"You want to know? Fine. It's because of a woman like you." He returns to the table and sits on a stool, flipping through a massive black tome. Dust puffs out of the pages, clouding him in a haze. "My father wanted to make the world a better place. He fought hard to put the most powerful fae in positions of influence and the less powerful in their rightful place. And he succeeded. Eneara was well on its way to becoming a perfect society. Unseelie was set to rule this world with all who opposed us under our boots.

"But my mother..." he seethes. "She found her mate and ran off with the usurper while she was pregnant with me. He convinced her that my father's ways were wrong. Twisted her mind. They overthrew my real father and acted like we were one big happy family. She let that damn vampire raise me like I was his. Meanwhile, they murdered my father. I found out the truth, found my real father's manifesto."

Oh no, not a manifesto. I sigh. It appears that the stories are true; I'd never heard they'd had a son, though.

"I spent years looking into everything and learning the truth. My mother was a terrible woman, but none of this would have ever happened if it weren't for that damn bond. So why am I doing this? I'm making the better world that my father wanted. Why am I doing this to you? I'm going to find a way to end mate bonds forever. Through you, I will better the world."

Wow, for the first time in my life, I am speechless.

He's crazy.

"So, mommy issues. Got it." Jade snickers.

I run my hand down my face. She's crazy, too.

"I do not have mommy issues," he growls.

"Well, if I'm getting all this correctly, you found out your mom left your dad, and your whole life was a lie. So, in your self-righteousness, you are exacting revenge on her for things out of her control. Under the guise of avenging Daddy. Mommy issues." Jade tries to shrug, but with her immobilized on the table, her back just flexes.

"Jade–" I warn as Ellis turns bright red.

"So, what are you gonna do if Beatrix finds her mate one day? Kill her? Kill her mate?"

"Those bonds are a nuisance, and I've already ensured that will never happen with her," he grinds out.

Does that mean he's already killed her mate? Or done something equally terrible to her? Gods, it's getting tough to hate the little crown digger. No, I still detest her. I empathize with what she's been through, but I don't think I can bring myself to like her.

"So, you just want to rule with an iron fist and make sure no one like your mom can possibly mess it up? Honestly, it sounds like you are making many of the same mistakes your father made. I mean, oppressed people eventually rise up and overthrow oppressors. It repeats over and over again in history."

"We are the oppressed. That's why we must rise up. Why should the more powerful be expected to put more power into the system than the less powerful just because we have it to spare?" His temper is back under control as he looks up from his book.

"Because we have it to spare." I deadpan. "It's for the betterment of everyone."

"It's robbery, and the lesser fae are the only ones benefiting. Why should I give more so that their lives can be better?" he asks, turning towards me with a lifted brow.

"Because helping each other ensures a better life for all. No one is overworked; people are happy. Everyone has shelter, and no one goes hungry. The jobs still get done because people take pride in their work, doing what they love. Why is that bad?" I ask. How can someone be so callous when he grew up with a silver spoon in his mouth like I did?

"Because they did nothing to deserve it. They have a good life because we gave it to them. Under my rule, the pitifully unpowered will be rounded up to do the jobs no one wants. They will have strict regulations on breeding and will no longer be allowed to mix with the powerful. We need to stop the mixing of and the diluting of the lines of the distinguished."

"Does your mother know you're here?" Jade quips.

Stop poking the bear, my love. Gods, she's just as bad as Rodan sometimes. I feel down the bond, fear, and anger twine together with panic that she is pushing away. I want so desperately to hold her, to help her. I don't know how much longer she will be able to stall him.

Anger flashes in his eyes, but leaves just as quickly. "I left ninety years ago. For all she knows, I'm dead."

Damn, he is way older than I thought. That means if Beatrix is close to my age, he could be nearly a century older. He's been grooming her, her whole life... I may throw up.

"Is that when you went to Light?"

He smirks. "Yes, it took me a while, but I earned the ear of the king and eventually warped his mind to my cause."

"Warped is right," she mumbles.

"You don't have to be such a bitch about it. I've told you all of this because there is no escape for you. I will run my experiments until I figure out how to rid the world of mate bonds. You will live the rest of your lives in these cells. However, if you understand what I'm trying to do here, maybe you could join me one day. I'm not a cruel man. Just cooperate and see reason, and this can all go away." He gestures around the dingy room.

I roll my eyes just as Jade snorts a laugh, and my heart sinks. Damn it, I need to get her out of here before she gets herself killed.

The beast within me finally awakens. Cracking its eyes open, the effects of that powder wearing off. So it has a limit on how long it lasts, good to know. I let the wolf take over with a fierce roar. Shaking out my fur, I bare my teeth at him.

Ellis startles and watches my pacing form. I snarl at him; I want him to be afraid. I want him to know that I'll rip his throat out the first chance I get. My claws rake into the stone, carving deep rivulets.

I will get free. And when I do, I'll remember everything he did to her.

Ellis raises a brow and shakes his head. Returning his attention to his book.

Jade closes her eyes and takes a deep breath. When they open, a tear drips onto the table, and a helpless whine escapes me.

I kick and thrash at the walls surrounding me, bouncing off the masonry. Dirt rains down, and a single stone shifts at the base. I breathe heavily as I sit next to it, glancing around to ensure he didn't see that. Running my claws along the rough surface, I shift it further. I will investigate this later.

Ellis stands, picking up a small knife, and my stomach drops. He lifts the back of her shirt and cuts into it. Ripping the fabric away, he exposes her back. Unclasping her bra, he lets it slide to the sides. Jade whimpers, stiffening.

The acrid tang of fear fills the air, nearly choking me. My ears flatten as I snarl and bark at him.

"Let's see if I can get this to work this time," Ellis murmurs.

Jade's face scrunches in anticipation.

There's nothing I can do to stop this.

Her scream shatters my heart as the knife digs and drags into her skin. Red bubbles out of the incision and drips onto the torn fabric of her shirt.

It's agonizing to watch helplessly. Everything in me wants to reach out and help her, to lash out and end her torture. I howl along with her cries to stop.

Butchering her, he slides the blade across her back, carving a circle. It's slow and calculated, methodical. The sharp metallic tang of blood fills the air. Her breathing becomes ragged as she grits her teeth between screams. Dizziness overtakes me as I slump against the wall, my tears rolling to the floor. Regret consumes me—I should have returned her to the mortal world when I had the chance. I never should have brought her back. I could have given up everything and spent my life making her happy. Saving my kingdom is not worth this.

"What the fuck are you doing?" Rodan growls from the doorway.

He slumps against the frame, fury in his gaze. His eyes trained on Ellis and the knife he wields.

My heart leaps.

If Rodan has broken the spell on him...

Ellis frowns. "I was attempting a ritual." He brings the blade around the curve of Jade's side. She screams, sobs racking her body.

Rodan grimaces, flinches, and rolls his shoulders backward. His eyes flash with blue light as he shakes with anger. He stumbles forward a step, collapsing to his knees. Blood drips from his shirt to the floor. He breathes in struggling, panting breaths. Electricity crackles up his arms as his face pales.

I crease my brows in confusion, looking back and forth between him and Ellis.

What the hell is happening?

Ellis furrows his brow, concentrating on Jade's back. He stretches the next patch of skin and brings his line down to her lower back. Flinching, Ellis sucks in a breath and pulls his hands away. His fingers are red and blistering as he stares in confusion. Jade's skin glows a pale blue, nearly imperceptible, flickering in its luminance.

Holy shit. What is that?

"Fascinating," Ellis says, straightening his glasses. A pulse of gray power flashes across his hands, and the blisters disappear. He stares dumbfounded at Jade's back as she sobs.

Rodan regains his feet and storms over to Ellis. "What game are you playing at?" he growls in Ellis' face, grabbing him by the collar of his shirt.

"Wha—what are you talking about?"

Rodan throws Ellis backward; he stumbles, looking wide-eyed at Rodan. With a snarl, Rodan pulls his shirt off, exposing his back.

I suck in a breath, returning to my fae form.

Rodan's back pours with blood; it's been carved up. A half circle drawn over one side of his body. The same marks that mar Jade's beautiful back. He turns away from Ellis, whose eyebrows raise in surprise. Ellis casts his gaze to Jade, then to Rodan, seemingly speechless.

"Well?" Rodan seethes.

"Fascinating," Ellis whispers.

"Wrong answer." Rodan moves to Jade, raising his hands over her skin, and blue light flickers over her back. Her body relaxes as the cuts close. Unstrapping her, he yanks her up by the arm.

She looks at him unblinking, stumbling to her feet. Tears stream from her red, puffy eyes. She sniffles as she studies Rodan's face. His grip on her arm digs into her muscles. He stares at her, watching her chest heave. Attempting to cover herself, she pulls at what remains of her top, her eyes pleading.

Rodan sneers, dragging her to her cell. He pushes her in, and I lose sight of her again. The door clangs loudly, and Rodan storms to the table, snatching his shirt and throwing it in Jade's cell.

Turning to Ellis, Rodan's eyes flash with barely contained fury. "Tell me what the fuck that was? Why was I being carved up?"

Ellis walks over to another bench, picking up a book and flipping pages. "I don't know for sure. Perhaps it's residual from the curse she put on you. A side effect?"

Or whatever he did to the bond. I sneer, wishing I could rip Ellis' head from his body.

"No one touches her, not until we figure out how to fix this shit." Rodan growls and picks up a stool, throwing it at the cell across from us. It clangs and rattles as he storms back over to Jade's cell. "I don't know what you did, but I refuse to let you be my weakness."

Jade's sniffles. "Well, I'll keep that in mind the next time I'm being carved like a turkey."

Chapter 39
Jade

Three days and not a peep from anyone. Two meals a day just appear out of nowhere. The torches light up for a few hours a day. But no one has been down here except Killian and me.

He knocked a brick loose, just big enough to reach through and hold my hand. I can fit my arm through, but it's not exactly comfortable. However, no matter how hard we try, none of the other bricks break free. Killian has tried to chip away at the mortar with his claws, but it's been fruitless.

We spend our days lying on the floor, reaching through the small opening, gaining that little bit of physical contact. Sometimes, we talk through the opening, his face a comforting sight. Killian shares stories of his youth, of adventures and mischief with Rodan. He narrates fairytales and the history of his world. We whisper about anything and everything we can think of.

It's almost peaceful.

Almost.

We are coping. I don't want to die in here, but at least this time, I have Killian. I'm not alone.

There's a hollowness inside me that, for once, isn't fear. It feels like part of me is missing. I know Killian can feel it, too.

"Is it really possible to take someone's heart?" I ask. With my body pressed to the wall, I stretch my arm through the hole, resting my hand on Killian's chest. It's an awkward position, but my skinny arms are paying off for something.

His chest rises as he takes a deep breath. "I keep going over it in my head. It doesn't make sense. You can't live without it, so I assume it can't be his physical heart. But I don't know. Ellis brought a dragon back from the dead, so anything is possible. I don't know much about dark magic. It's forbidden for a reason."

"I wish I knew how to get through to him." I sigh. "Not that I can do anything from this cell."

"The fates must be laughing it up right now. I can't believe they'd let this happen." He makes it sound incredulous. My poor wolf, so sheltered from the world.

I laugh softly. "They are fates; I doubt they care about the outcome as much as we do."

"They could have warned us."

"That would have changed things."

"Exactly."

"No, I mean, that could have made things worse."

He groans. "I still think a warning would have been nice."

"The world is often cruel. As you now know. I don't know if there was anything we could have done differently to prevent all of this. Ellis has been working on this for decades. He used the King of Light to curse Shadow and set the wheels in motion. All we can do is try to delay his plans until we figure out how to stop him." I sigh. "Maybe this was the only way. The fates appeared to be on our side. Plus, I never would have found you if all this hadn't happened." Or Rodan, even if he's being an absolute twat right now.

Killian squeezes my hand—warmth and love flowing down the bond to me.

"I shouldn't have brought you back here," he sighs.

"At least here I have you. In my world, I'd be in jail at Mark's mercy by myself."

The door slams open, and I yank my arm back, scraping my underarm and shoulder on the rock. Hissing, I quickly rub my arm as Killian slides the rock back in place. I sit up and watch the open bars of my cage.

Ellis stomps into view, his hair wild and his shirt askew. "This is your fault." He growls.

I furrow my brow and stare at him.

What now?

"You helped her escape, and now they've all vanished." Sweat beads on his forehead, dripping into bloodshot eyes.

My heart thunders as I attempt to understand what he's telling me. I keep my features neutral as hope gallops through my chest.

Cat.

"Tell me where they are." His face turns red, and his hands fist.

"I have no idea. I've been here. Did you lose someone?" Even if I knew, I wouldn't tell him.

Anger twists his face, demolishing his normally controlled appearance. Whatever Cat pulled off has royally screwed his plans. I want to laugh. His panties are so bunched he may explode.

"I know you know something. That many prisoners couldn't just walk out without help. I know it was your friend, but she couldn't have done it alone. Talk." He demands.

"I've. Been. Here," I drawl, to let it sink in since, apparently, he's daft today. How the hell should I know where his prisoners went? I have to fight not to grin. I'd rather not get sliced up again, even if I get healed after. That shit sucks. However, I will revel in the state that Ellis is in right now. He is unraveling by the second.

My cell door creaks open, and once again, I'm being dragged out on my knees as he pulls my arm. Good god, I could do without the manhandling. My knees scrape against the coarse, rough floor, tearing holes in my dust-streaked pants. He yanks me to my feet, his grip on my arm bruising.

As I feel the bruises form on my skin, I can't help but think of how they will blend with the old ones left from Rodan's assault on my arm. I am a canvas of old and new blooms of color. Who needs tattoos when you can have fingerprints decorate your skin?

My heart thuds in my chest, my head swimming with panic. The rush of adrenaline makes my limbs tremble, and I struggle to keep my balance.

Ellis hurls me into a chair, my arm suddenly free. I scramble to my feet, desperate to escape, but before I can take two steps, I collide with an unyielding figure. I breathe in the scent of rain before a storm. Shadows swirl around me and lock my arms to my sides as I look up into Rodan's intense, dark eyes.

Well, shit, it was worth a shot. Ellis should know better than to let me out.

I sigh and feign a smile. "Hey, honey, I was just coming to see you." I flutter my lashes at Rodan for good measure.

Rodan's eyes move over my head. "I thought I told you: no one touches her."

"I barely touched her; calm down. Thanks for catching her, not that she would have gotten far."

"Then why is she bleeding?"

I look at my arm, and sure as shit, it starts to sting. A small line of blood wells on my shoulder where I also ripped my shirt. Well, if I'm going to be a prisoner, I suppose I'd better look the part.

"I didn't do that. Ask her. I pulled her out to get answers. I want to know who Catria is working with."

Rodan pushes towards the chair and shoves me into it, his shadows securing me to the back. "Don't make me restrain you further."

"You'd like that, wouldn't you? Kinky." I smirk. It's impossible for me to resist poking the bear with him. I want to rile him up, shake his foundation, and rattle the sense back into that thick head of his. "I'd prefer not to have an audience, though. Maybe you could ask for some privacy? Unless you're into that sort of thing, I guess I could give it a whirl." I know he's in there somewhere.

Rodan growls at me, his eyes flashing blue for a second. His shadows convulse around me, tendrils flicking with irritation.

Ellis walks over to Killian's cell, and my smile falters. He pours a vial of dust into his palm and blows it through the bars. Killian sneezes and glares at Ellis.

"Can't face me without your tricks, huh?" Killian sneers. "Or are you afraid of the big bad wolf?"

Ellis throws his hands out, and Killian straightens. The bars open, and Ellis walks to the other side of the room. Killian struggles in his bindings as he is dragged across the floor.

"Let him go!" I shout.

"Be quiet, or I'll silence you." Rodan growls.

"You are being an asshole. What happened–" A shadow wraps around my mouth. I glare at Rodan.

Under some spell or not, I'll kick his ass for that.

He hoists Killian onto his knees in front of a low wooden beam. Ellis wraps a rope around his neck, tying him to the wood. Metal cuffs are clasped to his wrists, restraining them to the floor. He thrashes, but the bench is unyielding. Another board is flipped over his ankles and chained into place. Leaving him trapped on his hands and knees. His breath comes heavy as anger overtakes his features.

Frustration boils within me as I violently thrash against the unforgiving bindings, my clenched fists trembling with rage. I can't let them hurt him again. Glaring at Rodan, he walks away from me and leans up against a wall, crossing his arms over his chest like he is supervising a meeting. What the hell is making him act like this? It's bullshit.

Ellis walks over to a corner just out of sight, returning with a whip. My stomach sinks. My eyes grow wide as I weep through my bindings. I shake violently, sweat trickling down my back.

No, this can't be happening.

Ellis looks at me. "If you won't tell me where they are, and I can't torture you, then I'll take it out on him," he says with such calm coolness that you'd think he was asking for a recipe.

I thrash, my screams muffled through the shadow that gags me.

"Let her speak, Rodan," Ellis says, rolling his eyes.

Rodan shrugs, and the tendril drops from my face.

"Please, don't do this. We don't know anything. I haven't seen Cat since she escaped, and you have everyone else," I plead.

"No. I don't." Ellis sneers. "Somehow, your little friend got into my dungeon and freed them all. So now you are going to tell me where they went and what they have planned, or I'm going to make you wish you did."

Killian growls and shifts his weight, his back heaving. "We don't know anything. It's like she said, we've been here the whole–"

The whip cracks, cutting off Killian mid-sentence and turning into a groan of pain. His back stiffens, his face contorts in a furious grimace, and he exhales sharp, angry breaths, his eyes blazing with rage.

I suck in air through my closing throat as the blood drains from my face. Trembling, I know sound is coming out of my mouth, but I don't register what I'm saying.

The whip cracks again, lines of red well up on Killian's back. The lines drip down his sides as his breathing quickens. His face contorts in pain as he tries to breathe through it.

Sobs wrack my chest as I try to get to him, but my bindings hold me, growing tighter the harder I struggle. Rodan watches with impassive ease, raising an eyebrow at me as his shadows grow tighter around me. Dark spots cloud my vision as I try to fill my lungs, but my ribs are being squeezed. I gasp for air as the world tilts around me. Panic has me firmly in its grasp; even if the bindings weren't so tight, I don't think I could take in air.

Rodan scowls at me, his face turning a slight shade of red. He wheezes a breath, stepping closer and looking down at me. The tendrils loosen, but I'm still choking on air. The world grows dark around me. With every crack of the whip, my heart cracks further.

"Breathe." Rodan strangles out, his voice gruff and pained.

I can't; I'm too worked up, and every hit Killian takes steals more air from my lungs. His face is going pale, yet he doesn't cry out. Gritting his teeth in pain, he takes hit after hit.

I can't breathe.

I can't stop this.

It's all my fault. I let Cat out, and now Killian is paying the price.

"Stop." Rodan growls.

Ellis looks at him in question. "Is she ready to talk?"

Rodan clenches his teeth. "If she knew, she would have said something by now. This is pointless."

Sighing, Ellis drops the whip and walks over to the table where he keeps his books and tools. With a furious roar, he sweeps the contents of the table to the floor. Glass shatters, and papers float across the room. He kicks over a stool and throws a glass jar from a shelf. It explodes against the stone wall.

Killian slumps, his back relaxing a bit.

Another sob wracks my body as I take in a shuddering breath. The tunnel vision begins to recede, but my head pounds with pressure. Even with the binding looser, my chest is tight, and I hiccup with my sobs.

"Just put them back. I'll deal with them later." Ellis says, storming from the room.

Rodan looks down at me. "Go back to your cell," he growls.

The shadows fall away, and I rise from the chair, taking another look at Killian's prone body. His back is smeared with crimson. I don't even have the ability to heal him. He took the brunt of Ellis' rage because of something I did.

"Go." He growls again.

I step into my cell and collapse to my knees, not bothering to turn around as I hear the lock click into place. Folding over, I try to breathe as tears continue to pour from my eyes.

Killian grunts, and his cell door clangs shut.

I hear footsteps and a door slam before we are cast into darkness again. Pushing the stone through the wall, I reach my hand out, hoping to find Killian. My hand meets the empty, cold stone floor, and another tear rolls down my cheek.

"I'm sorry," I whisper.

A warm hand closes over mine, and our bond thrums to life, filled with tired but content feelings. How he can filter out the pain and sadness is beyond me, but it calms my racing heart and eases the pressure in my head.

I take a deep breath. "I love you."

"I knew you would eventually. Who knew getting whipped was the way to your heart?" he chuckles and then groans in pain.

I almost choke on a laugh. "You know that's not true. I just—I just needed you to know that."

"I love you, too, Emerald."

"Do you want me to try to heal you?"

"Baby, you turned your cell into an icebox the other day. Don't take this the wrong way, but I don't think I want to be your test subject today." He chuckles, his voice low and gravelly.

"Fair enough. I just wish there were something I could do."

"Just hold my hand and tell me you love me. I'm going to need you to say that at least a million more times," he sighs.

Chapter 40
Rodan

Ellis paces the room, ruffling his hair with his hands. I don't know if I've ever seen him look so disheveled. "It's too quiet. How did that many people just vanish? The wards prevent any portals. I still haven't figured out how to break the link between you and the girl. How can I finish my experiment if I can't use her? She is the key. I need her broken."

We've spent more and more time in his laboratory in the last few days. With Ellis' wards up around the border and the castle, he's more depleted of power by the minute. He drinks vials of a thick, black liquid that seems to suck the light out of the room. It's like staring into a void. Whatever dark magic he's using allows him to steal magic from those he drains, but it's only temporary.

Owari cuddles up to him, rubbing her hand across his shoulders. "Let's worry about that later. It's time to focus on me," she purrs in his ear. Her long leg peeks out from a slit going up the side of her gown. Shrugging off the strap of her dress, her small, pert breast is exposed, the tiny lavender scales shimmering in the light.

Shifting uncomfortably in my seat, I throw my legs up on the short table in front of me. The leather couch creaks, and I throw my arm across the back. I take a long drink of wine. This is going to be a tedious night.

"Fine," Ellis growls as he pulls her by the waist to the table in front of him. She sits and hikes up her skirt a moment before his belt is undone, and he's slamming into her.

Fucking fantastic.

Rolling my eyes, I turn my head away. Beatrix groans and slumps further into the leather reading chair. She taps her nails across her arm as she stares daggers at me.

"Problem, Doll?" I drawl, lifting an amused eyebrow.

"Well, you won't touch me, so yeah, big problem." Her tone is laced with venom. I'm unsure if I've ever noticed a woman pout so much. The thought of touching her is abhorrent. Jade, on the other hand, had me fighting a hard-on when she talked about fucking me in front of Ellis. I sneer as the mere thought sends blood to my cock again. How does she affect me like this? I growl and pour another glass of wine, trying to drown out the woman who haunts my every waking moment.

From my vantage, it's nearly impossible not to see exactly what's happening in front of me. Owari splayed across the table, her breasts bouncing in time with every thrust. A vision of silver hair fanned over the table while I thrust deep into that witch's pussy floods my mind. That sweet scent of cinnamon mixed with vanilla. Moaning my name as I send electricity sparking through her clit; squeezing my cock as I push her into another orgasm. Now I am rock hard.

Draining my glass, I pour another. I need to get that witch out of my head.

Owari screams her pleasure, her lavender hair splayed around her and her eyes screwed shut. Ellis turns his head to talk to Beatrix. "You just need to carry the heir to shadow, and there are ways to do that without him touching you. I just need my queen to have the rightful heir to Shadow, so we can legitimately claim it. I can just take his seed and put it in you. Honestly, pet, this isn't a big deal," he says, thrusting into Owari, who moans loudly.

I crack a smile and nod towards Ellis. "Why don't you just join them?"

Beatrix glares at me before lifting a brow at Ellis.

Ellis continues slamming into Owari. "Not right now, pet. We have things we need to discuss."

The man's dedication to his cause is admirable. Still trying to figure out how he can concentrate while Owari moans, but to each their own.

"We need to find out where they are hiding," Ellis pants.

Taking a sip of wine, trying to look anywhere but at him. Is this a multitasking thing? Surely there's a better way. "They can't have gone far with the wards in place. Just send your constructs through all the passages." I sigh.

"I've already sent all I have, but they destroyed all but a handful of them in their rebellion, and the replacements are not ready yet."

"How long can it take to throw together those disgusting things?" I ask.

"Weeks," he growls, upping his pace. The slapping sounds are almost comical.

I focus on the wall of books as one flies out and re-situates on another shelf. "What about one of those toothy things that tried to take a chunk out of me at the ball?"

"That was an experiment gone wrong. Recreating those exact conditions would be impossible."

"The black sludge?"

"I used the last of that to take care of the queen's cats during the siege. It takes months to ferment it to its proper state and far more dark magic than I like to use in one sitting. I won't risk corruption that way again. I'd made two batches months apart—" He sighs, pumping his hips. "Alas, the first was destroyed, and the second only lasted the night. The lifespan is just not worth the risk involved. Unfortunately, I did not know that when I made them. Damn. Fine. Print." He breaks up the words with thrusts.

"For fuck's sake, man," I murmur, swigging back the last of my wine before pouring myself another glass. I understand Owari needs an heir and that it's the right time of month to conceive, but couldn't they do this in ten minutes when we finished this meeting? Or postponed the meeting?

Are the rumors about sirens eating their mates once they conceive true? This is why their arrangement is problematic. However, that would make my plans significantly easier. There is still the problem of this link with Jade that plagues my mind. That witch did something to me, and now I have to make sure she doesn't get hurt for my own safety.

Does this mean I can't hurt her? If my inability to breathe yesterday as my shadows squeezed her is any indication, then probably not.

Until I'm free of her, I suppose I need Ellis alive.

"My queen, maybe you should go flush out the rats. Just take plenty of the shifting preventative powder with you."

"Why me?" she whines. "Make him do it." She points at me.

"Because you've done so well in the past. Plus, they were drained of power just hours ago; you'll have plenty of time to catch at least a few while they are weak." Ellis grunts out as he continues to rail Owari.

Beatrix huffs, walking over to a tray of vials on the table next to Ellis. She slaps his ass, causing him to thrust harder into Owari. Picking up a handful of the small vials, she pockets them and saunters out of the room.

With the room smelling like a brothel, Ellis finally collapses on top of Owari, breathing hard. Within a moment, his pants are zipped, and she is straightening her skirts and floating out the door. These fucking people.

Ellis pulls out a book and starts flipping through it as if nothing had happened. "I need to find the link. I need to break Jade to sever her hold on you."

Planting my feet firmly on the floor, I lean my elbows on my knees and fix him with a determined stare. A strange feeling of guilt and nausea mixes with an idea. She may have cursed me, but I hold a secret weapon-I know her worst fears. "I may know a way."

Chapter 41
Jade

Killian barely moves in his cell; his back is still screaming with pain. I feel his anguish in sharp beats down the bond. I wish I could do more for him, but all I can manage is holding his hand. If I could only get a hold of my powers, I could learn how to heal him, but this binding is infuriating. They don't even bother to drain my powers since I'm just one of many experiments.

Yesterday was rough; at least, I think it was yesterday. Two meals have been whisked into the cells on invisible hands. At this point, I don't even care how they do that; I'm glad they aren't starving us.

I don't know whether it's good or bad news that they haven't returned yet. The idea that the others have escaped gives me hope in this hopeless place. If Cat got the others out, help might be on the way. The torches flicker and cast shadows around the room. From my cell, my only view is the metal table and the cells across from me. If I lean close to the bars, I can make out the door frame leading to freedom.

Sighing, I lean back against the wall. If only I could make it through the bars in my otter form. Killian told me not to, but if I'm quick, maybe I could jump through before they closed in.

I doubt I'm that quick.

Maybe I'm focusing on the wrong things. Rodan seems to be

walking around freely. I was able to reach him when he had black eyes. Can I break through whatever they did to him again? His injuries mirror mine, and my emotions affect him. There has to be a way to get him off this villain arc he's on.

The door swings open, startling me out of my thoughts. Killian growls—it's a low guttural sound. His fitful sleep is broken by the footsteps coming into the room.

"So I found out something very interesting yesterday." Ellis muses as he comes to stand in front of my cell. "It appears you skipped out on your duty in the mortal world." He tisks, shaking his head. He opens the door and beckons me forward. "Easy way or hard way." He smiles.

I grumble as I move to follow him. I glance at the door.

"There's a ward on the room, so no trying to run."

Of course. I glance at the doorway and see the telltale flicker shimmer around the edges. I hope he chokes on a chicken bone.

He walks to the table on the other side of the room, his back to me. He shuffles books around, grabs a notebook, and flips it open.

I look over my shoulder at the open door again, longingly. Next to me are that accursed metal table and the chair I was strapped to. Killian struggles to his feet, his breath ragged. He leans against the wall, and I feel his strength run through me.

"After some digging and a long conversation, I discovered some fascinating things about you. So, being the gentleman I am, I made a deal," Ellis says, sitting on a stool and turning to face me again. His cryptic smile makes me uneasy.

Clearing my throat, I ask, "What are you talking about?" I am tired of his games. I take a half step back, wringing my hands.

"Come now, what would be the fun in ruining the surprise?" Ellis smirks.

"So, this is where you've been hiding," says a voice behind me. A voice that elicits chills down my spine and sweat to bead across my forehead. My heart slams in my chest as my stomach drops.

No, no, no.

This can't be happening.

Slowly, I turn, not wanting to accept this reality. My heart races, hoping against hope that I'm wrong and this impossibility isn't happening. The blood drains from my face as I gape in horror, my hope dwindling with each passing moment.

Standing in the doorway is a man of my nightmares. Like a halo of deceit, his blond curly hair is perfectly coiffed into place. His large frame, a looming shadow of my past, takes up most of the doorframe. But all I see is fury and amusement in his eyes, like a storm brewing in a sea of malice. This isn't the man who commanded authority in his world within the confines of the law. This is the man underneath who worked on the outskirts of the law, my ex-father-in-law, Mark.

"It's quite the setup you've got here. I can see why Ace wasn't good enough for your expensive taste. But ending up in the same place I would have put you is just comical. I mean, your downfall was thinking you'd get away. At first, I didn't know what to think when Ellis approached me. This all sounded outlandish. I thought he was crazy." He chuckles. "But seeing it, wow. Who knew?" His voice is lighthearted, but his face shows the monster beneath the surface.

"Stay away from me," I say, backing around the table to put it between us. Trembling, I glance at Ellis from the corner of my eye, trying not to let either out of my sight. He fiddles with a few vials and beakers, tapping on some and storing others, but his attention is mostly on me. The wicked glint in his eye is all I need to know about his intentions.

"Is that any way to treat family? Honestly, my son did a terrible job getting you under control. None of this would have ever happened if it had been me." He takes a few meandering steps forward, trailing his hand over the bars of Killian's cell. Tears prick the backs of my eyes as I think about all the times Mark ran his fingers down my arms. All of the inappropriate touching and comments he made over the years bring clarity I don't want to see.

"You lay so much as a finger on her, I'll rip you limb from limb," Killian growls, his voice so low it's almost a whisper, but I feel the promise in his tone.

Mark laughs, taking another step towards me. His eyes light up as the lines around them grow more prominent. "Oh, I plan to do much more than lay a finger on her."

Not again.

Not him.

No.

I retreat further around the table, trying to keep it between us. In denial of him, I shake my head back and forth. My heart ramps up, ready to launch off this crazy roller coaster. I clench my fists, my palms growing sweaty, and my muscles tense as I watch the predator stalk closer to me.

"You owe me an heir since mine disappeared."

What the fuck? The hell I do.

Ellis turns to me, animated amusement playing across his face. "Imagine my surprise, finding out another had claim over your firstborn. Boy, that would have been awkward. Don't worry; we worked out a deal to rectify that."

What? Rectify?

I fight the impulse to shake my head. I must clear my mind; I can't be hearing this correctly. This can't be real. I inhale deeply. My thoughts are in a whirl, grappling with their words. Bile burns in my throat as I struggle to make sense of this madness.

Firstborn...

Oh, fuck no!

I endured Ace. I will not even entertain the idea of enduring his father.

Adrenaline courses through me, panic rising with the nausea in my belly. The all-too-familiar sensation of my body freezing in fear takes hold.

Not again.

Not again.

Mark smirks and steps around the table.

My eyes widen, my vision tunneling as the sound in the room turns to a high-pitched whine. The feeling of panic cloaks my bones, a chilling reminder of my vulnerability. I can't let the fear win.

No.

I lurch to the side and sprint for the door, my determination to escape overpowering the chaos behind me. There's a clatter and yelling, but I don't look back. Colliding with the ward sends a shock through my system and makes me stumble backward into arms that close around my waist.

I stomp on his foot and throw my elbow into his jaw as he buckles forward. Turning to face a seething Mark, I aim a kick between his legs and try to dart around him as he crumples to the floor.

His arm reaches out and catches my ankle. I fall to the ground, trying to shake him off. I claw at the bricks for purchase. With a grunt, he holds my other leg and pulls me towards him.

I flip over and punch him in the nose, using all my strength. A howl of pain follows a sickening crunch. Blood blooms under his nose as he scrunches his eyes shut.

"Get off me!" I scream.

I know Killian is raging, but my world has narrowed to keeping Mark off me.

His eyes are lit with venom as he snarls. I kick wildly, trying to free my ankles from him. Swinging another punch at him, he lets go with one hand and catches my wrist, squeezing it painfully.

"I can do this all day, princess; you'll run out of fight before I do. My new friend made sure of that." Beneath the amusement in his blue eyes is the hate I often saw in Ace's.

"I'll never stop fighting," I growl, leaning forward. I slap his face with my free hand.

The hand on my ankle jumps to my other wrist as he snarls and pulls me closer to his face. Just the way I'd hoped he would. This is going to suck.

I throw my forehead as hard as I can into his nose. My head connects to a world of pain that ricochets around my skull.

Mark snarls, dropping my arms and holding his face.

I struggle to my feet, my breath coming in short, desperate gasps, my head aching. A quick check reveals no blood, but my desperation is palpable. Backing away from Mark, I scan the room wildly, my eyes landing on the wooden chair. I drag it with me, putting the table between us again.

I glare at Ellis, who casually writes notes in his book. Watching us like a spectator sport. I'd like to punch him, too, but as of right now, he's not an immediate threat.

Killian catches my eye; he smirks and nods his approval, mouthing, "I'm sorry."

I shake my head in response. If he could, he'd help me. I feel his pride pulse through the bond; this is what my training was for.

Breathing heavily, I watch as Mark clambers to his feet. His nostrils flare as he meets my eyes. Blood covers the front of his shirt as it drips from his busted-up face.

You stop fighting only when your heart stops.

Killian's words float through my mind like a forgotten memory. I let the shard of memory fuel me. Readying my stance, I place my hand on the chair.

"Ellis, are you just going to sit there?" Mark barks.

Ellis scribbles down some notes in his book, not bothering to look up. "Yes, this is very informative. Please continue."

I snort a laugh. "What's the matter, Mark? Can't you take the little girl by yourself?"

That's my girl. Show him what you're made of. Fight.

Killian's voice stiffens me. My eyes dart to him, and his eyes grow wide. "Do it," he growls.

I'll unpack whatever the fuck that is later. Speaking down the bond is a conversation for another time.

Mark slams his hands down on the metal table, baring his teeth at me. Not a good look, old man.

"Did you kill him?"

"I don't know what you mean." I smile, batting my eyelashes. I don't know how smart it is to bait the bear, but the angrier he is, the sloppier his fighting will be.

"You took my son; now you'll make me a new one," he growls.

Ew. How about not. I always knew this was where Ace got it from, but seeing it in action is unreal. There is no way I'm letting this man touch me.

"Fuck you," I seethe through clenched teeth.

"That's the idea, princess," he hisses, launching himself across the table, fisting my hair.

I scream and lift the chair, smashing it into him. He huffs but doesn't let go. Pulling the chair from my grasp. He yanks himself closer by my hair. The pull sets my scalp on fire. I claw at his face, grasping for anything that might make him let go. Yanking my head back, he forcefully slams my face into the metal table. He releases my hair and tosses me backward; I stumble back and fall on my ass against the cells behind me. Clutching my throbbing cheek, I arch off the burning bars, my head ringing.

In the next moment, he's on me. I scream as he pushes my back into the scorching iron. My clothes do nothing to stop the burn. I'm blinded by the pain, but I press my hands against his chest. Pushing with all my might, I try to get him off me. My strength is draining from me by the second. Mark's face contorts in pain, his back stiffening as he holds me down.

Somewhere, I hear Killian screaming my name, but it's clouded by my own voice.

I push against his chest with all my strength.

Not again.

Not again.

Not aga—

A choked sound comes out of Mark, and blood pours from his lips. He releases his hold on me. Leaning forward off the bars, my vision comes into focus again. His eyes are wide with shock, and his features blur. I blink several times, trying to make sense of things.

His face distorts, and he coughs more blood. The warmth splatters across my lap. His blond hair dulls and darkens, and his blue eyes melt into green.

He slumps to the side as I pull back my hand and stare in horror at a massive dagger of ice protruding from my palm. It lanced all the way through him like a giant, grotesque stake. Sliding free the foot-long icicle from the hole in his chest cavity, he rolls onto the ground.

What the hell?

Breathing heavily, I try to slow my pulse. I drop my hand and watch the blood run down the ice shard as it melts away. The blood twines between my fingers, coating my skin.

Pain lances through my head, and I scream, clutching it in my hands. Memories flood me as wall after wall falls in my mind.

Warrick, the bar...

Dinners with Killian...

A cave of starlight...

The prophecy...

Rodan saving me from Bravos...

Ellis and Owari taking my memories...

All the pieces slam into place. The memories, the dreams, everything.

I remember.

A pulse of crackling energy surges through the room, followed by an earth-shattering boom from outside, which quakes the stones. Metal tools fall from the wall, clattering to the floor.

Clapping pulls my attention back to Ellis, who stands and laughs. "Well, I wasn't expecting that. Bravo."

Huffing out a breath, I look over at Mark—

My blood freezes.

Long black hair fans out around an alabaster face, the scent of ozone mixing with the metallic tang of blood.

It's. Not. Mark.

Oh god, what have I done!

I scramble to my knees as tears prick the back of my eyes. Trembling, I reach out to him, unable to register where to even begin.

"No, no, no, no," I squeak. "Why would you do that? H—how?" Tears flow of their own accord down my cheeks.

Rodan is bleeding beside me. The hole in his chest pours blood. Crimson spreads like waves on a shore around him. His face is pale and unmoving. Dark lashes rest on his ghostly face.

"Rodan, say something. Please. It can't end like this. Please, Rodan." I frantically run my hands over him. Unsure of where to touch him or what to do. His chest is barely moving, and his pulse is almost nonexistent. My throat closes as I suck down painful breaths. I am so consumed by panic that I'm suffocating, drowning in despair and fear. I killed him. Oh god, I killed him. There is so much blood. I lost control—I didn't mean to.

"Rodan—" I whisper. "No. Please, no."

Sobs wrack my body as I caress his face in my hands.

"I guess my failsafe on your memories is gone. Pity, I thought I had something there, tying them to his blood. Damn. Still worked better than expected. I just never expected you to stab him," he murmurs.

Vibrating with fury and grief like I've never known, a keening wail rips from my soul. Ice fills my veins with promises of numbing the pain, and I just let it out. Nothing matters without him. We need him. I need him. My heart shatters, or maybe my soul does; fate said it would happen after all. What was all of it for if he was just going to die?

Dropping my head to Rodan's chest, I sob.

My world devolves into nothing but pain and cold. I let it take me as I straighten and lean my head back to scream. A rush of power floods me, and ice fills every molecule of my body, asking to be released. The pressure is profound; I unleash my fury.

Ice pours from my skin in an avalanche, covering the entire room in glimmering white and blue. Ice waterfalls off the metal table. Plates of frost cover every cell door. Glass shatters across Ellis' work table. Vials pop and splinter as the frost wave overtakes them. Ice twines around Ellis' knees as he turns red with rage.

My eyes fall on Rodan, his body suspended in the moment in solid ice.

"This is your fault," I whisper, my eyes unwavering from the smooth, glittering surface of Rodan's tomb. Ellis has taken him from me twice now. My heart is a storm of rage, but I steel myself. I hear Killian's desperate calls for me somewhere in my mind, but I tune out everything. My focus is fixed entirely on the relentless destruction of Ellis.

"You destroyed my experiments!" Ellis shrieks like a petulant child.

"You destroyed my mate," I growl, standing to face him. "You destroyed his kingdom. You maimed my mates. Twisted their minds, manipulated them…" A cool calm settles over my rage.

Red flickers through my vision, tunneling down to a single point.

"Not again," I grit out.

Pushing the power in my veins through my skin, it grows and dances in indigo flames across my body. The room is tinged with blue as Ellis sucks in a sharp breath and puts his arms up to cast.

"This shouldn't be possible! I bound your powers. I had it right this time. I know I did!" he yells.

Apparently not, since power writhes like a turbulent storm within me. Hell hath no fury and all that jazz.

He hits me with a blast of air that makes me stumble back a step.

Reaching into his pocket, he pulls out broken glass with a terrified look on his face. Red smoke floats out of his pocket like the fragile wisps of sanity that float away from me. The tendrils move around his body, wrapping him in a cocoon.

A wicked grin plays across my lips. "You thought I was weak," I bite out. "You bound my power, but I feel it coursing through my body, fighting for release and revenge." His own hubris shall be his downfall.

Forcing myself to my limits, I let my rage consume me. "Never again!" I shriek, funneling the blue flames at Ellis. They erupt like a hurricane, the wooden table beside him shattering like glass. He holds it back with a shield, quivering under the force. Panic overtakes his features as his own concoction from the shattered vial works against him. His body slackens under the assault of the crimson smoke coiling around him.

I see lines of blue power connecting my flames to my body; they glow brightly around me. Amid them, black threads twirl about Ellis. With a thought, I tie the blue ones to his, and the shield crumbles.

Flames instantly engulf him. He screams, falling over, trying to put them out. His movements are slow as he fights against the smoke containing him. Rodan, Arlin, and Yudoku flash through my mind as I stare at him. No amount of pain is good enough to make up for their loss. He took them from this world, and we will never know the good they could have done. So many innocent people died at his hands because of some misguided vendetta. I hope this is as agonizing as it looks. I hope my friends can be at peace knowing this is over.

He reaches for a frozen bucket, and on instinct, I let it thaw to see what he will do.

I watch through narrowed eyes as he pours the bucket of water over himself, and the inferno grows white. The water only intensifies the fire as he writhes on the floor. Numb, I turn away from him, satisfied. Everything is happening in slow motion around me as I move on autopilot. Blue flames dance along my skin as I take the keys off the wall and unlock Killian's cell.

His eyes are wide as he takes me in and sees Ellis.

Killian's back is shredded, and lines mark his beautiful skin. They crisscross in their cruel execution. Red threads seem to flow out of him, similar to the black ones on Ellis.

He slumps against the wall, staggering out of the cell. "You broke the binding." He smiles wearily at me.

I nod, taking in the flames on my arms.

"Think you could try to will your power to heal? It's mostly about trusting that you can do it. Be clear in your mind of your intentions and follow your intuition. It's okay if you can't right now; I've never been very good at it."

My power pulses, urging me to let our lines connect. I run my hand over the red threads connected to Killian, tying them together. My power glows bright, and the gouges across Killian's back shimmer, erasing one by one. I trust the power to guide me; it knows what to do. Not a single flame touches my mate.

Killian turns to me, beaming. "I'm so proud of you. You're incredible. Um, I wanna hug you, but I don't want to get cold fire burns."

"I killed him," I choke out.

"Ellis had it coming."

"Not him." I hang my head, feeling the next round of sobs as the numbness and anger melt away.

"Mark deserved it."

I look at him in confusion, then back towards Rodan. The table blocks my view from Killian's cell. From this side of the room, only his legs are visible.

He doesn't know.

I sink to my knees, and my fire goes out.

Chapter 42
Killian

My heart drops as I look at the block of ice encasing Rodan. I sink to the floor, running my hand over the smooth ice. How did this happen? This can't be real. My mind races like a cheetah shifter, not knowing where to stop. He can't be gone. I need him. She needs him. I am frantic and numb; every impulse contradicts the next. There's a gaping hole in his chest, but a solid two inches of ice between me and his skin.

Was it illusion magic? She stabbed Mark. I shake my head, trying to clear it. My breath catches in my throat as I squeeze my eyes shut against the tears that threaten to spill. Why would he do this? We both saw Mark.

Gods damn it, Rodan. How could you?

"I killed him." Jade chokes on a sob as she sits next to me.

"Was he dead when you froze him?"

"I don't think so. I—I didn't mean to—"

"Frozen doesn't equal dead. You may have given us time." Refusing to give up hope, I turn to her and tip her chin up, making her watery eyes meet mine. "You did what you had to. And it looks like you got your powers back." I give her a weak smile and look around. Thinking about his being gone will only cause me to lose it, so I change topics. "How did you know how to use them?"

"I just kinda let them take over. It was like turning on a firehose and just letting it go. There wasn't control, just anger." She sounds so defeated, it breaks my heart.

"Nah, you saw the threads connected to everything. That's royal-level power. You may not have realized it, but your magic showed you the way. You are a badass."

"I killed my mate. I killed your brother. I—I never got to tell him I love him. Not really, not to his face," she cries.

I pull her into my arms, grimacing at the chill of her skin. I need my fire powers back pronto because otherwise, she's gonna freeze my nipples off. I can't afford to fall apart, not when she needs me. If he wasn't dead when she froze him, there is hope. My chest tightens, and my eyes burn with unshed tears.

"I remember everything." She sniffles. "As soon as I stabbed him, it all came rushing back. Ellis tied his blood to my memories."

Holy shit.

His blood was the key to unlocking her memory? That's fucked up! I knew he said something about her memories, but I couldn't hear exactly what he said.

A rumble shakes around us, and dust rains down on our heads. Sounds like explosions rattle the walls.

"We should get out of here; with Ellis dead, his enchantments should be falling," I say, looking at the ceiling. I know we need to move and find the others, but my muscles feel like lead.

"I can't leave him like this."

Clinging to her, I tighten my embrace, my tears forming a steady stream that paints a path down my face. She's right. So we sit and hold each other because what else can I do when I don't know how to fix it? Even if Jade can heal him, we don't know if our Rodan will come back or if he will still be dead inside.

"Whoa, what the hell happened in here?"

I spin to see Warrick looking around in wonder as Cat careens into the room after him, Ryker hot on her heels.

"Jade!"

Jade spins, leaping to her feet and crashing into Cat in a massive hug.

"Are you okay?" Jade asks.

"Oh my god, after you helped me escape, I ran into Maysant. Did you know she's a freaking snake? Anyway, we snuck into the dungeon and turned off that creepy black orb thing. Then we busted everyone out. We've been hiding in the walls and taking out all of Ellis' lackeys. Where is he? I've got a serious score to settle." Cat's ramblings make Jade crack a sad smile.

Jade points to Ellis' still-burning body, the blue flames crackling through his bones.

Cat's face goes into a silent "O," and she grins.

"Warrick, what's going on up there?" I ask.

"It's what Cat said, but there's more. The curses fell; we all felt it. The moon is whole, and we are fairly certain the curse on Amara is gone. I don't know how, but it feels different."

When the blood of great love is spilled, dreams and moonlight become one; the fractured orb will mend.

"The prophecy has been fulfilled." I breathe. "The last shadow fell. The blood was spilled, the moon mended."

Jade takes in a sharp inhale. "Oh god. No, I was the precious stone, and I killed the last shadow!" Jade crumples to the ground in a ball.

Kneeling, I embrace her tightly.

Cat looks confused and frowns, looking around for answers. Seeing Rodan, she gasps, covering her mouth with her hand and shaking her head. She takes a step back as the color drains from her face.

Ryker surges forward only to stop in his tracks, his jaw going slack. Just a moment later, Warrick falls to his knees before Rodan.

"I didn't know," Jade wails. "He looked like Mark; I didn't know. I'm so sorry." Her body shakes as she sobs into my shoulder.

"Get Beatrix," Warrick growls. "I can try to heal him, but I need to know what Ellis did to him. I may not have been in control of my body, but I saw how he was acting, and it wasn't him. They had many conversations about Rodan when he wasn't around, but I never figured out exactly what they did."

Ryker shifts and flies out of the room.

"Ellis said he took his heart," Jade whispers.

Warrick's brows crease, and he looks over Rodan, running his hands along the ice.

"She's right—" Warrick says, baffled. "The essence isn't there."

"That's because I stabbed right through it!" Jade cries.

I rub tiny circles on her back. There is still hope. We've wasted enough time losing ourselves; I need to keep my head on straight. She is tired and depleted; I need to get her to bed. For now, I can let her rest and help her out of her spiraling.

"I hate to break it to you, but your aim was off. You hit a small part of his heart but really fucked up his lung." Warrick smirks. Jade glares at him over my shoulder, gritting her teeth. "There's a chance that since the essence of his heart wasn't there, he may have been unkillable. Hurtable, yes, but—"

"Too bad I froze him to death after I stabbed him," she retorts.

This is all making me slightly lightheaded. I am definitely not a hundred percent, and losing Rodan is not an option on the table.

Warrick shrugs. "Let me work, little mortal. You can freak out if I can't fix him."

"You can't fix him?"

Yep, she's gone hysterical, if that's all she heard. I'm not far behind. "Is the castle safe?"

"Yes, Lyra is patrolling the halls with Darius. Scarlette and Corsac are outside, commanding the remaining guards. The trustworthy fae are making sure everything is safe. The questionable fae are in the dungeon, enjoying the perks of the black orb." He smirks. "Most of the constructs just suddenly dropped. And any fae with black eyes just blinked back to normal. Once that happened, the round-up was fast, and we came down here to dispatch Ellis."

"You let Cat come to help defeat Ellis? She could have gotten hurt!" Jade scolds him.

"So, I kinda have this kick-ass power under control now, like I was gonna turn him into jerky. Plus, I had plenty of time to practice flying in that stupid box, so I could have flown away if that plan didn't work."

Warrick groans and looks pointedly at Cat. "I told her to stay behind. She claims she didn't hear me."

I scoop Jade into my arms, and Warrick gives me a hand to stand. "Okay, I'm gonna take both of us upstairs for a bath. Let me know immediately if there's a change with Rodan. Any news about my parents?"

"Not yet. Lorelai will send word if anything changes. Go clean up, you stink," Warrick says.

I groan. "Jerk."

Jade cried herself to sleep on my bed. She looks like a cute little fairy, nestled amidst the pastel blues and purples. I'm starting to understand why Rodan kept calling my room the fairy princess room.

Damn it. Fucking Rodan.

He can't die.

I slip out of the room, closing the door as quietly as I can, my determination to do something, anything, burning within me. Turning down a hallway, I spot Corsac running towards me. She collides with me, the fox shifter sealing her arms around my waist. She shakes her short, bouncy curls out of her face and smiles up at me.

"I'm so glad you're okay. I got Beatrix nice and roughed up for you. So you can question her now." She wiggles her eyebrows, stepping back.

I almost laugh. "I didn't ask for her to be roughed up." Pursing my lips, I lift an eyebrow.

"Okay... I did it for me. She touched my girlfriend; that's unforgivable." She turns on her heel and walks down the hallway.

I follow, chuckling. I definitely understand that.

Reaching the cell, Beatrix's long hair is matted, and chunks are cut from it. She's sporting a fat lip and a black eye. I glance at Corsac, who only shrugs.

Don't fuck with the fox. Got it.

The state of Beatrix calms some of the rage I feel for her, but justice has not been served. She is like the wicked queen in the stories, who has finally reached her end. In the dungeon, I spent hours thinking of all the things I would do to those working with Ellis. But now that I have her at my disposal, I feel the fight drain out of me. What I crave now are answers.

"What did Ellis do to Rodan, and how do we fix it?"

"I'll tell you everything. Just let me go." Beatrix rushes to the bars and sinks to her knees, looking up at me.

"Answers, and I'll consider it."

"His heart is in a jar; there's like a red snake holding it hostage. It's in a hidden safe in the lab." She rushes out. "It was in a book; there must be an undo spell. Now let me go."

"I see." I scratch the scruff that's grown on my chin. "Was he unkillable?"

"Gods no. It just took the love from his heart." Her flippant tone causes my blood to boil.

My wolf opens one very groggy eye. My anger rousing it out of the spell that kept it dormant.

"Well, you better hope he was because otherwise, I'll kill you myself," I growl.

"What? Why would he die?" She goes pale.

"The only thing you need to worry about is if he recovers. Thank you for the information. Corsac, play nice with your toy and maybe share her with your friends. Try not to break her," I say, winking at Corsac as I turn to leave.

"Wait, no! Please, Killian!"

"Ask Lyra to reach out to Lupos; she's diplomatic. Maybe we can offer her up to them for killing their princesses." Perhaps I can scare more answers out of her, or maybe I just want to torture her a bit.

"Oh, Nucifera can do it; Lorelai is working on fixing her wings. Or regrowing them? I'm fuzzy on the details, but I'm sure she'd have no problem talking with her parents," Corsac says.

"No, no, please! I'm sorry. Please don't trade me to the pixies; I'll be good. I can stay right here. Please don't send me there."

I turn, slapping my leg in recollection. "That's right; my dad was gonna give you to the bog lord. How could I forget? Let's get those wheels in motion. Hey, on the bright side, you'll still get to be a queen just like you wanted." The tension in the room is palpable as I turn away and walk out, leaving behind the sound of her screams.

"Killian, I didn't know you could be so mean," Scarlette says as I enter the hall.

I laugh. "Neither did I."

"How long you gonna let her think she's going to be a bog lord's bride?"

"I figured we'd let her stew on it, show her wedding dresses, flowers, all that planning stuff. Then, after a few months, see if she is worth rehabilitating. If not, then we will figure it out."

"Cruel but genius. I love it. Call if you need us," she says, returning to the dungeon.

After everything Beatrix did, it can't go unpunished. However, learning that psycho spent her entire life grooming her makes things more difficult. She deserves a chance at a better life. It won't be right away, but maybe she can be helped. I feel bad for her.

So many people are missing, dead. The halls are so empty.

Thankfully, most of Ellis' bullshit was kept to castle grounds, and my people were minimally affected. He instated curfews, and his constructs raised havoc, but for the most part, the people survived better than the court and the guards. I already miss spotting the queen's cats out of the corner of my eye.

The library is unscathed, not a book out of place. I walk through the stacks, headed for the passageway to Mr. Psycho-Pants' laboratory. I'm stoked that Ellis is gone, but there is still so much that we have to do. Rodan is our top priority; the clock is ticking, and if we don't figure something out soon, we may lose him.

As I round a corner, I hear a book shift and a small chirp.

I'd know that sound anywhere.

I frantically look around. Happiness and hope flood my body.

"Pop, it's me. Come on, man, tell me that's you."

A little chirp sounds overhead, and I look up to see a tiny black kitten face poke out from the top shelf. Pale green eyes blink back at me as his purr rumbles. He chirps again, and smoke wafts out of his nose. Leaping out of the stacks, he glides on tiny wings to my shoulder and rubs his spiky head against my cheek.

"Oh man, I thought we'd lost you! I'm so happy to see you." I pet him and cuddle him in my arms. "Such a good dragon, staying out of sight."

He chuffs another cloud of smoke as I continue walking to the lab.

"Did you protect the library from the bad guys?" I coo at him as we walk through the fireplace door and into the old passageway.

He growls his response and nips at my hand as I pet his belly.

I chuckle and scratch him behind his ears, holding him tighter. My brave little dragon.

The broken steps we encountered the first time we came down here have been repaired; no doubt Ryker's handy work with stone. As I reach the lab, I set Pop down, letting him walk into the room at my side. He enters with his little chest puffed out and yowls at Cat.

She turns, and her face lights up as fluffy orange ears pop out of the top of her head.

Rushing forward, she scoops Pop up in her arms with tears in her eyes. Her tail swishes back and forth as she carries him over to the book she was looking at. The two of them chirp and speak in that cat language I wish I could understand.

Ryker claps me on the shoulder. "Glad you're okay."

I smile at him. "Yeah, it was touch-and-go there for a while. Glad Ellis' hubris was his downfall in the end. You should have seen it; that binding spell broke on Jade, and she was like a goddess of wrath." It was so hot.

"So about that, Ellis is still smoldering. Think you can ask her to put it out? Because water makes it worse." He snorts a laugh.

"It's cold fire, man. Just take a torch to it." I laugh.

"Well, how the fuck was I supposed to know that?"

"A history book? She's not the first fae to have that power."

"No, just the first in a generation. I studied war tactics and earth magic. Not what crazy shit water elementals can do."

"We got the coolest powers." Cat singsongs to us from her perch, giggling.

"You got the scariest powers," he grumbles.

"You like it," she says.

His only response is a grunt, but the gleam in his eyes and smile he's trying to hold back tell another story. I stare dreamily up at the ceiling. We were so lucky with them. I just wish the cost weren't so high.

"I talked with Beatrix," I say.

"What did she have to say for herself?"

"She was very informative. Have you seen a safe in this room?"

Ryker tips his head in thought, his interest piqued. "I have not, but I'll feel around for it. Earth magic has its perks when it comes to hidden things. Speaking of, have you recovered any of yours yet?"

"I can feel my wolf beginning to stir, but I'm still pretty tapped.

How long did it take you to recover?"

"About a day for my powers, but Maysant snuck into the dungeon the night before they got us out. She turned off the orb and snatched the keys. Weirdest thing, waking up to a snake jingling keys across the floor and then winking at me."

"No shit. Damn, I'm glad I helped her escape."

"She and Cat showed up the next night and unlocked all the cages. We ended up in the passages. The remaining councilors were in pretty rough shape. We did what we could to heal them, but mostly, we stayed hidden long enough to fully recover our elements so that we could rain down hell."

"It was super helpful to have most of the monsters drop dead during the fight, though," Cat pipes in.

I bet. I guess dark magic no longer works if the one wielding it dies. That's definitely a lucky break, but it also shows just how much it's tied to the person using it. Sorcery is scary; I have no desire to see what else is possible with it.

Ryker runs his palms over the walls while we talk. "What's in this safe?"

"Rodan's heart, apparently."

Ryker whistles. "Yikes. Explains a lot."

Yeah, unfortunately.

I survey the room, noting the additional sofa and reading chairs in the middle. Ellis was definitely making himself comfortable down here. I look over Cat's shoulder at the book she's currently reading, with Pop curled up in her lap, purring contentedly.

She looks up at me. "How is she?"

"Sleeping. Using that much power knocked her out. I barely got her out of the tub before she started to nod off."

"That's probably a good thing. I'll go up there and watch over her; she shouldn't wake up alone. You two keep working on finding a solution for Rodan," Cat says.

I raise my eyebrows. Did she just order me around?

"Just go with it; there is no sense in arguing with her," Ryker says.

Cat smiles at him as she grabs the notebook and walks out, Pop following closely behind. "I'll let you know if I find anything useful in his notes," she calls as she waves, leaving the lab.

I sigh, drop into the chair she was using, and crack open one of the notebooks. There are a disturbing number of notes about Jade and her mate bond. For a guy who acted calm and collected, his notes scream his distaste. He really was insane.

"Should the wall be pulsing?"

I snap my head to Ryker. "No, I swear to the gods, if another spider is hiding in the walls, I'm going to lose it."

"Well, only one way to find out." He grins wickedly at me and pulls the wall apart with his bare hands, peeling back the stone like paper.

An eerie glow of red peeks through the wall as Ryker digs. It pulses smoothly, and a cold sweat breaks across my forehead. Uneasiness settles deep in my bones.

"I think you found it." I gulp.

Kneeling down next to Rodan's body, I place the jar with the red pulsing snake beside him. Warrick and Lorelai wait patiently, hands outstretched, ready to get started as soon as the ice melts.

Focusing on the fire of the torch Ryker holds, I close my eyes and pull the flames into me. Barely an ember flickers in my well, but it's enough to ignite my element and fuel my fire. Warmth spreads through my body as I feel for the flames around the room, snuffing them out one by one.

I open my eyes to the dark room and cast a single fae light to illuminate it again. Rubbing my hands together, I place them on the ice and let the power flow through me. Water trickles across the floor, soaking into our clothes as I melt away the ice coffin.

Once Rodan's body is exposed, Warrick and Lorelai push their hands onto him. Blue and yellow light shines through their fingers and spreads over Rodan's body.

"Now," Warrick tells Ryker.

Ryker opens the jar and turns it over the hole in Rodan's chest. I hold my breath as I watch the snake get unceremoniously flipped and coil tighter in the glass.

"Come on, do something," I growl as I thaw the ice and heat Rodan's body.

Ryker taps on the bottom of the jar, his eyebrows pinched, and lips pressed in a thin line. "What if the little bastard needs another spell?"

Lorelai takes a deep breath, pushing more light into Rodan. "Come on, go home. The love you contain is important." She coaxes the snake.

The red snake writhes as it pulses, glowing brighter. Slithering down, it pokes its head through the opening in the jar, its tongue tasting the hole in Rodan's chest. It uncoils and drops into the cavity in the blink of an eye. Momentarily blinded by white light, Ryker lets the jar fall away. As the last of the ice melts, the wound begins to close.

Warrick breathes heavily as he pushes more power into Rodan, and Lorelai looks ready to pass out. The last of the flames dies in my veins, and I just hope it was enough.

Chapter 43
Rodan

She stabbed me.
The crazy witch stabbed me.
Everything has gone white, and she fucking stabbed me.
Why is it so cold?

The blinding white is starting to fade.
But the frigid cold is no longer chilling my bones—if I have bones—because there is only endless white.

Pain lances through my chest.
Thud.
Thud.
The sound is deafening.
I scream, but there's no sound. Just the infinite beat of a drum, hammering its percussion.
Memories float through on a stream—pictures through glass—

Anger and hate drain from my consciousness, replaced by abject misery.

What have I done?

"Trouble," I groan. My eyelids feel weighed down by lead. "Trouble."

I suck in air, but my throat is dry, and I struggle with the labor of it, coughing violently. Tingles flood my body as if every nerve has been asleep and suddenly shocked into alertness.

"Oh, thank the gods. Easy man. How are you feeling?" Killian's voice reaches me through my tumultuous thoughts. His hand closes over mine, and his warmth is near scorching.

"Is she okay? I—I fucked up. Oh gods, I fucked up." I say, trying and failing to lift myself.

Hands grip my shoulders, helping me to sit up. A cup presses into my parched mouth, and I take tentative sips, the water going down like razor blades.

"We almost lost you, so cool your jets before you overdo it. I don't have enough power left to fix you a second time today." Lorelai scolds. I almost smile at her familiar presence, filled with gratitude for her care.

"Is she—"

"She's fine, just resting," Killian says as I finally manage to open my eyes fully and look around. "Are you, you again?"

The room is covered in thick ice. Ice waves cascade up frozen walls as they curl over on themselves. Cells shimmer with frost, covering the doors and hiding their contents. A few feet away, a blue fire burns over a pile of ash.

"I sure fucking hope so. Did I hurt her?"

Killian looks away, and my heart sinks.

Pulling myself to my feet, I balance against Killian and a table covered in a thick sheet of ice. "This is because of what I did, isn't it?"

Killian scratches the back of his neck. "Let's blame Ellis for taking your heart."

"Ellis—" I growl.

"Is dead," Warrick states before I get spun up. Relief washes over me.

Jade's hand presses against my chest as I hold her to the iron bars. The pain she experiences radiates down my spine as I try to control her. A sharp sting drives through my chest, and then the world goes white.

Shaking my head, more memories flood my mind, and nausea makes my mouth water. I feel the hole in my shirt and the unblemished skin underneath.

I would have destroyed everything if she hadn't stopped me.

Gods, I'm a monster.

"I need to see her." With a surge of energy, I break for the door, stumbling and gaining my balance on the walls.

"Rodan!" Lorelai calls.

"Let him be; there's no stopping him." Warrick chuckles.

"She's in my room!" Killian calls after me.

Opening the door to Killian's room, I am met by the demon known as Cat, as she shoves me out into the hallway.

Her lip pulls up in a growl. "Oh no, you don't. I'll drain every drop of water from your body if you even try to hurt her again. Where's Killian?" The fire in her eyes speaks of the danger within her.

I raise my hands in surrender as a grin pulls at my face. "Well, hello to you too, little hellion. I'm not going to hurt her. I just need to see her."

Wrinkles form around her eyes as she scrutinizes me. Her fingers pull my face down to hers, checking my eyes. She grabs me by the chin, pushing my head from side to side before again leveling me in her glare. "How do I know you're back to normal?"

It's a fair question. "She's my world, and if you don't get out of my way, I'll have a lot more groveling to do for knocking you out. I'd prefer not to add to my list of wrongs against her."

A grin spreads across her face. "There's the asshole we all know and love. Don't wake her; she needs to rest." She turns and strolls down the hallway. "Oh, and don't think you're off the hook; payback's a bitch, and her name is Cat."

Fuck my life. These girls are going to be the end of me. I will never live down the atrocities I put them through. All I have is the knowledge that I never would have done those things in my right mind.

Stepping into Killian's room is like entering a dream of clouds. The pale blue walls, adorned with fluffy, shifting clouds, create an ethereal atmosphere. Sheer curtains frame the large open windows, their lavender fabric rippling in the breeze. The four-poster bed, draped in translucent pastel panels that cascade like a rainbow waterfall, is the centerpiece. Bookshelves seemingly floating among the clouds line the walls.

Despite my attempts to convince him otherwise, Killian's room always seemed more suited to a princess. But then again, he's a romantic at heart. It suits him that his space reflects that his head is always in the clouds.

As I withdraw the drapes from the bed, I find Jade nestled among a heap of blankets and pillows. Her silver hair cascades behind her, forming a delicate halo around her curled-up figure. Even in sleep, I can see the dark circles that dim her features.

Frost speckles her skin like glitter, freckling her arms as she pulls the blankets snugly around her.

I did this to her.

Silently, I open the trunk at the end of the bed and pull out a golden comforter, carefully spreading the fluffy blanket over her.

Shifting into my panther form, I creep into the bed next to her and curl up, watching the rise and fall of her chest. She reaches out and wraps her fingers in my fur. I still don't want to wake and scare her. She felt safe with my panther once, and I just hope I can provide that to her again. She murmurs something and shifts into my body, burying her face in the fur of my chest, and sighs.

Laying my head down above hers on the pillow, I drape my paw over her shoulder and close my eyes, breathing in the soft scent of vanilla sugar.

"Mmm, warm." Jade mumbles, rousing me from sleep. "Void?"

I blink open my eyes to see dark blue blinking back at me. She's slack-jawed, and I can hear her heart ramp up in her chest. Silver lines her eyes and threatens to spill, her nose turning red with unshed emotion. She sits up and tentatively brings a hand to my face.

Bowing my head, I'm ready for her to dismiss me. I take a deep breath.

"You're you again, aren't you?" Her hand softly brushes the fur on my cheek, and I lean into it. If she doesn't forgive me, this may be the last time she touches me. I don't even deserve this simple caress.

She takes in a shuddering breath, and I dare a look at her. Tears spill down her perfect face as she cracks open. "I thought I killed you. I'm so sorry. I–" She hiccups and throws her arms around me. "I didn't mean to."

Stunned, I hold absolutely still.

No, I can't let that stand. I can't let her think any of this was her fault.

I turn back into my fae form, but her arms stay locked around my neck as I wrap her in my embrace. "You did what you had to. I am the one who got captured. I should have seen the trap coming. You saved me. Although I could have done without the hole in the chest." I smirk, pulling her back so I can look into her watery eyes. "Please forgive me. I didn't know I was capable of being such a monster. Or that I could feel so hollow, so empty."

"Except when you felt my pain."

"I still don't know how you made me cry," I say, wiping a tear with my thumb from her cheek.

"It's how I knew you were still in there somewhere, that our bond wasn't gone completely."

"I was going to do horrible things to you and everyone else." Grimacing, I drop my head to her shoulder. "I don't know if you'll ever be able to forgive me."

"Can we call it even since I technically killed you?" she sniffles and twines her fingers in my hair.

"I didn't die, Trouble."

"Um, considering we broke the curse on the kingdom and the gods. I think you did."

I rear back and study her. She drops her arms and fidgets with the blanket, her gaze cast down.

"How?" I stammer as I get to my feet and rush to the window. Would there even be a way to know? Glancing around at the garden beneath, nothing seems different until I look at the sky.

The large moon stands proudly in the sky, bright in the sun's light, and next to it, the smaller moon is whole. It glitters in the light, shining with its brilliance once again. My jaw drops, and I turn to see Jade stepping beside me.

"It's beautiful," she breathes. "Warrick thinks the curse on Amara is gone as well. Shadow may no longer be cursed..."

"What was the key?"

She takes a deep breath. "You."

Stunned, I look between her and the moons. I need to see.

"I'll be right back."

Her brows crease, and I pull my shadows around me and step

through. The tower is exactly how we left it. I never should have left her here alone. Rushing to the window that looks over Shadow, I suck in a breath. The fog is gone, and spots of green peek out from gray branches and trees. There is still a distinct line of demarcation on the border, but birds sweep and dive through the canopy, and signs of life once again are taking root in the kingdom.

My heart pounds as I lean against the glass to steady myself. The prophecy runs through my head, and all the pieces click into place.

I was the key.

If I died, Amara would fall. So how? Was it dependent on how I died? No, my blood was spilled. I didn't die. It's her. She was the key. She had to spill my blood. If I died, all would be lost, but the woman who loved me had to spill my blood to save us all. Gods, that's fucked up.

Thanks a lot, Fates.

I step back through my shadows and sweep Trouble into my arms, taking her off her feet with a squeak. "You did it, not me," I explain my theory of the prophecy to her, detailing all the events that have occurred until now.

The weight of two kingdoms lifts from my shoulders as I stare at this magnificent creature before me. She smiles up at me, and all I want to do is hold her and kiss her.

She runs her hand down my chest and stops over my heart, frowning. "Does it hurt?"

"No, but I wish it did, so I would have a reminder of what I did to you."

She scoffs. "You were an asshole, but what else is new?"

"But I was going to—" Her finger comes up over my mouth, silencing me.

She cocks an eyebrow. "And I stabbed you. I think we are even. Now kiss me."

I've scarcely acknowledged her words before my hands clutch the fabric of the front of her shirt. Pulling her into me, our lips collide. The bond hums in my veins, reawakened. It's faint at first as the threads find each other and twist back together. She moans as I deepen the kiss, and my nerve endings spark to life.

Her hands roam down my chest, deft fingers tugging at my tunic and finding their way to my bare skin. Every delicate touch sends electricity through my body. She rakes her nails over my pecs, and I groan, nipping at her bottom lip and pulling her flush against me. I grind into her with my hardening length.

The guttural groan that escapes her has me on edge as she breaks the kiss, discarding her top and dragging me towards the bed. She backs into the post, and I cage her in, pulling her arms above her head and kissing down her neck. "I was trying to grovel," I murmur.

"Then try harder," she whimpers. I nip at her neck, and the soft moans coming out of her are all the encouragement I need. Unfastening my pants, I let them drop as I suck her nipple into my mouth. Her hips buck at the contact as she tries to pull her underwear down with one hand.

I throw open the draperies surrounding the bed and move her to the edge. Sitting her down and pulling off the offending fabric between her legs. Dropping to my knees between hers, she squeaks as I dive in like a starved man and lick up her center. Pushing her thighs wider apart, my shadows hold her exposed to me as I devour her, sucking on the nub that has her moaning my name. I can't get enough of her taste as I graze my fangs along her folds.

I will spend the rest of my life trying to get her to make this sound.

I slip a finger inside her wet heat, relishing the way she bucks and pulls against me.

"More," she moans.

"Anything you want, Trouble," I say as I nip at her leg.

I slip a shadow within her, and she cries out as her back arches. Leaning in, I suck hard on her clit as I have the shadow twist inside her, growing its girth, stretching her to get her ready for me. She is so wet already that I could easily sheath myself, but I want her to come first. I want her to orgasm so hard she sees stars.

My dick is so hard it's painful as my shadow pumps and twists inside her; I can feel every part of it. But when I feel her get close, I back off and let her body calm. Slowing my pace until she is writhing within my grasp.

"Not yet." I tease, flicking my tongue against her.

"Rodan, I need to orgasm; stop edging me," she growls.

"Oh, but you liked it so much in the cave."

"Yes, I remember." She squirms, and I pump the shadow harder into her, leaving her with a moan on her lips.

She remembers, thank fuck for that. So lost in my elation, I lick and suck her with renewed vigor. I need to taste her come on my tongue. I want her pulsating around my shadow so I can slip my cock inside her and feel her come on me.

Her breathing increases in tempo, and her body squirms as I find a fast rhythm to toy with her most sensitive area. The shadow picks up its pace, curling into the spot deep within her where she is clenching the blankets in her fists and crying out. Her whole body convulses as I quickly stand and push my cock into her. Letting the shadow fall away. I slide in inch by inch while I play with her clit; she clenches around me as I push in, gripping her hips to hold her steady.

She groans and wiggles as my hips meet hers, fully seated.

Fucking hell, she's so tight.

With a shallow thrust, I flick her clit with a little jolt of electricity, and she rockets over the edge again. She clamps down so hard on my dick that I think I see stars as I thrust into her.

"Fuck, that's hot." Killian's voice almost throws me off as he comes up beside the bed. He stares down at Trouble as she reaches out to him. "Do it again," he growls.

Grinning, I channel my power through her body, and she crashes into another orgasm. I almost lose it in her heat as she squeezes my cock, her body pulsing with pleasure.

Killian strips and climbs next to her on the bed, leaning down and kissing her, muffling her moans. He runs his hands over her breasts, tweaking her nipple, causing her insides to twitch. Fuck me, that feels incredible.

I continue my slow thrusting into her and watch as she grabs his dick, stroking the hard length. A growl rumbles deep in his chest, and I know his wolf is out to play.

"I need to flip over," she says, looking devilishly at me. She gasps as I slip out and flip her. Her beautifully round ass bent over the bed. I spread her cheeks and line myself up with her pussy and slam into her. She groans at the invasion but pushes back against me, taking me in deeper.

"Greedy today, are we?" Killian laughs, but is silenced as she grabs his cock and pulls him towards her.

I keep a slow but punishing rhythm as I watch her tongue run up the length of Killian's dick. She circles the tip and flicks her tongue over the slit, taking the bead of pre-cum. His head falls back as his fingers lace through her hair. I watch, mesmerized, as she takes his cock in her mouth and swallows it to the point of gagging before returning to the top.

I'm so entranced by her I forget to keep moving; picking up the pace again, so does Trouble. My shadow moves to play with her swollen clit as I try to hold back my release. But as she moans and pushes into me, she forces me deeper with every thrust. I send a shock through her that sends us both over the edge; she screams as she shudders around me, and my legs almost give out. I slip from her, and I nearly collapse to the floor, catching myself on the bed. Killian picks her up, ready to thrust into her before I've even recovered.

My cum drips from her as he pushes in; she breathes heavily as he stretches her even further. Her back arches as he caresses her clit, and he glides into her until he's fully seated. I lean over and kiss her deeply as she moans her pleasure.

"Do you want to come again, baby?" I purr

"I can't," she pants.

Killian smirks at me and picks up his pace while massaging her clit. "Be a good girl and lick the come off his cock, my love," he says. Before I have time to prepare, she takes hold of my dick and positions it by her mouth.

She licks up the side like a damn ice cream cone and then swirls her tongue around my slit, making my hips buck and my cock instantly rock hard again. She sucks and licks, taking me so deep my eyes roll back into my head.

She grips me hard as she releases her lips from my tip with a loud pop and moans. Killian picks up his pace, slamming into her as he roars his release. Sucking me hard as she comes down, moaning around my dick, the vibration added to the visual I just witnessed sends me over the edge. I send my power through her again, prolonging her pleasure and causing Killian to curse as he pushes deeper inside her. I try to pull out to warn her, but she grabs my ass and sucks me even further down her throat; I roar my release, and she swallows every drop of my cum.

Fucking hell, this woman will be the death of me.

Chapter 44
Killian

Clouds float above my head in the canopy of my bed. The enchantment almost seems real with its calming effect on the soul, like a gentle breeze on a hot summer day or the soothing sound of rain on a tin roof. Jade lies nestled in the crook of my arm, her fingers tracing lazy circles along my chest. Rodan presses behind her, his arm wrapped possessively around her middle.

I can't believe he had her in my bed before I did. It's like a known rule not to have sex in your brother's bed, isn't it? Either way, I'm not angry about it because watching was extremely hot. Now I understand how Rodan felt the first time I was with Jade. Something in me says I should feel jealous, but I just can't bring myself to be. The obvious choice was to join.

"So what happens now?" Jade asks, propping her chin on my chest.

"Well, Lyra's father just arrived with his troops. Seems the barrier around the kingdom fell when you flambéed Ellis. Anyway, they captured Owari trying to flee with Calazar. They are now in the dungeon with Beatrix, awaiting judgment. Thankfully, the King has good ties with our kingdom and has agreed to help where he can until we get things figured out. He and Warrick are currently calling on all the other monarchs for aid and to call a royal conflux."

"What is that?"

Rodan groans, pulling her tighter into his arms. "It means that all the monarchs will meet to decide what to do from here. They will determine the fate of Shadow going forward and what will happen if we can't wake up our parents. It's meant to keep the peace, but it's also a colossal pain in the ass."

"We should go to my parents' chambers and see if there has been any progress waking them," I say, kissing Jade on the forehead.

Moving off the bed, we reluctantly get dressed and make the daunting walk to my parents' tower. With the wards dropping and the spells collapsing after Ellis died, I'd hoped that my parents would wake. Unfortunately, they did not, even after we had the orbs cleansed and set right. Lyra's kingdom brought as many fae as they could spare to help heal and rebuild. Within a few hours, the urgent matters were rectified.

Passing through the wards to my parents' room, the air is warm but stale. They lay side by side, breathing steadily. If I didn't know better, I would have assumed they were asleep. Perhaps this is a Sleeping Beauty-type curse, and they need their true love to kiss them.

"Hear me out—"

"Killian, I know what you're thinking, and this is not a fairytale," Rodan grumbles as he walks over to Mom and smooths his hand down her cheek.

"But if we just make them kiss, it could—" I whine. I know it's not dignified, but we can't say we exhausted all options if we don't try them all.

Rodan groans, glaring at me. "Fine, I'll turn Mom, and you push Dad towards her." He rolls his eyes. "This is by far the stupidest idea you have ever made me do."

"That's not true. I talked you into going to the river nymph party, and we almost got eaten by that hot chick who was really a bog witch. That was the stupidest idea I made you do," I say as I turn

Dad's head towards Mom.

Jade giggles, standing at the end of the bed.

I lift Dad up by the shoulders and shimmy my knee under him for leverage, rolling him onto his side. Gods, he is heavy. It is going to be hard as hell not to smash Mom with him. Rodan rolls Mom, but the space between them is still a little too far.

"You guys are doing this the hardest way possible," Jade laughs. "There is a much more dignified way that won't embarrass your parents. Rodan, scoop your mom up and place her on her back, touching your dad. Then, Killian, you slowly roll him and lower his face to hers. This has to be the worst version of playing with dolls I've ever seen."

"They aren't dolls." Rodan growls.

"Well, they aren't dead bodies either, yet you two seem to think that they can't be touching anywhere but the lips. There's still a good six inches of space between them." Jade retorts.

Grumbling, Rodan readjusts Mom in his arms and slides her into Dad. I've got Dad propped on his side, but I'm not sure how to lower his head to hers without just dropping him on her. There may be some major flaws in this plan.

Rodan looks at me expectantly and sighs. "I'll direct his head; you'll ensure he doesn't crush Mom. Gods, this plan is worse in execution."

With my arms wrapped around my dad's torso, Rodan reaches for his head, holding him steady. Dad takes in a deep breath, and we both remain still as his eyes blink open.

The world freezes as his eyes lock onto Rodan's shocked face.

"What are you doing?" Dad asks, his stern voice gruff with disuse.

"You're awake!" I yell, pulling him into me. I hug him tight in my arms, nuzzling into his hair. This is amazing. I can't believe we broke the curse. Did we break the curse? I don't even care because he's awake. My wolf does a little happy dance, and I know as soon as I shift, I'll be wagging my tail for hours. I haven't felt this good in weeks. Finally, everything is coming back together.

"Answer the question, son. What in the seven hells is going on?"

Rodan leans on his heels and scratches the back of his neck, looking sheepish. "You were under a sleeping curse of some sort, and Mr. Fairytale wanted to see if true-love's-kiss would bring you back... Damn it, Killian, it gets worse with every passing minute." Rodan runs his hand down his face. It's cute; he doesn't know how to show his excitement. He totally gets that look from Mom; she does that when I have great ideas, too.

"But it worked!" I say, hugging my dad tighter in my arms.

"They didn't kiss!" Rodan motions at Mom and Dad. "And Mom is still asleep!"

"What?" Dad booms, breaking out of my hold. He repositions himself to scoop up Mom's face in his hands. His eyes grow wild with unspoken panic. Creasing his brow, he leans down, kissing her softly.

She doesn't stir.

Dad turns, gets off the bed, and paces, running his hand through his hair. "What exactly did you do before I woke up?"

I looked down and fiddled with the blanket. "Uh, we moved both of you closer together. Then, I held you while Rodan tried to position your face over Mom's. Then you woke up."

His eyes light up, and he puts his hands on the bed, looking between us. "That's it; you both have to touch her simultaneously. That has to be it. Rodan was missing when we got cursed. It would have been impossible to wake us without both of you."

"That guy was seriously twisted in the way he built his curses," Jade grumbles.

Rodan and I reach out and place our hands on Mom's. My brows furrow as hope and fear tumble through me. "Please, Mom, wake up," I whisper.

She takes in a deep breath, and her eyelashes flutter. Dad roars in triumph before I've even registered that her eyes are opening. He lunges on top of her and pulls her into his arms.

"What in the gods name?" she stammers.

No one can get a word in before my dad cups her cheeks and kisses her.

Rodan and I look away as Jade tiptoes over to a chair and looks out the window.

"Someone, explain what is going on?" Mom demands.

"Hey, Mom," Rodan says.

Her gaze snaps to Rodan, and a smile curves over her lips. "Oh, my darling, you're back." She reaches her hand out and runs it through his hair. "What has happened?"

We send for Lorelai and food while we recount everything that has happened since I left for the mortal world. My parents sit holding each other, their faces a mix of horror at the dangers we faced and pride at our bravery.

"So the royal conflux is to happen in three days' time?" my father says over a cup of tea.

"Yes," Rodan says.

"There should be enough time to pull together the reports. I'm sure Warrick already has it underway. I'll sit down with King Lyris tonight and discuss a plan," Mom says. "We were great friends before I married your father. It seems like just yesterday I was a lady of the Serbea court." Her voice carries a hint of nostalgia.

"Mom, we have something else we need to talk to you about," I say, looking nervously at Rodan and Jade. My pulse quickens as I prepare to tell her.

Dad chuckles into his tea, and Rodan lifts his brow in question.

"Yes, I suppose we do need to discuss the other elephant in the room at some point. The three of you have something going on." She gives me a stern look, and I feel my face heat. "Don't look so shocked; we can smell it on all of you."

Blood drains from Jade's face as she looks down at the floor.

Rodan smirks, trying not to laugh.

"Damn, I didn't think about that. You see...it's kinda complicated..." I scratch the back of my head.

"She's our mate. We are both bonded to her," Rodan says. "It's not that complicated."

Dad smothers a laugh, pointedly avoiding eye contact with Mom, who looks a little lost for words.

"You...both? Huh...Okay then. That makes things both less and more complicated. It's not unheard of, but...we will figure it out." She dismisses her thoughts with a wave of her hand. "This is joyous news, and I guess I'm happy you finally figured out how to share. Jade, my dear, I suppose a welcome to the family is in order. We will have much to discuss and plan. I will wrap my head around this later, but for now, we must ready ourselves for the arrival of the royal conflux." Mom stands and looks down at her wrinkled dress; her face scrunches as she takes in her appearance. "I'll just go change..."

"Why don't you give your mom and me some privacy? We will see you all for dinner." Dad smiles and follows Mom into the bathing chamber. Rodan and I exchange a look and usher Jade out of their room. I recognize that look in Dad's eyes and have no desire to overhear what happens next.

"I can't believe the curse on your parents just required both of you to touch them at the same time," Jade says.

"Makes sense; he'd already sent Rodan to the mortal realm. The chances of our being in that room together were minimal at best. Ellis was a twisted little man," I say, a sense of relief washing over me. I'm overwhelmed with gratitude that we managed to break the curse on them. Because I did not have a Plan B after my kissing plan.

"You have no idea. You think Mom is freaking out about our bond?" Rodan says with a laugh, his voice tinged with a mix of amusement and concern as he scoops Jade's hand into his, kissing her knuckles.

I grab her other hand and do the same, winking at her. "Did you see her face? Of course, she's freaking out. The only other time I've seen her that lost for words was when we tried to make bread and flooded the lower west wing with sourdough starter."

"That's not even the same." Rodan laughs.

"But she had no words," I defend.

"Yeah, because she was debating murder. She's just caught off guard this time, not contemplating the ramifications of murdering her children."

He may not see it, but it's definitely similar. Mom is totally shocked but will be super happy once she wraps her head around it.

Jade squeezes my hand, and I meet her eyes. "I love you, Killian." Turning, she meets Rodan's gaze. "And I love you, even if you're an ass."

We both laugh and sandwich her in a big hug. "I love you, too, Emerald."

"I love you, Trouble. Even if you love a nutcase."

"You really shouldn't talk about yourself like that." She playfully chastises him.

I laugh, and Rodan lifts a brow as we continue walking down the hallway.

"I'll remember that, Trouble."

"Oh, what's the big bad cat gonna do? Spank me?"

"Don't give me ideas." He smirks.

I lift a brow as her face turns pink and suppress the smile playing at the corner of my mouth as I meet Rodan's eye. He winks, and now a whole new set of games plays through my thoughts. Oh, Emerald, we are gonna have so much fun.

Chapter 45
Jade

"It's been four days; how much could there be to discuss?" I ask, slouching onto a chaise lounge by the window. We've waited outside the royal conflux daily, our anticipation growing with each passing moment. The sun is once again getting ready to set, casting the large sitting room in a golden glow. Everything in this parlor is like shades of autumn, rich siennas, and burgundy, mixed with gleaming golds and splashes of forest green. It's one of the most opulent parlors in the castle.

Rodan sits down next to me, pulling my legs onto his lap. "A lot happened, and they have a lot to decide on. With Shadow's curse lifted, fae will be allowed to return. They will need a great deal of help to rebuild and schedule my coronation. With you being bound to two fae in line to take thrones, I'm sure they probably have their panties in a bunch. Not to mention the whole debacle with Light; Beatrix is an unfit successor." While he sounds confident, I can feel the tension rolling down the bond.

"Thank the gods, the King of Light came to his senses. However, they will probably want a replacement soon," Killian adds as he pours a cup of tea, standing at the gilded cart in the corner.

Cat groans as she slumps further into her chair. "So why do *we* have to be here? Waiting outside the doors with nothing to do? Can't they just collect us from the library when they are done?"

"Royalty doesn't wait on people," Rodan grumbles.

"But you're waiting..." I grin.

"We—that's not the point. We were told we could not attend until they called for us. Ask one of the guards to bring you a book," Rodan says.

"But they won't know what book I'm in the mood for." Cat smirks, the twinkle in her eyes spelling mischief.

"I know what you're in the mood for." Ryker grins. Cat smacks his leg as he leans over her for a kiss. Sometime between us getting here and being captured, she finally let her guard down and accepted that he wasn't going anywhere.

Killian brings me a cup of tea before settling in next to me, propping my head against his chest. "I honestly don't know why Mom told us to wait here. I tried to ask, but she gave me the scary mom look, and I caved."

"No. She told you to wait and stop asking questions." Rodan laughs.

"Same thing," he grumbles.

"Do you think it will be bad news?" I ask.

"Don't worry, my love; the worst thing that could happen is they sever the bond and force our kingdoms to remain separate." Killian's brows pinch as his words seem to register.

Gaping at him, I snap my head to Rodan for confirmation.

Rodan puts his face in his hand and shakes his head. "You cannot follow a statement like 'don't worry' with something like that. Fuck, man, I highly doubt they would do something like that."

My heart jackhammers in my chest while I try to pull air into my lungs. "How unlikely is that outcome?"

Both of them stare at the floor, and suddenly, I understand why they have been so tense the last few days. I didn't even know they could sever the bond. Wasn't Ellis trying and failing to do something like that? Okay, to be fair, who knows precisely what Ellis was trying to do? Maybe the royals have some method that wasn't what he wanted. He seemed bent on destroying even the possibility of a bond. But why would they force us apart?

"About fifty-fifty, depending on how it could affect the continent as a whole—" Ryker huffs as Cat's elbow collides with his sternum. "I love you too," he wheezes while patting Cat's head.

The large doors swing open, a sight to behold. Towering at twelve feet, they gleam as if covered in gold. Ornate carvings, intricate as a spider's web, cover the thick wood, with vines and flowers climbing up to the top of the curved doors, nestled in a grand archway.

We all stand as we are beckoned inside. Monarchs from every kingdom, a diverse assembly of sirens, pixies, foxes, elves, and other mystical beings, sit around an enormous round table. Their faces, like stone, reveal nothing of what may befall us in this room.

As Queen Aleena stands, we are guided to one side and positioned behind her. My heart thunders as Killian's fingers brush mine. He and Rodan are flanking me, while Cat and Ryker stand to Killian's right. A chill rolls down my spine as all the eyes in the room fall on me, anticipation building in the air.

The doors shut with a thunderous boom that causes me to flinch.

The queen picks up a long document and turns to address the other monarchs. "A new treaty has been decided here today at this royal conflux. Every royal line has agreed to the terms I am about to present." Her commanding tone has the attention of every person in the room. Curt nods from the other royals follow her statement.

"Killian shall remain the heir of Amara. Rodan shall be crowned as the King of Shadow one year hence. The borders of Shadow will remain open to all who wish to relocate, and aid will be sent from every kingdom to help rebuild."

Out of the corner of my eye, I notice Rodan's brows furrow in thought.

"Due to the unprecedented revelation that both princes share the same mate, the kingdoms have presented a suitable compromise for combining the kingdoms. King Corbin and I shall not step down for ten years. During this time, we will aid in rebuilding Shadow and preparing to merge both kingdoms. Prince Rodan, Prince Killian, and Lady Jade will travel to every kingdom to learn from its rulers. During this training, they will build relationships and alliances. They will learn policies and politics in the hopes of strengthening our ties. They shall be with each kingdom no less than one month. Together, they will shape a new country and an era of prosperity throughout Auburnigh."

Nearly dropping my composure, I school my features while the shock radiates through me. They aren't separating us. Relief washes over me, and the tension in my shoulders relaxes. I want to squeal with delight, but I feel this isn't the place.

"With only three known heirs to the Kingdom of Light at this time, we were left with few options. After much debate, it has been agreed upon that Catria is the rightful heir to Light."

My jaw drops momentarily as I watch the color drain from Cat's face. She gulps and watches on in horror.

"The fae that Catria and Jade hail from is the only other known descendant of the royal line. Beatrix is disqualified due to her treasonous actions. Seeing as Jade is already in line for two kingdoms, combining the whole of the north under one ruler was out of the question," the queen continues.

Cat clutches Ryker's hand between white knuckles. I can see the words she wants to say written across her face, but she holds her mouth in a tight line.

"The King of Light will officially name her heir and train her. Ryker will accompany her as her guard and consort. Scarlette and Corsac have agreed to go as her council. Catria will also attend the training throughout the kingdoms. The majority has consented to this alliance. But you must take your time in their kingdoms seriously and forge the alliances. I know we are throwing Catria to the wolves, but no others exist of the bloodline, with Beatrix being deemed unworthy and seen as a threat. Whereas Catria is unknown but powerful, with careful training, she would be a formidable ally."

In other words, they are afraid of her.

Cat raises her hand, and the queen nods for her to speak. "With all due respect, I don't know how to be queen." Soft chuckles whisper around the room, and she turns bright red.

"You will have decades to learn from all the country's monarchs. The King of Light has agreed to these terms. It is decided. You all have a lot to learn. Use the time well."

Cat and I lay on the floor of Rodan's bedroom, staring at the night sky that twinkles across his enchanted ceiling. It figures that his room is very similar to the cave he took me to. Everything is midnight blue or black with splashes of violet. Stars glitter from almost every surface. And he says Killian has a princess room. They need to watch way more princess movies and see how ridiculous they both are. However, where everything in Killian's room is light and airy, all the furniture here is dark and imposing.

I pop another piece of chocolate in my mouth. The rich, salty caramel flavor coats my tongue, instantly calming my racing thoughts. It's a small comfort in this strange, enchanted world, a reminder of the familiar and the ordinary.

"How long do you think it will take them to find us?" Cat asks as she feels around for the tray of chocolates. Her nose scrunches, and she rolls her head to the side to see that her hand missed the plate by half an inch. She grabs a bonbon and pops it in her mouth, lacing her fingers over her stomach.

"I imagine it's the last place they will look. Our rooms..." I tick off on my fingers, "The library, the gardens, the kitchen. We've got time."

"How the fuck are we supposed to be queens?"

"I have no idea." I sigh. This was never a position I saw myself being in. Granted, I never saw myself with two men, and look where I am. I trust they will make this transition easy, even if it seems daunting.

"I guess we have loads of time to learn," she grumbles. "Stupid Beatrix. This is her fault."

"No, it's our great-grandmother's fault for sleeping with some fae guy. I always thought it was a bit fishy that neither of our families knew who our great-grandfathers were. Go figure, it's the same guy, just spreading his children all over the place."

"Jerk."

We both laugh; that's all we can do at this point. "Remember when our biggest problem was trying to get Ace to sign the divorce paperwork?"

She laughs. "Seriously, what the fuck? Now, we gotta figure out how to rule a kingdom? This is bullshit."

"You're telling me. I was ready to be single forever, and now I'm bonded with two guys," I say.

"You? What about me? I was never planning to get married, and now..."

"Now, you couldn't imagine your life without him."

"Well, how else am I gonna rule a kingdom? This is his fault, so he has to help. There's no escape for him now. I'm putting that in the contract."

I laugh. "How is it Ryker's fault?"

"Because he went and fell for me, so I stayed. I could have been back in our world living like a—"

"Queen," I finish, laughing.

"Damn it. Be careful what you wish for, I guess." She laughs.

The door to the room creaks open, and I groan. "Damn it."

"I found them!" Killian shouts down the hall. I hear his soft footsteps coming towards us before he looms over me. "Rodan's room, really?" He smirks down at me.

"Seeing as we've never been in here, I figured it would take you a while to find us." I grin, popping another chocolate in my mouth and letting it melt across my tongue.

"Yeah, I know. I could hear you through the bond."

"What?" I squeak as Cat starts cackling, rolling onto her side.

"When your walls are down, sometimes your thoughts come through. But if you learn to control it, you can push through what you want me to hear."

So, did I really hear his voice when I attacked Rodan? I thought I imagined it.

"You didn't imagine it."

"Stay out of my head!" I shriek, getting off the floor.

This is terrible! How do I make it stop?

Cat is curled up in a ball and laughing so hard that her face is bright red.

Killian suppresses a smile as he looks sheepishly at the floor.

How long has this been going on?

"Not long, Trouble. But could you stop yelling? It's giving me a headache." Rodan says, leaning on the doorframe in all his sexy glory.

"Oh god. How do I make it stop?"

"I'm afraid I can't stop all my *sexy glory*, Trouble." He laughs, and I scowl at him.

"I'm out. I'll see you at dinner." Cat giggles, slipping past Rodan, who winks at her. This throws her into another fit of giggles, which I hear all the way down the hallway.

Rodan steps into the room. "Don't worry, Trouble; we will help you learn how to control it. And now that you have your powers back, we will help you learn how to use those, too."

"Great, even more for me to learn," I grumble. I am not cut out for this life.

"You'll do fine, my love. It's only because you are so formidable and took down Ellis that the other monarchs are afraid of you. Now, they want to be your ally as opposed to your enemy. Because of you, we have made so much progress with relations in such a short amount of time. Dad says that you and Cat scare the shit out of them. And since you are paired up with two gloriously sexy and powerful fae, they conceded to our terms." Killian smiles.

King Corbin walks through the doorway and laughs. "Gloriously sexy has nothing to do with politics, Killian. You three make a powerful force that no one wants to reckon with. Anyway, I just wanted to update you. We have the location of where Ellis was making his constructs—his base of operations, as it were. It's in the mountains on the northern coast of Light. A contingent from Colire is headed there now to shut it down."

"Beatrix, I'm guessing?" Rodan sneers.

King Corbin laughs and nods. "Oh yes, she said she didn't know anything about that, but then Owari shouted that she knew everything. That girl is out for blood; I'm at a loss for what to do with that one. So, to give Beatrix some incentive, I brought in the wedding planner. Molly wheeled in racks of wedding dresses and carts of flowers. You should have seen the look on her face. After that, she spilled everything. Who knew weddings could be so scary?" The king's eyes light up with mischief the same way Killian's do.

The three of them laugh as I look at the king in confusion. Killian runs his hand through my hair, smiling at me. "You'd be scared, too, if my dad threatened to marry you off to the Bog Lord."

"Are you really going to do that?" I mean, she kind of deserves it, but if she's that scared, I have a feeling that it's a much worse fate than I imagine.

"Nah, we are going to try to rehabilitate her. Owari is another matter, but the courts of Illa will probably deal with her. Her mother was unhappy with her part in Ellis' scheming," Killian says.

"Correct. Now, if you'll excuse me, your mother needs tending to, and we've been held up in a room for days."

Rodan and Killian grimace as their dad walks out of the room, and now I know where they get it from. Fae are horny bastards.

"That's not very nice, Trouble," Rodan says, closing and locking the door. He turns and levels his stare at me. "Let's start working on blocking your thoughts."

Nothing in their body language says anything about training me. These are predators, and I am absolutely their prey right now. Their muscles flex as they pull their shirts over their heads, exposing the hard muscles of their bodies and that delicious V that disappears into their pants. I lick my lips and take a step back.

How the hell am I supposed to concentrate on anything when they look like that?

"That is the point, my love." Killian grins.

"I don't like that you can hear my thoughts," I pout and retreat another step.

"I love it." Rodan smirks.

"Best way to learn is under pressure," Killian says, taking another step forward.

"You know you smell like those cinnamon rolls you like so much when you're turned on," Rodan purrs, tugging at the laces of his pants.

"I do not," I say, a bit breathless. Wonderful, my voice is even betraying me. Not that I'm not totally down for what's about to happen.

"It's true, you always smell like vanilla, but when you're turned on, you smell like cinnamon." Killian smiles, pulling the laces of his pants loose.

"Spicy, like those books you're so fond of."

"Is that why you gave me cinnamon in the library?" I ask Rodan.

"You said you wanted spicy books, and you smell spicy when you want us."

"And when I talk dirty to you," Killian adds.

"And the other day, when I said I'd spank you." Rodan grins as he and Killian glance at each other.

My knees hit the bed, and I almost fall backward into it.

"And right now." Killian closes the gap between us and embraces me with a kiss. His lips are soft against mine as I lean into him. He pulls back, and Rodan replaces him hungrily, marking my mouth as his.

They surround my senses in every shape of the word.

I love you.

Both of their voices fill my head, and it's the sweetest sound in all the world. A simple sentence, a vow, a thought carried down the bond that completes and reshapes my heart.

I may not be ready to be a queen, but I know in the depths of my soul that I have everything I need.

Epilogue
Jade

A year and a half later
Christmas

Twinkle lights dance a festive glow around the bright rainbow of colors in Mom's living room. A small tree stands prominently in the corner, its pot adorned with red and gold garlands. Ornaments hang from the branches, each a memory of our travels and my childhood. Paper snowflakes dangle in glittery glory from the ceiling like craft project exhibitions. The smell of cookies and apple pie welcomes me home.

I sit nestled and warm between my guys on the couch, sipping eggnog. Mom and Queen Aleena sit across from us in the teal high-backed reading chairs Killian's parents gave mine for Christmas. They wear nearly matching Christmas sweaters that they designed together a few weeks ago. The red-nosed reindeer gleams in all it's sparkly opulence. Dad and King Corbin have disappeared into the garage to tinker and drink beer as usual. It's shocking to see Killian's parents in casual mortal clothes, but I'm sure I'll get used to it someday. The cozy moments we share bring a sense of relaxation and peace.

It's become a tradition for Killian's parents to visit with us when we come home for Christmas and birthdays. They've even discussed taking a vacation together without the kids. I couldn't be happier with how our families have merged, though it hasn't been without its challenges. For instance, Rodan's eyes nearly bugged out of his head when they started plotting to have my parents move to the castle.

Just what we need—more parents looming over our shoulders. He'd sent down the bond, and Killian nearly spit out his drink. But moving to the fae realm would extend their lives, so I'm all for it.

Only took me a month of dedicated effort to master talking down the bond and not having them privy to every thought that flits through my head. The journey was challenging, but now it's a valuable form of communication between us, especially around other royals or parents. The struggle was real, but the triumph was sweeter.

"I was just telling Jade that her work in Illa was extraordinary. Her being an otter shifter really helped turn the tide in peace negotiations. She even helped plan a memorial to their fallen princess, which I'm sure went a long way." Queen Aleena says to my mom. A faint blush stains my cheeks as Killian squeezes my hand. It was the least I could do for Yudoku.

"So she's learning quickly?" Mom says.

"They all are. Quite a burden was placed on them, but they are handling it with the grace and poise that befits royalty."

Mom and I both snort a laugh before quickly regaining our composure. The room falls silent momentarily before Killian, Rodan, and Ryker burst into laughter. Glancing at Cat, perched on an ottoman in front of the fireplace, we hide our grins and look at the floor.

"It's a huge learning curve," Cat scoffs.

Aleena smiles. "That it is, and you're doing fine. It takes time to learn what our roles will be. Notice I make most of the official announcements because Corbin is quite excitable, like his son." She looks at Killian, who beams back at her. "I have to be the voice of reason. Wolves." She says, rolling her eyes. "You will have to be that voice of reason with my boys." She directs at me, our roles in this family becoming clearer with each passing day.

Rodan huffs. "I'm usually the voice of reason; their heads are in the clouds."

"Not when you're angry." She smirks, and Rodan sinks into the cushions, pretending to pout. "Now that you've finished your training with the other courts, you will sit in on everything with me. But that's enough talk of work."

Ryker leans over from his spot next to Cat and whispers, lighting up Cat's face. "Clair, I think it's time for dessert!" She bounces to her feet. I'll go get the guys from the man cave.

"It's a garage," Clair calls after her, laughing.

Rodan and Killian rise abruptly, leaving me confused and cold on the couch. Since when do they get this excited over cookies? They usually just roll their eyes when Cat and I act like this. But today, their excitement is palpable, and I can't help but wonder what's going on.

I steal a glance at Mom, who swiftly disappears into the kitchen, retrieving plates and a knife for the pie. My curiosity piques. I narrow my eyes.

Aleena studies the mug of eggnog like it's the most interesting thing she's ever seen.

I have whiplash from the sudden change in atmosphere, and the shift in conversation leaves me with a sense of unease. They are definitely up to something, and I seem to be the only one not in on it. I gulp down my drink, relishing the warm burn of the brandy, which I hope gives me liquid interrogation skills.

"What did I miss?" Standing from the couch, I put my hand on my hip to emphasize my annoyance. It would probably be more effective if I weren't wearing a giant knit sweater hanging almost to my knees with a sparkly reindeer on it.

"I'm dishing up dessert. Come grab the forks and put them on the table." Mom's voice sounds far too giddy, and she's concentrating too much on each cut she makes.

Killian dashes down the hallway with Rodan right behind him. "I need to wash my hands," Killian shouts.

What the absolute fuck is happening? They are all acting like loons.

Cat comes careening back into the kitchen, smiling from ear to ear, nearly tipping the chair she slides into. "I am so excited for pie!"

I cock an eyebrow at her as Aleena sits in the seat next to Cat and whispers in her ear. Both of them share a smile.

Dad and Corbin come in, backs straight, but stumble slightly as they take their chairs. Corbin leans into Aleena and kisses her cheek.

"I see you've drunk your weight in beer again." She smiles.

"Every time." Mom sighs. "You'd think we'd have learned by now not to leave them unattended."

"I didn't," Aleena protests. "What have you two done with Warrick?"

"Shots." Corbin beams. The men burst into laughter.

Mom and Aleena gape at one another just as the man in question stumbles into the room.

Oh hell.

I can't help the giggle that escapes me, which sets off Cat and everyone else.

Warrick slips into a chair and swings his gaze to me. "Well, hello there," he purrs, giving me the same charm he used the night we met. "I'd ask you to dance, but I think your men might kill me. Got a brother or sister, perhaps?"

"Dude, I think you're done." I roll my eyes, trying to rein in my laughter.

"Who's done?" Rodan says, coming back into the room and slipping into the chair beside me.

"Honestly, all three of them. But mostly drunky over here." I say, pointing to Warrick, who blows a kiss to Rodan.

"Nah, he's fine. Just fucking with you. Believe me, this is nothing;

you should have seen him at Ryker's bachelor party." Rodan waves it off.

"Which you're supposed to have before the wedding, not immediately following the engagement party." Cat laughs.

"Nah, we had to celebrate him finally wearing you down. Never thought we'd see the day." Warrick says, batting his eyelashes and feigning a swoon.

Warrick straightens and winks as my dad slides another shot across the table, which sloshes green over the wood. I do not want to know what's in that; it smells like acetone. Warrick downs it in unison with Dad and Corbin.

I guess I can't fault him; it is his day off.

Everyone continues chatting about the day's festivities and the presents we'd opened earlier as Cat helps Mom bring the plates to the table.

"What's taking Killian so long?"

"Poor planning," Rodan grumbles.

"Huh?"

Rodan leans over, kissing me on the forehead and lacing his fingers with mine. "Stop worrying so much."

"But you are all acting super cagey."

"Haven't you learned to trust us yet?"

Or do I need to excuse us from the table and show you? His suggestive tone rumbles through the bond, causing me to clench my knees together.

Not right now! Killian shouts in my head. I smother my grin behind my hand so I don't have to explain why I suddenly started giggling.

Killian bolts into the room, holding a large box covered in scraps of wrapping paper and duct tape. Mom purses her lips and shakes her head, and I instantly know Dad taught him how to wrap.

"Finally," Rodan grumbles.

He hands me the flat box, the type you would wrap clothing in, and extremely light. Confusion and excitement war within me. I thought we had already finished opening gifts.

Killian sits down on my other side as everyone watches expectantly. "Everybody pitched in on this. So we hope you like it." He smiles. "But if you don't, there's pie."

I see.

I glance at everyone and smile, looking down at the patchwork of Christmas paper and tape artfully arranged to look like ribbon. Every layer of this mystery makes me more confused.

"Thank you," I say.

"Don't thank us yet. Open it, Trouble." Rodan gives my leg a squeeze.

I tear into the paper and wrestle off the tape, flinging it onto the floor as it sticks to my fingers. I have no idea what this could be, considering I have everything I could possibly want.

My brow furrows as I lift the lid to find a newspaper neatly folded inside.

"Um...thanks?" I don't know what I expected, but it's not this. I lift an eyebrow and look to Killian for an explanation.

Killian leans into me. "Read it, Emerald, my love."

Picking up the paper, I unfold it, and my jaw drops as I read the headline. My heart beats fast in my chest as I continue down the page. Lowering the paper, my jaw is nearly on the floor.

"Took me the last year and a half to collect the evidence," Warrick says, smiling.

"Then I delivered it to the DA," Dad says, raising his glass to Warrick.

Cat's smile is so wide she can't contain it. "Mark has been arrested, and the entire department is being investigated for corruption!"

"We had Warrick do some digging and got a ton of evidence to prove his department's misdeeds," Rodan says. "There is a lot more, too; that guy was into some sick shit."

"They built a huge case against them that's so damning and ironclad that they will never dig themselves out of it. Then Warrick gave it to us to give to people who could do something about it." Mom beams.

"Now, you don't have to sneak around when you come home to visit. It's safe." Killian puts his arm around me.

I can't believe it; it's right here on the page, but I'm frozen in shock.

"But how?" I stammer.

Warrick knocks back another shot. "It's easy to get the evidence when you can portal into everything. Had someone duplicate every paper, video, and picture...and the delete button on their computers doesn't work so well when magic is involved. Took a while, but we have so much on them that they have no way out."

"With what they found, Mark is looking at life," Dad chimes in.

"In short, you are free, my dear." Aleena's eyes crinkle with joy, her soft smile finally letting everything sink in.

Tears prick the back of my eyes as I look down at the newspaper again. His mug shot is large and imposing on the page. Mark looks furious as he stares down the camera. Visions of his face as I stabbed him rush into my mind, and my heart rate kicks up.

"Quick, give her the pie before she cries," Mom says.

Rodan pushes the paper down onto the table, and Killian places a plate of apple pie on it. The pie is so loaded with cinnamon that it resembles caramel puddling onto the plate. Vanilla ice cream drips down the sides of the warm pie. The smell is sweet and calming, reminding me I'm home and bringing me back to myself.

"I don't know what to say... thank you."

"Now we don't have to look over our shoulders whenever we come back! We can go shopping and out to eat without having to be in other states or countries. Although I still wanna do that," Cat says and stabs at her pie.

The tears that streak my cheeks cause Cat to frown in confusion, and then laughter bubbles out of me like a manic witch.

I can't believe it. They did that for me? Who am I kidding? Of course, they did. "Why didn't you tell me?" I laugh, wiping the tears from my cheeks.

"We wanted it to be a surprise!" Killian hugs me and plants kisses all over my face.

"You should have seen the look on his face; it was all over the news." Mom laughs.

"I'll pull up the clips," Cat says, picking up her phone.

"This was Rodan and Killian's idea. Can't have a queen afraid to visit her parents," Aleena says.

"Thank you so much; seeing him face justice means the world to me. But I'm still confused by the pie."

"We were worried it would stir up bad memories, and we wanted to replace them with something good," Rodan says, holding a fork full of apple goodness to my mouth. I happily take a bite.

As we eat and chat, Cat shows me videos of Mark's house surrounded by SWAT, as he refuses to open the door. He screams that he's the chief of police as they drag him out. His face is a mixture of rage and terror. I laugh until my face hurts.

Mom brings out the cookies as Dad dishes more ice cream. Dessert is never done by halves in this house. It's a very serious part of a holiday meal.

"Merry Christmas, Trouble."

"Merry Christmas, my love."

"Merry Christmas. You know, everyone was acting so sketchy, I was afraid you two were planning to propose." I laugh.

Rodan smirks. "And if we were?"

I roll my eyes, facing Rodan. "I don't know. I'm still undecided. This whole queen thing seems like an awful lot of work, especially since we will have to combine the kingdoms. Queen does have a nice ring to it, though," I say, flipping my hair over my shoulder.

"Hum, guess we fucked up then. Should have known better."

Rodan sighs. "Maybe next year, Killian."

I lift a brow at Rodan. They teased me like this last Christmas, too. My cold feet have become a holiday tradition. Never mind the fact that we are practically married, considering the mate bond. We just haven't done anything official or publicly yet.

"In elven culture, it's tradition to present a grand gesture before you propose marriage," Killian says, standing. "That's why Ryker brought all of Cat's books and belongings from her apartment to the castle. It was a grand gesture."

Does that count as a grand gesture? For Ryker, probably. "I thought it was because he wanted her to move in?" I look at Cat, who just shrugs.

Rodan pulls my chair out from the table, and both my guys move to kneel before me. "Tonight, we presented our grand gesture," he says.

I look at Mom, cradling her face in her hands with a dreamy grin. The queen smiles, and Cat looks like she's caught the canary.

When my stunned face lands on the guys, Rodan smirks. "You brought it up."

They both take my hands and kiss my knuckles. "We were bound by fate, but it's still your choice," Killian whispers. "You are the air I breathe, my heart made full."

My heart thunders in my chest. They aren't joking this time. They are serious.

"I've never met someone so brave as to bring me back from my own destruction," Rodan says. "I'd burn the world to keep you by my side. We are not whole without you. So now we ask you."

The answer is trying to fall out of my mouth, but I clamp it shut. Pulling my lips into a thin line.

Let them finish.

"Will you do us the honor of marrying us in front of the world? Making this last part of us official? I mean, we know you're kinda against getting married again, but we practically already are with the mate bond—"

"Killian—" Rodan growls, stopping Killian from his rambling.

"Yes," I breathe. "Of course!"

As if choreographed, they pull rings from their pockets and present them. Killian slips a dark ruby with tiny emeralds adorning the band on my finger. Rodan's fits snugly against the first, interlocking the two large stones into a heart. Its stone is a deep onyx with blue sapphires lining the band. Each one is a perfect representation of us together.

"They're beautiful," I breathe.

"Lorelai and Ryker made them, but we designed the set," Killian says with a shy smile.

Beaming, I leap into Killian's arms. I can feel the warmth of his body, the strength in his embrace. I kiss him long and hard before grabbing Rodan by the back of his neck and doing the same to him. The taste of his lips, the scent of ozone—it's all so familiar and comforting. When I come up for air, I see everyone has a glass of champagne and the celebrations have just begun.

"I'm telling you, Belle should have chosen the Beast *and* Gaston. It's the perfect match," Rodan says.

Killian looks affronted. "He's the bad guy. There's no way. He was an arrogant asshole. Belle had better sense than that," Killian growls.

"But he's way better looking. That blond guy at the end was terrible. Even Belle was like, damn, I kinda want the beast back."

Killian snarls, his wolf coming out to defend the princess's honor. I fall over in a fit of laughter. This happens whenever we watch an animated movie. Rodan absolutely loves to goad Killian by saying the princess should have ended up with the villain. I don't know why Killian takes the bait every time.

It's late; everyone else has gone to bed or returned to the fae realm. Only the three of us stayed behind, wrapped in the warmth of our Christmas tradition. We're continuing our cozy night of watching movies until the sun rises. After breakfast, we'll go home and sleep.

As I watch the two of them argue, I admire my rings with fascination. They represent so much more than just our wedding or mate bond. They symbolize how much we've all changed, how far we've come, and the love that binds us together.

"Hey, lovebirds, cold, soon-to-be wife over here who could use some warming up," I tease.

Their heads snap to me so fast I instantly feel like prey. Their heated gazes rake over my body, and they have a silent exchange that they've left me out of. Heat floods my core as they close in.

"I think we forgot to give her one of her Christmas presents," Rodan purrs. My eyes dart between them as I bite my lip.

"You're right; it's a rather important one, too," Killian says with a sparkle in his eye.

I bite my lower lip in anticipation.

"Better run, little wolf..." Killian growls.

Acknowledgments

Dear Reader,

This story was a labor of love. I know it was a wild ride to get to the happily ever after, but it makes the ending even more sweet. Thank you for taking a chance on a first-time author. I never thought I'd publish a book or that people would actually read it. So, from the bottom of my heart, thank you.

I wrote this book with my mom in mind because I know she would have loved it. I wrote the kind of story that we would have read together and called each other gushing about. My mom is where I get my love of romance and the fantastical. I hope wherever she is, I've made her proud.

I want to thank my dad for supporting my many endeavors over the years. He is the rock my waves crash upon that never lets me down. He told me that anything was possible, even if my head was somewhere in the clouds.

Thank you to my husband for hyping me up when I'm feeling down. He was critical for bouncing ideas off of and helping edit. He always kept true to my vision and added a much-needed perspective on my characters. I'm still unsure how he knows them better than I do.

I'd like to thank Maddy for pushing me to write, alpha reading, editing, and motivating me to put my story out there. If she hadn't shown me what was possible, this story never would have made it past the first chapter and a plethora of notes.

I hope to only grow as an author and refine my writing. I do plan spin-offs from this world, so I hope there are many more stories to come.

Books By J. Grenz

Labyrinth of Crimson

<u>Shattered Moon Duet</u>
Soul of Fractured Fate
Fate of the Broken

About the Author

J. Grenz is a self-published author living in the Pacific Northwest, where she hopes to one day fall into a fairy realm or bump into a vampire. Her love of romance, fantasy, and whimsical places lead to her debut book, Soul of Fractured Fate. Her husband and teenager help keep her grounded in reality, while her four cats and two dogs pretend they don't understand English.

www.ingramcontent.com/pod-product-compliance
Lightning Source LLC
Chambersburg PA
CBHW032114310726
48972CB00001B/213